The Hunt

BOOK THREE IN THE BRIDGE SERIES

ANN HOWES

The Hunt

BOOK THREE: THE BRIDGE SERIES

Editing: Sue Seabury
thetechnopeasant.wordpress.com

Author's Note
Sawmill is a made-up town in a made-up location near Redding, Northern California.

Thank you for selecting this book and for taking the time to read.
Enjoy!

To those who have helped me along the way, you know who your are~~I love you.

Chapter One

"Got eyes on the target, Sarge."

Carmine Niccoterra sighed and shook his head. Though technically his rank was Staff Sergeant, his army days were long behind him. "Don't call me Sarge, Brady."

"Right, sorry. Got eyes on the target, Boss-man." The kid, his badass in training, leaned against a white pillar in The Westfield Mall, downtown San Francisco, pretending to ignore all the Halloween shoppers. He looked like any young adult dressed in jeans, Converse All Star's and a plain black hoodie, talking on his phone. The target, however, was Carmine's latest job.

"He's wearing a dark gray suit, sunglasses, hair all scraped back. What a douche. Dude's got a swagger like Jagger and an ego bigger than Canada."

Of course, the target had a swagger—he was about to meet the woman he was screwing, who happened not to be his wife.

"Stop speculating about his ego, Brady, and tell me what he's doing."

"About to get on the escalator going up—the one with the Nordstrom sign."

"Alone?"

"Alone on the escalator?"

Christ.

He rolled his eyes to the elaborate dome and bit down on his impatience. "No, Brady. Is *he* alone?"

"Oh, sorry Sarge. Yeah he's alone."

"Carrying anything?"

"Got a brown leather man-bag with a long strap, stuffed like the Pillsbury doughboy."

Interesting. Overnight plans? Or maybe just in need of a change of clothing in case his second woman—or was it the third—reeked like an Ann Klein commercial.

The job was outside of normal channels, too small for his regular skills, but a favor for an old friend. Therefore, a perfect opportunity to train Brady in the art of covert surveillance. The question of the day was, who was the unfaithful husband cheating with this time?

"Going up one more floor, boss."

Carmine, from his position on the second floor, saw the top of the man's dark head appear, then the rest of him as the escalator rose. He stepped off onto his floor and turned to the right.

"Got him. Stay on the phone and follow at a distance. Don't let him notice you, as we may need to switch off again."

"Affirmative."

He adjusted his San Francisco 49ers baseball cap over his dark curls, bringing the bill down low and pushed mirrored sunglasses up his nose, hiding light green eyes. Eyes that were not normally a hindrance when it came to inviting women into his bed, which he did often and successfully. But for surveillance purposes people tended to notice them.

Carmine followed, staying hidden behind a man about his height walking in the same direction.

Suddenly the man stopped and abruptly spun around, eyes wide like he'd seen a ghost.

"Shit!" he uttered, his voice laced with panic. Dodging left, he narrowly missed clipping Carmine's shoulder. "Do me a favor, man," he said, blinking hazel eyes rapidly and scraping a hand through light brown hair, mussing it more than it already was. "She can't see me. Please, just stay in front of me."

What the hell?

Had he been made? Was this a deliberate distraction so his target could pull a Houdini? He studied the man's eyes and determined the alarm in them was genuine.

"Who can't see you?" Carmine asked as he looked over the stranger's shoulder, keeping his target in his line of sight. For the moment, this wasn't messing with his tail, but he couldn't fall too far behind.

"My ex. She's gonna kill me if she sees me."

He swept his gaze past the lanky dude, looking through the throng for anyone that might pose a potential danger. All he saw was a group of high school girls, an oversized South Pacific Islander dripping with muscles and a slim, deceptively harmless, yet deadly member of the tong that controlled Chinatown––his little girl dressed in a pink ballet tutu hopped beside him, ponytails bouncing as her tiny hand clasped around her father's index finger.

Other than them—nothing. Just regular mall goers getting their Halloween spook on even though it was still early in October.

He took it one degree further and looked past them, until he saw *her*.

A cute, curvy little thing, dressed in skinny jeans with uneven ragged bottoms, a long rust-colored blouse and brown ankle boots.

Strange how his body recognized her before his brain did, thumping him in the chest like the back legs of an angry mule.

That Helen chick!

The same woman who'd dominated his frontal cortex for days after she'd rejected his admittedly weak come-on at his buddy Zander's bar.

A cascade of auburn hair swished across her collarbone as she moved, caressing the top of her milky cleavage, reminding him of the urge he'd had to get his hands on those ample breasts.

"Cody!" She yelled and quickened her pace to a run-walk heading straight towards him, a shiny Nordstrom shopping bag bumping up against slim legs. "Stay right there, you coward."

What?

He scoffed, and looked at the dude who was still trying to use him as an invisibility shield.

"*She's* your ex?"

He'd thought she was a lesbian, or that was what she'd told him at the time. He shook his head at the coincidence almost too bizarre to be true, but no way he was gonna miss this.

Carmine lifted his phone to his ear. "Brady, continue on, I've gotten sidetracked."

"Gotcha, boss. On him."

Cody, aka the idiot, squeezed his eyes shut and mouthed *fuck*. Then his chest heaved and, taking a deep breath, he hesitated a beat before he turned to face the oncoming tempest.

Carmine continued on but stopped at an electronics store about twenty feet away, keeping his head down pretending to be interested in a rack of phones.

"Where's my money, Cody?" Helen asked. He couldn't decide if he was impressed with her balls facing a man who stood almost a foot taller and outweighed her by at least eighty pounds or horrified for the same reason.

"Jesus, Helen, keep your voice down, you're making a scene."

"Oh!" she said. "You have no idea the kind of scene I'm willing to make and I don't care if I make a fool of myself. I want everybody around, *everybody,*" she emphasized and swept her hand indicating the shoppers, "to know what you are. A thief! A big, tall, skinny-ass thief who stole two thousand dollars I could *not* afford so give me one reason, just *one*, why I shouldn't call the cops on you."

"Shhh." Cody took her petite shoulders in his big hands which she promptly slapped away.

"Don't touch me!" Those pretty russet brown eyes narrowed and flashed. "You've lost that right."

"Shit, Helen. Okay, look, I'm sorry, I've been meaning to call you, I really have. I've got your money and I swear I'll get it to you. I just can't right now."

"Your promises mean nothing, you lying piece of crap. I need that money, Cody. My parents had to pay my rent. Do you have any idea how humiliating that was, lying to my family. Especially my brother because we both know what Petey would have done if he knew what you did." One index finger jabbed him in the chest. "But you're" —*Jab*— "not" —*Jab*— "worth him going to jail." *Jab*.

Carmine was fascinated—unable to take his eyes of the exchange, like a rubbernecker stuck watching a freeway collision. The woman had enough fire to burn most men. And at least the loser had the decency to look embarrassed as he glanced around.

Or was it worried?

Hm.

"Helen, stop."

Jab. "No." *Jab*.

"Ow, dammit. Don't do that!" Cody glanced over his shoulder, then at his phone.

Yep, dude definitely looked worried.

"I've gotta be somewhere," he said, trying to back away.

"Don't you dare brush me off."

"Helen!" His voice got sharper, and Carmine bristled at his tone. "I can't do this right now. I swear on my life, I'll call you when this is done."

What's done?

Studying him further, Carmine readied himself to intervene should it become necessary. Cody had a vibe about him, a sense of desperation that set his senses on high alert. Though he didn't seem the type who'd want to attract attention, it didn't mean that someone else who might be watching wouldn't.

"Brady, you still on the target?" he spoke into his phone.

"Like a leech stuck to my balls, Sarge."

Carmine cringed then shuddered at the visual that presented, failing to categorize it as unseen. "Right, just stay on him."

"What's done?" Helen echoed his own thoughts from a moment before, but something had changed in her voice. It sounded sad and loaded with disappointment as her face crumpled. "This is your last chance to make it right, Cody."

"I know." He leaned in quickly, put a palm to her cheek and kissed her before she had a chance to move out of his way. "I swear I won't let you down." Then before she could respond, he hurried away.

There was an unfamiliar churning in Carmine's gut, yet also a sense of relief. He didn't understand it but was glad that hadn't come to anything more than just a minor public disturbance. That she wasn't harmed, at least outwardly.

For several long seconds she stood frozen seeming to watch Cody's retreating back. Then her head tilted slightly forward, that gorgeous curtain of shiny auburn hair hiding her face. Her shoulders hitched, and her hand came up to her face.

Damn. Girl was crying.

That shouldn't affect him—but it did, making his jaw spasm. For some reason he wanted to comfort her, and he'd only met her once before—where she totally blown him off and told him she didn't do men. But he'd seen her with dudes on the dance floor grooving to Terra's band while he'd done a diagnostic on the bar's surveillance equipment. Granted it had been on video and he might've rewound it a few times more than necessary. And yeah, since he was being honest, there was that one other time when he'd driven passed Provocative, the lingerie store she worked at and saw her through the window serving a customer. For some unknown reason besides her obvious beauty and spunk, something about the woman drew him.

Helen walked into the shoe store next to the electronics shop, moving out his sight line. He relocated to the glass railing opposite and watched her sit on one of those fancy little cushioned benches, her profile to him.

"Boss," Brady murmured into his ear. "He's going into a sports store on level three. What do you want me to do?"

"Stay outside, keep watching. See who he's meeting and video. Make sure you get the name of the store."

"Will do."

"Now's your opportunity to change your appearance. Reverse your jacket and put on your beanie."

While he spoke, his eyes stayed on Helen. She flicked her hair over her shoulder, then searched in her purse, found a Kleenex and dabbed at her eyes and nose. After touching up her make-up and lip gloss, she re-stashed her cosmetics and offered a smile to the approaching shoe saleswoman. A few words were said, then Helen left the store, continuing in the same direction as before.

He wanted to follow but stayed put as she stepped onto the escalator going down, getting off on the concourse level. Just before she disappeared from his sights, a man joined her. Involuntarily, his back and shoulder muscles tensed, then became rigid when she tipped her chin and he kissed her on her lips.

Damn.

Why was that so disappointing?

"Boss," Brady broke into his thoughts, laughing. "You're never gonna believe this. The douche is locking lips with another dude. He cheats both ways and I got it all on my phone."

Carmine sighed, not surprised. Though to him it wasn't a laughing matter. He'd always known it, having been on the receiving end of an unwelcome come-on from the target about six months prior to him marrying his client.

Naturally he'd told him to fuck off. One, he wasn't into dudes and two, his fiancée was a friend. She'd come to him last week with her suspicions he was cheating, now it was his displeasure to confirm that news. Generally, he had no opinion on anyone's sexuality. Who people slept with or fell in love with was their business, but he did have a strong one on infidelity. He'd seen what his father's cheating had done to his mother.

He exhaled.

Relationships.

The only serious one he'd had hadn't ended well either. When that...died, he'd vowed he'd never fall in love again. The pain of which he still dealt with, though it had softened over time. Three hard, long, difficult years.

"Good job, Brady," he said, staring at the last spot he saw Helen. "Meet me in the food court. I'll buy you a burger."

"Excellent. Do I get fries with it, Sarge?"

"Not if you call me Sarge again."

"Sorry Boss-man."

He hung up and immediately his phone rang again with a number he didn't recognize.

"Niccoterra," he answered.

"Hey, um, this is Carly."

Carly?

He searched his brain but couldn't come up with a face.

"You gave me your card a while back in case I saw someone you were looking for?"

"Yeah?" His ears pricked up, his heart beating harder. He only had one other unresolved hunt. After exhausting all leads, he'd come to a dead end. Could this finally be the one he'd been waiting for. "Where are you Carly?"

"I'm in a town just off 78 in Arizona, near the river."

Holy shit!

"The Colorado River?"

"Uh huh. The girl you're looking for, I'm not a hundred percent sure it's her, but I think it is. She stole a pair of shoes from my dad's store. We have her on video. I just thought you might want to check it out."

"When did this happen Carly?"

"An hour ago."

Damn, this could be it.

He took the necessary information from her then called Brady back. "Raincheck on the burger. Get your ass to the Jeep."

Chapter Two

The following evening, Helen sat on the seat of her living room bay window, one leg up on the cushion, chin on her knee, watching the traffic pass––the incident with Cody replaying in her mind.

""Dudes, I'm freaking out!" Terra's slightly panicked voice broke into her thoughts. She was running her fingers through her mass of strawberry blonde curls. If she noticed Helen's unusually somber mood, which as her best friend she would, she wisely didn't say. Not in front of her other friends anyway. "I'm in a music video! How cool is that? But I have one *massive* problem."

"What's that?" Rory, her video buddy asked.

"What am I going to wear, obviously."

Helen focused on the man relaxing on her couch. Rory had one ankle draped over a knee and was strumming his guitar, while Truman, Shelly's overweight English bulldog sat next to him on the couch. Each time Rory hit a particular chord, the dog attempted to sing along with often hilarious yet abundantly cute results.

"What kind of vibe are you going for?" she asked, trying really hard to snap out of her funky mood.

"I'd say earthy," Shelly joined in, curling a strand of her long, dark hair around her fingers. "Terra's got that bohemian thing going on. Play it up."

"You think?" Terra stopped pacing.

"I concur," Rory said. "Sort of Stevie Nicks back in the day, except tight jeans and a sexy top. Lots of jewelry and definitely the nose bling," he added. "Show off your ass, because that's what everyone's gonna be looking at anyway."

"Ha! It's always about asses for you, isn't it?"

"Well, yeah." Rory paused his strumming, looking at Terra like she was crazy. "I'm a dude."

Helen sighed. Their banter, interesting as it was, failed to lift her mind out of her Cody funk. She glanced at her phone one more time, then out her living room window at the rising orange moon. Why hadn't he called? He'd seemed so genuine when he told her he would, she'd actually believed him.

And therein lay her problem.

Always wanting to trust, to believe, to think the best of someone. Until she couldn't. Didn't make her heart hurt any less. Though no longer shattered, it was still bruised. His broken promise a jab to the center, most sensitive part of that bruise, like her bratty little brother Petey used to do when they were kids.

Rory strummed a chord. He and Terra began to harmonize the chorus and Truman joined in. "*Howooowoo,*"

Everyone burst out laughing, Helen included. Truman's jowls quivered as he sang into Rory's ear.

"God, Truman," Shelley half laughed, half cried. "I'm gonna have to muzzle you."

"You should have him in the video," Helen giggled. "He'll make it go viral."

"Ohmigod, we should!" Terra sat up straight. "Shelley, can we?"

Her phone rang, making her jump and her breath catch. Until she saw the caller ID.

"Hey Mamma, what's up?"

"Oh, sweetie I'm having a hell of a time."

Sudden fear shot through her at the scratchiness of her mother's voice. "What's wrong? You having heart palpitations again?"

"No, honey, not that kind of time. Something else. I hate to ask this, but do you have Nana's ring—the ruby one?"

"No, why would *I* have it?"

"I thought maybe you borrowed it and forgot to tell me."

"Mom, I would never take your jewelry without asking. The one time I did that, I got grounded for like a year, remember?"

"I do, but you were fifteen, and anyway it's eventually going to be yours if I can ever find it again. I was just hoping you maybe took it. Dad's got a work function tonight and I wanted to wear it. Obviously that's not going to happen anymore, but I really just want to find it now."

"Did you look in your jewelry box?"

"Of course I did. It's not there, that's why I'm calling."

"Okay that was a stupid question. What about your purse?"

"I looked there too."

"Between the couch cushions?"

"Ditto."

"When was the last time you wore it?"

"Well, let's see. I would have been wearing red because that's the only time I wear that ring and I always take it off right away afterwards, because, you know, I'm so worried the stone will fall out."

"And when was that?"

"The last time I wore red was...oh! When we went out to dinner. For your birthday. That was right before..." her mother's voice trailed off.

She and Cody broke up.

In fact, it was the last date they had. The following day she'd come home from work to find he'd packed his clothes, forged her signature on a check and disappeared with two thousand dollars.

Her stomach dropped. That night, she'd seen Cody leaving her parent's bedroom. Had thought it odd at the time but he'd said he was looking for toilet paper as there was none in the guest bathroom. That had happened on occasion, so she'd hadn't questioned it further, just wondered why he never asked her to get it from the pantry where her mom stored it.

Would he really stoop so low as to steal from her parents? Then again, he'd stolen from her, *why not* her parents.

"I can't stand the idea I might have lost it," her mother went on, "and I was really hoping you had it. Any other ring, even my wedding rings, but not that one."

Indeed, not that one.

Nana's ring was the one relic from a terrible time in their family history—Nazi Germany. The only member of her family left alive, her teenage grandmother had swallowed it before jumping into the Rhine, preferring to die by drowning rather than get taken to the death camps. She'd hidden clinging to the underside of a log and got swept away with the current, somehow surviving. Then crossed the border into Belgium with a small group of Jews and sailed to Dover. She later met and married her grandfather, an American soldier stationed there.

"Mom, I'm sure it will turn up," she said, crossing her fingers and praying it to be true. "You probably put it somewhere for safekeeping and forgot where that was."

Her mom sighed. "I know, that's probably what happened, but I just thought I'd ask."

"Well, have fun tonight anyway."

"I'll try, but I'm actually quite sick to my stomach."

Helen leaned sideways, resting her temple on the glass. Holy hell, could it get any worse? Nana's ring?

"Helen?" Terra's hand slid over her shoulder. "You okay, babe?"

Her head jerked up. "Huh?" It was then she became aware everyone had gone quiet and was watching her.

13

"What's wrong? You're feeling sick?"

"I'm fine." She forced a smile. "Just got the beginnings of a headache. I'll take something for it. You all want more wine?"

"I could use a fill up," Shelley said. "Rory's driving so I can partake."

Besides Rory being Terra's video buddy, he was also one of Shelley's bosses. He co-owned a chain of high-end salons with his sister Cas, though didn't actually do hair himself. He mostly provided the financial backing and scoped out new locations.

Helen entered her tiny kitchen and stood next to the butter-yellow tile counter, taking a few breaths before retrieving a bottle of Zinfandel tucked neatly in a corner next to her matching butter-yellow fridge. Come hell or high water, she had to find that ring. But first she had to find her ex. She thumbed through her contacts, then sent off a text.

What the hell Cody? Can't you ever follow through?

She refrained from asking about the ring. That she'd need to do eyeball to eyeball to gauge his expression.

Of course, there was no response. In all actuality she wasn't even sure he hadn't blocked her number. Wouldn't put it past him just to spite her.

When she saw him, she was going to kill him. Nana Resnick didn't survive the Nazi's to have a scrawny ass, pencil pushing accountant steal her ring.

She'd get it back.

No matter what it cost her.

Chapter Three

Carmine flipped the light then tossed his car keys onto his desk. He strolled to his office window on the first floor of his building, opening it and letting in the breeze. San Francisco's summers were typically engulfed in fog, mostly non-existent except for September and October. Therefore, no need for air-conditioning, and the majority of older buildings in the city were not equipped with it.

Today had broiled with temperatures into the high nineties, but thank God it wasn't the desert.

He unbuttoned his white linen shirt, leaving it hanging open over his jeans and stood in front of the window allowing evaporation to cool him.

Thankfully this hunt was over. It had been a doozie.

A year ago, his client, a wealthy Silicon Valley venture capitalist's daughter, followed her boyfriend into the Sonoran Desert in favor of a nomadic life off-grid with a small band—or as they preferred to be called—a *grove* of modern-day druids. Their leader did not believe in technology and convinced—make that forced—his followers to disengage from the modern world by confiscating and destroying all their devices. But not before emptying their bank accounts.

Finding her hadn't been easy. They'd put in countless hours over a two-month period tracking the grove's movements, and always several steps behind. Carly's phone call had changed that.

He didn't envy Isaac, his client, for what came next, but the relief and gratification he'd delivered was why he did what he did. In return his little agency had received a hefty check for their efforts, enough to give all his men and Verity his office manager a decent bonus.

He strolled through the back end of the bakery––past the dungeon as it was called, where his men did the things he hired them to do, to the weight room they used to keep themselves strong.

It was empty now.

Discarding his jeans and button-down, he changed into shorts and a tee shirt. Chugged a bottle of water he pulled from a fridge and started his routine. A hundred pushups, thirty pull-ups, squats, lunges and then thirty minutes on the treadmill.

After a shower, he headed back to his office and planted his ass in his chair. He needed a vacation. They all did.

The photo, the one he couldn't bear to put away just yet sat slightly askew, which meant his mother had cleaned his office again. No matter how many times he told her not to, she did it anyway. Touching his thumb to the woman in the photo's smile, he let out an extended breath.

"Hey baby. How're you doing today?" he whispered.

It was the last one taken of them together, two days before they went on leave, still dressed in army fatigues. Her blue eyes sparkled with laughter, but her face hid the fact his hand was squeezing her ass.

Three years.

When did the hurt and the guilt finally go away? Did he want it to? It had lessened somewhat, but letting go of it completely meant letting go of her and he wasn't there yet.

He moved the frame into its usual spot before retrieving his phone from his back pocket.

One voicemail, and he debated returning the call right away, figuring it wasn't going to be good, but it probably meant a job. Snake, President of the Redwood Rebels Motorcycle Club, aka Double RMC, didn't call out of the mighty blue yonder to shoot the breeze.

He hit the call back button.

"Took you fucking long enough to get back to me," Snake grumbled.

"Well, hello to you too, dickhead," Carmine responded as he parked his heels on his desk. "It's been a while." Since he'd recovered a bushel load of cash for the club when one of their hang-arounds had disappeared with it after a particularly lucrative drug run. Had taken risks for that job, but he was young, fresh out of the army with a death wish. Gave him experience and quite the reputation. Men like Snake were better to have in your corner and of course, never short of referrals.

"Yeah, whatever." Snake's tone was gruff, but Carmine detected the hint of laughter in his voice. "Got a job for you. My fucking bookkeeper has gone AWOL. I need you to find him."

"You never considered the poor sap went on vacation, just forgot to mention it to you?"

"Not this asshole if he knows what's good for him."

"How about getting a new bookkeeper?" Carmine leaned forward in his chair and jiggled the mouse on his computer, bringing up the Facebook page he'd resisted stalking. Mostly because he'd been busy with Isaac's case. But now he had down time and seeing that little redhead again had caused an itch. One he had a definite need to scratch.

"Because the asshole knows the ins and outs of my operation. Probably too much, now that I think about it."

"Because...?"

"You don't need to know the why, Niccoterra, you just need to find him."

"That's not how it works, Snake." He typed Helen's name into the search bar, already losing interest in the dude's caginess. Maybe he could beg off this one. When her profile picture popped his breath almost stopped. A cascade of pretty auburn hair shining in the sun, and those russet eyes looking directly at the camera —at him.

"Would be nice to know what's at stake before I put my life or the life of my men on the line."

"Used to be you weren't so cautious or discriminating."

"Used to be I didn't have employees. Times have changed."

"Yeah, well, he's a fucking boring, thick as shit bookkeeper, how dangerous could he be?"

"Not so boring if he decided to ditch your gnarly old ass."

"I'll have you know, my old lady happens to like my gnarly old ass, asshole."

"Lucky for you."

Snake grunt-laughed on the other side of the phone. "You want the job or not?"

On the one hand they could use a nice, easy, ass planted in the chair job looking for a boring bookkeeper. Most of it could be done online checking patterns, social media, and Badger was a master at finding precious little nuggets if he had enough information to work with.

However, all his men needed a break after the hours they'd put in. Besides the missing daughter, they'd hunted and located a husband who was suspected of murdering his wife, who'd somehow convinced a judge to grant bail and then skipped across the border to Mexico. They'd brought him back and received a decent reward from his bail bondsman. Cash flow was the least of his problems—burnout on the other hand, was.

"I was thinking about heading to Hawaii for a week. Get some sun, and surf. I can refer it out."

"Fuck that shit! I need *you* on this, Niccoterra. I don't beg, but I don't want nobody else."

Hmm.

Indeed, Snake did not beg—ever. So, this must be big.

"Fine," he sighed while he scrolled through Helen's photos, hoping to find one with her and the dude he'd seen her arguing with. He'd like to do a little digging on him and maybe the douche was tagged. "What are the deets and I'll consider it."

"Knew you couldn't resist my gnarly old army charm."

"Army something, but I haven't said yes yet." Though Snake was an army vet like him, they hadn't served together. Being almost thirty years older, his tour had come way before Carmine's. The man had driven Humvees during Desert Storm, while he'd dodged enemy fire, though not always successfully, in Afghanistan.

"You will. Not like you to let a little old boring bookkeeper outfox an intelligence grunt."

Carmine snorted. The man had him pegged, but he'd yet to prove the job he proposed was a challenge.

"Anyway," Snake continued. "He belongs to one of the brothers and he's been cleaning shit up since we got our permit to grow marijuana. Using one of those software programs, Quickly something, I think it's called."

"QuickBooks," Carmine corrected while he clicked on a selfie of Helen cross-eyed and sticking out her tongue. She was with Terra at what looked like some kind of street festival. One of those arts and wine thingies chicks flocked to. He smiled at the image. The woman was quirky for sure.

"They were supposed to check in a couple days ago." Snake broke off to cough. "He and Hunter, the brother who brung him into the club and who's responsible for his skinny ass went to your neck of town for some personal business but neither are answering their phone. That makes me worried."

19

"So, who am I supposed to be looking for? The bookkeeper or your brother?"

"Technically both, but I trust my brother. The bookkeeper, not so much."

"Like I said, maybe he took a vacation."

"Thing is, the little prick has, or had a coke habit. He's managed for the most part to keep it under wraps. He's gone on benders before and I'm thinking this could be one more."

"What the hell you doing using a coke-head to do your books?"

"Wouldn't normally but he's a fucking genius."

Wait...what? "I thought you said he was thick as shit?"

"Thick as shit in life. Got not a club-whore's ounce of common sense and a real ability for attracting trouble. But when it comes to taking care of the books and keeping the IRS off our asses and out of our business, he's a...what's that word when someone's retarded but clever in one thing?"

Carmine shook his head and raised his eyes to the ceiling at Snake's insensitivity. "You mean savant."

"Yeah, that. Only reason we tolerated him, *and* he's Hunter's old lady's brother."

"You checked with his dealer?"

"Kai, another brother, did that. Said he hasn't seen him in a while. Believed he'd stopped using or found another dealer."

Carmine opened up Excel on his computer, found the spreadsheet he needed, and printed out the standard customized profile form he used when he started a new job. He retrieved it off the printer, then wrote *bookkeeper* down in pencil.

"What does he love to do?"

"What do you mean?"

"Is he into sports, gambling, motorcycles...what?" A person could run and hide, change their hair, their face, their appearance —but they couldn't change what they love. That was always his starting point and it usually saved him masses of time.

"Shit. I'm not sure. Didn't spend much time chatting, he was kind of a nerd. Didn't have much in common other than him keeping my books clean. He was quiet, most of the time I didn't even notice him."

"Woman?"

"Supposedly had one in the City, but I don't know much about her. Like I said, quiet and never talked about anything other than the books, at least not to me."

"What about his sister?"

"Losing her shit. She hasn't heard from them either."

"I'm going to need a photo."

He heard the flick of a lighter as Snake lit up a cigarette, take a deep drag, then exhale before he spoke again. "It's weird, but I don't got any of those either. I'll get one from Candy and send it to you."

"Was that intentional, or coincidence?"

"That I have no photos?"

"What I mean is, did he avoid the camera on purpose or was he just never important enough to be in the shot?"

"A bit of both I think."

Hmm. "Ugly?"

"Decent-looking in a nerdy way. Tall, a little on the skinny side. Reserved, but not shy."

Figures. Always the silent, observant ones a man had to worry about. His gut and experience told him things weren't exactly how Snake described. Men who employed men like himself usually hid something. Snake was no different.

"Before I give you anymore, you gonna take the job?"

"Rates have gone up."

"Of course they fucking have."

"Got overhead and employees now."

"I hear that."

"I'll do it on one condition."

"Always with the conditions."

21

"I need you to tell me, why me?"

"What do you mean 'why you?'"

"Why not have your club look for him? As you said, a boring old bookkeeper. Can't have gone far."

There was a long hesitation before he spoke. "It's sensitive, man."

Uh huh—like he thought. Dude was hiding something, which upped the stakes, and his interest level.

"How sensitive?"

"He's got something that belongs to the club. They don't know it's missing yet. I'd like to retrieve it before they do, and this stays between you and me. I need your word."

Carmine pushed back from his desk and sat up straighter. A fine tingle started at the base of his spine, which raised the hairs on the back of his neck. Shit had just gotten interesting.

"You have it." he said, after a moment and put Snake on speaker phone. "Give me his deets."

After Snake had hung up, Carmine plugged the bookkeeper's name and other details into a registry. It pulled up several hundred possible hits. He eliminated the obvious ones by ethnicity, age and location until he was left with just three.

One of those interested him immediately. "Holy mother of God," he muttered.

He screen-shot the image, then emailed it to Snake. *This him?*

Snake's response was immediate. *Yep.*

Since he didn't believe in coincidences, the universe had to be fucking with him.

Chapter Four

Where was he?

Helen drove around the busy parking lot looking for Cody's blue Toyota 4Runner. Unable to find it, she waited for an octogenarian gentleman pushing a shopping cart filled to the max to move before she pulled into a vacant spot and checked the time again on her phone. Then his text message.

Safeway parking lot at 7pm.

Yep, he definitely said seven. As it was seven twenty-two, it meant he was late—as usual. No surprise. She was sick to death of his bullshit and pushed back her seat to try to relax a little. Her feet throbbed, and never mind her stomach grumbling from hunger she was in desperate need of a glass of wine.

She tried his number, but it rang until it went to voicemail. Again—no big surprise. It was one of the things that drove her hair-pulling crazy when they dated, and it definitely wasn't one of the things she missed—she could never reach him when she needed to.

She fired off a text. *I'm here. Where are you?*

As she waited, she kicked off her shoes and rubbed her aching soles, while she scrolled through her social media pages, liking several posts until her phone made a pretty little *ting* sound.

Cody: *Inside the main doors. You need to hurry.*

Oh!

Well how about that? He's late, but she needs to hurry? Typical. She ran her tongue over her teeth while sucking in a breath through her nose and thought about that bottle of rosé chilling in her fridge.

Whatever. She could do this. Only a few more minutes, she'd have her money and be done with him forever. After jamming her feet back into her cute low-heeled pumps, she hooked her purse strap over her shoulder and exited her Fiat, then walked towards the main entrance of the grocery store, smoothing down her suit jacket.

All kinds of unholy hell raced through her mind—the kinds she'd like to rain down on his unpredictable ass. But she'd refrain, and she'd already sworn off the sticking any pins into the voodoo doll she'd bought as a joke, only because she was too hungry to get arrested. It would be fun, no doubt satisfying and long overdue, but Cody wasn't worth Terra having to bail her out of jail.

He must have seen her coming, as she was barely halfway through the parking lot with the wind whipping at her hair, when he stepped through the doors loping towards her. His head moving side to side, like he was keeping a lookout for something.

He seemed skittish, even more nervous that he'd been in the mall, or perhaps he'd overindulged in the white powdery stuff again. Cody's eyes widened and his step faltered before he froze completely. She followed the direction of his gaze. Two men dressed in jeans and dark hoodies, the taller of the two was white, and the other a young African American man with a baseball cap approached him. They didn't exactly give off a menacing vibe, but their demeanor wasn't friendly either. Although, perhaps Cody thought differently because he spun and ran.

Poop!

The taller dude, anticipating his move, chased and caught him within just a few steps. She didn't know whether to be happy they'd caught him or sad he hadn't gotten away. Until he pushed Cody against the wall, twisting his arm up behind his back, while the other took a position behind him, as if standing guard.

Holy hell! It occurred to her suddenly. They were mugging him!

No!

This so wasn't happening. Cody could *not* get mugged!

"Hey," she yelled, waving her arms. One of her faults as everyone, especially her family lovingly pointed out, was she didn't think; she just did. "What are you doing? Get off him."

The shorter, leaner dude standing back pegged her, his eyes expanding to the point his irises were completely surrounded by white.

"Leave him alone."

"Fuck, Boss," he blurted. "We got incoming."

"Block 'em," the taller one answered. A second later, Helen launched herself onto his back, wrapping her legs and hooking her feet around his waist. She locked an arm around his thick, strong neck, fisting a chunk of his dark hair and pulled like Cody's life depended on it.

"Get off him!"

"What the hell?" Tall dude grunted and staggered back a foot.

"You can't mug him," she yelled. "I won't let you. Cody, run!"

Reeling to steady himself, he released his grip on Cody, but before Cody could run, the younger man wasted no time stepping in to take his place.

"That's my money, you can't take it."

"Money? Holy shit, woman, we're not mugging him."

"Helen—what are you doing?" Cody yelled at her, his voice pitched high. "Don't be stupid. Get outta here."

"Don't call me stupid. Jesus, Cody, fight back. For once in your stupid life."

"Helen?" The tall dude asked. There was a note of surprise in his voice as he tried to twist his neck to get a look at her. "Helen? Are you kidding me?"

"Yeah, that's my name, butthead." She turned her attention to the other guy who was stiff-arming Cody. "Don't mug him. Let him go or I'll bite your friend's ear off." She captured his lobe between her teeth, along with a bunch of dark curly hair.

"Ow fuck, woman!" he growled as she bit down. She felt it vibrate angrily through his body which was currently pressed to her stomach. "Release my ear, I told you we're not mugging him."

"Wike I'm ghonna faw for zat," she mumbled, her breath blasting hot against his head and bouncing back in her face. When she took a breath through her nose, his citrusy-scented hair smelled surprisingly good.

Which was against all that was holy. Muggers weren't supposed to smell good.

"What?" he asked, exasperated.

"Wike I'm ghonna faw for zat," she repeated. "Wet whim gow!"

"You let *me* go," he snapped, fingers digging into her calves. "And I may let you both live."

This made her squeeze them tighter and hook her feet for a better grip, silently blessing both yoga and her figure eight classes.

"Tell her we're not mugging you, Cody. We're here because of Snake."

Wait.

They weren't?

For the first time, she realized she may have misread the situation and pulled her mouth from tall dude's ear, spitting out a mouthful of hair which had gotten stuck to her lip gloss. "Do you know these people, Cody?"

"Jesus, Helen." Cody sounded scared, straining against shorty's arm. "This has nothing to do with you. I'm sorry, I didn't want to get you involved in this."

"Involved in what?"

"Listen to him. We're not interested in his money. I just need to talk to him, and you're being a slight impediment to such. Now let go of my hair and get off my back."

"Cody?"

"Woman, relax your legs."

"Or...what?"

"Or so help me God, I'm gonna dump your tiny ass onto the concrete."

Tiny ass?

It was small, but in proportion to her body. Besides how did he know that?

"Who are you?"

"I'm not telling you again. Relax your legs." When she didn't immediately, he began to bend at the waist, and it was then she saw the peril of her situation. If he bent all the way forward, she would slide off his back onto her head.

"Okay, *okay*! I'm relaxing."

"Let go of my hair."

Fine.

She huffed, and loosened her grip on his hair, then her arm around his neck, and slid down his back to the ground.

A strangled snort came from the younger man. He was still stiff-arming Cody, but his lips were stretched over startling white teeth, shoulders shaking.

"What the fuck are you laughing at, Brady."

"Boss," he strangled out, shaking his head, tears forming in his eyes.

"Dammit, Helen," Cody said. "You fucking fruit loop. What were you thinking?"

"I wasn't thinking." She turned to face him. "Are you taking their side? I thought you were getting mugged. What do you want me to do, stand by and watch?" She tossed out her hand, palm up. "Give it."

"I can't give it until he lets me go," he said with a sideways glance at the kid named Brady.

"Let him go," she ordered. His eyes shifted from hers to his boss who was standing behind her. She could feel him bristling.

"Tell him..." She spun around and stopped. Her eyes locked onto the prettiest, light green eyes rimmed with the blackest lashes she'd ever seen. They were so pretty they almost looked fake. But what wasn't fake was the ultra pissed off vibe emanating from them and his hard body. And she recognized him. That over-the-top hot dude from Zander's bar.

"Oh boy."

She didn't know much about him, but what she did know from Shelley was if Carmine was hunting for you in a professional capacity, you were deep in it. "What do you want with him?"

Without ripping glinting eyes off her, he pointed a stiff, angry finger at Brady. "You deal with Cody." Then he crooked that stiff, angry finger at her. "You, come with me."

"What?"

"Come. With. me." Hard fingers wrapped around her upper arm and virtually dragged her a short distance away.

He leaned down and got in her face. "What, for the love of God, was *that*?"

Yes, he was tall, and big, and she was only five-two, maybe five-four in heels. She had, however, grown up with a much larger little brother. His size didn't intimidate. She squared her shoulders and stuck out her chin.

"I was trying to help Cody. What did it look like I was doing?"

"You put yourself in danger for that idiot?"

Idiot? *Oooh!*

"Where do you get off calling him that? Yeah, Cody is an idiot. But he's *my* idiot. You don't even know him."

"You're shitting me, right?" He stared at her before stepping back, putting his fingers to his forehead, like he wasn't believing his ears.

"I am not shitting you. I do not *shit* people."

"Well, I've got news for you, lady. I don't know much, but what I do know isn't especially good."

"So, he's made mistakes. That just makes him human."

"Mistakes? If you really knew him, you'd keep away from him —unless *you're* the idiot."

"Ohmigod, you don't get to judge me. You know nothing about me and anyway, it's none of your business."

"Woman, we have mutual friends. We run in the same circle."

"So?"

"So, *Helen,* that means, because you mean something to my friends, and because my friends mean something to me, you're in my vicinity that by default makes you my responsibility and my job to protect you."

"Your responsibility?" She laughed. "God, you're something, aren't you? I'm not a child."

"That idiot,"—he pointed in the direction of Cody—"has done something really, *really* stupid, pissing off a really dangerous man. And if you'd pulled that stunt on him, what do you think would have happened?"

"But it wasn't him, was it?"

"Not. The point."

"It *is* the point. You don't need to worry your"—she made a circular motion with her finger,"—your pretty little curls about me. I can take care of myself."

"Listen Tomato Head, that was not smart. You could have gotten hurt."

She pulled her head back and wrinkled her nose. "Tomato Head?"

She'd been called all kinds of things, like ginger nut and chili pepper. One kid in junior high even called her lobster top. But Tomato Head?

"That's just rude," she responded. "Now take your rude,

29

obnoxious self and get out of my face. I need to get my money before Cody bails on me again."

"He's not gonna bail. Brady's got him." Then his gaze narrowed. "Why does he owe you money?"

"None of your business."

"I'm making it my business. Why does he owe you money?"

"He just does."

"Try again."

She folded her arms and pursed her lips. "No."

Little crinkles formed in the corners of those phenomenal eyes. "Why did you tell me you didn't do men?"

"Seemed like a good idea at the time."

"You make a habit out of lying?"

"Just to you."

"Sarge," Brady yelled with enough panic in his voice to make both their heads jerk in his direction. "We got trouble."

A big black Harley with high handlebars rumbled between parked cars narrowly missing a woman in his way and headed straight for them. Something in the rider's extended hand glinted.

"Down," Carmine yelled, quickly engulfing Helen in his arms, he shoved her behind a row of shopping carts, then rolled his body onto hers, squishing her ears between his biceps and his chest. The rapid thump of his heart thundering in her head was almost drowned out by the obnoxious, menacing roar as the bike came closer.

Then *pop...pop...pop...pop!*

Bullets hit the stucco on the building above their heads, and then shattered the glass of the main entrance sliding doors. It was deafening, how she would imagine a war zone sounded as people all around screamed.

Pop, pop, pop, pop!

The bike accelerated erratically, giving the impression the biker didn't know how to control it properly, which was weird. Then it gained speed as it veered out of the parking lot over the sidewalk and around the corner out of sight.

Car alarms mingled with the human cries of chaos. Carmine lay on her, his chest pressed to hers. Both their hearts beat double time and his breath rasped in her ear. As the Harley's roar faded, he lifted his head and stared into her eyes. His were wide––his pupils dilated.

"You okay?" he asked, his voice hoarse, cracking a bit.

She nodded, though she found it difficult to breathe with his weight crushing her, at the same time she was grateful for his body shielding hers.

"Who...who are they shooting at?"

"Not sure, but do you get me now when I said these are dangerous people?"

Did she get him? Yeah, she got him—all six-foot-one of his solid, muscular body.

"Cody." Suddenly fear struck deep and hard, stealing what breath she had left in her lungs. "Ohmigod, Cody!" She pushed at his hard torso until he grunted. "Get off me, I need to check on him."

Something dark flickered in his eyes, but he didn't waste a moment doing as she asked. In one lithe movement, he sprung to his feet. Then gripping her hand, pulled her up. When he was sure she was steady, he let her go and sprinted on sure legs to where Cody and Brady last were. She followed, though not so quickly on legs made of rubber.

Several people were crouched low to the ground behind cars and shopping carts. Two lay flat—one was a woman covered in red.

"Help her," a man on his knees next to her cried, looking around frantically. "God, somebody help her!" Another man ran towards them and she turned her attention to the one she knew. Cody. Except he wasn't where he was supposed to be. She did a wobbly three-sixty but there was no sign of him—anywhere.

Then she saw Carmine, also on his knees, pulling his hoodie over his head.

Nine-one-one!

Good God, she needed to call nine-one-one. Why hadn't she thought of that? Pulling her phone from her pants, she stabbed the numbers. While it rang, she bounced on the balls of her feet, still looking for her missing ex.

"Nine one one, what's your emergency?"

"There's," her voice hitched. *Stay calm, she told herself. Just stay calm.* "there's been a drive-by shooting. A man on a Harley... he...he shot at us." Despite her admonishments to herself, her breath continued to come in short, quick breaths.

Where was Cody?

"The...the main doors... at the Safeway on Webster. Please hurry, at least two people are down but I'm sure there's more. There's blood...ohmigod...there's so much blood and we need ambulances. Lots of them."

Where the fuck was Cody?

"Ma'am, can you give me your name."

"He...Helen Resnick, but I can't talk any more, I have to help. Please hurry."

"CODY?" she called, looking every direction. What if he was injured, or maybe dead?

"Ma'am..."

"Hurry...just hurry. I can't find Cody."

"Ma'am?"

She hung up and checked behind the wall where the shopping carts were stashed, then inside the store doors. This was good, yeah? If he could move, he was okay...?

But then she caught sight of Carmine crouched over a flattened Brady. *He* clearly wasn't okay as blood spilled from his side. She ran over to help, pulling off her own jacket. Carmine had clumped his hoodie into a ball, using it to put pressure on the wound, but it was already soaked. Brady's beautiful chocolate skin had turned an ashy gray.

Carmine muttered, "C'mon, bud stay with me." He angled his head to look at her. "Helen, this is important. Put your hands here, maintain pressure, as hard as you can. I'm gonna get something out of my car."

"There's more blood coming from underneath him," she said, removing, then balling her own jacket up. "Lift him just enough I can put this under him."

Carmine nodded without looking at her, and somehow maintaining the pressure on Brady's side, rolled him.

"Aww, *fuuuuck*," Brady moaned. "That hurts,"

"I know, I'm so sorry," she acknowledged as his moans cut through her, but she had to find the source. It was currently dispersed by his clothing. When she did, she slid her jacket under him, making sure the surface was flat and smooth with no buttons pressing into him to increase his discomfort. After it was in place, Carmine rolled him gently back, then directing her to hold his balled up hoodie in the other spot on his stomach. When she had it, he ran somewhere. To his car she presumed, but it was out of her sightline. She continued to put pressure on the top wound, and therefore by default, on the bottom as well. Moments later Carmine came back carrying something. He passed her a black plastic package that looked like an oversized condom wrapper.

"Do what I do," he ordered. "And don't be squeamish. If you do, he will die." Nothing like the "D" word to make a girl pay attention. She watched him rip open the wrapper and pull out white gauze. He rolled Brady over again and to her surprise started shoving the gauze *into* the wound in his back, ignoring Brady's cries of pain. "I'm sorry bud, I'm so fucking sorry, but I gotta do this."

He nodded at Helen and barked. "Do it now!"

She swallowed, found a little notch on the side and opened the second package, then did exactly as he was doing.

"What is this?" Helen asked, unpeeling a section and then forced it into his stomach wound.

"It's a coagulant. It'll stop the bleeding."

"Just shove it in?"

"Exactly, little bit by little bit."

They worked quickly. When the wound was packed, he showed her how to fold the remainder and use it as a pad. He then pulled off his tee shirt and tore it length wise, using it as a bandage to hold the pads in place. It worked. The flow of blood had slowed, then after a few moments more, stopped. He placed the empty packages under the tee shirt at both locations of the entry wounds.

"Why are you doing that?" she asked, not really focusing on the why, just needing to stay engaged.

"It lets the paramedics know what we used."

Helen glanced around, wondering about the woman who'd been shot as well. Others were helping her, but she turned to Carmine. "Does she need some too?"

"Don't have any more," he answered. There was so much regret in his voice, she couldn't almost process it. "Sorry, but that's how it is in a war zone."

"I hope she makes it."

"Me too, but right now we need to focus on what we can do."

She understood the concept of triage. It was an unfortunate fact of life, doing what you could to save the ones you could. Therefore, she focused only on Brady. It was a miracle he hadn't passed out, and his breathing was short and shallow.

"Did you get a look at him, bud? Carmine asked. "Anyone we recognize?"

"Shaw a patch, Sarshe. One per...shenters...backtoback errs."

"Fuck," Carmine mumbled, his brow forming furrows in his smooth skin. "Back to back R's? You sure?"

"One percenters?" she asked. "What does that mean?"

"Outlaws."

Holy hell.

34

She was aware there were actual outlaw biker cultures, but why would one be shooting at them?

"Cody...made a runner, Sarche."

"Don't worry about that, Brady. Just focus on staying with me."

"Shaw 'em before me...went white-er..." Brady grimaced as a wave of pain reverberated through him. "Fuuck...hurts."

"I know, bro...I know. The medics are coming." Carmine looked up, the same question on his face as she was thinking.

Why were they taking so long?

It seemed a lifetime had passed, but in reality was only a few minutes. Helplessness overwhelmed her. What else could she do? She didn't know him, but she could comfort him. Taking Brady's hand, she squeezed his fingers gently. They were cold, but his eyes slid to hers and he gave her a weak smile.

"Listen, you," she said, holding his gaze even though his eyes were glazing with pain or lack of blood, she couldn't say. "I can hear the sirens." Which was true, they finally could. "They'll be here very soon. You hang in there, otherwise you're going to have to deal with me, okay?"

His lashes flickered, he was fading.

"Hey, look at me. I need you to keep looking at me. Do you have a girlfriend?"

"Nooo," he groaned.

"Well that's a shame. When you get through this, I'll introduce you to a few of my friends, okay?"

"Sounsgoo...uugh!"

"Bro, don't talk, Carmine interrupted him as the first ambulance arrived. "Save it. They're here. They're going to take care of you."

Like stormtroopers, medics descended, and Helen and Carmine stepped aside to let them work. Carmine turned his back to her and ran his hands through those dark curls.

It was then that she saw them— the scars on his back and

shoulders. Vicious, deep, ugly things that could only have caused him immense pain. At first glance, they looked like ropes of agony and while their severity shocked her, she had a compulsion to touch them. Run her fingers down the furrows of twisted skin and soothe them. Only stopped because at that moment the police arrived and started separating witnesses.

What was *that* story? Not a pretty one by any means, she was sure.

Carmine seemed oblivious to her observation, while he spoke to several of the cops. She hovered close, and very quickly a handsome Asian-American cop with almond-shaped, black eyes and a name tag that read Lee zeroed on her. She had trouble focusing on his questions but managed to give a quick recap of why she was meeting Cody.

"Do you have any idea why a member of a motorcycle club would shoot at your friend?"

"I don't know, I mean I don't know anything about motorcycle clubs or bikers, or whatever. Or why they'd shoot at Cody. He had issues, sure, especially money issues, but I'm not part of his life anymore so I don't know what he's mixed up in now." Turning, she spied the bullet holes in the stucco. They were head height, and but for Carmine's quick thinking, she could be one of those being treated. It made her shudder. "They may have been aiming for Brady over there for all I know."

"We'll be investigating that angle too. Do you have an address for your friend?"

"I don't." Tears started to burn in the backs of her eyes. *Where the hell was he?* "He used to live with me, but we broke up, and I have no idea where he moved to. Frankly, I didn't want to know, you know?"

"Bad break-up, yeah?'

"Yeah."

He asked a few more questions before wrapping up. "Thanks for your time, Ms. Resnick." He took her information, jotting it down in a little black book. "We'll be in touch if we have any more questions." She slipped his card into her pants pocket, and he left her to talk to the other witnesses.

Helen rubbed her arms. She was still shaking from the adrenaline surging in her system. Looking around, she saw the medics load Brady into the ambulance. Her teeth began to chatter, but her unfortunate jacket was soaked in blood and unusable, probably a complete loss, which was a pity. But all things considered, she didn't care about a piece of fabric.

As the ambulance pulled out, she noticed Carmine on the phone. While he talked, he picked up her jacket and took it with him to a four-door army-green Jeep with super tough, super wide all-terrain wheels parked one row away. He opened the back and unzipped a gym sack. After pulling out a black plastic garbage bag, he dropped her jacket into it. She expected him to hand it to her, but he instead stashed it in the back corner. It was ruined, therefore she didn't push it, and anyway who needed the reminder.

His expression was grave, yet he seemed completely focused while he multitasked, pulling on another tee shirt and talking. Unlike her, who could barely keep it together.

"You did good," he said to her after he hung up and shoved his phone into his back pocket. "You okay to drive?"

Helen nodded. "My apartment is only a couple blocks away."

"I can have one of my men drive you."

"Not necessary. Do you think he'll be alright?"

"Christ, I hope so." The emotion in his statement made her throat tighten. He held her gaze for a beat longer, like he was about to say something but changed his mind. "I'll follow you home," he said, rubbing his hand over his jaw.

"It's not…"

"Red." He paused and looked at her from over his shoulder. "I don't have time to argue. Just do it please. Where's your car?"

"Okay," she acquiesced, pointing to the next row of cars. "It's that little red Fiat over there." He nodded and she felt his eyes like military-grade laser beams on her back as she walked to her car and climbed in.

He followed closely behind, and she made the drive home without killing herself—or thankfully anyone else. Though she hesitated too long at a stop sign and the car behind the Jeep let her know it. Her hands still shook when she parked her Fiat in her spot, which technically wasn't her spot. Her car was so small, she could squeeze into an area between the last carport and the neighbor's fence. She'd parked there for years and the landlord hadn't complained. Tenants who'd moved in after her knew no different. Therefore, it had become her spot.

Surprisingly, Carmine was still double parked as she walked up her driveway and to her lobby. Obviously the man wasn't going to be satisfied until she made it inside. Unlocking the front door of her one-bedroom apartment, she gave it the necessary extra shove before giving him a wave to let him know she was in.

He nodded, then drove away.

Somehow it seemed a completely inadequate goodbye for what they'd just been through, yet she didn't know what else she expected. He had other things to do, like chase an ambulance to the emergency room.

Heading straight to her couch she immediately parked her butt and dropped her head back onto the backrest. How could this be her life and what had Cody done to deserve this shit?

Digging her phone from her purse pocket, she called him. It went straight to voicemail, which prompted her to text. *You okay? Call me. Please.*

Perhaps the shooting partially explained his strange behavior in the mall and why he'd been so anxious to get away from her. Was he in some strange way trying to protect her? But even more mystifying—how was any of it connected to that over-the-top hot dude, Carmine?

And who the hell was Snake?

It was too much for her brain to contemplate, her thoughts

jumbled together like the pieces of a jigsaw puzzle and she had no guiding picture to make sense of any of it.

She scraped her hands through her hair, but her fingers caught strands that were hard and crunchy. On further examination, she found dried blood, gum and dirty motor oil from the parking lot, and not just in her hair. Her white fitted button-down blouse was stained, as were her fingernails. She pushed up from the chair and began stripping, dropping each item in her laundry basket as she walked to the shower.

Her apartment was old by San Francisco standards and had not yet seen the light of any architect's modern-day vision, but the plumbing had been redone, affording her a powerful spray when she turned the faucets to full. Hot water pummeled her skin and hair, easing the tension, but did not decrease her anxiety. Neither could half a bottle of shampoo get rid of the crud in her hair.

She dressed, did her best to comb around the clumped-together strands, finally giving up and pulling it into a ponytail. She then called Terra.

"Hey, babe."

"If I were to ask what kind of sandwiches a certain smoking hot dude known to your current beau ate, would you by any chance have a way of finding out without being too obvious?"

"Wait, let me process that for a moment," Terra answered. "If I were to...okay, got it. *Zander*?"

"Freckle." She heard in the background.

"What kind of meat does Carmine like on his sandwiches?"

Jeez!

"Tee," she hissed, palming her forehead. "I said don't be obvious."

"I know, but I'm not sure how else to ask without being nonsensical. Just a minute."

"Fine." There was a muffling noise, no doubt due to Terra putting her phone to her chest as she had a habit of doing.

Several moments later, she came back.

"Zander says Carmine's a man. A pretty woman brings him food, doesn't matter what it is, he'll eat it."

"Doubtful he thinks I'm pretty. Bat-shit crazy? Absolutely."

"Oh dear," Terra said in her exaggeratedly understated way. "What happened and why are you wanting to take Carmine a sandwich?"

"Um...he might be hungry?"

"Oh...my...god," Terra's voice dropped to a whisper, and she pictured her cupping the phone so Zander couldn't hear. "You two grinding it out on the low down and you haven't told me?"

Grinding it out?

Whoa Nelly––she wished! The cobwebs between her thighs weren't wispy, delicate things—they were so calcified she could build bridges with them.

"Of course not."

"Then...?"

"Because he's probably sitting in the emergency room at ZGH waiting on news of one of his employees."

"He's at Zuckerberg General?" Terra's husky voice pitched higher. "Why the hell is he there?"

"Because we almost got our heads shot off."

"What...holy shit."

"Exactly, it's probably on the news by now."

Chapter Five

"When you have your flight details, let me know. I'll pick you up."

"Thank you," Brady's mom whispered over the phone. "He always said you were a good boss, Carmine. The best he's had.

He rubbed the back of his neck, but it did nothing to alleviate the tightness in his throat, forcing him to clear it before he could speak again. "I'm the only boss he's had outside the army, Mrs. Wilson. I'm no better than anyone."

Anyway, a good boss would protect his trainees, not leave them to be used as target practice for a hostile fucker on a Harley.

"Don't blame yourself, Anyway, that's for him to decide, isn't it? My boy knew what he was doing when he started working for you."

Yeah, he did. Brady was a vet, just like all his men, but he let it go. After they hung up, he blew out a long breath. The band around his chest had loosened somewhat by Jules, the on-call doctor's prognosis. They'd met when his uncle Billy spent time in the ICU after being run down by the Russian mob. They'd fucked a couple of times, or maybe it was three—he couldn't remember—but none of that mattered. Brady would live.

He'd never lost an employee, and he had no intention of starting now. Close calls? Absolutely. It was the nature of his business and his bad-asses knew the risks coming in—he made sure of that. The reason he only recruited ex-military, battle-hardened men. Besides, they had skills a regular civilian could never hope to have. But often those skills came with baggage.

He knew, he bore enough scars to prove it.

And hospitals—the smells—the bustle had a way of stripping him naked. Too many bad memories, too much heartache.

But dwelling on that wouldn't help him now, so he shook it off and called Thomas, his surveillance specialist.

"How's he doing, boss?"

"Lost a lot of blood, but last I heard he was stable."

"You need me there?"

"I need you to get whatever camera footage you can of what happened. Not just Safeway's. I want the ATM, the stores across the street, the gas station, every angle you can get. I don't care who you need to bribe, what markers you need to call in or who Badger needs to hack, just get it."

"I'll do what I can."

"I know you will. And Thomas?"

"Yes, boss?"

"Thank you."

He disconnected.

Who was on that bike and what the hell was Snake playing at? Was his reason for finding Cody Grant to put a hit on him? It went contrary to everything he knew about Snake and didn't feel right. The man could be brutal and unpredictable, yeah. But a public execution drawing unwanted attention to the club wasn't Snake's style.

He scrolled through his recent calls and found the number.

"Niccoterra," Snake's gravelly voice boomed through the speaker. "You got what I need?"

"Tell me you didn't do it."

Silence, then, "Do what, motherfucker?"

"Set me up to find Grant so you could put a hit on him."

"What the fuck you jabbering about?"

"Don't play stupid, Snake. It doesn't suit you. Tell me one of your brothers did not just do a drive-by, almost killing my trainee, my target and myself, never mind random, innocent victims who just happened to be in the vicinity."

There was a sharp sound, like a breath being sucked in. After a long pause, Snake said, "No, Niccoterra, one of my brothers did not just do that." Snake punctuated the last five words with spaces.

"Then we've got a problem. Somebody is setting one or both of us up. Any clue who?"

There was another long silence, not counting Snake's rasping breath which grated on his nerves.

"Tell me why you think it was one of mine."

"I'm working on getting the footage, but a dude on a Harley wearing a Double RMC patch rode through a parking lot, aimed and fired at Cody and my man. Where's your brother Hunter, Snake? You heard back from him yet?"

"Don't, asshole. It's not him."

"How are you so damn sure?"

"'Cause it's not. Gimme a couple hours. I'll get back to you." Snake hung up. Carmine resumed rubbing his temples, picturing the crowded parking lot again trying to recall the minutia. The hellcat climbing his back, biting his ear. If it hadn't hurt, he might have found it funny. Even so, and despite the seriousness of Brady's situation, the fact that he was sitting in the waiting room of the trauma unit, his lips turned up for a moment.

She was something.

Too much woman for a little runt like Cody Grant, and in his opinion better off without him. Woman like that needed a man strong enough to handle her feral tendencies. He suspected those feral tendencies translated into feral jungle sex in the bedroom. He cleared his throat again. *Getting off topic, dickhead.*

Think.

He'd heard the Harley before he saw it. That in itself wouldn't have alarmed anybody. It was San Francisco—people rode Harleys.

Brady said Cody turned white when he saw the biker. Why? How had the shooter known where they would be? As an army recon scout with an intelligence background, he was trained to watch for tails. They would've spotted if someone had been on them, and with two pairs of eyes, it would've been virtually impossible to miss one.

Didn't mean they hadn't. So, tailing Cody then...or the woman?

Shit.

A sharp, icy shiver sliced down his spinal column, settled in his tailbone. This was no longer a simple case of looking for a boring old bookkeeper. This had become something much darker, more dangerous.

And what triggered the drive-by? Was it planned or in response to him approaching Grant?

He typed a new text to Badger. *Dig deeper into Grant. Wanna know everything.*

Badger: *Roger that.*

Pinching his fingers, he moved from rubbing his temples to massaging the bridge of his nose. A stress headache had started at the base of his neck, accompanied by a hungry rumbling in his stomach. There was a vending machine somewhere, but he didn't want to leave the waiting room. Keeping his eyes closed, he leaned forward and rested his arms on his thighs. It had been too close a call. Should've bailed on the job like he'd first wanted to—like his gut told him to after he'd seen who his target was—and taken that damn vacation.

Should be sitting on a beach, riding the surf or sipping a beer.

"Any news on his condition?"

His head jerked up, and he blinked—twice. Was he hallucinating? Then her subtle honeysuckle scent touched him. He took a couple greedy hits. A refreshing change from the antiseptic smells he still hadn't gone nose-blind to.

Girl had poured herself into tight yoga pants with roses running in a line along the side of her legs and a long sports tank. From his point of view, a lot better to look at than the drab blue and white vinyl. She was also carrying a fat white deli bag and the thought of food made saliva pool in his mouth.

"What're you doing here, Tomato Head?" he asked, keeping it cool in spite of his now speeded up heart and the not-so-random thought he wanted to get carnal with her ASAP.

Her lashes fluttered, annoyance sweeping across her face at his nickname. He kinda liked it got beneath her skin. If that made him a prick, oh well.

Helen squared her shoulders, and he found he liked *that* even more, though he couldn't actually allow himself to like *her*. Not until he figured out her angle. But the woman had spunk—and she'd helped save Brady's life.

"I couldn't sit at home thinking about him. I needed to know how he was doing."

He got to his feet, rolling his shoulder muscles in an attempt to release some of the tension. "He's still in surgery. The bullet went through his side, and he might lose his spleen. But he would have lost more blood if it wasn't for you."

"You did all the work. That magic stuff you used, the blood clotter, that helped?"

"It helped."

Again, her lashes fluttered bringing attention to her irises which were an unusually pretty brown—like warm maple syrup drizzled over pancakes, with a liberal splash of chili-sauce.

He mentally checked himself. Nope. Not liking her. Respect? Yes. She'd earned that, in buckets. However, somebody needed to notify his groin, because it seemed to like her a whole fucking lot.

"This is for you," she said, holding out the white paper bag. "I stopped at my cousin's deli on the way and brought you a sandwich. I figured you'd still be here, and you might be hungry."

He stared at her, forgetting for a moment how to use his words. "You brought me a sandwich?" he finally managed, his voice having gone all Lou Rawls on him.

One auburn brow popped into an arch and she studied him like he was crazy to think she wouldn't. Like it was the most natural thing in the world to feed a man in the hospital. "Food just makes everything better, you know?"

Shit. That's something his mother always said, and it was also the kind of statement designed to fuck a man up in the head. If Helen ever met his mother, he was pretty sure Paola Niccoterra would start planning their wedding.

Too damn dangerous.

"Thank you," he muttered, finding it difficult to stop staring, or reconcile in his head why she affected him so. It wasn't like women hadn't fed him before, but that usually ended with them fucking. And right now, he knew that wasn't on her agenda. "That's really thoughtful."

The ICU doors swung open and Jules flounced out. Her blue eyes taking in Helen before they came to rest on his.

"He's going to be okay," she said, touching his arm. "He's stable but will be out of it for a while. We managed to save his spleen and barring anything unforeseen, I don't see any reason he shouldn't make a full recovery."

The elephant on Carmine's shoulders stepped off and he took a deep breath. "That's good news, thank you." His head dropped with relief and exhaustion.

Jules stepped forward and slid her palm on his upper arm. "I'm so relieved for you, honey," she said. Then in a bold and completely unprofessional move, stepped into his space and pressed her body to his. "I'll touch base with you later, maybe we can get some coffee."

He knew Jules well enough to know coffee was code for drinks then sex. And considering she'd just helped Brady and the fact they'd been intimate in the past, it shouldn't have felt wrong. But it did. He wanted to step back, put distance between them. Instead he gave her a smile that he didn't feel in his eyes and cast his gaze over her shoulder to Helen. She turned away, toeing a spot on the vinyl floor, though he didn't miss the flush moving up her neck.

"On a job, Jules," he said softly into her ear, not wanting to embarrass her. "I'm not going to be free for a while."

He felt her stiffen slightly against his body, then her cheek slid against his in a single nod. "Maybe some other time," he said, softening what he knew she would think of as a rejection.

"Will Brady be able to have visitors?" Helen asked as Jules stepped away.

Her question surprised him and pleased Carmine at the same time. She had no reason to visit Brady. She didn't know him, but he like she cared enough to ask.

"Are you his girlfriend?" Jules responded.

"No, I...uh..."

"Visiting will be restricted to family only for now." Her tone was a little cutting, a little dismissive. He put it down to what had just happened between them and it annoyed him that he was the cause of Jules talking to Helen in that way.

"She was with me when Brady got shot," he clarified. "She helped slow the bleeding."

"Oh?" Now Jules was the one surprised. "I see." Her eyes darted between them. "She works for you?"

"Helen."

"What?" They both turned to her.

"My name is Helen, and no I don't work for him. But I don't want to intrude any further on...um." She waved a hand between them, obviously not knowing what to call it. Honest to God, neither did he. "I just wanted to make sure Brady was going to be okay." She swung her eyes up to his, then to Jules'. "You hold someone's hand and look them in the eye when they're bleeding like that, you kind of develop a connection, you know."

Connection?

He didn't know how to feel about that, but whatever he was feeling wasn't good. Just because he couldn't like her, sure as hell didn't mean he wanted her developing any kinds of *connections* with his trainee. That shit was not happening.

"Yeah, I guess you would." Now who was the snide one? Funny how he didn't like Jules sniping at her, but he had no issues taking shots himself. Where the hell was that poke of jealousy coming from? "But as you heard the doctor say, he's going to be out for a while. You should go home and get some rest."

She scoffed, and shook her head, disbelief plastered on her beautiful face.

"I'll let him know you came by."

Looking him up, then down, leaving no doubt she thought him a dick, she murmured, "Don't bother, Carmine. I'll come by some other day. In the meantime, you enjoy your sandwich." With that, she spun on her heel and walked away. If her perfect heart shaped ass could've, he was sure it would have flipped him the finger.

It would've been well-deserved. As it was he had a hard time looking away.

"I'm sorry, did I not read the situation right?" Jules asked, snapping his ass out of it. She was staring at him, a questioning look on her face.

"What?" he asked.

"Did I overstep my bounds?"

"What are you talking about?" He feigned ignorance.

"I didn't think you were with anyone."

His brow scrunched. "I'm not with anyone, Jules."

"Okay, Carmine." The smile on her face widened, if you could call it that, since at a second glance it looked more like a smirk. Clearly, she wasn't buying his bullshit. "Whatever you say, honey. It's no big deal."

He grunted, but was saved from further comment as right then another emergency caused a stir at the doors. She pressed her lips to his cheek in a much more platonic way than before.

"I'm glad Brady's going to be okay. I am a little worried about you, though." She glanced down the corridor where Helen had made her exit.

"I'm fine."

"Sure, you are. But there's really nothing more you can do here. You should take your own advice and get some rest yourself."

She patted his arm, then rushed to join the other doctors and nurses, not giving him a chance to answer. Not that he had one to offer.

He attempted to shove his hands into his pockets, and realized he still held the white deli bag. Figured he'd eat in his car, if whatever sandwich she'd brought was still edible and not a soggy mess. When he hit the parking lot, he opened it and examined what was inside.

It only took him a couple of seconds to feel like an even bigger dick.

All the contents were separate, yet ready to be made into whatever he wanted. Rosemary ciabatta bread, and in separate plastic baggies, prosciutto, roast beef, turkey, Swiss cheese, lettuce, sliced tomatoes, pickles, and in small to-go containers, mayonnaise and dijon mustard. The woman had even thought of adding napkins, a plastic knife and a small bottle of water.

He sighed as he took in the bright lights of San Francisco, the city he loved so much.

Without a doubt, this wasn't going to end well for him.

Chapter Six

"Come in." Shelley peeked her head through the open salon door and beckoned. "Quick, before anyone thinks we're open for business." Which of course they weren't as it was Sunday.

"Thanks for doing this on your day off," Helen said, hugging her. "I can't tell you how much I appreciate it."

"No worries, I'm just sorry I couldn't fit you in yesterday." She pointed to her chair. "Take a seat." After Helen slid in, Shelley pumped the foot pedal and swiveled the chair so she faced the mirror.

"Holy crap," she said, after snapping out her drape and securing it around Helen's neck. "What happened here? You stick your head into a tar pit?"

"It got caught between Carmine's arm and a parking lot while we were being shot at."

"He...you got...what?" Shelley froze. "Wait!" She held up her hands. "This I have to hear, but I don't want to interrupt you so tell me what you want to do with your hair first, then I want every tiny little detail."

Helen sighed, blowing a loose strand that had escaped her

ponytail out of her face. She'd done her best, but it ended in a battle between her hair and the brush. Her hair won.

"I'm guessing we're going to have to layer it 'cause I can't see any other way around getting rid of that muck, but I can't make up my mind if I want to bang."

"Depends on *who* you want to bang." Shelley's cognac-colored eyes gleamed.

"Ha! You funny girl," she scoffed, yet couldn't help feeling a little jealous as she was the only one in her circle not getting banged. "Both you and Terra are sexed-crazed, but who could blame you with willing, testosterone filled bad-asses to bang at will."

"You could too, you know."

"With Ben?" Who did absolutely nothing to raise her temperature or make her glands squeeze out sex hormones, not even at gun point.

Shelley took a section of her hair, covered her forehead with the ends. "Bangs and layers it is. Are you still dating him?"

"If you want to call it dating. He's handsome enough and sweet enough, but he doesn't ring my buzzer."

"He's cock-blocking."

"What...no. We go to the movies and maybe dinner but that's because we agreed to be each other's plus-one when we need it."

"Babe, think about it. He knows you don't want him that way, right? But he still dates you. Why?"

"Because plus-one?"

"Plus-one my ass. He doesn't want anyone else to have you. If he's good-looking and sweet enough, he could have a girl who wants him, and there are probably a few. So, why you when he knows there's no chance?"

"Shell, it's not like that."

"Sweetie, it *is* like that. I've seen the way he looks at you. Trust me, the man wants you for more than just plus-one. I'm not gonna tell you what to do, but it might be best to cut him loose before he gets in too deep and gets hurt."

Helen sighed while eyeing Shelley through the mirror. In her experience, it was always her who got in too deep, but her friend had a point. Ben had gotten much more touchy-feely lately and having experienced her own heartbreak recently she did not wish that on someone she considered a friend.

"Okay," Shelley relented, making a grimace face and led her to the shampoo bowl. "Enough heavy, tell me about the gunk in your hair."

To which, while her friend shampooed, cut and styled her, she proceeded with the Cliff notes of the drive-by but nixed telling her about the hospital visit. She didn't want to give the impression she was interested in that arrogant, yet impossibly compelling man. Because in all reality, she might've been just for a moment, until she saw his interaction with the willowy doctor.

After locking up, they walked to Provocative to meet Terra. The lingerie store had the honor of being situated equidistant between the salon and Tony's Taqueria, the happening seventies-themed Mexican joint which was their ultimate destination. Sunday was Karaoke night, her favorite of the week.

"Holy hell, babe, look at you!" Terra exclaimed when they entered Provocative, ringing the tiny bell situated above the door. "That is spicy hot."

Helen grinned and tossed her new 'do, only now there wasn't as much to toss as almost half her length was in the trashcan.

Shelley moved to the plush red velvet French settee in the middle of the sales floor and pulled a bottle of champagne from her purse.

"You got any glasses back there?" Shelley asked.

"Do hippies live in the Haight?" Helen responded with a slow smile. It wasn't unusual to have a pre-drink before they hit Tony's, but it was usually homemade margaritas which they blended while Terra closed up shop. Though she didn't question it, she liked bubbly just as well and entered the break room to pull three flutes off the rack above the counter. Provocative was high-end, designed to look like a French mistress's boudoir and offered bubbly to their customers in the hopes of loosening their grip on their credit cards. It worked and more than offset the cost of the sparkling wine, which Anna, Provocative's owner, had a connection to a Napa Valley vineyard and bought by the case.

Then, because she still hadn't heard from Cody, she ousted her phone and typed another quick text.

Are you alive?

While it travelled through the cellular networks, she returned the phone to her purse and snatched the glasses.

She was worried.

Actually, she was more than worried, and it was no longer about money. It was about Cody's safety, and yes, okay she was a terrible person, but it was also about Nana's ring. Not the cash value, but what Nana had gone through to save it—the fucking Holocaust.

"Champagne?" Terra asked, looking between Helen and Shelley when she re-entered the sales floor. "We're celebrating something?"

"We are indeed," Shelley answered, getting to her feet with a smile so big her face could split. "I've been dying all day keeping this quiet, because I have an announcement to make and you two are the first to know. I'm getting married to Gianni-fucking-Cadora, the one and only man of my dreams."

Chapter Seven

Carmine found parking half a block from Tony's which weirdly enough put him right outside of Provocative. The window display of crotchless teddies and bustier's was enough to induce fantasies. But knowing Helen sold that stuff, and therefore probably owned some of that stuff, had his head spinning visions he could currently do without.

Her ass in yoga pants was distracting enough.

The bar was packed, loud and vibrant as always. Music pulsed through mid-century walls. The signature disco ball hung from the ceiling, and a mosaic of a thousand tiny mirrors reflected the humans below it.

He noticed Gianni Cadora immediately. The man stood half a head taller than most and carried an aura that bled generations of mafia. He leaned against the wall, arms crossed against his chest, an amused grin splitting his mug.

And he instantly saw why.

The redhead was on stage hamming a version of "Bitch" that wasn't bad and *if* she lacked finesse, she made up for it with enthusiasm and showmanship. In his book, that counted for more than technique. Right as the words "Goddess on her knees" left her lips, by some weird cosmic coincidence she looked up straight into his eyes. And damn him if he didn't feel that somewhere he'd decided was off limits until further notice.

He exhaled though his mouth and exercised his jaw muscles. One more visual he didn't need in his head.

"What are you doing here?" he asked Gianni when he got close enough he didn't have to yell.

"Giving my tipsy-ass woman and her friends a ride." Gianni, still grinning dipped, his chin to the dance floor where Shelley and Terra were doing their thing. "What's your excuse?"

"Working a hunt," he answered, doing his best to keep his eyes off Helen, noticing she'd gotten her hair cut. How was it possible that made her even more attractive? Cody had disappeared—completely. The more he learned about the bookkeeper, the less he seemed to understand. And that woman on stage singing dick-enlarging lyrics may have some of the answers he needed.

"Got a skip I'm trying to trace," he said to Gianni, nodding at Tony behind the bar who winked at him, a flirtatious smile plastered on his face. "Helen's ex. Cody Grant."

The amused grin slipped off Gianni's face and got replaced with a frown. "Why are you hunting him?"

"You familiar with what happened a few days ago?"

"The drive-by?"

"Grant was the target, but something stinks. On its face, it looks like a Double RMC hit, but Snake, their president who happens to be my client, denies it. The deeper I dig, the crazier shit gets."

"You believe this Snake individual?" Gianni adjusted his position, standing with his feet apart, arms folded and now facing him.

"Not his style. If he was gonna do a hit, it wouldn't be a drive-by drawing attention to the club."

"Unless that's what you're being made to think."

"I've considered that, but one of his brothers is missing. And that brother is connected to Cody through his old lady."

"You think this brother has gone rogue?"

Carmine shook his head. "Bikers are like mafia. They have loyalty to each other, and the penalties are harsh should one break the code. Besides, it would leave his old lady vulnerable."

"Hmm," Gianni grunted.

"None of it makes any sense."

"Why was he here in the first place? The club looking to expand their marijuana business into the Bay Area?"

"My understanding is it was personal business, but I don't know what yet."

"Interesting." Gianni caught his eyes. "Just keep it away from my fiancée."

Carmine's lip twitched. That was a given—and what was more, Gianni knew he would, it didn't need to be said. Rules in their world were clear. His statement had more to do with him making an announcement.

He couldn't stop the grin from cracking his face. "You put a ring on it."

Gianni's lips did a little twitching of their own.

"About time, brother." He stepped into Gianni's embrace and gave him a brief power pat on the back. "Shelley's the right woman for you."

"She's the only woman for me. Always has been."

There was that twist in his chest, the sharp, familiar pain he still felt after three years. He'd had that. A part of him still missed it, and actually envied it, but there was no place in his life for a woman. His job was too damn dangerous. Not unlike that little redhead on stage he couldn't seem to keep his eyes *or* mind off.

He caught Tony's attention behind the bar and ordered a beer. Tonight, the dude wore black bell bottoms with a fat line of sequins up the sides and a black ruffled pirate shirt. One of his more muted outfits. Shelley said Tony had a standing appointment at the salon and considering his matching glittery black fingernails, he didn't doubt it. The dude had a definite

Steven Tyler vibe from Aerosmith, and he carried it off with style.

Tony slid an IPA across the bar, and Carmine dropped a ten, nodding his thanks. While he sipped, he surveyed the room catching more than one pair of female eyes. He chose not to linger on any of them.

That was the other thing of late, he realized. He loved women, and partook often, but he was a hunter by nature. And he'd become bored with how easily they followed him to his bed with little more than a cheesy pick-up line and a smile. Case in point, his recent encounter with Jules. Though he liked her on a personal level, the main reason he'd fucked her, was she reminded him of Jaz. Messed up, he knew, but it was what got him through the grief and guilt early on. Something his VA shrink had spent a disproportionate amount of time analyzing—pervy asshole.

Speaking of women and before he could control his hungry eyes, they swerved back to the redhead. This both annoyed and fascinated him, because what the fuck? She'd rejected him outright before, then he'd pulled an asshole move at the hospital after she'd brought him food — not to mention helped save Brady's life. What kind of prick does that and why the hell was he so intrigued?

Her song ended, garnering whistles which the girl rewarded with a bow and blown kisses like a true diva before stepping down to join Shelley and Terra on the dance floor. He had to work at keeping himself from rubbernecking. Showing more than a minor interest in front of his buddy would no doubt earn him a ribbing only a newly engaged man could dish out.

Not happening, so he kept it tight.

As the three girls made their way through the crowd towards them, his heart sped up. But before he could even tell it to calm the fuck down, she veered off. Unfortunately, his view was blocked by Gianni hooking his arm around his woman's neck and tipping her chin to kiss her on the mouth.

He'd just located her again when Terra greeted him.

"Hey," she said, pulling his attention and giving him a quick hug. "Glad to see you're undamaged and thank you for protecting my girl. God, I can't believe you went through that. How's your employee doing?"

"Brady's getting there. His mom's here which makes it better." Usually he enjoyed talking with Terra and definitely appreciated her concern, though at the moment he was finding it difficult to maintain eye contact due to the slightly familiar tool Helen had stopped to talk to. The dude's body language expressed his interest and wouldn't have bothered him too much, until she tossed her hair and smiled at him. That made his knuckles whiten around his beer.

He kept them in his sights as Terra chitchatted about her upcoming video shoot. When there was a natural lapse in the conversation, he tipped his chin towards Helen. "Do you know if she's heard from her ex lately?"

"Cody?" Terra's curly, strawberry-blonde head canted to the side. "She hasn't said. Why?"

"He's gone missing."

"That's not unusual. Cody's bailed before, and frankly I hope he stays missing."

"Except I need some background."

"On what?"

"He's connected to the case I'm working. I'm hoping she can give me intel I don't already have."

"Oh, Jeez." She blew out air then looked at Helen. "It never ends with that dude."

"What doesn't?"

"The bullshit."

That piqued his interest. "He bullshit her often?"

Terra's eyes rolled before they came to his. "Don't get me started on Cody Grant. It just pisses me off. If I didn't have a conscience, I'd sic Vasily on him."

"Melnikov?"

"Know any other Russian mobsters that could hurt someone and not get caught?"

"A little over the top, don't you think?"

"Maybe, but the bastard hurt *her*. Forgive me for fantasizing in a little revenge. I'd bet Vasily would probably do it for her too."

Something crawled up his ass, straight into his gut at her supposition, giving him something like heartburn. "Why do you say that?"

She shrugged. "He likes her, and she needs a man like him in her corner."

"And you're convinced that man's Vasily?" he asked, thinking he wasn't going to like what he heard.

"They'd make a hot couple, don't you think? She's all fire, he's all ice."

He sucked in air through his nose. Yeah—he definitely didn't like what he heard. As he fought the curl in his nostrils, a big Latino dude hopped onto the stage and started rocking Elvis's "Can't Help Falling In Love." The tool pulled Helen back onto the dance floor and slow-danced her.

"What about him? You know that dude?"

"That's Ben. They're sort of dating."

Sort of?

Did that mean they were sort of fucking? That too made him bristle. "I need to talk to her."

"Well, she kinda looks a little busy but you know where to find her during the day. She works the late shift tomorrow. Why don't you stop by then?"

He could, but he didn't want to wait that long. For some reason still unclear to him, what he wanted was to break that slow dance shit up. And what was worse, though he couldn't take his eyes off her, the woman had yet to look at him again. There was no doubt she was avoiding him, and he couldn't deny it was his own fault, but the harder she played, the more determined he got.

"How are you all getting home?" he asked, formulating a plan.

"Gianni's giving us a ride."

"I'll make sure she gets home safe."

"Um..." Terra laughed and flicked her gaze to the dance floor. "You're big and badass and undoubtedly charming, Carmine, but I think that's up to her, and perhaps Ben."

He narrowed his eyes. "Well, *Ben* looks like he might have had a couple too many."

Terra scrutinized him intently, like she was trying to settle something in her mind. Then she shook her head in warning, causing her tiny nose bling to catch the light.

"Don't."

"Don't what?"

"Don't fuck with her, Carmine. That girl is one of my favorite people. She's like my sister and you've got that look in your eye, like she's a game you want to play."

His brow furrowed as he threw her words back at her, surprising himself. "I'd think that would be up to her, wouldn't it?"

"Don't be a dick, Carmine."

"Not being a dick, Terra. For one, I don't play games with women."

"I mean it. You've barely taken your eyes off her since you've been here."

Damn. He hadn't but he didn't want it to be that obvious either. "That's because I need to ask her a few questions, find out what she knows about Cody that I don't already know."

She eyed him with skepticism, which he supposed he deserved, but it wasn't going to stop him from doing his job. Or so he told himself.

"Promise?" she asked after a long moment. "You won't mess with her?"

"Pinkie promise." He held up his little finger and waited for her to hook hers into his. When she broke it, she positioned her fingers into a V, directed them first at herself, then at him. The message was clear. *I'm watching you.*

Yeah, well he was watching himself, though undeniably doing a bad job at it. Terra walked back onto the dance floor and spoke into Helen's ear. There was a brief exchange that he wished he could hear, or even lip read. Perhaps that was a skill he should look into learning.

When she came back, she and Shelley were ready to leave. He kissed Shelley's cheek, congratulating her on their engagement and then shook hands with Gianni. All the while pretending not to notice Terra's warning glare.

After they left, he leaned an elbow on the bar sipping his beer. A brunette pulled in next to him.

"Hey," she said.

"Whassup?" He smiled, only giving her half his attention, but her smile was so big, he couldn't miss it.

"Whassup yourself, Carmine. Can I get you another beer. I'm buying."

He sighed. It wasn't like he wasn't flattered women noticed him. He was. It was just that once in a while, he wished for more of a chase.

Wait, she knew his name?

He looked closer at her dark hair and multiple piercings in her ears. Who the hell was she? Mutual acquaintance—had he fucked her?

"You never called me," she said after she gave her order to Tony. "I was disappointed."

Maybe he had been too, which is why he didn't remember. However, just then the song had ended. Helen and her *friend* left the dance floor and seemed to be in the process of saying goodbye to some people and then headed towards the entrance. He took a last, long swig of his beer, then set it down and winked at the brunette. Never one to burn his bridges, as he liked to keep his options open, he said, "Catch you later, babe. Gotta go."

"Do you even remember my name?" she called after him.

It wasn't his habit to blow off women, but it had become his top priority to keep Helen from driving home with *him*. Cutting through the crowd and stepping through the door, he looked left, then right, preparing to speed up his pace, but spotted them immediately under a streetlight several cars down.

"You're not driving, Ben."

"Helen..."

"Please get an Uber."

"I'm fine."

"You're not fine," she argued, reaching for his keys but he held them above his head. "Don't be stupid about this."

It was a perfect opening, and Carmine used it. "Yo, listen to her."

"What?" The tool said, wobbling like the over-indulged idiot he was as he turned in his direction. "Who are you?"

Oh man, he sighed inwardly. Dude was going to get belligerent. Why did they always do that? "I'm someone who is telling you to listen to her," he said in a deadpan voice.

"Butt out, man, this's between me and her and you're not invited."

"Yes, Carmine." Helen took his side which he found slightly irritating, considering he was trying to save her life. "Butt out."

"Not going to do that, Helen."

"You know this man?" Ben whined.

"I do...sort of," she said. "Just a second, okay. Let me talk to him." Turning her back to Ben she took a step towards him, placing herself between them. She then put her hands on his chest and gently pushed on him, indicating he should step back a few. The top of her head didn't reach his chin, yet she faced him off like a little warrior. Most women getting pushy would piss him off, but for some reason it sent a curl of heat through his blood.

"Hello, Red." He smiled. "What is it with you and the weakass men you choose?"

"What?"

"They should be taking care of you, not the other way around."

"Just stay out of it, Carmine," she said in a firm, quiet voice. "I need you to let me handle this."

In contrast to Jules's advance, the combination of her touch and being so close in his face felt somehow right and was beginning to do uncomfortable things to him. If he didn't watch it, he'd spring a boner. Warning lights flashed bright and loud in his head, and in spite of his intellectual commitment to not liking her, it didn't mean his body listened to his brain. He leaned his head in a bit and dropped his voice to match hers.

"Were you going to ignore me all night?"

"I wasn't ignoring you."

He was pleased to note her color rose a little and the hunter in him paid close attention. He wanted to believe he was having an interesting effect on her, but that could be just his ego talking. Or a trick of the streetlight.

"I got sidetracked."

Hmm. Sidetracked.

"Helen?" Ben called from behind them. "What are you doing? Let's go."

"Just a second."

"C'mon, let's go. Who is this guy anyway?"

"Hey!" Carmine interjected. "We're talking and she said give her a second."

"Carmine, stop it. I asked you to let me handle this."

"I would," Carmine answered. "If I felt confident you *were* handling this. None of us need him to drive home drunk and get himself or someone else killed."

"I know that." Her lids fluttered. "But there's no point in antagonizing him. And I'm going to repeat, just stay out of it, please."

He stared down at her for a long moment, the heat from her

hands seeping through his shirt and as innocent as it was, felt...intimate. He had to admit he liked it. But this was business, and he'd promised Terra he wouldn't mess with her. He sighed. "Fine. Do your thing."

"Thank you." Her fingers curled slowly against his flesh before she removed them. The sensation that caused in his chest headed directly south, straight to his dick. Made his nostrils flare.

"He's right, Ben," she said, turning towards the other dude again. "The city is cruising with cops, and you don't want a DUI." Her tone softened as she now put both of those pretty little hands she'd just had on his chest on the Tool's. He bit down hard, straining his jaw muscles. It felt like those pretty little hands were cheating on him.

Fuck.

"It's not worth it," she said. "Let me get you an Uber."

"Better yet, baby. Why don't you drive me home? We can leave your car here."

Baby?

Baby?

He growled inwardly. Okay. He'd had enough.

"Or." Carmine stepped forward, leaving no space for her to accept the prick's proposal. He wanted this done, and this dude gone, even if he had to get him gone himself. "I'll drive you both."

"That's not gonna happen. I'm not getting in a car with you."

"Then get an Uber."

"Fuck you."

"Ben!"

"I'm helping you not get a DUI, *Ben.*"

"Well just stop helping, okay?"

"Both of you," Helen yelled. "That's enough! Ben, you can't drive."

"Fine!" Ben's hands went up in the air, palms out. "I'll get an Uber." Then he took one of Helen's and moved it to his heart. "But I want you to come with me."

Carmine stilled while he waited for her answer.

"No," she said softly. He had to move closer to hear. "It's late. I work tomorrow."

"Not 'til noon."

"I'm not coming with you, but you are taking an Uber."

She took his phone and typed his address into the app without having to ask where he lived. He found that more annoying than it should have been, but not as much as her sliding her arm around the douche, shoving his phone into his back pocket. What further pissed him off was the prick took advantage and pulled her into his arms—and she let him.

For the first time in his life he felt like a third leg, but he had questions to ask, and he wasn't leaving.

It only took a minute for a Ford Focus to show up—thankfully. Then, cherry on top, he endured Ben's sloppy attempt at a goodbye kiss. She artfully turned her face just enough the dude's lips landed next to her mouth. Any other time, he might have found that amusing.

When the car finally pulled away with Ben inside and she attempted to walk away, he placed himself in front of her.

To which she sidestepped.

To which he parried and blocked her again.

"What?" she huffed, flicking her new 'do off her shoulder.

"I'll give you a ride."

"No, I'm Ubering it too. I just wanted to make sure *he* didn't drive."

Girl had intriguing layers. Bitch on the top, but caring underneath. Squished somewhere in-between was stubbornness and the need to feed. All of these he found interesting. She cared about her friends, even weak-ass boyfriends who needed babysitting.

He softened his tone. "Red, save your money and let me give you a ride."

"Do you ever take no for an answer?"

"I have an ulterior motive. Like I said, I need to talk to you."

He pointed down the street. "My car is this way. We can save us both a lot of time if I drive you."

"Did you follow us out?"

Yeah, he had. "Nope."

"You just happened to be walking in the opposite direction of where your car is?"

"Heard you arguing. Figured you needed help convincing his drunk ass not to drive. Wasn't wrong, was I?"

"I would've handled him."

"Maybe, but who's going to handle you?"

"Excuse me?" She stopped walking and angled her head to look up at him. "Handle *me*?"

"Uh huh."

"I don't need handling."

"Yeah, you do."

"Do not."

"Do too."

"I suppose Red is better than Tomato Head, but my name is Helen. He...len. Two syllables. Should be simple enough for you to remember."

"Know your name, woman," he said, chuckling. "But *you* should know I like tomatoes." They'd reached his vehicle and he beeped the locks open.

"Holy hell."

"What?"

"I didn't notice the other day how rugged that Jeep was. You repurpose it from the military?"

"Nope, bought it new."

"What do you do with that thing? Climb mountains."

"My job, you never know where you need to go. Gotta be prepared for all circumstances. Hop in." He opened the door, and waited for her to get settled, then climbed in on his side and stuck the key in the ignition.

"What do you need from me?" she asked as he waited for a car to pass before pulling out onto the street.

"I need the whereabouts of Cody."

"You and me both. I haven't heard from him since the shooting."

"Well, then let me pick your brain. He ever mention a connection to the Double RMC's?"

"You mean the ones who shot at us?" She shook her head.

"How about a man known as Snake?"

"Only when you mentioned it to Cody." She turned in her seat to stare at him. "Why are you asking this? Does it have to do with what happened?"

"That's what I'm trying to figure out." They'd stopped at a light and he met her stare. "What do you know about Cody's family?"

She was quiet for a long moment, then she gave a slow blink.

"This is going to sound weird, but he never really talked about his family except for his sister, Candy. I think he was close with her, but he always seemed to dodge my questions. Cody was very reserved and private. Maybe too private, which should've been a red flag. I tried to respect that and after a while stopped asking."

She plonked her elbow on the window ledge, fingertips to her temple, face scrunched. "Do you think he owed money to these bikers as well as his dealer? Or maybe his dealer was that biker?"

The light changed and Carmine turned his attention back to the road, moving the Jeep forward.

"He owes something. Don't know what yet though."

"What do these bikers do?"

"You mean besides ride bikes?"

She tilted her head in a way that said *of course stupid*.

He snort-chuckled. "They grow pot."

They'd just crossed Bush Street when she called. "Wait...stop the car."

"What?"

"Can you please stop the car?"

"Give me a reason, Red."

"There's a pawn shop across the street. The lights are on and I want to go inside."

What the hell?

"Again...reason."

"I need to check something."

"Red," he almost growled. "Tell me the fuck why."

"I want to see if they have something of mine."

Of hers?

"This better be good because any pawn shop open at this time of night doesn't exactly deal with the clientele you're used to."

"I'm aware of that."

"And yet you still want to go in there?"

"Yes."

Hmm.

He found a spot and shut the engine off. Before he could retrieve his handgun from the console between their seats, she had the door open and trotted towards the pawn shop, heels clacking on the sidewalk.

He shoved the gun in the back of his jeans underneath his jacket. "Dammit, Tomato Head. Slow down."

"I want to make sure I get there before they close."

He was beginning to get the feeling that nothing with this chick was ever going to be easy. "Wait up," he grumbled as he jogged to catch up with her.

She tried the door, but it was locked *as it should be* at this time of night.

Good.

Maybe someone just left the light on. The woman rapped her knuckles on the glass—loud enough to wake the homeless person sleeping in a cardboard box in the alley they just passed.

Inside, two men looked up—one, a muscular black man with a cool, silver streaked 'fro was behind the counter. He made eye contact with Carmine through the glass, shaking his head and mouthing "We're closed."

"They're closed," he reaffirmed to Helen.

"Hmph," she huffed, then planted a big smile on her face and knocked even louder.

When the black dude raised his head a second time, she waved at him. Carmine saw the man's shoulders drop. He hesitated for several seconds before he ambled from behind the counter to the door.

"We're closed," he said again through the glass.

"I need five minutes," she countered. "Please?"

Surprise, surprise, the man unlocked the door and before Carmine could stop her, Helen darted into the spartan space, he had no choice but to follow. Did a sweep of the store, no weapon on the owner and the other person didn't represent a threat either. He relaxed—somewhat.

"Hey little lady, we're closed."

"I know and I'm so sorry, but I'm kind of desperate. By the way, I'm Helen and this is Carmine."

"Hm hmm," he nodded. "Alright."

"Thank you for letting us in." She smiled again but even from his position slightly off to her side, he could tell it wasn't a happy smile. "Can I ask, what's your name?"

"You can call me Al." The black dude studied her for a hand full of seconds, then his stance softened. Carmine assumed he read the same sadness in her expression he did and wasn't surprised. There was something compelling in her tone that nudged his protective bone.

"Thank you, Al. I promise I won't take up much of your time, but I'm looking for a ring."

What?

"You're shopping, Tomato Head?"

She ignored him.

Al's face wrinkled but he pointed to a case over to the right.

"Rings are over there, and you got five minutes, okay?"

"Thank you." Helen did not waste one second going to the glass case.

Al gave Carmine the squint eye. "She don't look like she's gonna pop out a baby so I'm guessing it ain't a shot-gun wedding. You couldn't wait till the mornin' to get your woman one?"

Carmine shook his head and held his hands up in a gesture of surrender. "Don't ask man. I sure as shit don't know."

Al stared at him, then chuckled. "Sheeyit! You oughta be takin' her to Tiffany's, man. Not some broke-ass motherfucker pawn shop."

"Hello," Helen called, looking up briefly. "I'm right here and I'm not his woman."

Not yet.

Wait.

What the hell kind of thought was that?

"In any case, it's not here." Her voice got all husky, like she was fighting hard to hold back tears. "Do you have another case of rings or any in the back you haven't yet processed?"

"Maybe. What you lookin' for, Helen?"

"My grandmother's ring. It's antique...a ruby surrounded by yellow diamonds."

Carmine narrowed his eyes, something unpleasant tickled his tailbone.

"Have you by any chance seen it?" she asked.

Who pawned her grandmother's ring?

As her words sunk in, a wave of rancorous disgust moved through him. Cody fucking Grant. Who else?

"Nah," Al's expression got serious as he listened. "But if you give me your number and it comes in, I can call you."

"You'd do that?"

"Sure would."

"I can't tell you how much I'd appreciate that. The ruby has a distinctive flaw and it's not about the money, but it has...it has deep sentimental value to my family. I'll do almost anything to get it back."

"I'll give you *my* number," Carmine stepped in and pulled a card out of his wallet. "You can call me if it comes in."

Al caught his eye, then nodded. "Fair enough. Now get yourselves outa here. I gotta close and go home to my woman before she comes after my late ass with a shotgun."

They shook, then Al hustled them out the door and they walked back to the Jeep. When he opened the door for her, he didn't like her deflated expression, or posture. As she went to buckle herself in, he took the strap, reached around and did it for her.

"Thank you," she mumbled, catching his eye. The disappointment flowing from her was contagious.

When he climbed back in, he asked, "How long you been looking?"

"I just started. I only found out a couple days ago it was missing. My mom"—she stopped, then swallowed—"she thinks she might have misplaced it, but I'm pretty sure Cody took it."

"You're not sure?"

"I'd ask him, but he won't return my calls."

Of course he won't.

"Anyway, he probably wouldn't tell me if he did."

"Doesn't mean he pawned it."

"Why wouldn't he if he needed cash?"

"Pawning an item is like a loan," he explained. "You get a fraction of what it's worth and you have to pay the loan and the fees associated within a certain period of time to get your item back."

"Yeah, so...?"

"How convinced are you he was going to get it back?"

He watched her stop breathing, then her eyes widened.

"You mean...?"

"It's possible Cody sold it outright, Red."

"Oh God, no," she groaned, leaning forward with her arms

wrapped around her waist, and looking like she might actually throw up. "Please don't say that."

But he had, and the possibility of it being the reality didn't settle well in his gut. He shouldn't care one way or the other about some sentimental piece of jewelry. But he did—because she did.

And he had a nasty, unsettling feeling no matter how hard he tried to keep this just business, he was going to fail miserably at it. Famous last fucking words.

Chapter Eight

"You can just drop me off here," Helen said as they approached her building. Not unpredictably, he didn't listen. "Um...hello?"

"I'm looking for parking, Red."

"Why? There's no need. Parking's impossible at this time of night. Just drop me off here."

Naturally a moment later a free spot appeared, making her a liar because that was her luck lately. A ridiculously attractive smirk played on his lips as he parallel parked the Jeep like a pro.

"Impossible, huh?" He extracted the key fob from the ignition then pressed the snap on his seatbelt buckle. "I'm just doing what every gentleman should do and making sure you get inside okay."

"You know my apartment is right there." She pointed to a glass lobby. "Just inside those doors. I'll be fine." Though in reality she didn't feel fine. She was tired and emotionally beaten with the possibility of Nana's ring being gone forever. And this man's sexual energy radiated like the Fukushima nuclear plant. It was bad enough sitting next to him in the compact space of his car. How would she handle it inside her apartment? "I mean, what is it you're expecting?"

"Expecting?"

The Jeep's interior lights were dim, but it wasn't hard to miss his eyes hardening. "I'm not expecting anything, Helen. Have I given you reason to believe otherwise?"

Sadly, that was a negative.

"Uh...no." If anything, she suspected he found her annoying. Other than that one incident when he'd flirted for a nanosecond in Zander's bar and she'd shut him down, he'd shown absolutely no further interest. Which was disappointing and not awesome for her ego.

"Right. I want to make sure your apartment is secure because if you're a target..."

"A target?" Her eyes widened. "What do you mean...why would I be a target?"

"Has it occurred to you that whoever shot at Cody may think he's hiding out with you?"

"Are you serious?"

"As a heart attack."

Holy hell.

It *hadn't* occurred to her. What's more, what just had, was Cody hadn't returned his key after he left. Why she hadn't thought to ask her landlord to change her locks was beyond her, but if her ex needed a place to hideout could she really deny him? Especially after being shot at.

Yes, yes, she absolutely should—just as a matter of practicality. God alone knew what dangerous things Cody was into and those dangerous things would probably follow him wherever he went, like right into her apartment.

"Okay." She swallowed, reaching for the door handle. "Satisfy yourself, but I'm sure you're wrong."

As she slipped out of her seat, he reached behind his and retrieved a flat white plastic package off the floor and tucked it under his arm. The locks chirped and he joined her on the sidewalk. They walked side by side in silence until they reached the narrow pathway leading to a brightly lit lobby where he let her go first. It was decorated with mailboxes, two potted ficus trees and a huge, faded print of an aerial view of the city.

Her apartment was the first on the right. As usual the door stuck.

"Dammit," she grunted, giving it a shove, but it refused to budge. Tried again, to no avail.

"Here, let me," he said stepping up close enough to brush her back with his solid chest. "Hold this." He curled an arm in front of her and handed her the package he was carrying. She couldn't spend the brain cells to wonder what was in it as his body heat emanated through his thin shirt, as did his clean man-scent. Magnetic and irresistible. Was it just her, or did the air really seem to crackle around them? Her hormones definitely woke up and took notice.

He chuckled, which made her look up and over her shoulder into those enigmatic green eyes.

"You need to step aside, Red, unless you want to be sandwiched between me and your door."

"Oh," she said, flustered as the mother of all blushes moved up her neck at the visual that inspired inside her dirty mind. But she took a step to the left, giving him the necessary room to work.

There was that smirk again. Like he knew exactly what she was thinking as he put his shoulder to the door and gave it a nudge. It popped free on the first try. Of course.

Dropping the little bunch of keys into her hand, his fingers brushed her palm. It was the smallest of touches, but his hand jerked before he snatched it away as if she'd zapped him with a jolt of electricity.

He didn't follow her immediately inside, instead scrutinized her lobby. He was a handsome devil anyway, but what was it about a man who hadn't shaved in several days? How that dark stubble emphasized a hard, strong jaw and a gorgeous nose with just the slightest of bumps on the bridge. And she wasn't even going to mention those luxurious curls that gleamed under the lobby lights.

He'd stepped inside and that sexual energy she'd experienced in his car spilled over and swamped her apartment. Unable to be contained by an untucked button-down linen shirt the same color as his irises. Or the way his faded jeans curved around a solid ass. They clung to his thighs and emphasized the hard lines of his legs.

Unfortunately, and to her undoing, she'd seen what lay beneath that shirt. Tossing him a quick glance, hoping he hadn't noticed the slight sheen touching her forehead, she noted there was no judgement in his scrutiny of her apartment. Just an acute attention to detail. Her building was old, but decent and well kept, the rent reasonable for the city. An eco-warrior, her little unit reflected her quirks, her love of repurposing old and discarded furniture and was eclectic as she was.

"Okay," she stated, needing to put an end to this—whatever *it* was. "You've seen, now you can go,"

Other than a slight narrowing of his eyes and a short breath expelled through his nose, his expression remained impervious.

Good. If he thought she was rude, maybe he would leave. It took several ticks of her wall clock for him to turn his head. When that green gaze landed on her, he said, "You're on the first floor."

"Yes?"

"I need to check your windows."

"What?"

"They're wooden frames."

She glanced at the windows in question that were covered by the floor-length kick-ass drapes she'd found at Marshalls for a steal.

"How do you know they're wooden frames?" *She* wasn't even sure they were...goodness, they *could* be wood, but he knew this in...what...like five seconds?

"I pay attention, Tomato Head," he said tapping the side of his eye with his pointer and moved deeper into her living room. Stepping past the newly re-upholstered couch she'd acquired from

Goodwill, he pushed her curtain aside to jiggle the latch securing the window.

She tossed the package he'd her given onto her coffee table, unsure why she was still holding it. "Stop calling me 'Tomato Head.' You're going to make my head explode, which would be unfortunate since I'm the one who'd have to clean it up."

"Why?"

"Why would it be unfortunate?"

"Why would it explode?"

"Because it's disrespectful and I don't like it."

"Not trying to be disrespectful. If *you'd* been paying attention, you'd remember I mentioned I like tomatoes. Your hair color is close to an heirloom variety I have a particular fondness for. My mom grows them."

"Oh," she whispered, because that was all she could manage. That was actually quite charming.

"Yeah...*oh*."

"I thought you were just being cliché, you know, like every other sixth grader I once knew."

He grinned. It was then she realized it was perhaps better to have him annoyed with her. Then he wouldn't smile. Because his smile was devastating and made his eyes sparkle.

"I'd bet a dozen doughnuts you didn't let it stand then either."

"Jamie Hopkins called me 'Lobster Top' in middle school. I jumped on his back, like I did with you. Only, I didn't bite his ear." She wrinkled her nose. "'Cause his ear was kinda gross. I gave him a noogie. Got blisters on my knuckles, but he never called me Lobster Top again."

A slight lip-twitch was the only indicator he may have found that amusing. "I count myself lucky."

"You should. I made him cry."

"I have a feeling you've made a lot of guys cry. Is that how you got to be such a ball buster?" he continued while checking the deadbolt on her door. "Because of sixth graders like Jamie Hopkins?"

"Have you seen my brother?" Her auburn brows arched. "He's six-four. I'm two years older but he outgrew me at age eleven. I had to be."

"Must've been fun growing up."

"We almost killed our parents trying to kill each other, but we're okay now." Since they were sharing little life details, she couldn't resist asking. "And you? Any siblings you dominated or terrorized?"

Carmine shook his head. "Only child."

He'd moved into the kitchen and paused at the window above her sink. She'd attached a small rack to the wall and added a few potted herbs and a red impatiens for color as the view was of the building next door's ugly paint-peeling exterior. He slid a couple pots aside before doing the same test as he did in the living room.

"My dad bailed when I was five. It was just my mom and me until I joined the army."

"Oh...sorry."

"About what?" he said, breaking off a basil leaf, then rubbing it between his fingers and bringing it to his nose. The sharp, enticing scent filled her kitchen and she suspected she'd never cook with basil again without thinking of this moment. "My asshole dad ditching Mom? Don't be. He was an abusive drunk and did us a favor."

"Oh?" she repeated, because seriously, what did one say to that. "That must've been hard."

"Not really. My mom's brother, Billy was more of a dad to me than that prick ever was. Your window latches in here and your living room are okay. I just need to check the one in your bedroom."

She blinked.

Him in her bedroom?

Benign reasons aside, it had been a while since any man had been in there.

"Um," she cleared her throat, "is that really necessary?"

She turned away, but before she did, caught his questioning gaze. There was a long pause, then his voice dropped low and got all gravelly. "Why are you afraid of me in your bedroom? You leave your panties on the floor?"

"Excuse me," she said, scoffing. "That's kind of personal, isn't it?" They weren't but she had a sudden visual of removing said panties and dropping them on said floor. "I just don't think you need to be in my room, that's all."

"Seen plenty of panties, babe. Nothing new to me. But in case you're thinking the other thing, I'm no threat to you. However, someone else may be, and for that reason I'm also going to add a sliding lock to your door." He said that as if he had every right to do it, her landlord be damned.

"Wait...what?"

"One more layer of protection. I'd also recommend window alarms. That's not happening tonight but the sliding lock is."

"Why do I need a sliding lock?"

"If someone tries to break in it gives you more time to call 911."

Okay, there was logic to that. Especially if that unwelcome someone had a key.

"Um, you're making me feel kind of paranoid and...and unsafe and I don't get scared easily."

His gaze dropped to her lips, and the way it lingered for more than a couple seconds and then the way he swallowed sent a thrill up her spine.

"The point is to make you safer." He cleared his throat. "A little paranoia, however, may not be a bad thing for you right now." Her heart beat several times while he watched her before closing his eyes and looking away. "I'm going to my car to get something," he said when they opened again. "Lock the door behind me."

His car? For what—a sliding bolt?

He moved past her, giving her a wide berth, like she'd been infected with some mysterious virus. The man confused her. How could he one minute be so close she could feel his heat, his breath on her neck, and the next like she had some undesirable communicable disease? He made her dizzy.

Once he was out the door, she locked it then kicked off her shoes and carried them into her room. She slipped into a pair of sweats, the least sexy she owned, a ragged old faded, bleach-stained gray tee shirt with the neck cut out that she used to clean her apartment in and her fluffy blue slippers. She checked her reflection.

Heh. No mixed signals there. Then she pulled her hair into a messy bun on top of her head. The newly-cut shorter strands escaped from the bun, giving her a disheveled look but there was nothing she could do about that.

Okay, so she didn't have panties on the floor, but she did have new lingerie laid out on her bed. She shoved them into her top dresser drawer just as a double tap on her door knocker sounded.

To be sure, she peered through the peephole before opening, surprised that he carried a toolbox and a small colorful, carboard package.

"You make a run to the hardware store?"

"I carry extras in my car."

"You just happen to be driving around with a sliding bolt in your car?"

"Security is part of my gig, Red. I always have something or other pertaining to it in my car." He stepped over the threshold then stopped next to her, waiting for her to look up. When she did, his eyes were flat but his jaw was tense. "Is that what you usually sleep in, or is that for my benefit?"

Okay, so he had her number, which was good. She jutted her chin an inch upward. "It is what it is."

Carmine's mouth tightened, then the corner of his eye ticked. Without further ado, he placed his toolkit on the floor next to her door and dropped to his knees—stretching those jeans over strong, beautifully muscled thighs. Extending one arm out in front of him, he curled his fingers around the fabric of his sleeve, manipulating it up. Then repeated the action with his other arm. After, he flipped the latches on the toolbox. Unable to look away, she was mesmerized by those corded forearms. The way they rippled and tensed made her nipples harden and scrape against the fabric of her tee-shirt. This in turn caused pleasurable sensations to surge through her body, and a flush to move up her face.

She blew out air and left the room––went to the kitchen, poured a glass of cold cucumber water. While sipping it, she moved the little herb pots back into their original positions. Then she prepared coffee for the morning, sorted and folded laundry, brushed her teeth and washed her face. The gentle hum of her ceiling fan drowned out any noise, but suddenly, her skin prickled. She didn't need to hear him to know he was behind her.

That potent, male energy he emanated completely dominated the tiny space. When she looked up, he was leaning his shoulder against the doorframe, arms crossed. Their gaze caught in the medicine cabinet mirror above the sink. She saw something she hadn't seen since that first time they met.

Interest.

It made her toes curl. Looking quickly away, she put her toothbrush back in the cup. The air grew heavy as she grabbed a towel to wipe the tiny blotch of foamy toothpaste from her lips.

"Bedroom latch is a little weak," he said, blinking. "The wood has dry rot. Have your landlord take care of that as soon as possible."

"Okay."

"What time do you get off work tomorrow?"

"The store closes at eight, but it takes about thirty minutes to finish up. Why?"

"I want to rig an alarm on it until it gets fixed."

Okay...wait...what?

"Don't you think you're over-reaching? I mean, what if I don't want you to?"

His eyes flickered before they narrowed. "That would be stupid. You don't want to take chances with the people who are looking for your boy."

He had a point. She really didn't, but she also really couldn't afford to spend any more time with him even if she wanted to. There was only so much a girl with a healthy sexual appetite who could use some mind-blowing sex could stand. Everything about him, from the way he moved, the gentle bulge of his package that indicated the man was indeed packing, to those elegant full lips suggested sex with him would without a doubt be mind-blowing. But she wasn't the kind of girl who could randomly hook up.

"I can install it."

"Red..." he growled.

"I'm pretty handy with a screwdriver and I can follow instructions."

"It's going to take more than just a screwdriver to install what I'm thinking you need." His voice was low and rumbly as he took a step deeper inside the bathroom. She sucked in a sharp breath, which wasn't easy. The air had disappeared. As if the testosterone he exuded had absorbed every molecule of oxygen.

She squared her shoulders. "My brother will help me." *If* she could drag him away from his current hottie of the week. Petey's mission in life at twenty-three was to be a badass and his heroes were men like the one in her bathroom right now.

As if reading her thoughts, he said, "I don't trust you to get it done in a timely manner."

"You're saying I'm not trustworthy?"

"Helen," he growled again. "Stop putting words in my mouth. You need to let me do this for your safety."

What she *needed* was to get out of the bathroom, but what she wanted, well that was a whole other story. "You," she said overly bright, "should have a little faith in a girl. How would that alarm work?"

Skirting past him, her arm accidentally brushed against his abs. His stomach flinched. Hers, on the other hand did flip-flops. A dense, heavy silence descended on them until she was well inside her bedroom, standing on the other side of her bed. When she looked back at him, the intensity in his stance, the way his jaw ticked, suggested there was definite tension there. On her side, it was all sexual. On his?

"It's a pretty simple concept," he said flatly. "Someone opens the window past a certain point, the alarm goes off, and unless you're dead, you wake up."

"Okay well, I'll think about it," she said in the same neutral tone she'd use on a difficult client, or when she was nervous. Because the way he was looking at her, the way she couldn't read him — and she could read most people — definitely made her nervous. "If that's everything, it's getting late and I'm guessing you want to go."

He tensed. "Don't do that," he warned, tilting his head.

"Do what?"

"I'm getting odd signals here, babe. You're acting like you're unsure of me, like you think I'm going to hurt you."

"Odd signals?" She turned as if to look at something on the wall, gave a slight shake then turned back to him. "I'll tell you what's odd. Yes, I guess I am a little nervous. And the reason I'm nervous is because you're looking at me funny."

"Funny?"

"Uh huh."

"Funny as in you think I'm the kind of man who'll take you by force?"

"I never said *that* and why would you even say something like that? Are you thinking it?"

"Jesus...of course not."

I just don't know what your intentions are, doing all this"—
she waved her hand in a sweeping gesture—"stuff for me. I mean, I
didn't ask you for a ride home, you insisted on giving me one. I
didn't invite you into my apartment, you decided you just had to
come in and check it out. Then you decided you needed to install a
sliding bolt on my door. You also insist on being all badass and
freak the shit out of me with your scare tactics, making me think
whoever is after Cody may come after me. Now I'm telling you,
I'm tired and I want to go to bed. I don't think there's anything
odd about that."

"My intentions?"

"Yes."

"Okay, Helen." His voice dropped to a low growl as he took a
step forward. "My intentions are to make sure you're safe in your
home. That if someone on a mission decides to break in, you at
least have a warning, a chance to arm yourself. So you don't get
surprised by waking up to an intruder pointing a gun, or something worse, at your head."

She swallowed hard because he painted an ugly picture. And,
she'd come to realize, he only used her real name when he was
pissed.

"Are you deliberately leaving yourself open to having midnight
visitors with guns pointed at your head, or are you just that
thickheaded?"

"Thickheaded? Okay, I'm done with your insults. You need to
pick up your toolbox and leave."

"I'm leaving, but not until you get it through your stubborn,
thickheaded brain how fucking important this is. How much
trouble Cody is in and that there's dangerous people out there,
how both of those things could mean bad things for you."

"I got it. It's important, Cody's in trouble and those bikers are
dangerous."

His lips flattened, and if she'd thought his eyes were green
before, his anger intensified them to emerald.

"Are you always this annoying?"

"So I've heard." She blinked and swallowed. How could she literally just minutes ago have had fantasies about this *rude,* overbearing, high-handed and admittedly sexy man. Just more good reasons she needed to avoid him.

"The door's over there." She held her arm out. "Please send me the invoice for the sliding bolt and your services."

"You've got to be fucking kidding me." He clipped. He impaled her with his eyes for a long moment, then shook his head and moved to the living room to pick up his stuff.

"I insist." She followed him out and planted her hands on her hips. "Send me the invoice." God knew, she did not need to owe him anything, let alone favors.

He threw her a dark look as he yanked open her front door.

"Forget it, Helen. There'll be no invoice. I didn't do this to make money. I did it so I can sleep tonight."

With that, he stepped over her threshold into the lobby and pulled her door shut. Which left her staring at the empty spot he left.

So *he* could sleep tonight?

Holy poop.

She dropped her forehead against her front door and squeezed her eyes shut. The question was, would she? As she was returning to her room, she noticed the package he'd brought with him was still on her coffee table.

"Dammit."

No way was she going to run after him, but she picked it up to examine it more closely.

Huh.

Her name was printed on the label. What the hell? Was this for her? Nibbling her lower lip, her curiosity got the better of her. She opened it. Inside was an identical replacement for the jacket she wore when Brady was shot. Brand spanking new with the Nordstrom's label still attached.

* * *

Helen kicked off her quilt for the umpteenth time before getting cold and pulling it back on.

Damn him and his beautiful eyes.

And his beautiful lips.

And those abs...and pretty curls.

And his thoughtfulness.

Reaching behind her, she gripped the old iron gate she'd salvaged from a wine estate sale, painted white and repurposed into a headboard.

"Argh!"

It rattled against the wall, before she remembered she shared a common wall with her neighbor. "Oh shit, sorry, Mrs. Jackson."

The poor woman had suffered through many of her late-night battles with Cody, and their make-up sex afterwards, which perhaps wasn't as make-up as it suggested. At least, not for her. Cody had been a decent lover, but she wouldn't classify him as great. Now that stupidly sexy hot dude would probably be incomparable considering the amount of experience he had.

Ugh. Why couldn't she get him out of her head?

Her nightstand lit up from her phone's home screen as it vibrated. Reaching over to grab her device, she checked the time. Holy hell! It was three-thirty in the morning. This couldn't be good. Then she saw the caller ID and sat up straight, her eyes wide open.

"Ohmigod, do you realize what time it is?"

There was a ragged, breathy kind of wheezing on the other end.

"Helen...I need help."

Chapter Nine

Wake your ass up, soldier.

The army base's warning siren blared, splitting his eardrums. He rolled off his army issue cot and reached for his Glock. What's happening...we got incoming?

It's your phone, squadie.

His eyes sprung open. A godawful wailing reverberated through his bedroom. It took several blinks to remember it was the tracking device he'd put on the redhead's car.

Sitting up, he snatched his phone of his bedside table. Then rubbed the sleep from his eyes before studying the blinking red dot. Girl was on the move. Squinting at his window, he noted there was no natural light seeping through his drapes. Only the street lights. Where the hell was she going at this time of the morning?

Unless someone had taken her car. It was entirely possible Cody had kept a spare key. His phone indicated it was four-oh-five and while he watched the little red dot move on the tiny street grid he scraped the remaining sleep from his face. He'd only had a couple hours. That girl had him twisted into knots and he still wasn't sure what to do about it.

The blinking dot stopped for longer than a traffic light would force her to. Studying the location harder, he tried to recall the details of her neighborhood. Her car was on Steiner Street. There was that church, a philanthropic foundation, then just a block down, a gas station.

As he rolled out of his king-size bed, he got a bad feeling––that tingle in his tailbone, the one he paid attention to. One thing he'd learned in that damn rockpile, one of the reasons he was still alive, he trusted his gut. And since her schedule didn't start till noon, work was out of the question.

Holy mother of God. Not a booty call?

He let out a low growl at the thought.

There was definite tension between them and if she was half as frustrated as he was, could he blame her? On the way home from her apartment, for about two seconds, he'd considered stopping at Jules' apartment to relieve some of that tension but couldn't make himself turn the wheel in that direction. Then to further frustrate himself, he'd refused to take matters into his own hand. Because the girl had pissed him off. Didn't need her owning his ass even if she didn't know she did. Which she absolutely fucking did not.

Shit.

He dressed, brushed his teeth and threw on a zip-up hoodie without a tee shirt, collected his wallet, his gun and an apple. Grabbing his work bag and his keys off the polished concrete counter, he locked his front door then jogged down the stairs to the bakery.

His mother, Paola Niccoterra, was preparing a fresh batch of dough for the fryer and wasn't surprised to see him. She was used to him or his men coming in at odd hours and gave him a smile.

"Hey, honey," she said.

"Hey, Mama." He gave her a quick kiss on her still smooth cheek, then filled a to-go cup with coffee and half and half.

"What are you doing up so early," she said, her liquid brown eyes showing her concern. "I thought you were taking some time off."

"I was, but I'm on a hunt."

"Honey..."

"Ma, not now." He grabbed two chocolate doughnuts from the day before's batch and placed them in a small box. "I've got to go."

"You're tired, my boy." She paused her kneading. Having run their family bakery in Trenton, New Jersey until she sold and came out here when he got out the army, she still did things the old school way. "I can tell you haven't slept. Why can't one of the others take this one?"

"The others need a day off too, and anyway, this is one I have to do myself."

"I'm worried about you."

"I know, Ma. You're always worried but when this one is done I promise I'll take a week off." He headed towards the back entrance that led to the underground parking garage he shared with his mom, his uncle and their tenants.

"You need more than that," she called a parting shot as he jogged down the stairs. "Otherwise you're going to lose those good looks and ruin your chance of giving me grandbabies."

He chuckled and shook his head. "Wishful thinking, Ma." Babies were not in his future as far as he could tell. Jaz hadn't wanted kids, and he'd been okay with it, figuring if it was meant to be it would. Then it wasn't at all. Did the redhead like kids?

Jesus.

He needed to stop with that.

If she wasn't his only lead to Cody, he'd avoid the hell out of her. Girl was trouble. He knew it as surely as his balls ached. But so far that hadn't worked out so well for him. Yeah, it was inevitable they'd bump into each other considering their circle of friends. But dammit, that didn't mean she was allowed to take up all the available space in his head.

He wasn't supposed to like her, remember?

He opened the back of the Jeep and checked his bag. Everything he needed for every situation was in there, as it should be. Then he folded into the driver's seat, placed his phone into its holder on the dash and almost dropped his coffee.

Her car was heading east—over the Bay Bridge. "What the hell are you up to?"

A long breath escaped him, and he was suddenly grateful he'd filled up the Jeep last night before he'd hit Tony's. As it was, she had a good thirty minutes head start, but he'd catch up. He always did in the end.

In the meantime, he needed to make some calls.

"Hey Siri, call Snake."

"Calling Snake."

After several rings, the man, growled into the phone. "Really, asshole?" His gravelly voice made even more so by having just been woken echoed in Carmine's ears. "This couldn't wait till the goddam birds were chirping?" Carmine heard a woman mumble in the background. Snake said, "Go back to sleep, honey, it's nothing." The sound of a lighter flicking, then the man taking a deep drag from a cigarette.

"Got a situation, and you never called me back."

"Yeah, well, fuck you, I got my own situation and a business to run. Gimme a second."

Carmine heard a door open, then close again before Snake continued. "I had to ask around, then, based on what I learned from you, had to bring all the brothers to the table. This shit takes time."

The quality of the sound coming through his phone changed to something more echoey. He realized he'd been put on speaker. Then the unmistakably noise of a urine stream hitting water inside a toilet bowl, and a fart.

Carmine rolled his eyes.

"Hunter is still missing," Snake went on. "No one, including his old lady, has heard from him. Normally this wouldn't be an issue, but considering what you told me, the patch on that drive-by bandit, has me seriously worried. Candy's beginning to think he's fucking around, got some pussy somewhere south, so she's losing it. And until I hear from him, or he contacts her or shows up back home, I can't speculate. But between me and you, I think something has happened."

"Like what?"

"I don't know but the piece of metal I got in what's left of my tibia is telling me it's bad."

Carmine blew out air. "This isn't just me looking for a boring old bookkeeper anymore, is it?"

"Not gonna lie to you, but that is how this started. There's been a little tension in the club lately. Not all the brothers agree with going legit with the pot and want to keep their sidelines."

And there it was.

"Like what?"

"Can't talk about that, 'cause it ain't got nothing to do with our business."

"So how does Cody fit into it?"

"He doesn't as far as I know. You making any progress on that?"

"Following a lead right now." Carmine rubbed his temple, then took a long drag of his coffee.

"But why the hit on him? That's what I'm not getting."

"Don't know, but you better find the little fucker before whoever shot at him does it again. I need my shit back."

"What shit exactly do you need back?"

"That's not for you to know."

Okay. Couldn't blame him for trying.

With one eye on the GPS tracker, he noticed Helen had exited off the bridge and was headed north east on 80.

"Does Cody have property out your way?" Badger had looked but couldn't find any deeds in his name, but that didn't mean he didn't own any. Just meant it hadn't been recorded.

"Not that I'm aware of, but like I said, I don't know much about him. That's your job."

"What about Hunter, or his old lady?"

"They own a house near the compound outside of Sawmill."

"Anything else?"

"Yeah...maybe. I think Candy's family may have a hunting cabin up in the forest. Don't know where though."

"I need Hunter's real name and to talk to his old lady. Any chance you could set that up?"

"Jeremy Chase with an 's' and I'll find out."

Chase? Guess that explained Hunter as his road name. "Copy that," he said. Snake hung up.

Carmine checked the distance between him and the redhead. He'd gained a little now he was on the bridge.

"Hey Siri, call Badger."

"Calling Badger."

He could wait for Snake to call him back, but that could take hours and he had a feeling he might not have hours. He had a better plan—the exact reason he hired Badger. The man was tough, resourceful and knew more about IT and intelligence than anyone he knew.

"Boss? Everything alright?"

"You're not up yet?"

"Very funny," the man said through a yawn.

"I need you to find me everything you can on Jeremy Chase, a member of the Double RMC. Road name is Hunter. What deeds or mortgages are in his or his wife, Candy's name. She's Cody Grant sister and I believe they live in Sawmill, a little town east of Redding, and anything else you might find interesting."

"When do you need it boss?'

"Ten minutes ago."

"On it."

"And when you get into the dungeon, have Verity help you if

she has time. She wants to learn more. FYI, I'm on the road, but I'll check in as per protocol."

"Roger that. Following a lead?"

"Following something."

There was a brief silence and he thought for a moment Badger had hung up. Then the man spoke, and he could hear the grin in his voice. "Is she a cute, feisty little thing with long red hair by any chance?"

He snorted. Brady had a big mouth.

"Fuck you, Badger." A moment before he hung up, he heard his man laugh.

Chapter Ten

After two hours of driving north, Helen pulled off Interstate 5 at the town of Williams. She followed the app directions and found a Starbucks. No sleep and an early morning road trip demanded an extra dose of caffeine and food.

After placing her order for a caramel macchiato and a protein box, she snagged a table in the corner. It was still too early to call Anna, her boss, so she left a text message relaying her emergency. Then she sent one to Terra.

As she munched on an apple slice, her phone rang.

"Hey babe," Terra said, sleep still evident in her voice. "You okay?"

"Did I wake you?"

"It's my own fault for sleeping with my phone next to my head. Can't seem to stop it, even though my mom's not with us anymore. What's up?"

"I just needed someone to know where I am in case things go badly."

"Oh, good God," Terra groaned then yawned. "What have you done now?"

"It's not what I've done, it's what I'm about to do."

"Resnick, tell me you are *not* about to take the walk of shame."

"I find it amusing that's the first thing that comes to mind."

"Carmine was pretty determined to drive you home."

"Well as it happens, he did drive me home, but he's got nothing to do with what I'm calling about."

"Um, you still haven't answered me."

"No, no walk of shame." But if she was honest, in retrospect she wouldn't have minded. Might have slept better. "I'm doing something even crazier. I'm halfway to Sawmill, California."

"What's Sawmill—an amusement park?"

"I'm not exactly sure if it *has* an amusement park, but it's a town somewhere east of Redding. Though it's so small if you sneezed, you'd miss it."

"Wait, I'm not awake yet. You're on a road trip?"

"Of a sort."

"With who?"

"No one."

The Starbucks barista called her name. Still holding her phone to her ear, she accepted her coffee then dropped a couple dollar bills into the tip jar. "And that's the reason I'm calling. God help me, but Cody's in trouble and I'm going to help him."

She sat back at her table close to the window and took a sip.

"You are so not."

"I so am."

"Are you crazy? Wait...don't answer that because I already know you're crazy. You've run off, on your own, to help your ex-boyfriend who stole from you and got shot at, almost getting you killed in the process because...why again?"

As Terra ranted a text came in. She pulled her phone from her ear.

Cody: PW&%#@2241.*

Probably a butt-text.

"Hello?" Terra called at her silence. "Are you still there?"

"Still here, but you're going to wake Zander if you keep that up." Then it buzzed again. *Duncan gift vid tovas Menlo.*

Okay, definitely butt texts. Any way she looked at it, it made no sense. Smirking, she ignored them. At least it proved he was still alive and his fingers were working. He hadn't sounded so great when she'd talked to him.

"Because he needs me, Tee. He's hurt."

"Physically hurt?"

"Yes."

"Then he should get medical help, Helen."

"I know that, but I bet he hasn't. That's why I'm going to make sure he does. I can't let him die."

"Why not?" Terra asked, sarcasm dripping from her tone. "Have you considered he's manipulating you?"

"Thought of that, but I have to go for the same reason I wouldn't let you die. I loved the guy once. And he promised to give me my money back." As well as hopefully tell her where to find Nana's ring.

"Alright. But you shouldn't have gone alone. I would've gone with you."

"Babe, you've got the video thingy tonight."

Terra sighed. "I do but I still would've."

"Oh no, I'm not going to be responsible for messing with that. Anyway listen, I've got to get back on the road. I only stopped to get coffee and use the bathroom. I'll call you when I get there."

"'Kay, love you. Be safe."

She hung up and finished her boiled egg and string cheese. Then hitting the restroom, she washed her hands and splashed cold water on her face. Not having bothered with makeup — as who did at four in the morning — she looked washed out from lack of sleep under the fluorescent lights. Well, she wasn't out to impress anyone, so whatever.

The sun was just a few inches above the horizon when she

stepped outside. A bright, burning semi-circle of orange and already the temperature was in the mid-seventies.

Oh, California.

Wait?

Where the hell was her car?

She did a second sweep of the parking lot, and realized it was hidden behind that obnoxious double-parked Jeep.

Her heart slammed into her throat. Those super-wide rugged tires looked way too familiar, as did the man whose ass was leaning against the side of the hood. His arms were folded, and the top half of those gorgeous curls were pulled into a folded ponytail.

Oh brother! So much for avoiding him.

"Morning, Tomato Head," his growly voice greeted her as she approached him with apprehension. His face showed nothing, and his mirrored sunglasses aimed at her prevented her from seeing his eyes. It was so unfair he had all the advantages.

"You're kidding me, right? This cannot be a coincidence."

"Nope."

"Why?"

"Why do you think?"

"I'm your golden ticket to the chocolate factory?"

The beginnings of a lip quirk started to show, then as if he thought better of wasting a smile on her, disappeared again.

"Actually, I'm a little surprised it's you I was following. I thought you might have given him your car. Or he stole it."

"Obviously it's neither of those, but I do want to get moving. Therefore, I'm going to need you to please move yours."

"Nope."

She stopped a foot in front of him and tilted her chin, studying the way his jaw muscles convulsed. Damn him to hell. Even grumpy-faced he was sexy. And *he* didn't look washed out so early in the morning. In fact, much to her dismay, he looked excitingly dangerous. Perhaps she shouldn't look at him.

"First, let me say this," she said to the dip in his throat. "Thank you for replacing my jacket. It wasn't necessary, but thank you anyway."

"You're welcome, Tomato Head."

"Second, move your stupid car."

"Nope."

Hmph.

What to do? She couldn't physically move him, and she got a feeling level-ten bitch factor wasn't going to work, therefore she was pretty much out of options. Unless she resorted to trickery.

"Stop thinking," he ordered.

"That's impossible but give me one good reason why I should."

"Because whatever that devious little brain is planning isn't going to happen. But if we work together, we can help each other."

"What exactly is it you want?"

"I want you to take me to Cody."

"What makes you think I'm going to Cody?"

Carmine's eyes narrowed. "Know anyone else who lives in Sawmill?"

Poop.

She looked at his Jeep then at those mirrored glasses before she remembered she wasn't supposed to look at him. How did he know all this?

"Well, you're just going to have to keep following me to find out. If you can keep up." With any luck she'd lose him in the traffic, though she doubted it. The Fiat was speedy and zippy, but by no means incognito. "Okay, this is getting old and you're wasting my time. Could you please move your car?"

"Nope. Your car stays here. You're driving with me."

"I am not."

"Are too."

"Am not." She folded her arms, mimicking him and stuck her chin out. "How did you find me anyway? Did you sleep outside my apartment?" She didn't remember seeing his Jeep when she left, and she definitely would've noticed it.

"Stuck a tracker on your car. Did he call you?"

She sighed. The man was a step or two ahead of her. No matter what she did, she apparently wasn't going to win this one.

"Fine!" They really were wasting time and Cody could have septicemia or be bleeding out while she argued with his insufferable and immovable ass. She would just have to remember not to look at him.

But that didn't mean she couldn't smell him. His deodorant and his particular delicious man scent seeped through his hoodie and made her want to shove her nose inside and sniff him.

"Let me get my stuff." She cleared her throat. "But if my car gets stolen, or if the slightest little thing happens to it, so much as a scratch or a dent, you're responsible."

For the first time he smiled. And it was a good smile, sending butterflies in her tummy into a flurry. "Not to worry, Red. We'll keep the tracker active, so even if some idiot decides to steal it, it'll be easy to find."

She rolled her eyes. "Well, that's comforting."

"Or better yet, I can have one of my men collect it and drive it back to the city."

"And leave me at your mercy?"

"If that's how you want to see it."

"I'll think about it."

"Don't break your brain by thinking too hard."

"Ugh...you're an ass."

He snorted, then held out an arm, indicating she should precede him, and after glaring at him one more time, which only made him broaden that wicked grin, she did. Much to her chagrin, victory looked good on him.

While she retrieved her carry-on, he opened the back of the Jeep. Taking her bag from her, his warm, calloused hand curled over hers. She couldn't tell if it was deliberate or accidental, but that now familiar electricity zapped up her arm and into the rest of her body. Their eyes locked. His nostrils flared.

Holy hell.

He totally felt that too!

Carmine Niccoterra, man-whore extraordinaire was affected by her touch. She wouldn't have thought it possible, except for slight break in his voice. "Planning a romantic getaway?"

"Hilarious," she managed, though she wasn't sure how, as there was no air left in her lungs.

"Just saying, that's a lot of stuff for going to see an ex."

"You have ex-ray vision now? Anyway, a girl can never be too prepared."

"Prepared for what, though," he muttered, as if the was talking to himself when he shut the back.

Choosing not to answer, she did however allow him to open the passenger door for her. And though she wasn't happy he'd followed her, she had to secretly admit his car was much better suited for where they needed to go. According to the pin Cody sent and google maps, the area looked pretty rugged and off the beaten path—off any path for that matter.

"You got directions for me?"

How did he do that? Always seem to know what she was thinking.

She pursed her lips in annoyance but gave him her phone. He entered his number into hers, then sent the pin to his device. After, he punched a few buttons on the onboard screen, and it wasn't long before they were back on the road heading north on 5. It struck her at how tricked-out the interior was. Like a luxurious tank with black leather seats, tinted windows and the big screen displaying a map and a small stationary red dot.

"Is that my car?" she asked, pointing to it.

"What do you think?"

"It's my car."

Again, he smiled, but this time it was warm, lazy and lethal, even though she could only see it from the side.

Not even his profile was safe to look at.

Note to Helen—do *not* fall for him.

If only she could follow her own orders.

"Got any music—so I don't have to listen to you thinking."

"Have at it." He pointed to the radio. "Or use the aux cable if you want to listen to your own playlist. I'd rather not have you poking at my thoughts anyway."

"Yeah, who knows what nasty little thoughts are crawling around in there."

He smirked but kept his eyes on the road. "You don't want to know."

She played around with the radio until she found the only station that came through clearly. An eighties station which was fine with her.

"You've never heard of Pandora or Spotify?" she asked over Journey's "Small Town Girl." "I'm pretty sure in cars like this it comes standard."

"This car is an extension of my office, not a karaoke bar. I don't have time to listen to music."

"So, what do you do when you're on a date? Make phone calls?"

"Don't date, Red."

She shook her head, scoffing. No, of course not. A man like him didn't need to fork out dough in order to stick it in a woman.

She tried calling Cody. It went directly to voicemail. Odd. Why would he turn his phone off if he knew she was coming? What if she needed more specific directions?

The further they drove, the harder it was to relax. Yet Carmine navigated the heavy traffic with confidence and ease. Behind those kickass sunglasses, he seemed completely relaxed, but as for her, the tension between them seemed to grow thicker with each breath she took and every passing mile.

And it was getting hot. Only some of that she could blame on the late Californian Indian summer. But she was grateful she'd worn denim cutoffs and a tank under her off the shoulder coral colored sweater.

After kicking off her brown leather sandals, she put her feet up. Expecting him to rebuke her for blaspheming his precious dash she was surprised when he did not and actually caught him once or twice glancing at her legs.

Well at least there was something about her he appreciated. She dropped her seat back a bit and closed her eyes in an attempt to block out his intensity. At some point she dozed off and woke again when she felt the Jeep slow down. They were approaching a small town.

"Are we almost there?" she asked, raising her seat and rubbing the sleep from her eyes.

"Yep. You want to stop and pick up a few things or freshen up before we head into the forest?"

"How far is the pinned location from here?" she asked, retrieving her phone from her purse to try calling Cody again.

"Couple miles into the foothills, according to the GPS."

"He isn't answering. I'd rather head straight there. I'm worried."

Carmine gave her a sideways glance. "Why are you worried?"

"He's injured."

"What? How bad?"

"He wouldn't say, just that he thought it might be infected."

"Not too bright, is he. Why didn't he get medical help?"

"He's probably not thinking straight if he's got a fever." To be honest, she wasn't sure he'd ever thought straight, but that was neither here nor there.

Again, she felt Carmine give her a look, but refused to meet it. He said, "Ever consider he might be manipulating you?"

"Of course, I have." Good grief, why did everyone think she

was so easy to manipulate? "But if there's one tiny chance he's got my Nana's ring, I'm taking it."

"You ask him if he has it?"

"It's something I want to do to his face."

"Hmm."

Soon, they came to the end of town. It was as tiny as her google search had suggested, with only one stoplight in the center. What the google search didn't show was the several depressingly empty and boarded-up buildings. Like they never fully recovered from the oh-eight financial crisis.

They passed through, following a road with maybe one house every few hundred yards. Eventually the asphalt turned into dirt. As the elevation rose, the pines got fatter and closer together, and the air got cooler. In another mile they took a right onto what looked like a private road and a short driveway. Hidden behind a canopy of wild elderberry and a Blue Oak stood a remote logger's cabin. Nearby a stream bubbled, fed no doubt by the ample snowmelt.

Carmine parked at the bottom of the drive in a shaded alcove behind the elderberry and turned the engine off. He observed the cabin and its empty driveway for a long minute before pulling the handle on his door.

She scrambled out before he could open the door for her and, raising her arms above her head, stretched out the kinks.

"Any chance you'll get back in the car while I check this out?" he asked, his head still turned to the cabin.

"Nope. Cody's not going to open the door to you. Not the way you went after him before the shoot-out."

He pushed his sunglasses up onto his head and his thick, dark brows rose, highlighting a snarky glint in those phenomenally green eyes. "The way *I* went after *him*?"

"You know, you don't need to keep bringing that up."

"You almost chewed my ear off, Red. It still hurts, but whatever. Just stay behind me and if I tell you to do something do it, okay? No questions."

"Why?'"

"You want to come with me or not?"

"Fine. God, you're so bossy."

Carmine in the lead, they trod up a winding narrow path made of flat granite slabs, then up five stairs onto a wraparound wooden deck. It was eerily quiet for being in the woods. Her mountain experience wasn't overly vast, but even she knew birds and insects could be noisy.

"Watch your step," Carmine said softly, looking at her feet, his jaw tight, tension rolling off him like smoke.

"Oh...crap." She narrowly missed stepping on a gnawed on dead rat. They must have disturbed whatever killed it for it to leave it there for the taking.

He used the side of his fist to rap on the hard, naked wood door, but even that sounded hollow, and not like a cabin that supported life. He tried the doorknob. Locked.

"You sure you got the right directions?" he asked, but his eyes weren't on her. He was in scout mode, eyes sweeping the building and the landscape like a searchlight.

"It's what he sent me. I didn't change anything."

"Try calling him again."

She did, and as before, to no avail.

"Something's wrong. I can feel it."

She didn't disagree. For one, where was Cody's car? No sign of his Toyota 4Runner.

"Stay here," Carmine said, pulling his weapon from the back waistband of his jeans. "I'm going to check around the back."

Whatever he was sensing, she began to feel it too. Despite the heat, a cold sweat dampened the back of her neck under her hair.

Something definitely *was* wrong, and a tickle of fear started in her spine. "I'd rather come with you."

He eyed her for a second, and must've seen it in her expression because he nodded. Staying close to his back, they went around the corner, checking in windows until they came to a second door. It was when he looked through a small, diamond-shaped window at eye-level that he stiffened. He put his hand to her chest, fingers spread wide, keeping her away.

He didn't have to say anything, the look in his eyes, his stance told her not to move.

"What?" she mouthed.

He pointed to a spot somewhere far from the window.

She nodded and moved back a few paces.

His expression remained grim as her heart pounded in her throat. He pushed the latch, then with the side of his palm, inched it open and peered in. Then he exhaled through his nostrils.

"Stay," he ordered.

The seconds ticked by. Each one fraying her nerves a little more. The only sounds were those of creaky floorboards and the high-pitched yip of a coyote somewhere on the hill behind the cabin. She waited as long as she could stand it before peeking. He had his back to her looking down at something. The atmosphere inside was heavy, cloying with an undefinable gag-worthy metallic odor, and there was a faint but consistent buzzing.

Then her eyes adjusted to the gloom and she saw it.

A person lay sprawled on the couch, legs hanging over the arm, apparently napping, but the pool of dried blood on the scuffed wooden floor said otherwise.

She gasped, "Oh God."

Carmine whipped around. "Christ, woman," he snapped. "Don't you ever listen? I said stay outside."

"I know you did, but...oh God, is that Cody?"

"It's kind of hard to tell," he said, his tone grim.

"What?" Helen lunged forward. "Why?"

His eyes widened the second before he sprung forward and blocked her from reaching the body. He circled his arms around her shoulders, pulling her against his solid chest. "Fuck, no, you don't want to do that."

"Let me go!"

"Not a good idea."

"Dammit...I need to know if it's him!"

"Red...listen to me," he said against her ear. "Let me do that for you. Let me see if it's Cody. You don't want this in your head."

"He said he was injured, ohmigod, did he bleed out?"

"This isn't from an injury. This is an execution." Still holding her, he eased her back outside into the fresh air, despite her efforts to fight him.

"Execution?"

Carmine exhaled hard, then released her to wipe a hand over his face. "This happened after you spoke with him."

"How can you be so sure?"

"Because that man, in that condition, didn't do any talking."

It's not Cody. It can't be.

She darted past him, evading the hand that shot out to stop her.

"Fuck, woman!" he called as she made it through the door.

She didn't have to go all the way in to see half his face was gone. Gory brain matter covered in flies was left in its place. One arm was lifted in a defense posture, as if he tried to stop the bullet with his hand, which no longer existed. Or rather was now blended like course ground beef and shards of bone with what was left of his skull.

There was no doubt. She recognized the gray Kings of Leon tee shirt, and if that wasn't enough, the lone wolf tattoo on the underside of his forearm.

All the air left her body. Saliva began to pool in the back of her mouth. "Oh...God, no." She gagged and barely made it outside before vomiting over the railing. It kept coming in waves but when she was finally done, she spat out the remnants and wrapped her arms around her waist, then sat with her back against the cabin wall.

"Noooo," she cried. "No, you idiot, what have you done?"

Carmine thoughtfully gave her space and for that at least she was thankful. After a what seemed a lifetime of doing God knew what inside because why would anyone want to be in there, he rejoined her outside. Dropping down to his haunches, he touched her lightly on her shoulder. "You okay?"

"No," she answered, her breath hitching. "I'm not...I didn't... expect this."

"Not sure anyone does. I'm sorry, Tomato Head, but we need to get you away from here, yeah? There's nothing you can do for him."

He took her arms and pulled her up as he stood, then gently turned her so her back was to his front and put his hands on her upper arms, guiding her towards the front of the cabin.

"He didn't deserve that," she whimpered.

"Nope, nobody does."

They'd come to the front stairs. She turned to face him. Carmine pulled her close, wrapping a hand around her head and clutching her to his chest. She got the feeling he needed it as much as she did. Beneath her ear, his heart thumped a steady drumbeat that was comforting and reassuring. She leaned into his warmth, clung to his hard body, his scent making her feel safe and protected. "Why would they kill him—who would do that?"

"Don't know, Red." His voice rumbled in his chest as his fingers tangled in her hair, gently tugging, compelling her to look into his eyes which were so beautiful, yet clouded with determination. "But I'm going to find out. That I promise you."

Chapter Eleven

He got her settled then left her sitting on the bottom stair and walked to the Jeep to retrieve a bottle of water and a few sheets of paper towel from his kit.

Unfortunately, this wasn't his first rodeo. He'd seen much worse in Afghanistan and most of it would never leave him. He'd learned to cope, but damn, he shouldn't have enjoyed holding her so much.

He was a sick, sick man.

Girl was devastated yet all he could think of was her warm, small frame pressed against his. The points where her breasts hit his chest were aching, empty spots. He rubbed them, blew out air in a long steady stream and shook his head. Sick.

As he made his way back to her, he slowed his pace, allowing himself time to pull his shit together. However, this girl tested that ability every second he was with her. And probably going to when she wasn't, as he found out last evening.

"Here you go, Red." He gave her the water and the paper towels.

"Thank you," she murmured and accepted them. He made sure not to touch her. Spotting the dead rat off to her side, he eased it further out of her sight. Its presence seemed a little more ominous now. A message maybe. But for whom?

"I'm going back inside. Stay put."

"'Kay," she mumbled in a small voice that was so unlike her and gave a clue as to how messed up she was.

Entering through the back door, he skirted around the body and opened the front, leaving it wide so he could keep an eye on her and to air out the place. Not entirely sure what he was looking for, he canvassed the area, figuring he'd know it if he saw it, videoing as he did so. The cabin was small enough it didn't take long. A single medium-size room with a bed in the corner, a dresser, table and a couch which was now ruined. The kitchen was rustic with rudimentary plumbing and a small closet with a composting toilet and a sink. Drawers had been opened and emptied.

Only thing that stood out was a destroyed cell phone on the floor next to the body.

He called Snake.

"You heard from your brother Hunter yet?"

"I've sent texts, but he still hasn't checked in."

"That's worrying."

"No shit."

"I've got an update for you, but it's not good. I'm at a cabin in the woods, about two miles outside Sawmill, and Cody Grant is inside."

"You found that motherfucker." Snakes voice carried his excitement. "Give me directions, I'm on my way."

"Did you hear the part where I said it's not good?"

Silence followed. "Fuck."

"He's dead, Snake. Executed. Somebody blew his head off."

"If he's got no head, how're you sure it's him?"

"Got a tattoo on his forearm, like you described. I have his ex with me, and she confirmed it. It's him."

"He have anything on him?"

"Haven't checked his body, but the cabin has been tossed. Shit everywhere, like whoever did him was looking for something."

"Damn!" Snake yelled into the phone. Carmine jerked it from his ear. "Fuuuck." There was further ranting, and he heard what sounded like something smashing. He suspected Snake was using his boots on anything breakable. It was a minute before the man came back.

"Dammit, I need my shit. Chances are it's gone forever. *Fuck!*"

This time Carmine was prepared and held the phone a foot from his head.

"I'm going to need to call the cops."

"Not yet. Fuck! I didn't like the asshole, but I didn't want him dead. Sure as shit don't want to be the one to tell Candy her brother is gone either. Where in hell's name is Hunter?" Carmine suspected Hunter was a casualty too, but he wasn't going to say that out loud. Not yet. There was more ranting and he waited patiently, looking at the floor while the man got it out of his system. His eyes landed on the iPhone a few feet from Cody's body. It explained why she couldn't get through. Question was, who crushed it—Cody or his killer?

Snake finally spoke again. "This is a cluster-fuck."

You don't say. "The longer I delay calling the locals, the worse it's going to look for us."

"Us?"

Did the man not listen? "Like I said, I have his ex with me. I had a tail on her, and she led me to him. We found him together."

"Give me directions and do not touch anything. Make sure the woman doesn't either until I get there."

Carmine looked out through the window at Helen. She leaned against the rail, her arms squeezed between her knees. That auburn hair hid her face, but he didn't have to see it to know it was cloaked in grief. Her posture, the slump of her shoulders, her bowed head told him. It made his chest burn.

"She's cool," he said, rubbing the back of his neck. "I got her. How much time do you need?"

"I'm at the clubhouse. Give me thirty or so."

"I'm calling the sheriff in twenty."

He disconnected and sent the promised pin to Snake, then stepped outside and sat on the stair next to her. He reached out and tucked her hair behind her ear. Like he suspected, tears rolled down her cheeks.

"He's gone," she whispered. "Maybe if...."

"Maybe what, Red?"

"If we'd gotten here sooner, or..."

"Maybe if we'd teleported we might have made it, but then we might be dead too."

She blinked at that.

"Don't blame yourself, there's nothing you could've done. I'm no expert, but Cody's been dead several hours."

"How do you know that?"

"I've seen enough dead bodies."

She turned to look at him and he met her gaze. The sunlight slanting through the trees made her irises a deep, reddish brown. Though her lashes were wet and spiky, the white's a little pink, he had a sudden, almost overwhelming urge to capture her mouth and kiss the fuck out of her. His dick whole-heartedly agreed. Something warm bloomed in his chest, then inconveniently in his pants at the way she looked at him. He got the impression that for the first time she really saw past the exterior he presented to the world––and saw *him*. And what a damn turn-on.

"Oh, that's right. You were army."

"Yep, Afghanistan."

"Those scars on your back, those dead people...they were yours."

He liked how it wasn't a question. That she wasn't fishing, she was acknowledging. He nodded, waiting for that warm feeling to be replaced with the familiar hollowness that filled his chest whenever he thought about Jaz.

It came. But not like it usually did. Not the deadly tidal wave that swamped and drowned him in emotions too painful to bear, it sometimes made it hard to even breathe. It was softer, slower and a little less empty—like when you began to grow apart from an old friend, and that gap was slowly filled by someone else. He'd clung to that feeling for three years. Its sudden and rapid mutation caught him off guard, made him feel disloyal. What the actual fuck was happening to him? Before anything showed on his face, he turned away to look at the slope on the other side of the stream and rubbed his temples.

Lack of sleep—it had to be. The alternative, her getting beneath his skin, filling that gap with her pretty hair and pretty eyes and those fuckable, kissable lips weren't an acceptable option at this time.

Or were they?

What would Jaz want? What would *he* want for her if the boot was on the other foot?

To be happy, soldier.

"What do we do now?" she asked, breaking into his thoughts.

He took a moment to school his face before turning back to her. "I'm going to call the sheriff, and we're waiting for the club to get here."

"Why are we waiting for them?"

"We're in their territory. It's the thing to do. Last night you mentioned his sister, Candy?"

Her brows came together. Then she gasped. "Oh God, somebody's got to tell her."

"Somebody will. That'll fall to Snake." At least he had confidence in that. Snake may be a dick sometimes, but he wasn't a heartless dick when it came to his brothers and theirs.

"Who is this Snake you keep mentioning, and why are we deferring to him?" This time her nose wrinkled. It tickled his adorable nerve, along with his weary, watch out for the red flag one.

"President of the Double RMC, and my client. Cody did their books."

"Oh." She sniffed. "I never knew who he worked for, just that he had several clients." Another fat tear spilled and she made no move to stop it. He watched its glistening path roll down her cheek, then land on the pale flesh of her knee.

She was silent for a while, then blinking, looked at him again. "Do you think being out here is a good idea? Maybe whoever did that"—she glanced behind her—"maybe they're still around?"

It was a good question, one he'd already considered. But just to be sure, and to reassure her, he went still, breathed in deep, then out. He scanned the trees, the rocks, the skyline, like he'd learned in the Province—to feel the landscape, the energy and sense what shouldn't be there. He was good at it, better than most.

He felt no human presence, only the critters that should be there. But there was something—not an immediate danger, nothing that raised any hairs. Just more like a dissipating ripple, an after-effect.

"You're right," he said, standing, taking the opportunity. "I should make sure." Mostly because he hadn't yet reconciled his brain with his past woman, and the conflicting emotions he was beginning to have with this current one. "Get in the Jeep, Red, and keep the doors locked. I'll do a quick recon."

For once she didn't argue and he waited until he heard them click before he left. The cabin was set on an incline and anyone surveilling would more likely go higher based on the landscape. He followed a natural path uphill, then circled around looking for any clear sight lines to the cabin. The sun was at its zenith. The breeze, tempered by tall pines, kept the temperature in the mid-eighties, but the exertion still made him sweat a little. After about five minutes, about one hundred yards above and to the right of the cabin he discovered a large boulder set into the hill that gave the best view. A perfect spot to see without being seen.

It didn't take long to find crushed lichen and cigarette butts, all of the same brand, and fresh. As far as he knew, Cody wasn't a smoker. A cokehead, sure. But he didn't do cigarettes. He took photos then called it in to the local law enforcement. As he started his descent, he heard the distinct rumble of more than one Harley coming closer, then their sudden silence.

Helen facing Snake and his brothers on her own was not what he intended, and he picked up his pace until at last, the Jeep came into view. Then three parked Harleys.

Snake sauntered over and tapped on the passenger window. He growled when Helen rolled it down and after a couple words being exchanged, *got out the damn car!*

What the hell was she thinking?

He moved into an urgent jog, his feet crushing dried pine needles but as he got closer, it was obvious he needn't have worried. All three men were staring at her, and he couldn't see her expression but her hands on her hips demanded their avid attention.

They wore similar outfits: faded jeans, faded henleys and faded black leather cuts with the Double RMC emblem of back-to-back Rs fashioned into a skull. He recognized one of the men with Snake. Torque was the club's Sergeant at Arms and enforcer. A man he had a not-so-comfortable history with.

Carmine's annoyance rose further at Torque's fascination with Helen's tits. Impressive indeed, but that didn't mean he appreciated the prick ogling, especially not when the woman was vulnerable. Asshole made no secret about it either.

"Yo," he called as he got closer, directing their attention away from her. Keeping his eyes on Torque, he communicated *do not touch.*

Asshole was good-looking—too damn good-looking, with

striking denim blue eyes and sandy blonde hair that touched his shoulders. The top half was covered with a red do-rag.

The prick smirked, no doubt encouraged by his annoyance—and Helen's fluttering lashes. Carmine's fingers tightened into a ball, wanting to smash that smugness into oblivion, but Snake stepped in between them, back slapped him in a loose hug and introduced him to the third biker.

"This is Kai," he said of the bulky man with a black skull cap. "He and Hunter are close. He wanted to be here." Carmine offered his hand, looking him in the eye. They shook, then Kai separated off. Sunlight glinted of highly polished silver-tipped boots as he walked away and stood in the shade under the Blue Oak and started texting. Far be it for Carmine to judge people how they deal with stress or grief, but the dude was cold as ice.

It had only been a couple years since he'd seen Snake, but he'd aged. His brown man-braid was salted with extra silver and the crags in his face were deeper. He still carried himself like his army days were just behind him, but the man looked thinner. A lot thinner.

Snake pulled a pack of cigarettes from his vest pocket just below a patch that marked him "President" and lit one with a cheap Bic lighter.

"Locals are on the way," Carmine said. "Just called them so do what you need to."

"This is now a club matter," Torque answered, his tone dismissive. "You can leave the sheriff to us."

Carmine bristled. Adjusting his stance, he hooked his thumbs into his pockets. He didn't take orders from this asshole and looked at Snake to communicate this.

Helen's head tipped as she stared at Torque, then at him. "Shouldn't we wait for them since we're the ones who found him?" Her voice was still thick from crying.

"This is club property," Torque repeated. "Therefore, a club matter. There's no need for you to stay."

Ignoring Torque, she looked at Carmine.

"What does he mean 'club property'? This is Cody's sister's cabin."

"It means I'm going to need you to get back in the car, Red."

"What...no!" Her chin lifted higher in defiance, red-rimmed eyes flashing. "Don't dismiss me like my opinion doesn't matter. That's *my* ex that's missing his face in there."

Christ. Though he loved her instinct to protect her own, her ability to put her grief aside and fight for what's right even in horrible circumstances—now was not the time.

"Red."

"I'm not getting in the car, Carmine. Cody needs justice. *I* need justice and if you're not going to make sure he gets it, I will."

Snake, speaking in a calm, yet no-room-for-argument manner, said, "He's gonna get whatever justice is due, darlin'. You don't need to worry your pretty little head about that."

Dragging her eyes away she directed her bold gaze at Snake. "How can I be sure?"

The man said nothing more, only looked down at her. Then he looked at Carmine, expecting him to clean his own house.

Fuck.

Carmine scraped his hand over his stubble. Club justice meant something completely different from what she might think it was, but he wasn't going to explain it to her in front of them. This was their territory, and the man was still his client. The sheriff was probably in their pocket anyway.

He sighed, then put his hands on her shoulders, turning her towards the car. She balked, but he dug his thumbs into the tender spots of flesh just below her neck, forcing her forward. In her ear, he spoke quietly enough so only she could hear.

"Listen to me. Now isn't the time to cause a scene." When he had her front against the hood of the Jeep, his hips pressed to her back, arms around the front of her shoulders, he continued softly into her hair. "These are dangerous men. Not the kind of dudes you want to throw your attitude at."

"I don't care."

He inhaled, which was a mistake. He pulled in her warm, feminine scent and had the sensation of slowly tipping over the edge, falling. "Maybe you don't." The muscles in his arm flexed around her front for a moment, like he was trying to steady himself. "But I sure as hell do. I know what these men are capable of, so just trust me on this." He let that sink in for a moment as his heart beat solidly against her shoulders. "Anyway, I have some private business to discuss with Snake. I need you to give me a minute."

"Why did you call them before you called the sheriff?"

"The cabin may belong to Cody's sister, but she belongs to the club. Therefore, club territory and club rules. But I need to talk to Snake before the cops get here. Just to make sure things don't get any uglier."

She shuddered against him. "Uglier than this?"

He didn't know if that shudder was caused by his words, his breath against her ear, or his body pressed up against hers. Didn't matter. His cock wanted to grind into the gentle valley in her lower back and began to react in a way that that was highly inconvenient. Yet somehow he resisted, but her pull on him was fucking growing. He didn't know how much longer he'd be able to keep his hands off her. For that reason, he needed this done and for them to be back on the road homeward bound.

Nevertheless, he still needed to send a message.

"Much uglier."

And was it just his hopeful imagination, or had she pushed her ass a fraction backwards? He looked down over her shoulder and found yet another valley; her cleavage. It was peppered with a soft smattering of light freckles he wanted to lick and bite off her skin. He'd bet dollars to doughnuts her nipples were pink. A surge of lust, hot and base rolled through him, stronger than he'd felt in a long while.

"Do your friends know who did that to him?"

He had to end this, before his boner became a tent pole. "I'm not sure, but at the moment they think it's none of our business."

"But it *is* our business, or at least it's mine. It's the reason I'm here."

"For the love of all that's sacred, Helen, just get in the fucking car."

Something in his voice must have struck her, because she looked over her shoulder to study him. A rash of goosebumps popped on her neck and in that delicious cleft between her tits. He swallowed hard. Their eyes connected and he thought he saw in hers what he was sure was in his. It took a millennium before she nodded, not in defeat. Recognition.

Holy fuck.

Part of him wanted her to know how much he wanted her, but that would make him an even bigger asshole. Girl was grieving and he wanted to stick it in her. Bad.

Sick!

With need heavy in every fiber, he schooled his face, stepped back and opened the door. She slid in and he shut it before she was settled needing the barrier.

Distance.

Putting distance between his horny ass and her beautiful one was imperative.

Snake and Torque watched, arms folded as he walked back to them, but Kai had his eyes trained on Helen. Carmine was a hunter, and he recognized the look in the dude's eyes as he watched her. It was predatory. But there was something else in the flat blackness he couldn't identify. What was his deal? As long as he kept his distance, he could look all he wanted. It was still a free country.

"Your woman under control?" Snake asked pulling his attention back.

His woman.

The words pinged around his head and didn't hit any negative points. It had been years since he'd called one his, but Helen was none of their business.

"She's grieving. You should hope your woman would do the same."

Torque barked a laugh. "So, you're the rebound fuck. Again."

"Fuck off, Torque," he growled, stopping close to the man.

"That's a whole lot of woman in a small package. You sure you can handle that?"

"Stay away from her."

"You've claimed her?"

"Gentlemen," Snake grumbled. "Get your heads out of your buttholes. We don't got time for dick measuring. We got a big fucken problem on our hands."

Neither man budged while they read each other's eyes. Then Torque put his palms up and smirked. "Just getting a little payback, man."

"This isn't about Lilly."

"Shut it, ya fucken assholes!" Snake ordered. "And keep your shit with my daughter out of it. Torque, get your butt-ugly self in there and make sure there's nothing the sheriff don't need to see. I gotta talk to Niccoterra alone."

"Right," Torque grunted, clearly unhappy, but did as his President said.

Carmine waited until he disappeared around the back, then said, "Like I mentioned, the place has been tossed. Didn't see any obvious contraband, which may or may not be what they're looking for."

"Yeah, I don't fucken know, but it better not be what that little shit took from me."

"You ready to share?"

Snake regarded him for a long beat but shook his head.

Carmine's jaw spasmed. "Something else you should know.

Cody stole from her. Took her grandmother's ring. She needs it back if you find it."

Blue lights flashed through the trees, then a black and white Chevy Tahoe with a gold stripe down its side crunched gravel and parked next to the Harleys.

"That was fast," Snake complained.

"Probably don't get to many homicides in your territory."

"Most of 'em are *accidents*."

That's what he figured.

The cop took his time getting out the Chevy, but when he finally rolled out, his gut proceeded him. He took a handkerchief from his pocket and wiped the sweat beading his balding head before ambling over.

"LaGrange," Snake said in greeting, lighting another cigarette.

"Snake," he answered, his voice was surprisingly high and reedy for such a large man. "You Niccoterra?"

Carmine nodded.

"Okay, take me through it."

Chapter Twelve

"Ya got anything else to add, Ms. Resnick?" the meaty sheriff asked, sticking his pen behind his ear. "You touch anything inside that cabin?"

"I don't think so." She shook her head, though, in spite of it being gross, she wished she'd had a moment to check Cody's pockets. But she wasn't about to tell the sheriff that. "If you find my Nana's ring, I'd sure appreciate it back. It's a family heirloom."

"You got it."

He took her contact details, then waddled over to Carmine, Snake and Torque who were deep in conversation. The latter two had their butts to their Harleys, heavy motorcycle boots crossed while Carmine presented her with a perfect profile. While the sheriff checked Carmine's gun and deemed it not to be the murder weapon, he'd pushed up his sleeves and unzipped his hoodie to cool off, allowing it to flap in the afternoon breeze. He was shirtless beneath, and each time he moved, she got a glimpse of hard, flat abs and a hint of his happy trail. It made her mouth water.

It would be easy to keep her distance if he wasn't so ridiculously sexy, and something had definitely shifted between them.

The air had practically ignited when he had her against the Jeep. There was still a wet spot in her panties to prove it.

After a minute, Carmine approached in that cool, confident swagger, his expressionless gaze homed in on her. Not one scintilla of that heat she'd experienced earlier, which was profoundly disappointing. Still, she found focusing on his walk, the way he moved with such relaxed ease, helped keep Cody's mutilated face out of her head. It didn't hurt he had yet to zip up his hoodie.

"You doing okay, Red?" he asked, sliding into the driver's seat. His voice low and calm, yet threaded with a measure of displeasure. He popped the console between their seats, retrieving a pack of wet wipes and handed her a couple.

"Thank you." She accepted them. A sharp piney disinfectant smell filled the car as she cleaned her hands. He did the same, then taking her used ones, he tossed them into a plastic garbage bag hanging behind his seat.

Was she okay? She didn't know. On the one hand, she was horrified by what she'd seen inside that cabin. Yet on the other, some primal instinct, something written deep into the human genetic code that when death was a factor, the need to propagate the species overrode one's logic. She wanted to climb into his lap, free that impressive rod in his pants and ride the man into a bright orange, orgasmic sunset.

"What do you think?"

He started the engine, then took a few seconds before answering. "I think you're in shock."

Maybe. And in lust. She crossed her legs, seeking a little relief from the ache between her thighs. It was not forthcoming. "Is that what you want to call it?"

"Well, what would you call it?"

"I don't know. I've been mad at Cody for so long for the shit he's pulled. Now he's dead, maybe because of some of that shit he pulled. And I don't know what to feel. But mostly I'm still mad. And frustrated. And very, very sad." She dropped her head back onto the headrest and pressed her eyes with the heel of her palms. "Ugh...if he wasn't dead already, I'd kill his stupid ass for getting himself dead."

Carmine half turned to her, one wrist draped over the steering wheel, the other resting on the console between them. His steady, probing gaze stayed on her face until she looked at him.

"What?"

"Your emotions are understandable. But your actions aren't."

Wait a minute? He was blaming what happened between them on her? But then he went on.

"And I know you do not have a hearing problem so it's not that. What I'm frustrated with, is your inability to follow directions."

"Um...excuse me?"

"Next time I ask you to stay in the car with the doors locked, stay in the car. With. The doors. Locked."

Oh.

"Alright, I hear you, I got out the car when I probably shouldn't have. I apologize, but there's no need to get testy. It worked out okay."

"Testy?"

"Yes."

"I do not get testy."

"Yes, you do. You're testy right now."

Carmine closed his eyes and took a deep breath. He then shook his head and slowly let out that breath. Then he turned to the front, waited a handful of seconds before studiously putting the Jeep into gear. They rolled out onto the dirt road, took a left down the hill.

"Does the sheriff expect us to stick around?" she asked to break the tension that was heavy as a wet wool blanket.

"Nope."

"Don't you find that strange?" Her nose pulled into a wrinkle.

"I mean, how does he know that we're not the killers? Surely, he can't just take the club's word for it, can he?"

"Two things. One, my weapon hasn't been fired and second, different caliber bullet. Mine's a nine-millimeter. The one he removed from the cabin is a forty."

She thought about that while he drove, grateful for what he didn't say. That the bullet was removed from what was left of Cody's head. And since she didn't want to think about that, she was left to consider their chemistry. How volatile and combustive it was, at least to her. And how he had seemingly either forgotten about it, or maybe he was just that unaffected. The man was a sexual being. He probably got turned on by a hotdog.

Which left music. The eighties station didn't come in clear, but a country one did. Gretchen Wilson's "Redneck Woman" filled the car and she sang along focusing hard on the lyrics until they hit the first stop sign in town. He turned the music down and said, "I need to eat."

She side-eyed him, and coincidentally her stomach chose that moment to agree.

"And so apparently do you."

"I shouldn't be hungry, taking into account what I just saw. I should be nauseated."

"But?"

"I'm starving," she confessed.

"Believe it or not, that doesn't make you a terrible person. Just human and hungry. There's a diner a couple blocks down."

While he parked, she noticed his mood hadn't improved, probably because he was hungry. Or perhaps the man was permanently broody or whatever badasses of his ilk were. Or maybe it was just her.

She stepped onto the curb, when a strange tickle at the back of her neck happened, causing her to shudder for the second time. Noticeably enough Carmine stopped and stared.

"What?" he asked.

"Just...you know, just the breeze."

He uttered a caveman grunt but didn't look convinced at her explanation. In all honesty, neither was she. She rubbed her arms, soothing the chill-bumps on her skin in spite the afternoon heat. It was like a ghost had touched her.

Cody's ghost?

They passed a bank with an alley between a small mom and pop hardware store that had a rundown, abandoned-looking shack behind it. There seemed to be a lot of those in this town. Then they went up a couple stairs. He held the glass door open and she ducked under his arm when her bare shoulder brushed against his chest. A tingle migrated through her, down her torso, and surged to her lower belly when he put his hand on her back, guiding her to a window booth.

Was she alone in this?

Did he not feel that?

She glanced at him as he sat opposite her, moving a small vase with a dyed blue carnation to the side. Sunlight shining through white lace curtains illuminated those thick black curls and stunning sea glass eyes, but his expression was impenetrable as always. Except for the way his jaw ticked. But broody or preoccupied or whatever, his beauty was devastating. The kind Michelangelo would devote his time to sculpting.

Note to Helen—in caps, bold and underlined—DO NOT FALL FOR HIM!

The waitress arrived and place well-used, cracked-at-the-edges laminated menus on the white formica table. "Can I get you started with drinks?"

"Coffee for me, please," Helen said glancing up, but the woman wasn't looking at her. How predictable. Her eyeballs were falling out of her head as she stared at Carmine.

"Same, and water please," he said, glancing up briefly from the menu.

"We...ah...serve breakfast all day if...ah...that suits."

"Thank you, but we need a couple minutes."

"Sure," she announced a little too merrily. "I'll give you all the...ah...time you want." With that, she shuffled back to the counter to prepare their coffee, a bright flush staining her cheeks.

Helen pursed her lips in and pretended to look out the window. She almost felt sorry for the poor thing.

Almost.

"What are you having?" he asked when she didn't pick up her menu.

"French toast."

He lowered his, then regarded her over the top like a wayward child. "You always eat like that?"

"Like what?"

"Carbs and no protein?"

"What do you care if I get fat?"

"It's not about you getting fat, Tomato Head, which I couldn't give one shit about. I'm just wondering if it explains some of your irrational behavior."

Her chin pulled in. "My irrational behavior?"

"I'd like to keep that to a minimum."

"What, you mean like sugar highs?"

He peered at her, eyes narrowed, then tossed her own words back at her. "Is that what you want to call it? Because I'm beginning to wonder if it isn't a personality disorder."

She stared at him, then her head angled to the side. "You know, for a second there, up in the hills after we found Cody, you and I had a moment. Sort of a bonding thing, discovering a body together. Or at least it seemed that way to me. I mean, how many people get to share that kind of shitty experience? And stupid me, I actually believed for one nanosecond you might be a nice guy. Did I get that wrong?"

Silence.

"Okay, well don't answer that, but you know what? I am who I am. You don't have to like me, which is overly obvious you don't.

And anyway, you're the one who's having irrational mood swings, brooding like you are. I just can't seem to win with you so I'm not going to try anymore."

His fingers stilled. "That was you trying?"

She glared at him.

"For the record," he drawled. "I do not brood. Neither did I say I didn't like you. I said you behave irrationally sometimes. Like getting out of the car when I told you not to." Those eyes stayed on her, even as the waitress placed their coffee and water on the table—the intensity making her shift in her seat.

"You ever going to let that go? I apologized already. Or do you want flowers too?"

"Are you ready to order?" Missy, according to her name tag, asked.

It was a bunch of seconds before he turned his head to address her.

"We are."

"Alrighty, I'm listening," she practically purred. Clearly, she'd recovered from her stammer. And, probably having witnessed their battle of words and glaring contest across the table, surmised correctly them not to be a couple.

Well, fuck her.

"French toast for her." Carmine tipped his chin in Helen's direction." Eggs Benedict for me, and an extra-large side of sausage and bacon."

Missy turned slightly towards him as she retrieved the menus, giving him a prime view of her bouncing cleavage. She was blonde, curvaceous and pretty, more than tempting for any red-blooded straight man. But she couldn't say if he was tempted. He'd given no sign, but that was just par for the course. The man was an enigma. He could be drooling buckets on the inside for all she knew.

She sighed.

So what if he was?

He wasn't hers. And she hated having thoughts like those. Just because she'd thought they'd had a moment of electrifying chemistry up in the hills when he had his body against hers, and just because he sat opposite her now didn't mean he was on her side. After all, he'd used her to find Cody and now Cody was found, her usefulness done, he was in full asshole mode.

She'd do well to remember that while she endured the next few hours until they got back to Williams so she could collect her car and be done with *him*.

"Why did Snake hire you to find him?" she asked, mostly because the silence between them had become palpable, despite Keith Urban's "God Whispered Your Name" which she loved, by the way.

"Because he went missing." He'd begun spinning the vase of carnations between his fingers.

Her eyes rolled at his non-answer. "You know what I mean. He has a whole motorcycle club at his disposal. I'm sure some of them are skilled enough to track Cody down. Why hire you?"

"I can't discuss my case, Helen."

"I see. What you really mean is, you can't discuss any of the illegal things your client is into."

Carmine's gaze held steady, but he said nothing.

"Okay, well how about this. You said the hit at Safeway was made to look like a club hit, but what if it really was a club hit?"

His spinning paused. "What do you mean?"

"What if Snake wanted Cody dead, and hired you as a distraction…to give himself cover, or an alibi, or whatever."

"It's an interesting theory, but not really credible."

"Why not?"

Lucky for him, their food arrived. He was spared answering her —for the moment. He sat back while Missy placed his plate down first, then the bacon and sausage in front of him. As soon as Helen was served her French toast, Missy asked breathily, "Is there anything else I can get you?"

Helen's bullshit meter spiked.

There was a whole lot of innuendo in that question. Was she really that bold, not really knowing their situation and suggested that the 'anything else' was *her*?

"We're good." Carmine smiled, because it was obvious he heard her come-on too. But to his credit, he didn't give the wench the full teeth version like he'd done that one time with her—the first time they met when he actually flirted.

But it was enough to make Missy linger for a moment longer than was necessary. She only left when Carmine picked up the plate of sausages and bacon and he scooped half onto Helen's plate.

"What are you doing?"

"What does it look like I'm doing?"

"I don't want sausage and bacon."

"You're a vegetarian?"

"No."

"You don't like bacon?"

"No..."

"Sausage?"

"Dammit, Carmine, that's not the point..."

"Actually, it is. I'm mitigating, Red."

"Mitigating what?"

"That," he pointed at her with his fork. "Your attitude. I've got to live with you for the foreseeable future, and since I don't know what sugar does to you, I'm mitigating with protein."

"Ohmigod, you are such a controlling jerk."

He grinned. "And there it is."

Her mouth dropped open. Fortunately for her, she had yet to put any food in it.

"You keep proving my point, Red. So, stop bitching and eat your protein."

"I do not bitch."

"Yeah, you do."

"Oh, you know what?" She held up both hands. "Whatever."

Fine.

Picking up the syrup, and just to be annoying she poured the equivalent of a small barrel onto her French toast, drowning the slices and edging up to the sausage. Cutting a small square she brought it to her mouth. It dripped and she caught the sweet goodness with her tongue.

"Mmm, yum." She closed her eyes and dragged out a moan as the sweet maple and warm butter combination exploding on her tongue made her taste buds and saliva glands come alive.

"Ohmigod, that's so good." She looked up and caught his eyes on her. "You want a bite?"

For several long seconds his gaze did not waver, then he shook his head. But it was there in his eyes. He couldn't hide it. One tiny flash of that heat she'd seen before.

Heh.

"Your loss."

They ate in silence, other than Dolly Parton lamenting "Jolene". She finished one slice of her French toast, then just to further show she was playing nice, picked up a sausage and rolled it in syrup, using her tongue to draw it in before taking a delicate bite.

The forkful of eggs Carmine held in his hand jerked, losing their bounty. She didn't have to lift her eyes to know he was looking at her as the eggs dropped onto his plate. She felt it. His gaze was burning a fiery hole into her skull. Butterflies took flight in her chest and tummy and the air between them became so charged, she was sure her fork would start to arc and glow.

He did feel it. Though for some reason he was fighting it, or he didn't want her to know it.

Her phone rang, breaking the spell.

"Would you listen to that," she said, out of breath. "We have cell service." It took four rings before she located it under her makeup bag at the bottom of her purse, because her fingers were shaking. Then she saw something that was unfamiliar. A black thumb drive.

How did that get there?

"Ben!" She said, grabbing the call before it went to voicemail. "How's your head?"

"You aren't at work."

"No."

"Well, shit, Helen." To her ears, he sounded a little petulant, or perhaps he was just hungover from the previous evening.

"I know," she sighed as reality of the reason she wasn't at work began to resurface.

"I wanted to take you to lunch, but Terra said you're on a road trip."

"Yeah, something came up."

She pretended not to notice the man in front of her take his last bite of bacon then push his plate away. Two can play at his game. He doesn't want to show he might be attracted to her, well, she had the Ice Queen down pat. Through her peripheral, she saw him wipe his mouth, and toss the napkin onto his plate before he slid long legs out the booth, stood and stretched. Those equally long arms stood tall above his head. A sliver of cafe au lait skin appeared over the waistband of his jeans, reminding her he was commando underneath his hoodie. Was he commando under his jeans as well?

She pictured him naked.

"What 'something'?" Ben prodded.

"Huh?"

"What came up?"

"Oh...um." *Holy hell.* "Cody got himself killed." Suddenly it all became real again. And there she sat with this weird mix of carnal want for one guy, sad anger for another and talking to a third, trying to make the first jealous.

What the hell was wrong with her?

"Your ex Cody?"

Carmine ambled over to the waitress and pulled his wallet from his back pocket, then his credit card from his wallet. He handed it to the blonde, who—Helen was one hundred and ninety nine percent sure—intentionally touched his fingers when she took it from him. And even though most of his back was to her, she could feel his smile.

"Yeah...um, it has something to do with that shoot-out I told you about."

"Jesus, Helen. And you went running after him after what he did to you?"

"I know."

"Are you okay?"

The wench laughed. A little too loudly, Helen thought, but hey—who was she to judge?

"Helen?"

"What?"

"Are you okay?"

"No...I don't think I am."

"You need me to come get you from wherever you are?"

Good lord.

"No, Ben. I'm not sure what's happening but I'll be alright. I'm not here alone."

"Who're you with?"

"Carmine...you met him last night."

"That dude at Tony's? Wait, you spent the night with him?" His voice raised a little in pitch. "Are you...and him...a thing?"

"God, no! I didn't spend the night with him and we're not a thing. I don't even like him."

Pants on fire!

She squeezed her eyes shut at her lie. "We just kinda got thrown into this thing together. Look, I have to go. I've got to deal with this..."

"Shit." She heard Ben release a long sigh. "I'm sorry. I'm being an ass. Does Pete know where you are?"

"He does not, and neither do you. You're not going to tell him." Because Pete, her insanely annoying little brother, was also insanely protective. And one of her best friends, behind Terra of course. "Don't say a word to him. You know how he feels about Cody and if you care about me or him, just don't."

"Helen..."

"Please, Ben. Don't."

Another long sigh. "Ugh, I hate this, but okay. If you need me, for anything, call...okay?"

"Okay...and thanks. I mean that."

"I know you do. I just hope you know that I mean it too."

She hung up and slid out the booth, straightened her tank top and shorts. Carmine was leaning his hip against the counter, still chatting up the waitress.

"I'm going to hit the ladies'," she said passing them, not checking to see if he bothered looking up, or acknowledged her comment. She followed the little dancing lady sign down a passage to behind the kitchen.

Helen flipped the light switch with her elbow (because God knew what cooties lurked on light switches) and locked the door. It was an ugly, unisex thing used by all and sundry—and then some, judging by the ratty-looking ginger cat sleeping in the corner on an equally ratty blanket, in an ancient, ratty wicker basket.

"Hey," she said. When the cat opened an eye, she wiped the sudden tears from her cheeks. "Don't mind me. Keep doing your thing." The cat yawned and went back to sleep.

Then she caught sight of herself in the speckled mirror and was horrified. No wonder Carmine preferred the company of that wench.

Her eyes were red-rimmed and bloodshot. Her hair was in dire need of a brush and she still had no makeup on. When she'd left this morning, who knew she'd be intercepted by an arrogant, beautiful badass of man with a tracker on her car.

Shit.

Her life.

Business done, she made an attempt at looking decent with the help of eye drops and a little mascara. Last, she added a touch of gloss. It would have to do because that was all she had on her. She was not prepared for this. Dropping her makeup bag back into her purse, she saw the thumb drive again. After further examination, she determined it was definitely not hers. She stuck it in her shorts pocket as a reminder to check it when she got home.

"Yo," she said to the cat, giving the basket a nudge. It raised an eyelid. "Catch you later." The cat stretched and made a rough little meowing noise.

"Okay, you're cute." She dropped down to scratch its chin. "You ever need a home, you call me, alright?"

She left the cat purring, and another call came through just as she exited the bathroom.

"Hey."

"Calling to give you a heads up..." Terra said.

"Thanks, but you're too late. Ben already called."

"Sorry, I was with a customer, I couldn't get away, but I didn't tell him where you were."

"It doesn't matter anyway."

"You don't sound good. What's going on?"

Where to start?

"Tee," her voice got tight as that familiar burn started behind her eyes. "Cody got murdered."

"What...are you serious?"

"Deadly...oh fuck, I shouldn't say that but yeah, I really mean deadly." She blinked hard as she passed Carmine still chatting with *Missy*. Pretending to ignore them, she refused to give him the satisfaction of acknowledging his flirting. It took stepping outside before she could breathe again. "He's really dead. Half his face is gone..."

"Helen."

"We found him..."

"We? Who's 'we'?"

She stopped walking and pressed her hand to her forehead. "I'm with Carmine."

"Okay, I'm not hearing right...did you say Carmine?"

"Yeah, he put a tracker on my car and followed me. We found Cody at his sister's cabin halfway up a mountain and..." She stopped again, to take a few shaky breaths as her chest felt too tight. Like she was having a panic attack. "God, I've cried so much today, I didn't think I had anything left in me. Ooh, I need a minute. I feel weird all of a sudden."

"Honey, you sound weird. Sit down."

Helen looked around, but there was nothing to sit on. Instead, she put a hand on a light pole and anchored herself to it, leaning her forehead to the back of her fingers. Hoo boy.

"Where's Carmine—is he with you right now?" Terra was starting to sound a little freaked herself.

"He's um...flirting with some chick inside the diner we just ate at."

She removed her head from her hand and glanced around. The handsome butthead still hadn't exited.

"Tee, something's not adding up. I mean Cody fucked up, but this is so much worse than him just fucking up." She took several deep breaths, and the dizziness slowly passed. And since her destination was only a few cars away, she continued walking. Why did the Jeep look lopsided? More lopsided than the other cars in front or in back of it.

"Oh no!"

"What's happening?"

Two of those ridiculous, indestructible tires were flat. But how?

A shadow crossed over her. She turned to point it out to Carmine. Except it wasn't him. A man with greasy acne scars, black eyes and black ear gauges stretching his lobes grabbed her hair and yanked her head back. He twisted behind her and covered her mouth with a sweaty palm, cutting off her scream. Her phone slipped and dropped as she clawed at his fingers. He forced her into the adjacent alley behind several newspaper vending machines and a tall potted bush, and kept dragging, and dragging. He kicked the door open and shoved her into that little abandoned shack she'd seen earlier. Then, yanking her head back and to the side, he pushed her front against the rickety wall.

"Give it to me." His breath stank of alcohol and some foul spice as he hissed into her ear.

"Mmmmph!" She screamed against his hand. What did *give it to me* mean exactly?

Her body?

God, no!

She tried to scream again, but he shoved his hand higher, covering her nose. Real fear and real panic rushed through her.

"Shut up," he snarled. "Give it to me."

Using her eyes, she tried to communicate she didn't understand. While he used his weight to hold her in place, he reached around and pulled his gun from his jeans and put it to her temple.

"Scream, and you're fucking wasted."

She nodded, and he relinquished the pressure on her nose and mouth, but kept his fingers pressed into her cheeks.

She sucked in air, her breath hitching as she did so.

"Please, I don't... know...what you want."

"I want what Cody had."

Where the fuck was Carmine?

"Give it to me or I'll fucking blow your head off."

Give him what? He wasn't making sense but whatever it was, Cody may have died for it.

And so might she.

"TERRA CALL CARMINE!" she yelled, praying she'd hear, though her phone was way over there at the entrance of the alley. She had to try.

"Bitch!" Her assailant smothered her mouth again, his eyes wide as he looked around frantically. "I said shut the fuck up!"

She struggled against his body, trying to bite his palm as the sharp edges of the wood dug into her flesh, scratching her cheek.

"Yo!" Carmine boomed just outside the door. "Over here motherfucker!"

The man froze, and like some real-life version of The Flash, Carmine was there. Gun drawn, arms straight, one hand cupping his other and aiming at him. The man adjusted his hold, tightening his grip on her hair and then again, pressed the barrel of his gun to her temple.

"Back the fuck off," he grunted to Carmine. "Give it to me and I won't kill her."

This was it—the end of her story.

"Give you what?" Carmine asked slowly, his tone cold, eyes narrowed, and laser focused.

"I'm serious man, I'll fucking kill her."

"Calm down and tell me what it is you want."

"She has it. She knows what it is."

"Red?"

"Shoot him."

"What?" they both said.

"SHOOT HIM." Her legs went slack. His grip in her hair caused him to stumble and lose balance as she went down.

Carmine charged forward and slammed the butt of his gun into his forehead.

"Ah *fuuuuck!*"

His grip loosened and she pulled free, scrambling for cover out of the shed into the alley. Carmine dove onto the man, there was a ruckus, grunting, wood splintering and loud, wheezy breathing.

Carmine had him face down on the ground, knee to his lower back and both wrists trapped in one of his hands and pushed up high.

"Red," he said, panting. "Get my keys from my left jacket pocket."

"What?" She asked, stunned.

"Keys in my left pocket," he repeated calmly.

Her legs were shaky, but she crawled to him and reached for his pocket. His phone was vibrating.

"Other left, Tomato Head."

"Oh, sorry," she breathed and fumbled her way into his pocket.

When she had them, he said, "In the back of my Jeep is my toolbox. Inside are handcuffs. Get me a pair."

She nodded, got to her feet and beeped the Jeep open. Her hands shook and it took a couple tries to unlatch the two-foot wide metal box––the same one he'd brought to her apartment last night. The cuffs were in the second tray she pulled.

After giving them to Carmine, she stepped away and sat with her back against a brick wall, arms wrapped around her knees, pulling them close. Her entire body shook, her teeth chattered, her breath came in quick, shuddery little gasps. Her floundering heart thumped against the walls in her chest.

Carmine dragged the man on his heels, and though his arms were pulled tight and bent behind him, he still tried to fight.

"Quit it, or I'll break your arm," he growled. Then he cuffed him and secured his wrists around the leg of a bicycle rack.

When he was done, he closed his eyes and turned his back to her, put one hand on his hip, the other in his hair.

Moments later he turned around and aimed those sea glass eyes at her, his face tight with fury.

"That was fucking stupid," he said between clenched teeth. "*Really* fucking stupid."

"Don't yell at me."

"Do you understand you could be dead!"

"I realize that..."

"Oh!" Long furrows formed in his brow. "*Oh*...she realizes

that? You"—he jabbed a finger in her direction— "are *ridiculous.* Ridicu-fucking-lous!

"I said don't yell at me, you jerk! This isn't my fault. You weren't paying attention. You were flirting."

He regarded her, breathing deep through his nose. Then he shook his head and closed the distance between them, grabbed her under her arms and yanked her to her feet.

"Don't *ever* do that again."

She was struck by how rough his voice was just as he gripped the back of her neck, pulled her hard against his chest and kissed her.

Chapter Thirteen

His mouthed crashed on hers.

His lips hard and punishing as he held her against his chest, their heart's battling each other. Every ounce of anger, of fear surging through his veins, he took out on her mouth. On those fat, juicy lips that tasted like French toast— sweet, and dangerous.

She had no right to put herself in jeopardy. To scare him like that.

No.

Fucking.

Right.

A mewling sound escaped her, and he realized he was hurting her. He forced himself to relax but it became quickly apparent that was a mistake, like everything about her. Every ounce of the woman was a big-ass, giant mistake designed to *fuck him up*. But he couldn't help himself. That pent-up lust he'd barely been keeping at bay since he'd left her apartment rushed straight to his dick and his balls and his brain. And everything changed. It became less about punishing and more about those sumptuous, tempting breasts against his skin, the curvy hips and flat stomach that fit so well against his groin. That tantalizing heat between her thighs that called to his primal core.

Her taste.

Her smell.

The hunter in him wanted to conquer and punish and devour. She was so exquisite, she'd slipped under the radar, under his skin, into his flesh and his blood. And he had that disconcerting sensation again of falling, of sinking, like his feet were in quicksand and he was being sucked in and about to be buried. Deep.

His phone vibrated again. And thank fuck he came to his senses. He dropped his arms but it took everything to push her away, for his sanity's sake. While he caught his breath, he swiped a hand over his mouth, but her taste lingered on his tongue, delicious and intoxicating. Torture.

How had she turned this on him?

This chick was too dangerous for his peace of mind. He couldn't afford her and right now he didn't trust her. And he didn't like it one tiny fucking bit.

"That does not happen again. You get me?"

She blinked, confusion written on her face. "What doesn't happen again? That kiss...or...?"

Both.

He turned away, unable to look at her. He needed to keep physical distance from her until this case was over. Until he understood exactly the depths of her involvement and what the hell she had that was so damn important somebody would kill for. His phone buzzed again, and his cock was still rock solid, it hurt when he fished the device out of his jeans.

"Tell me you've got her." Terra's panic was palpable even through the phone. "Tell me she's okay. Carmine. She's not answering."

"I've got her, Terra. She's fine."

"Oh, thank God." Her voice was thick, and he remembered it wasn't that long since she'd lost her mother. "Let me talk to her, please."

He held the device out to Helen, keeping his face blank. She accepted it without looking at him while leaning against his car, using a paper towel to wipe blood from a scrape on her cheek.

Shit.

Something broke in him. He hadn't even noticed she was hurt. He'd been so damn angry and so damn focused on what he wanted, what his dick wanted, he hadn't seen past his rage.

Snap out of it, Sergeant.

As she talked, he retrieved her phone from the gutter next to his car. It seemed fine, just scratched. Then he opened the Jeep's passenger door and found a latex glove in the middle console. After which, he went to the rundown shack and using the glove, he picked up the dude's gun. He carried it back and placed it on the hood.

Surprisingly there were no witnesses. At least none that had come out of any buildings and made themselves known. Then again, it had happened out of sight from any store front windows.

A soft touch on his arm caught his attention. When he looked down, Helen held out his phone. As she slid it into his hand, their fingers grazed. He felt it, deep in his groin, but managed not to react. A least not visually.

"Should we call the police?" she asked quietly.

"I will, but not yet." If someone hadn't already done it.

She went back to his car, and he turned to the dude hand-cuffed to the bicycle rack. "Who are you?"

"Fuck you, let me go. You got no right to restrain me."

"You're under citizen's arrest for assault and battery on a lady, asshole. I have every right. Who do you work for?"

"*Fuck* you."

"Okay, that's how we're going to play it. Well, let me do a little surmising then. I'm thinking ballistics from that gun are going to match the bullets in my tires. Am I right?"

By the way the man blinked, he'd probably guessed correctly. "That's vandalism. You're going to pay. Those suckers aren't cheap." Then he moved behind the dude and searched his jeans pockets. It wasn't hard. He wore them oversized and low—gangbanger style.

"Guessing you weren't expecting to be caught, thinking that little redhead would never outsmart a lowlife like you. You thought wrong."

Though he wasn't expecting to find ID, the idiot had a fat, brown leather wallet jammed in his jeans along with a silencer. That explained why nobody heard gunshots. He removed them both and flipped open the wallet. There was one credit card and a wad of cash as thick as his thumb. According to the name on his California driver's license which matched his credit card, James Falk had a Redding address. Inside his shirt pocket, he found a half pack of cigarettes—same brand as on the mountain.

"You kill Cody Grant with that weapon?"

"Fuck you, you cocksucker. You're not the cops, I don't need to talk to you."

"No, you don't." Carmine said, taking a photo of the dude's ID, then sent it to Badger, along with a message. *Find out if there's a warrant on this prick. Fast.* "But all this effort for what? Explain to me what it is she's supposed to have that's so damn important, worth killing for?"

Falk said nothing. Just leaned against the bike rack, legs stretched out, head back, eyes closed. His cheek was swelling. A bruise was beginning, and a trail of blood tracked down to his jaw.

"I need medical attention," Falk finally said. "Or better yet, just finish it, man."

"You're not worth the cost of the bullet."

"Just do it."

"Why you want to be dead? Who are you so afraid of?"

Falk opened his eyes and for a moment there was genuine fear in the man's eyes. Something he could play with.

"What a pussy." He let out a derisive laugh. "You got bested by a woman, who may or may not have something you want. Just out of curiosity what makes you think she does have whatever it is?"

"None of your fucking business."

"See, now that's where you and I differ," Carmine said. "You laid hands on a woman, put a gun to her head, made her bleed. That makes it my business. Who do I call first? The cops?"

He waited a beat.

"Or the MC?"

There it was—a subtle widening of his eyes. But why? Was whatever Helen supposedly had in her possession the same thing Snake was looking for?

"If I were you, I'd go with the cops. I'd bet my Jeep jail would be kinder on you than those motherfuckers. We know they own this town and what they're capable of. Tell me what I want to know, and I won't mention this little incident."

The prick closed his eyes again and swallowed.

Carmine's pocket buzzed. "You stew on that for a second," he said, then turned his back on him. Walking back towards his car, he pulled his phone from his jeans.

Badger: *Miserable Bastards Bail-bonds in Redding have an open bond.*

Perfect.

Call them. Let them know we've got him.

While he dropped a pin for Badger, he stopped in front of Helen. "who's got a spare key to your car?"

"My brother," she answered without looking at him, which was fine with him. He still needed to cool his ass down and the more distance she kept, the better for his ability to focus.

He then made arrangements for Verity to pick up Helen's car

from Williams and drive it back to the city. They weren't leaving town tonight.

Was that a siren? Damn. Seems like somebody *had* heard or seen something and phoned it in to the local law enforcement agency.

He called Snake while examining his tires. They were blown to hell, with zero chance of being repaired. They'd need to be replaced.

"Aw, you missed me," the man answered with a smoky cough.

"Got a situation."

"What's new asshole, so do I."

"I don't have time, so shut up and listen. Sheriff done with Cody?"

"As far's I know, he's waiting on the coroner. Why?"

"Thinking my situation is related." He tucked the phone between his ear and his shoulder while he field-stripped his weapon and removed his license to carry and bounty hunter identification, leaving them on the driver seat. Then he placed Falk's weapon on a paper towel and left it on the roof. His experience dictated it was best to be up-front and pro-active with law enforcement. Prevented all kinds of problems.

"Helen got attacked in the middle of town by some asshole who goes by James Falk. You know him?"

"Falk?"

"Medium height, acne scars, gauges in his ears. Has an affinity for beating on woman."

"What the hell you talking 'gauges'?"

"Those barrel things people use to stretch their earlobes. I have a feeling he might be who killed Cody."

"Figures you'd do the sheriff's job for him." Snake wheeze-coughed.

Carmine shook his head. The man needed to see a doctor.

"Why did he attack the woman?" Snake asked after a long pause, suspicion lacing his voice. "She okay?"

"Seems to be, and don't know yet. He's not talking but I'm hearing sirens. Sheriff got a deputy?"

"Yep. Young gun named Ryan. Not on the club's payroll so watch what you say."

He sighed at the confirmation.

"She got what I'm looking for?"

Carmine tapped a foot, beginning to lose patience. "Like I said, Snake. I don't know anything yet. This just happened and I haven't had time to figure it out."

"You do that, and while you're doing that, don't forget who's paying you, or let a piece of snatch get in the way."

He growled, "Don't talk about her like that. And anyway, I thought my job was done."

"Changed my mind. I need you to find what Cody had."

"What am I looking for?"

"It's a memory stick. I need it back."

"Any distinguishing markings I should be aware of."

"It's black."

"Along with a million others, Snake."

"Find it! Now is there anything else? I gotta go."

"Two of my tires have bullet holes in them. We're stuck here until I can get them fixed. Know of a good place nearby?"

Snake's gravelly laugh filled his ear, grating on his still irritated nerves. "Torque owns a garage in town."

"Of course, he does." Carmine dropped his head back to look at the sky between the two buildings. Right then, the sheriff's SUV rounded the corner, lights flashing. And over that, he heard Snake take a drag of his cigarette.

"I'll send him. He'll tow you to his shop and get your tires fixed. There's a hotel couple blocks east of Main Street. The owner is a friend of the club. Tell him I sent you, then sit tight. We'll meet later."

"Copy that."

As he hung up, a fresh-faced deputy with a short regulation cop do, top gelled into place climbed out of the SUV.

"Look at that." Carmine said to Falk, injecting disappointment into his tone. "Saved by law enforcement. If you survive this, James, I'd suggest a career change. You don't seem cut out for gang-banging. In the meantime, you might want to find some religion. Just in case you don't."

"Got a call about a disturbance," the deputy interrupted as he strutted closer. He looked at Falk attached to the bike rack, then back at Carmine. He confirmed the name Snake mentioned stamped into the gold star pinned to his khaki shirt.

"This piece of shit assaulted me!" Falk yelled, spit spraying from his mouth. "Uncuff me, right now."

"Yeah?" Ryan looked at Carmine.

"Shot my tires and assaulted the lady." He chin tipped in Helen's direction.

The deputy's gaze bounced between Helen and Falk. "That right, Ma'am? Who did that to your face?"

Helen pushed back from the Jeep and smoothed down her tank. She was a little unsteady, but pointed at Falk. "He shoved me up against the wall inside that shack and put a gun to my head." She pointed at Carmine still not looking at him. "He stopped him."

The deputy's brow wrinkled. "How did he do that?"

"What she means is," Carmine interjected, "I hit him with the butt of my gun, which is currently sitting with the magazine removed on the driver's seat of my car along with my license. His gun, and ID"—Carmine pointed to Falk—"are on top of my car. This town got CCTV?"

"You kidding, right?" The sheriff gave him a look.

"Then I'm sure it's all caught on that camera." He pointed at the ATM across the street.

The cop smirked, then asked them both, "Drivers licenses."

Helen still shook as she retrieved hers. Carmine took it from her, then handed it to the cop.

"Stay right there, please," Ryan ordered, then walked to his vehicle and climbed in. While he called it in to his dispatch, Carmine stood with his hands on his hips and stared at her until her lashes fluttered.

"Don't look at me like that."

"Like what, Helen?"

"You know...like you'd rather it was me handcuffed to that bike rack."

For the love of Christ! The visual that inspired.

He leaned in, his cheek inches from her warmth.

"You putting thoughts in my head, Red?" he asked dangerously. "Because believe me, I'm fucking fantasizing. Only not the way you're thinking."

"You don't know what I'm thinking."

"Now that's where you're wrong. I read you like the obstinate, stubborn woman you are."

"What do you want from me? I'm—"

"Shut it."

"But—"

"Shut. It." He iterated through clenched teeth, not entirely sure where his anger was coming from, or where it was really focused. At her? His weakness—his inability to contain his filthy mind, or the fact she might have what he needed. "We'll talk about it later, when we're alone."

"Oh...you think I'm going to be alone with you while you're acting like that, you're mistaken, buddy."

"Trust me, I want nothing more than to rid myself of your ass right now, but *unfortunately* for both of us, we're stuck with each other."

"Wow," she gasped, hurt in her eyes. "Okay...you really are an ass. This isn't a surprise...I don't know why I would think you had any redeeming qualities."

Shit.

For some reason that stung. But he deserved it.

"Don't let me keep you from leaving," she added, sticking her chin out. "Ben will come get me. Or I can rent a car or something."

"Not happening. *Ben* doesn't know his drunken ass from an apple. He can't protect you and if you don't start being truthful with me about the real reason you're here, neither will I be able to. So, I suggest you get honest and tell me what the fuck he's talking about. What do you have?"

"Hey," She jabbed hard at his chest. "I thought we weren't talking about this, so drop it."

"Drop it?" A deep growl rumbled from his chest.

Her eyes flashed. "Yes, drop it!"

His nostrils flared and he moved in. Lucky for her, or maybe it was for him, his phone buzzed.

He continued to glare, while he pulled it from his pocket.

Badger: *It's a go. Agreement in your email.*

Fan-fucking-tastic!

He switched to his email account and read the pertinent parts of the paperwork then gave Badger the go ahead to sign just as the deputy wrapped up his inquiries. He climbed out the SUV and stood in front of James Falk.

"Okay, so what's your story?"

Falk spat blood onto the sidewalk, narrowly missing Ryan's highly polished boot. "Lawyer," was all he said.

"First smart thing he's done all day," Carmine said, regarding the disgust on the cop's face. "I'm sure you've already figured out this lowlife has a warrant on his ass."

"Indeed," Ryan drawled. "And *you* know this how?"

"Come on, Ryan." Carmine hooked his thumbs into his pockets. "You ran my ID. You know I'm a bail enforcement agent."

Ryan grinned. "Help me get him loaded into the car. I'll put the order in for you to collect a body receipt. Should be ready for you this afternoon."

. . .

A few minutes later, as the Sheriff transported Falk to the local jail, Torque unfolded out a primer gray tow truck with Larson Towing emblazoned in glow-in-the-dark yellow on the sides. He had a black hair tie caught between his teeth.

"Hey, Trouble," he drawled at Helen, scraping that blonde mop back, capturing it into a doubled-over ponytail.

"Hey yourself," she answered, a sweet, yet sad smile playing on her lips while Torque eye-fucked her head to toe.

Carmine rolled his eyes. *Somebody shoot him.*

"Shit," Torque murmured, after finally turning his attention to where it should be; his tires. Scratching at his short blonde scruff, he continued, "Don't have any of those in stock, they're special order. What's a city slicker like you needing ridge grappler tires for?"

"Just do."

"Not an answer, dickhead."

"Can you get them or not?"

"Could take a couple of days."

"Put a rush on them."

"As long as you pay, I can do whatever the hell you want, but it's still gonna take at least a day, depending on who has them."

"Fine. But while you're standing here, they're not getting themselves ordered."

Torque smirked and shook his head.

"What?"

"Snake's right. You are an impatient asshole."

Carmine sniffed, ignoring him, not giving a rat's ass what the man's opinion of him was. His ultimate concern was for Helen being out in the open, and possibly someone else's target.

"Red, get inside the tow truck," he said in a softer tone. "Not good for you to be out in the open longer than necessary."

Without looking at him, she did as she was told, and shoved his hand aside when he offered to help, climbing nimbly into the back-seat of the rig. Supposed he earned that. While she settled, he retrieved their overnight bags and his field kit, which included his laptop, from his Jeep. He placed them on the seat next to her and waited for her to look at him.

When she did, he said softly, "Look, we've got some shit happening that I'm not fully comprehending. Until I do, and we've had a chance to talk alone, say nothing about whatever it is you may or may not have to Torque."

She blinked. "I don't know what it is I'm supposed to have."

"Alright. In that case, and I know this is hard for you, but I'm going to need you to follow my lead. Let me do the talking, understood?"

Those gorgeous eyes shimmered, all signs of fight diminished. It was a rude, very real reminder she'd had one helluva day. What-ever she may be hiding, her ex was still dead.

"Okay," she said softly, and turned to look out the truck's window. Apparently, the view out there was better than the view he presented.

He sighed. He was making a mess of this. What was it about this woman that turned him inside out, made him lose control the way he had? He'd never kissed a woman in anger before. Taking a step back, he moved onto the sidewalk and closed the door. A little space might be best for both of them, but no matter what, she was still his responsibility.

Torque had switched the spare with the back tire and had begun to hook it to the tow bar. While he waited, he sent another text to Badger. *How's Brady?*

Badger: *Awake, asking for the girl.*

He narrowed his eyes at the text. Brady didn't have a girlfriend. *What girl?*

Badger: *Duh boss. The redhead.*

Despite himself, a smile touched his lips. Damn. She collected hearts wherever she went. *We got the surveillance footage from Safeway yet?*

Badger: *Thomas is working on it.*

Carmine: *Need it ASAP. Do what's necessary.*

Badger: *Copy.*

"Need your keys," Torque said, interrupting his texting.

"What?"

"Gotta put your car into neutral."

Carmine tossed them to him. Torque worked efficiently then climbed into the tow truck. Carmine followed, taking the seat next to him. Before he fastened his seatbelt, he checked over his shoulder. Helen's temple lay against the window, and her eyes were closed and there was a small, wet smudge on her cheek.

He exhaled through his nose.

Torque started the truck, took the first left, then a right and stopped outside a building, two stories high. Painted brick red, it resembled an inn from an old Western with a wrap-around balcony trimmed with an iron railing. The kind of ornate affair you might find in New Orleans's French Quarter. It had old-timey charm and no doubt did a booming business after work hours—as the brightly painted "Happy Hour~Five to Seven" sign notated.

"Thanks for saving our butts, Torque," Helen said, swiping her thumb under her eye.

"No problem, Trouble." Torque answered. "If I see you later, I'll buy you a drink."

"That would be nice, although it's probably me that should buy you one."

Dude grinned at that, then watched Helen's ass walking through the swinging saloon style doors.

Carmine's nostrils flared. If he didn't need the prick, he'd reach through the window, grab him by his henley and punch him in the nose. "Send me the quote for my tires."

"Think I want you in my town longer than you need to be, Niccoterra?"

"Nope," he acknowledged, then shut the door. Out the corner of his eye he watched Torque pull away. "Don't suppose you do," he muttered when the truck turned the corner and disappeared behind a small hardware store.

Only then did he follow Helen's path into the hotel.

Chapter Fourteen

"What do you mean there's only one room?" Helen squeaked. "Are you sure"—she squinted at the thirty-something blonde's name tag—"Nancy? Can you please check again?"

"There's only one room left, ma'am."

"You can call me Helen. Well, is there another hotel in town? Or maybe a motel...something? Anything?"

"The nearest motel is five miles out of town east of here."

"Can you give us their number. I'll give them a call."

"May I remind you Tomato Head, we have no car."

"Well, we can Uber, right?"

"Um," Nancy interjected, "there are no Uber drivers in Sawmill. Not enough business for them."

"No Uber? Okay, well how about any Airbnbs?"

"If there are, I'm not aware."

"We'll take the room," Carmine said, not enjoying the prolonged cold shoulder. This was their only choice, and yeah, he got it she was pissed at him. Couldn't blame her, but when was the last time a woman wasn't happy to share a room with him?

Never.

"Just wait," Helen snapped. "We haven't explored all our options yet."

"I'm not exploring any more options." He handed his credit card to Nancy. "This is our option and we're taking it."

"Says who?"

"Says me."

She frowned, then faced Nancy again. "Does it at least have two beds?"

"Uh...sorry."

"Holy hell. A pull-out couch?"

Nancy grimaced and shook her head. "There is a chair, but it doesn't pull out."

"There's always the floor, woman." He looked at Nancy. "Can we get extra pillows and blankets?"

"Certainly, I'll have housekeeping bring them up shortly."

"I'm not sleeping on the floor," she bitched. "You sleep on the floor."

"Nope. I'm paying, I get the bed."

She darted a glare at him. "Not one ounce of gentleman in you, is there?"

"You want gentleman?" He placed his elbows onto the counter and leaned closer to murmur in her ear. "I suggest you cut the attitude."

"I don't have an attitude."

"You're full of attitude. Not one single inch of you isn't."

"And there's not one single inch of *you* that isn't jerk. And you're twice my size."

Nancy emitted a loud snort.

They both looked at her. She was looking down at the computer screen but her lips were pulled in. Without looking up she turned to retrieve a piece of paper from the printer behind her, taking much longer than it should have and Carmine swore her shoulders shook. When she faced them again, her red complexion and overly bright eyes were a dead giveaway.

"Sign here please," she said, pointing to little "x" with the tip of her pen.

He scratched his autograph, then dropped the pen on the counter as she handed over two large keys.

"Number nine, up the stairs, last door on the right. Enjoy the room."

Helen took the lead up the stairs. And swear to the Almighty, he tried to keep his eyes off that perfect heart-shaped ass and those smooth thighs. But her damn posterior gave off more attitude than she did. How could he not look?

When they reached their room, he shoved an actual key with a shiny brass metal tab stamped with '9' into the lock, turned it, then stepped across the threshold.

The room was surprisingly light and airy, with a queen bed and soft blue wallpaper spotted with tiny white flowers. The decor leaned more to the feminine side but was countered with a mounted pair of cow horns above the broad wooden headboard, and on the opposite wall, a large flatscreen TV. No couch but in the corner of the room sat a chair with wooden arm rests.

Ha!

Ain't nobody sleeping on that!

He dropped his bags on the floor, and waited for her to do the same, though she chose to put hers on the chair instead. Taking a badass stance, with his hands on his hips, feet apart, he positioned himself in front of her. Her widening eyes told him she knew exactly what came next and tried to dodge past.

"I need to use the bathroom."

"Ah!" he parried, sticking out an arm, blocking her path. "No, you don't. Not until you explain to me what all that was about. And you better satisfy me as to why that prick targeted you."

"How should I know why he targeted me?"

"No clue whatsoever, huh?"

"No."

"You're lying, Red."

"I do not lie!"

"Hand it over."

"Hand what over?"

"The thumb drive."

"Thumb drive?" Her nose wrinkled. "Oh...*ooh* shit." Her face pinked up adorably, and every ounce of his previous anger melted from him. "Okay...wait. I'm not saying I have any such thing, but if I did have such a thing, why do you want it?"

"I was hired to find it."

"By who...Snake?"

"Doesn't matter who. Do you have it or not?"

"Maybe?"

"Red!" he growled in frustration.

"Um...well, here's the thing. There *was* a thumb drive in my purse, but I swear on my Nana's ring I do not know how it got there. Or when it got there. I just noticed it for the first time when I dug in my purse to answer my phone earlier when Ben called me."

He stared down at her, watching those thick lashes flicker. Either the girl was an excellent actress or that was genuine puzzlement that crossed her features.

"Any chance Cody could have slipped it in there?"

"He must have. Who else could've done it?"

"Hmm."

"So that's why you were looking for Cody? Because of this thumb drive?"

He nodded.

"But wait a minute, what proof do you have that Snake is telling the truth? What if it belonged to Cody and Snake wanted to steal it from him? Did you think about that?"

Damn.

Girl had a point. But it didn't matter—he'd been hired to find it, and now he knew she had it, there was only one thing left to do. Get it from her.

"Hand it over."

"No."

He took a step closer, dipped his head. "Red, I'm serious, give me the damn thing or I'll be forced to take it off your person." Which, if he was honest, he was kind of hoping would be the case, his better judgement and earlier conviction to stay away from her notwithstanding.

"It's not on my person."

"It's in your shorts' pocket."

"What?" Her eyes popped wide. "How would you know that?"

"I'm a man, babe. *I look.*" He glanced down, making a point of letting his eyes rove over the outline in the fabric. "And since those shorts are hot and tight and designed to make me look, I'm gonna look even harder. And unless what I'm spying in your shorts is a teeny, tiny penis, which by God, I hope is not, that's a thumb drive."

Helen's head moved back in disbelief. "You think I have a teeny tiny penis?" she squeaked. "That I'm a...herma... maphra...whatever?"

"Hermamaphra-whatever?"

"You know what I mean!" she yelled.

He sucked in his cheeks, almost had to bite himself in order to control his laugh, because fuck, she was cute when she got flustered. "No, I do not think you're a hermaphrodite. I think you're all woman which is how I know that's a thumb drive in your pocket."

"You can't have it."

He inched closer. "Give it, Helen."

"It doesn't belong to you. It belonged to Cody and if he stuck it in my purse, he obviously entrusted it to me. And I'm saying you can't have it. Especially since some dickhead tried to shoot my head off for it."

"Do you know what's on it?"

"Of course not. How could I possibly since I only just discovered I had it."

Hmm.

"And why would I trust you with any information?" She said this walking to the chair where she looped a hand through her bag.

"Give me the thumb drive."

"Or what?"

"Or I'm going into your pants to get it."

"Oh no, no no no." She stepped back, wagging her finger. "You're not going into my pants."

"Then give it."

He held her eyes, saw her brain spinning, calculating how serious he was. Seemingly, she came to the correct assumption—he was serious.

"Fine." She huffed, and threw the hand not attached to her bag in defeat into the air. "Turn around."

"Why do I need to turn around?"

"You said yourself, my shorts are tight. I need to unzip them."

"Are you always this difficult?" He asked, narrowing his eyes suspiciously, but it wasn't an unreasonable request.

"Only when it comes to you." There was the sound of a zipper being pulled, then a rustling noise. In his head he saw her shimmy out of them, sliding them down those firm, smooth thighs, her delicately stepping out, one pointed, painted toe at a time. His cock thickened.

"You done yet?"

"Yeah, I'm done, but before I hand it over, I'm taking a shower." The bathroom door closed, then the lock clicked and engaged behind her.

He spun and stared at the shut, flimsy door. *She fucking played him!* Scraping both hands through his hair, he dropped his mouth open and continued to stare at the most definitely shut door.

Maybe he needed to rethink this whole sharing a room thing, because he couldn't use his noodle around her. The woman fucked him up. But the hotel was his only choice. There was however, something else the hotel had.

A bar.

Good thing too, because for the love of Christ, he needed a drink. Grabbing one of the little notepads on the desk, he wrote a quick note. DO NOT LEAVE THE ROOM! Then he swiped one of the keys and exited into the hall and jogged down the stairs. At the bottom he called to Nancy who was on the phone behind the front desk. "Bar?"

Her eyes flicked up and pointed straight ahead.

He followed where she directed and found *The Noon Day Gun*. Dark wood paneling, shiny from years of polishing made up the walls while Baroque chandeliers hung from four by eight support beams. It offered a homey welcome. He picked the closest available stool and planted his ass.

"Whiskey, neat," he ordered from the inked-up bartender.

The dude dipped his bearded chin, then lifted a bottle displaying the label for his approval. Carmine nodded, planting his elbows on the bar, steepling his hands together. Truthfully, he didn't care what he drank, as long as it had enough burn to erase her image from his head, and her taste from his lips. Her naked, full soapy breasts, nipples ripe and taut in the same shower he would later use.

He sucked air through his teeth and squeezed the bridge of his nose. Then exhaled hard.

"Make that a double."

Chapter Fifteen

The abundant hot water of the hotel's shower helped cleanse her emotions, but not her head—leaving her more confused than ever.

How had that thumb drive gotten into her purse and what was on it that was so important?

And who was the real owner—Cody or Snake?

Or perhaps the freak who tried to blow her head off?

Before she gave it to Carmine, conditions had to be met and guidelines established. *Hard* guidelines she would not cross.

Wiping the vanity mirror clear of condensation with a corner of her fluffy white towel, she noticed her lips were still a little puffy.

Yeah—and there was that.

How it started was angry and brutal, but how it finished was something else. Something she hated to admit, but something she'd liked and her sex-deprived body wouldn't mind more of. Sometimes it really sucked to have a healthy libido.

Her new 'do fluffed, mascara applied and her body lotioned with the special brand made for and sold exclusively at Provocative. She changed into ripped jeans and a white low-cut tee shirt, and prepared for battle. Only to face an empty room—except for a faint trace of that delicious man smell and a note on the desk.

Stay in the room?

Screw his handsome ass.

Anyway—she needed wine. The mini-fridge was a sad disappointment, therefore, the bar it was.

Extracting her credit card from her wallet, she snagged the second key off the desk and headed down the short, carpeted hallway and staircase, which was edged with a pioneer-style wooden bannister. Nancy intuited her need and pointed to the back.

She veered right. Metallica's "Enter Sandman" made it easy to find and she recognized his shape immediately amongst the other bodies in the bar. Even in the low light he stood out, making her stomach tumble over itself. How was that fair? Those thick, black curls that framed that solid jaw and sexy nose attracted attention wherever he went.

And he wasn't alone.

Missy the waitress was practically in his lap, her jiggling cleavage within a foot of his face. Okay, maybe two feet, but whatever.

She ignored them and approached the bearded bartender who, with a rough, back-country biker aura was his own kinda hot. Coupled with a nice smile and beautiful ink, it made it easier to keep her attention on him.

"Hey," he greeted as she stopped a couple feet behind Carmine. "How ya doin'? What can I get ya?"

"You got any rosé?"

She was pleased to note Carmine twitched on his seat at the sound of her voice.

The barman's grin got even wider. "Seems fitting—rosé for a redhead."

Carmine turned to look over his shoulder, his gaze scraping over her shredded jeans and tee shirt. She couldn't tell if he approved or not, but the middle-aged dude next to him did. This was proven when he pulled his eyes from Missy's cheap Walmart bra to her cleavage instead.

Noticing the man's rubbernecking, Carmine snapped, "Eyes forward, soldier."

The man almost spilled his beer in his hurry to look away. "Sorry, man," he mumbled. "Didn't know she was yours."

There *was* a slight possessiveness in his voice that made her hormones happy, and apparently was obvious enough Missy retracted the boob porn further from his facial vicinity.

"Oh, look who's joined us," she said, with a serious amount of let down in her voice but covered it by sucking up something pink and blended.

Was that what was happening when she was getting a gun held against her temple? They'd agreed to meet for drinks? Wow—what a dog!

"Red, what the hell? I told you to stay upstairs."

So he could have a date?

Again, she ignored him. "Can I get a bottle for the room, please?" she asked the bartender, because Carmine's note notwithstanding, she wasn't under any circumstances hanging around. She'd rather stick porcupine quills in her eye than witness whatever they had planned.

"No problem," the dude answered, flicking a look between her and Carmine, clearly sensing the tension but settling on Missy with something in his expression that suggested he'd seen this before. Perhaps the wench made a habit of sticking her claws into single, male out-of-towners. Then he dropped behind the counter and popped up again with two bottles, one in each palm.

She moved closer, stepping between Carmine and his neighbor, pressing her chest to the bar. Her hip unintentionally brushed his spread thigh, which she swore was not there a moment before. Without really studying the wine, she pointed to the one she was familiar with. It had a simple yet cute label of a laughing pig.

"Good choice," he nodded, catching her gaze and helping to break the tension that was thick as mud. "Not that I drink rosé, but my old lady tells me this is her favorite."

"Your old lady," she said with a smile, adding her own version of flirt because why not. "who I'm assuming isn't old has good taste."

He chuckled, using the point of the corkscrew to cut the foil. "It's just a term we use for our women. She's about your age, and just as pretty."

There was a hard bump on her leg. Her body jolted to the right and she careened into the other man. He looked up with a startled *oh shit I'm in trouble* look.

"Oh, sorry," she muttered, before turning her head to glare at Carmine. "What?"

"You thirsty, Red?" he countered, shooting the barman a glare.

"I am," she answered, tossing her hair over her shoulder, then looked pointedly at the tumbler his fingers were curled around. "Apparently so are you."

"How many glasses?" asked the barman as he proceeded to uncork the wine.

"Two please."

"Two?" Carmines eyebrows inched up. "I don't drink rosé."

"Who says the other is for you?"

"Someone joining you?" There was ice in his voice, a warning that could not possibly be jealousy, if he was that kind of guy. Which she had no idea if he was or wasn't. But anyway, who could she have had time to arrange a date with, unless he was thinking of Torque. He *had* said he might see her later.

"Look at you," she turned her side to the bar, giving Carmine a full frontal view of her chest, because why should the wench have all the advantage. "Acting like my babysitter." And anyway, Helen's bosom was just as impressive, and her bra was of far better quality. Not that she was competing for the arrogant beast. It was just a matter of principle.

"You got a date?" He asked, his eyes dropping to her cleavage.

She smirked. "That's a ridiculous question."

"Why's it ridiculous?"

"It just is. Unlike some of us, I didn't have time to arrange a date." She said this glancing at the woman shooting snake eyes over Carmine's shoulder at her.

"Then why two glasses?"

"Oh, who knows." She shrugged, making a show of looking around the bar. "Maybe I'll get lucky."

His lips went flat, which she pretended to ignore. Then directed her attention at the barman who seem fascinated with their exchange. "Could you fill one of the glasses with ice please?"

"Sure thing. Charge it to the room?" he asked, while grabbing tongs and adding cubes to the second glass. In answer, she slid her credit card over the bar. Carmine slid his ass forward on his stool. Then his hand clamped over hers stopping it from sliding it further.

"To the room," he instructed, keeping his eyes pinned on her.

She jerked her arm, but instead of letting her loose, his grip tightened. "I can buy my own wine."

"Goes without saying, Red."

"But?"

"But nothing. I'm buying it for you."

"Why?"

"There needs to be a why?" he challenged, one eyebrow arched.

"Yes."

He held her gaze, his unrelenting––yet there was something softer in it. Or perhaps it was just a trick of the mellow bar lights.

What the hell—if he wanted to buy her wine, so be it. The moment she gave in, he let go of her wrist and slid two warm fingers into her front jeans pocket—allowing them to linger, before he pulled it wide enough to slide her card in. He did it slowly, and with intention, his subtext clear. Holy hell. Warmth, sudden and tingly spread from her lower belly to pool between her legs.

What was going on here? First his angry kiss, now this imparting of some seriously sexy juju when all she'd received prior was nothing but stony-faced grump? Had she somehow boarded the crazy train and lost her ticket? But that didn't explain why her body wanted to melt into him while her brain was screaming *Run*.

When the card was all the way in her pocket he paused, and those eyes came back up. They had darkened, yet there was a twinkle—a challenge in them that invited hot, filthy bedroom suggestions.

He was the devil!

If she kept looking into those eyes, she would ignite like a cheap Chinese firecracker. As it was, her fuse was already lit, and she was powerless to look away.

Without warning, he yanked her closer, causing her to lose her balance. He spread his knees and hooked a calf around her legs, keeping her trapped with her breasts pinned against his chest. Her heart thundered when he slid a hand around her waist, slowly spreading and flattening against her lower back until the tips of his fingers dipped into her waistband. The other snaked up the back of her neck and gripped her hair, gently tugging her head back.

She gasped. "What are you doing?"

His mouth came within a whisper of her ear. "Remember when I said, follow my lead?"

She stared, incapable of doing anything else. The thump of his heart against her, his body heat, his man scent and the faint touch of whiskey on his breath induced the synapses in her brain to misfire. Her mouth was temporarily unable to form words, yet her lips inexplicably wanted to latch onto his. To suck on him, taste him. Bang him. None of which was lessened by his hot breath seducing her earlobes, making goosebumps explode on her skin.

"What exactly did you mean by that?" And holy poop but wasn't her voice all throaty and dripping with lust.

"I'm thinking it means I want to kiss you again."

Oh no. No no.

This was dangerous. Didn't matter she wanted that too.

"I'm thinking I need some space." Before she jumped onto his lap and licked him all over like a hungry, horny cat, bar patrons be damned. She pushed against his chest, hard enough his face turned serious, creasing that enigmatic brow.

"Helen."

"Let me go," she whispered. "Please."

How had he seduced her into lowering her defenses so? She was no damsel, and she certainly wasn't in distress but holy hell, she couldn't fight his magnetism. He was like a chemical reaction her brain's pleasure centers couldn't resist.

He sighed, letting the air out slowly. The hand on her waist dropped away, and she missed it immediately. Then his fingers untangled from her hair, sliding through the strands, and she missed that too, even more so. Then no part of him touched her, but he didn't move or put any real space between them. That was on her.

"Thank you," she said to the barman who was openly watching them. He nodded, and she grabbed the wine and glasses and did not look back.

The lobby was empty when she entered, thank God, and Nancy wasn't at the desk. Again, thank God. Free from observation she was about to release it all, let it hang out when a rough, newly familiar voice called, "Is that second glass for me?"

She paused, scrunching up her face for a second before turning and spotting Torque stepping through the front door.

"Hey," she answered, clearing her throat and blinking hard. "I didn't think you were serious when you said you'd see me later."

"I never say what I don't mean, Trouble." His eyes narrowed as he scrutinized her. "You okay?"

She nodded, taking in his damp hair. It was brushed back off his face and hung loose to his shoulders, making his denim-blue eyes pop. He'd changed—the jeans he wore earlier were faded and dirty, these were faded and clean.

"I've just had a shitty day."

His shoulders dropped at that. "Yeah, sorry about your ex. Saw his face and it's fucked you had to witness that."

She swallowed, blocking the image in her head and studied him instead. He was beautiful, plain and simple. Tall, strong, broad shoulders, narrow hips. In short, like his Viking ancestors, because there was no doubt he was descended from Vikings. She could imagine him in a past life leading a motley crew of Nordic raiders.

"Thank you."

"Where's your other man?"

She flicked her eyes to the bar. "He's in there."

His head pulled back a bit. "He's in there, and you're heading up to your room alone looking like you're about to cry. What's wrong with that picture?"

"What do you mean?"

"A man doesn't leave his woman when she's grieving."

"He's not really my—"

"Have you been outside on the patio yet?"

"There's a patio?"

He shook his head. "Figures." Taking her by the shoulders, he turned her around. "Keep going down that hall, past the bar, through the double doors and find a table outside. I'll see you there in a couple minutes. I have a quote for dickhead's tires and need his signature before I order them."

Ah.

That.

"Okay." She followed his directions, because it was a better plan than drinking upstairs alone. The back area was enclosed with a nine-foot redwood fence loaded with potato vine and cascading baskets of red, orange and yellow nasturtiums. It wasn't crowded and she chose a table in the corner with an umbrella. Once seated, she poured a glass of rosé. It was chilled to perfection and tasted even better.

The sun had not yet dipped behind the fence. Its warmth and the low hum of conversation helped her to relax. Well, at least her body. Her mind on the other hand, spun. Too many questions and right now she didn't want to think.

She called Terra.

"What took you so long to call?" Her friend sounded a tad freaked. "Are you seriously okay? I mean, you're not in some hospital lying to me?"

"I'm okay, except I'm trying to block it. There's a bunch of strangers around me, and you know me, if I cry, I'll make a boob of myself."

"Babe, you need to process, who cares if you make a boob of yourself?"

"I care. I mean I know I said some shitty things about Cody after we broke up, but Tee, never in my wildest....okay, the voodoo doll aside, I never wanted this."

"Babe," Terra whispered. "You tossed the voodoo doll. I wish I was there, and I feel like a shit I'm not."

"Don't do that, you'll just make me feel more guilty."

"You've got nothing to feel guilty about. What happened to Cody isn't your fault."

"What I meant was, I was supposed to be there for *you*. You know, the video?"

"Never mind that. Are you still coming tonight?"

"I'm still in Sawmill."

"You're spending the night?"

"Um...yeah."

"Uh oh. I don't like the sound of that. Please don't tell me you're sharing a room."

"Uh..."

"*Ohmigod,* Helen!"

"We had no choice! There was only one left."

"Girl, you find a chastity belt, and you wear that chastity belt because that man gets his penis anywhere near you, you're going to want it."

Boy, did she get that.

"Um...okay...but I find it ironic I'm having this conversation with you. Remember, I said the same thing about Zander and that turned out okay for you."

"That was different. Whatever you do, don't do it. Where is he anyway? I want to talk to him."

"He's...at the bar, possibly hooking up with some chick he met earlier. So, no worries there. Anyway, I'm not his type."

Though in all honesty, between the car incident and the bar incident she had thought for one moment she *might've* been his type. But that was probably just the whiskey talking.

"Are you kidding me? He's trying to hook up with someone else while he's there with you? What a dog!"

"Wait...I'm confused. You don't want me to hook up with him but you're not happy he's...? Actually, never mind. Have a little faith in me, would you?"

"Sure, just so long as you're aware."

"I'm aware." She sighed and fingered an ice cube from the second glass, dropping it into her wine.

Torque appeared through the back door, bearing a frosty pint of foaming beer and what looked like an ice bucket. The biker didn't walk—he swaggered. Every female's head turned and watched him place his beer and the bucket on the table in front of her. There was no sign of Carmine.

Perhaps she should consider moving. This tiny little Northern Californian town seem to rain hot men.

"Look, Tee, you're busy, so I'm gonna let you go, but don't worry about tonight. You'll be your awesome self and slay the hell out of that video."

"Thanks, babe. Send a 911 text if you need an intervention."

She disconnected and placed her phone on the table.

"Is that for me?" she asked, pointing at the ice bucket.

He pulled out a chair. "I don't see anybody else at the table, do you?"

She smiled. "That's sweet, and kind of unexpected."

He grinned back, and she had to admit, it was a really awesome grin, and probably kept him busy between the sheets. "That's because I'm a sweet and unexpected kind of guy."

A soft giggle bubbled up but was quickly shut down at the sight of Carmine bursting through the back door. Narrowed eyes locked on hers as he marched over, causing whiplash from the same woman who'd admired Torque. His gaze impaled her as he moved a chair so it was facing her, not the table.

"I thought you went to the room," he growled, parking his rather fine ass down, brushing her knee in the process. "What are you doing out here?"

That buzz she experienced whenever he touched her swelled up her leg at the friction.

She moved hers away. Taking a slow sip of her wine, she used the moment to give her time to gather herself. "I got redirected."

Those strong nostrils flared, and that green gaze stayed steady as he moved closer, then placed his hand on her thigh, just above her knee. She flinched, but he squeezed, not too hard, but enough to keep her leg in place.

"What did I just say to you in the bar?"

Where his palm came into contact with her skin through the rips in her jeans felt hot, and radiated delicious thrills upward, right to her lady parts.

"I don't know why I need to do that," she answered, trying to ignore what was happening to her insides. "You haven't explained it to me."

"Don't need explaining. You just need to trust me."

"Again." Her lashes fluttered. "I don't know why."

He sighed. "Right." Reaching behind her head, he pulled her in and kissed her.

Her mind went blank.

Then shock wore off and sensation set in. It was softer than before but loaded with tongue. Hot, wet, slippery, *fantastic* tongue. It took a long, heady moment for her brain functions to recommence, by which her lips defied logic and began to respond with equal fervor. His scruff rubbed her skin, igniting nerve centers she didn't know she had. And his whiskey taste only made her want to drink him in. He groaned when she leaned in, which resonated all the way through her center to her curling toes. Everything and everyone was forgotten, but just when it got really good, and really hot, he pulled away.

"Holy fuck," he muttered, breathing hard, though it seemed he was talking to himself.

Pulling her up with him, he rose, and because she was too stunned to do anything, she let him.

"Excuse us," he said to Torque in a gravelly voice, then shoved the wine into the bucket and tucked it beneath his arm. "We've got business to attend to."

"Fuck you, asshole, no need to rub it in." Torque smirked then gave Carmine the finger. "Guess I'll see you later, Trouble."

She had no time to respond, other than to offer a stunned wave while Carmine guided her on wobbly legs to the patio door. He didn't look at her, and he didn't let go of her hand. In fact, held on until they reached the lobby.

Wait.

What business?

Was he referring to the horizontal kind of business? If his erection was any indication, yes he was! And Lordy, she needed to get laid something terrible, her panties could attest to that, but she wasn't ready for this.

She wasn't ready for *him*.

Not yet.

Maybe not ever. Just a minute ago he was almost getting it on with the town wench and she wasn't going to be a substitute for her. She tugged on his hand. He ignored it and continued on until she tugged harder, pulling him to a stop.

"What was that?" Her voice was breathy and a little shaky.

He stopped, looking at her. "Seems pretty obvious to me, Red."

She extracted her hand. "Well, it's not to me. I don't know why you keep doing that."

He blew out a long breath, then shook his head. "I'm asking myself the same question, but this is not a conversation I'd like to have in the hotel lobby."

"You actually planning on having a conversation, or...are you thinking you're just going to have your way with me?"

He was silent for a several seconds, then his face went stony again. "Yes, I'm planning on having an actual conversation. You wanted clarification, I'm trying to give it to you, but I'm not giving it in front of him or here. We're doing this in the room."

Had she totally misread him––thinking there was more to that kiss than he did? Because that would be humiliating.

"Okay." she said, hustling around him before he could see her face turn bright red.

Fortunately, he stayed behind her, and once inside he bolted the door, placed the ice bucket and glass on the desk. He looked down, with his feet planted solidly apart, emanating an energy that came off as a man skirting the edge of losing his grip on his control. When he finally lifted his head, she didn't know what to think. His mouth was a flat line and those eyes had a glittery quality to them.

"What's your beef with me talking to him?" she asked, before he could launch into her. "He was keeping me company while you were doing your thing."

That caused his jaw to tick. "I have a history with that dude, not a pleasant one. It wouldn't surprise me he fucks with you to get to me."

"What history?"

"None of your business, Red."

"Oh, no, no no." She took a step forward and tilted her chin. "You don't get to tell me 'none of my business' when you try to dictate what my actions should be. You give me a reason or butt out telling me what to do."

"I don't trust him."

"Why?"

"I don't trust anybody until I figure out what the hell is going on with that thumb drive. I don't trust you, I don't even trust my fucking client right now."

"You don't trust *me*?"

"Not until I know what your part in this is."

"Good grief, I'm just the damn courier. An unknowing and unwilling one at that. And guess what, buddy. I don't trust you either."

"Is that right?" He folded his arms across that hard, broad chest. "For your information I'm the only one you can trust right now, because *I'm* not out to hurt you."

"Aren't you?"

"Not. At. All."

"So, what's with the 'follow my lead' stuff?"

"Just trying to protect you."

"From what?"

"From shit you don't know about. The last thing you want to do is get involved with a man like him."

"A man like what? He seems nice to me. Thoughtful, actually. He brought me that ice bucket without me asking."

"Thoughtful because he wants between your legs."

"And there's something wrong with that?"

He paused at her question and a long silence stretched between them and the air thickened with tension.

"You want him?" he asked finally. His voice was soft, yet strained, and there was more in that question that she could identify. Not that she was fool enough to jump to conclusions again.

But no, she didn't want Torque. But that was not his business, therefore she met his stony glare with silence.

"Helen, you need to listen to me," Carmine continued, "and listen good. Despite the legal pot business the club runs, it's a front and they're involved in shit I can't talk about. They're outlaws to the bone and don't answer to any kind of authority other than their own. Torque's their Sergeant at Arms. Do you know what that means?"

"Not exactly."

"It means he's their enforcer. When people cross the club, it's his job to make sure they get what's coming. If what happened to you today is somehow connected to them, you don't want a man like that interested in you."

Well, when he put it like that. "Then I'll make sure not to piss him off."

"Fuck, Red..." He dropped his head, then placed his palm over his forehead, hiding most of his face. It was so out of place, he almost looked defeated. But she knew that couldn't be right.

"Did you make a date with her?"

His chin tilted up slightly. "What?"

"Missy. Did you make a date with her?"

His hand fell away so she could see his expression again. There was no snark, just what she suspected was his version of incredulity, which looked really good on him. "Are you serious right now? Why would I do that?"

"Well, you spent a lot of time chatting her up while I was getting a gun pointed at my temple. Then she just happens to show up at the bar in the very same hotel we're staying in."

"News flash, Red. This is the only hotel in town. Probably the only bar too, so it doesn't surprise me she showed up here."

"Well whatever you're planning on doing with her, you're not doing it in here."

"What the hell do you think I'm planning?"

"I don't know."

"You think I want to fuck her," he said, a grin spreading across his smug, handsome mug. "You jealous, Tomato Head?"

"Of her?" Okay maybe she was, just a smidgeon. But she'd rather die than concede that point. "Of course not. If anything, the way you acted around Torque, I'm thinking you're the jealous one."

He said nothing, just watched her, weighing her words. Yet strangely, he didn't deny it.

She didn't know what to make of that, but anyway she was tired of fighting. Tired of the constant conflict and just plain exhausted. She sighed.

"Can we call a truce. Please? I just kinda want to have a glass of wine, forget about today and not fight anymore."

His chest deflated as he leaned back against the desk, dragging his fingers over his face, then through his curls, mussing his hair and making him look even more roguish and impossibly sexier.

"Fuck. You're right. I'm sorry," he muttered, sounding as tired as she was. "There's something about you that yanks my trip wires, but that's no excuse for being a dick. It seems impossible, but I keep forgetting you just lost your ex."

Dammit.

Now he was being nice. She'd asked for nice, but she clearly couldn't handle nice. Tears started to threaten again. She sniffed, snatching a tissue from the box on the desk and dabbed her eyes.

"You kinda are a dick. But in all honesty, I'd do almost anything to forget about what I saw in that cabin. Including fighting with you."

He continued to watch her, then he nodded slowly. "All right, Tomato Head." He pushed away from the desk and pulled the bottle of wine from the ice bucket, then poured a glass and handed it to her. She noted he was careful not to touch her fingers.

"Let's put our shit aside and try to work together, yeah?"

"I don't know if I can trust you."

"You have my word. If what's on that thumb drive doesn't

belong to Snake, he'll never know about it. But if it does, I need your word you'll do the right thing and hand it over."

"What if it's neither of theirs?" She traced a finger, making a sad face in the condensation on her glass. "What if it belongs to that dude who tried to blow my head off? Then neither of us have any rights to it."

"Since he tried to blow your head off, we've earned the right to find out. Don't you think?"

"Yeah, fuck him."

He grinned at her statement. How that made the creases in his cheeks deepen, which in turn caused her heart to rage out of control should've been criminal. Trying her best to act cool, she added wisps of hair with her fingernail to the sad face on her glass.

"Fine," she said at last when she was sure her voice wouldn't betray her. "But if you double cross me, Carmine Niccoterra, I'll find out where you live and sardine your heating vents."

"What?" He scoffed in surprise. "Sardine my heating vents? What exactly does that mean?"

"You don't want to know."

"Actually I do. You've done this before?"

"I will neither confirm nor deny."

"What unfortunate fool has been on the receiving end of... actually," he shook his head, holding up his hands in surrender. "You're right. I don't want to know."

"Wise choice. Just know this though, you've been given fair warning."

"I consider myself warned." He held out his hand. "Shake?"

She hesitated, eyeing him warily.

"My fingers don't bite, Red."

She captured her lower lip between her teeth and slipped her fingers into his––her skin sliding against his warm, rough palm. Her blood heated instantly. Good grief. If that's how she reacted when he shook her hand, how would those palms feel on other parts of her body, caressing the tender skin between her legs, or her breasts, or the soft, pliable globes of her ass?

She hoped he couldn't see what she was fantasizing about. His face was blank, revealing nothing. But his eyes? Those lids were heavy, lowered seductively and his jaw ticked in a way she'd come to recognize as him fighting for control. The energy between them stirred, became dense. Then, just like that, he released her hand and shoved his fists deep into his pockets.

Pretending she felt nothing, though her breath had stopped in her throat, she set her glass down on the desk and quickly bent to her bag hiding the hot, needy flush creeping up her face.

She'd love to say that spending the night in the same room with him was going to be easy, that it was just an unfortunate adventure they both had to get through.

But pigs couldn't fly yet.

And something was happening between them. Something she knew he felt, even if he tried to hide it. Like she did. Whether it be for her sake or for his, she didn't know. It had been there from the beginning, a sexual energy powerful enough to consume her, destroy her, churn her up and toss her out. And she no longer had any strength to stop it.

But she could delay it. For how long? That was up to him.

The thumb drive was stashed in the side pocket of her carry-on bag, and she took longer than she needed to retrieve it. Until she knew desire wasn't branded all over her face. Only then she stood. It was hard, but she kept her gaze on his face, and off the phenomenal package in those jeans that she knew if she let it, would have the power to break and undo her.

Carmine removed one hand from his pocket and held it out.

"I'm trusting you," she said, pressing it into his palm. "Don't let me down."

If he only knew she wasn't just talking about the thumb drive. She was also talking about his new and growing ability to destroy her heart.

Chapter Sixteen

W ords to live and die by.
Don't let me down.

He'd played women before for his job, he'd admit it. He wasn't a saint. Anything to get it done. And he'd taken *this* job because he'd seen what happened in the mall between her and Cody and he couldn't deny he was intrigued. Those Fuck Me eyes and baby blue lace panties peeking out the top of her jeans when she bent to get the thumb drive? Jesus. He had a nasty suspicion it was he who was going to be let down.

And he'd seen countless women in various stages of undress from sexy underwear to buck naked, so why was that tiny hint of lace getting his dick so fat? He'd said it before, and he'd say it again —this one was designed to fuck him up.

Time for some serious space, otherwise he was going to burst a blood vessel, or drill her beautiful ass against the wall and get them tossed from the hotel.

Ugly thoughts.

Stanky, sweaty-hairy-ass, ugly-dudes-in-the-gym thoughts.

Except, the only asses he could conjure in his fevered brain was her gorgeous naked ass and his...

Fuuck.

"We'll check it out after I shower," he gritted out. Snatching up his bag, he entered the bathroom and shut the door. Held onto the damn doorknob while he considered turning the lock, but Holy mother of Christ, if she wanted to join him, he wasn't about to put any barriers between them.

What was it about her that messed him up so?

No other woman!

Not even Jaz had fucked him up this way, except when he lost her. Then his soul had fractured. Left him an empty, guilt-ridden shell with nothing but his dick to offer any woman who bothered. For a time, sex was what got him out of bed, his medicine—the only thing that made him feel anything. But it wasn't for the want of caring. He cared too damn much.

Gingerly, he freed himself of his clothing, placing them neatly on the vanity. He stepped into the shower and stared at her shampoo in the caddy suctioned to the faux marble.

Turning the water to hot, he let it sluice off his shoulders until he could no longer stand it. When his balls were about to explode, his dick throbbing to the point of pain, he poured a quarter sized dollop into his palm. The subtle scent surrounded him. He breathed it in, absorbed it, not needing to commit it to memory. It was already embedded.

Helen and honeysuckle—forever shall the twain be stuck together in his brain.

Finally relenting, as that horny, hungry fucker between his legs wasn't going to leave him alone, he leaned his forearm against the tile and braced himself. With a low, agonizing groan deep in his throat, he palmed himself. Squeezed his eyes shut at the delicious sensation shuddering through his body. Goosebumps exploded on his flesh. He was so hard he could ram through a solid wooden door.

She did that to him.

One hungry look from those gorgeous, sensuous eyes did that to him.

Adjusting his stance, he caught his breath and began to stroke, needing relief like nobody's business. He'd refrained from taking matters into his own hands the previous night because she'd pissed him off. But his lack of action didn't negate the fact he'd wanted her——bad.

It didn't take long before his thoughts ceased, blanking his brain as his balls pulled up tighter and his dick got even fatter. Almost bit his tongue suppressing the roar building in his torso along with his orgasm. Sort of lost his balance when his legs faltered as he finally let it go but caught himself on the handicap bar screwed into the shower wall. Then he started laughing as the much sought after relief flooded his system. Or maybe he was crying.

Damn woman did shit to him, messed with his brain, his sanity, and the one thing he prided himself on—his control.

And he didn't have the slightest clue what to do about it.

* * *

There were two files on the thumb drive. The first, a video six minutes long. Carmine glanced at Helen. She'd changed into black form-fitting yoga pants and a black tank and made herself comfortable on the bed. Resting against the headboard, she sat crossed legged, hair piled on top of her head. A few loose strands fell about her face, giving her a soft, seductive look.

He usually slept naked, but of necessity, he'd put on a tee shirt along with his sweats, as he wasn't sure he could handle it if she looked at him like she had before. Adjusting his laptop so it was equally situated between them, and praying the video wasn't porn, he clicked on that file first.

It was raw footage, dark and shaky and appeared to have been shot on a phone. After the first fifteen seconds, and though he was relieved it wasn't porn, the content was far worse. His stomach turned.

A voice barked orders in a foreign language but was overlaid with the photographer's heavy breathing.

"Oh no!" Helen gasped when she comprehended what she was seeing, her hand covering her mouth. "*No.*"

Center stage, on the backside of a delivery truck was a row of humans. About twenty in all, female, young with their hands behind their backs. From what he could tell, mostly caucasian, probably Eastern European by their features.

He turned up the volume and listened closer to the voice. Russian?

Christ, it never ended.

He had knowledge of a faction in San Francisco that trafficked humans, but last he heard, it had been shut down thanks to Vasily Melnikov. Dude didn't like it and didn't allow it in his territory. He hit pause.

"Don't," she whispered, taking hold of his forearm and squeezing gently.

"Red," he cautioned. "You don't need to see humans being trafficked. It's a whole different reality and we don't know what's coming. Could be bad."

"If they lived it," she insisted, "I can stand to watch it."

He stared at her—torn. He wanted to spare her, but one thing he'd learned, she had resolve and an inner strength that he couldn't help admiring.

He tried again. "Helen."

She held his eyes, and there was determination in them that appealed to both the soldier and the hunter in him.

"We have a deal," she reminded him—as if he needed reminding. Nevertheless, it caused him to groan inwardly. In hindsight he regretted making that deal. If she'd been his woman, he'd have forbidden her to watch the rest until he'd screened it first. But she wasn't and here they were.

He nodded, knowing he was probably making a big mistake, but still he hesitated restarting the video.

"Do it," she said.

Once he did, her fingers lifted from his arm leaving a cold, lonely spot on his flesh. He swallowed.

A man of medium height, paunchy with dark slicked-backed hair cracked a long bullwhip. Some of the girls cowered and whimpered.

The man taking the video whispered, *"Fuck, man this is fucked. So fucked."*

Carmine paid close attention to the voice. He stopped the video, and replayed that section again. It didn't sound like anyone he knew. The third time he played it he asked Helen, "Sound familiar to you?"

"No," she shook her head. Her face showed nothing either.

Not Cody then.

At the same time, he examined Paunchy's face. It triggered nothing. A new player perhaps? For sure he wasn't one of Vasily's crew, which was a relief.

He'd studied Melnikov's operation in depth after the thing that involved Terra's mother, and he was familiar with the players. Which begged the question: was Melnikov aware of this new faction? Pretty sure he wouldn't tolerate it if he was.

Paunchy walked the line barking instructions, running the whip handle up between a girl's legs, lewdly rubbing there, then over her breasts. Smirking, he grabbed his crotch when she cringed.

If he ever came across this prick, he was going to *hurt* him.

Then he did the same to another girl who took umbrage, spitting in his face. Paunchy froze, then wiped it off with the back of his hand. He seemed to examine it for a second, then like lightning punched her hard in the face. She staggered back half a step, collapsed into a heap at his feet, blood spilling from her nose. Another girl broke away and tried to help but received a lashing on her shoulder. She cried out and moved away. No one tried anything after that.

Okay. Strike that. He vowed to *destroy* him.

As he walked the line, he tapped a few of the women on the head, and a second man, much taller and leaner who appeared from behind the truck, pulled the chosen girls aside.

Carmine's skin prickled. Hairs on the back of his neck rose. There was a lot familiar about dude number two, and he leaned in to study him closer. He'd seen him before for sure. He just didn't know where.

Paunchy continued on, reaching the end of the line. The selected girls were led inside a large house by a female who'd just joined them. She had dark hair pulled into a stylish ponytail on top of her head, jeans and heels.

It was a mansion really, now that he'd had a chance to focus on it. The unchosen were herded back inside the truck, including the one he'd punched and the girl who tried to help. Too spirited, and not worth the trouble would be his guess.

Tall dude reached up and pulled the door closed. Latched it by pulling a handle at the bottom, after which his head turned and faced in the direction of the camera, like something had attracted his attention.

"*Shit*," the photographer whispered. The moon was full enough to shine light on the tall dude's face, giving a full, clear look. Carmine's heart slammed into his chest.

Fuck!

He paused the video and stared at the still image for several seconds, eyes wide. He took a screenshot before restarting it, barely noticing the man climb into the passenger side of the cab. There was a third man, he realized, as the truck backed up. The driver. He paused it again and took another screenshot of the license plate. Then the video ended.

"That's a brothel, isn't it?" Helen's voice broke into his thoughts.

He nodded, sliding his gaze away from the screen to take her in. She was pale and shaken. It pissed him off that was in her head now.

"What do you think happened to the girls in the truck?"

"Probably sold."

"Sold?"

"Online or at auction."

"You mean like a cattle market?" she asked. "They do that?"

Again, he nodded, and took a deep breath. "On the dark web. It's an ugly world with a lot of ugly people."

"Why did Cody have this video? I can't...compute he was involved in something like this. I mean surely I would've known, because this is...evil."

"Wish I could answer that, Red." Using his track pad, he went to a different folder on his laptop, selected another video file, opened it beside the first and hit 'start.'

"What are you doing?"

"I need to compare something," he said, dragging the progress button to midway through the video.

It only took Helen a couple of seconds. "Wait, is that Zander's bar?"

"Yep."

Then came the footage he wanted; two men entering through the front door, paying the cover fee and receiving their stamps from Petey, Helen's brother.

She gasped. "Holy poop...*him*!" She pointed to one of the dudes. "He's in both videos!"

Indeed, he was. There was no date stamp on the phone video, but the men were wearing summer clothing. And so were the girls. He'd need to get it analyzed further to get a possible geographical marker of where it was taken. If Thomas could clean it up, they may get lucky.

Carmine sat back against the headboard and closed his eyes.

Whoever made the video didn't want to be discovered, that much was obvious. Put themselves in danger to get it.

"The photographer's voice, Tomato Head. You sure you don't recognize it?"

"It's not Cody, if that's what you're asking," she said, slipping off the bed and heading towards the bathroom. "It's too deep and rougher than his."

He agreed with that. It was rougher, but not as rough as Snake's either.

A yawn took him by surprise. Having operated on only a couple hours sleep his body felt heavy from exhaustion. But while she was in the bathroom, he took the opportunity to check the other folder on the thumb drive.

It was a MultiBit file.

Unlike the video before, Carmine knew exactly what it was for —a Bitcoin Wallet. For receiving or sending cryptocurrency.

Growing marijuana, though legal in some states, was still illegal on the federal level. No government-insured bank would accept money from a grower, leaving them with a cash problem—too much of it. Cryptocurrency made absolute sense.

Before he closed his laptop, he verified one last thing; the dates and times on the MultiBit file. It had been modified earlier, at seven-oh-two that morning—close to the time of Cody's death.

Why?

What had he changed?

And who the fuck took the video?

Chapter Seventeen

"**M**y turn, Sergeant?" *Jaz pulled the Humvee to a stop, put it in park and made to get out. It was pitch black, with no moon and their lights were off. Their image enhancement night vision showed a huge boulder blocking their path.*

"Negative," he answered. "We got it, just keep the engine running. On my six, Alvarez," he said to his fellow squadie, grabbing his weapon.

He'd needed to stretch his legs, get some air anyway. This was the fourth they'd come across, thanks to the six-point-five shaker that rocked Nuristan a couple days prior. Rockslides had become the norm in the area they scouted.

The fourth in their squad, Smithy, who despite his Anglo-Saxon name was as black as his Bantu roots, slept in the back catching much needed and overdue shuteye. He chose not to wake him. The grunt needed his rest.

He and Alvarez exited the Humvee. They scanned the area and the hillside above them, communicating through hand signals. The boulder was big, but round enough they could roll it and several smaller rocks closer to the hillside clearing the way for the Humvee.

The road clear, Alvarez was already heading back, when something odd behind the boulder caught his attention. He stopped, dropped into a squat to check it out when the energy in the air changed. His skin pimpled. Then he heard it—a high-pitched whistling.

Jesus, fuck no!

He didn't even have time to turn before his eardrums burst as the Humvee exploded into a giant, orange fireball.

Carmine jolted awake covered in sweat. His heart pounded in his ears while he stared at his surroundings. Nothing looked familiar.

Where was he?

His breath came in fast and short as he fought to orient himself. The balcony door, the desk with a bottle of wine, a mini-fridge. Hotel. He was in a hotel. He looked at the woman sleeping next to him.

The redhead. She was okay.

Just his dream—the same one he always had—with one new, terrifying variation. The face watching him through the windshield when that missile hit wasn't Jaz.

It was Helen.

In three years, the main details of the dream never varied, except for small things, like time of day, location, amount of rocks, that sort of thing. But the people who were with him on that mission, the ones who were incinerated never changed. He scraped a shaky hand over his jaw, then through his hair.

What was that about?

Tension bunched in his shoulder muscles; he sat up and rolled them. His tee shirt stuck to him, scratching his scars. They weren't normally sensitive, but always after the nightmare they burned and itched for a while. Reaching behind his head, he yanked his shirt off and tossed it on the floor. Evaporation cooled his skin, helped slow his heartbeat, and so did watching her breathing.

Helen lay on her side, under the covers facing him, one arm

under the pillow. It pleased him she'd slept on the bed instead of on the floor. Not that he would've let her if he hadn't fallen asleep first. He wasn't a complete asshole.

The slow, steady rhythm of her breath, her chest falling and rising instilled calm back into him. The problem was, the more he watched her, the lovelier she got. The kind of lovely that deserved her name—like that chick the Trojan's went to war over.

Dangerously lovely.

The moonlight shining through the sheer curtains couldn't dull the richness of her hair, or the translucency of her almost flawless skin, marred by that scrape on her cheekbone and the shadow of a new bruise forming underneath.

A ghost of a smile formed at those appealing, perfect breasts squished together. Yeah, okay, he was a perv, but he couldn't stop staring at them and blew out a frustrated breath. A man could die happy in those.

Careful not to wake her, he slid off the bed, used the bathroom, washed his hands then walked to the fridge for a bottle of water. Chugging half of it, he then opened the balcony door, leaning his shoulder against the frame, letting the cool night air wash over him.

The tiny town was quiet, lit by an obese moon partially covered by clouds. It had rained at some point. He could smell it in the air. An owl hooted somewhere, its haunting cry the only sound echoing through the narrow street below.

Carmine's gaze tacked onto movement in the far west corner of the hotel, near the parking lot. A ginger feral cat wiggled its butt, stalking dinner next to the dumpster.

It pounced.

Some unlucky critter emitted a series of high-pitched squeaks. He turned away, unwilling to witness the carnage. Not that he blamed the cat—it was nature and it had to eat, but he'd seen and heard too many desperate sounds of death. They still rang in his ears. He didn't need to add to it. Mercifully, the cat was efficient in its killing and it stopped. Probably too hungry to play with its prey.

Shutting the balcony door, he walked back to bed, lifted the blanket aside and slid under the sheets. She shifted, mumbling something that sounded like "Cody". The emotions that word conjured coming from her mouth were not something he particularly liked. But look at him, getting all bent over a dead dude taking up space in her dreams, when he'd just woken from one of his own damn nightmares. Difference was, she'd been in his.

A strand of hair had fallen across her face and he reached over to brush it off with his thumb. Her lashes flickered, then her eyes opened. Those sleepy brown irises caught his.

"Mmm, hey. What time is it?"

"Late, Tomato Head. Go back to sleep."

"Why are you awake?"

"Couldn't sleep," he said, leaning back against the headboard, rubbing the rough on his jaw. "Bad dream."

"Yeah, I know. You called out...kept saying something about... jazz, or jasmine."

He swallowed, but said nothing and when she didn't press it, he didn't know if he was relieved, or disappointed, or some weird combination of both. Nevertheless, they were quiet and he'd thought she'd fallen back asleep.

Until she whispered, "I can't stop seeing Cody's head, or those girls."

No...quite frankly, neither could he. But he'd seen worse.

Much worse.

"And the flies...ugh." Her body shuddered under the covers.

He didn't know what to say. *That's what you get for not listening*? Dick move.

"But those poor girls, they're so young. What kind of life is ahead of them?"

One he didn't want to ponder, but he sure as hell could guess.

She rolled onto her back, pressing her palms to her eyes, her chest rising with each breath. Her tank rode up, exposing a section of her smooth belly.

"Why did you kiss me?"

Jesus—out of left field. He stopped breathing for several ticks of the clock. Because, how the hell did he explain that in that moment he'd been compelled to. That his body had overridden his brain and he'd lost control. So he went with the generic.

"Why does any man kiss a woman, Red?" He'd have like to add a touch of neutrality into his tone, hoping she'd drop it, as thoughts of him kissing her were not good for his situation, but even to his own ears, he sounded...hopeful? More like fucking desperate.

"Usually a man kisses a woman when he wants to have sex with her."

Okay.

Now his heart was doing interesting things. Dangerous territory, bringing up sex—like he wasn't already fantasizing about fucking her. Had thought about it constantly and abused himself with her shampoo in the shower because of it.

He cleared his throat. "Usually that would be correct."

"Usually?" she asked softly, her gaze drifting over his face, then down his chest, lower, lower. He felt every inch of that gaze on his six-pack, gooseflesh rising in its wake. And something else rising too.

"You're going to have to be a little more specific, babe." Because he was getting crossed wires, not sure where she was headed with this, but hoping he did. The pulse in his throat became noticeable.

"Well, the first one after...you know, felt angry."

Yep, he'd have to agree with that.

"But the second one downstairs in front of Torque seemed more...possessive? Like you were staking a claim."

And he couldn't disagree with *that*.

"But that wouldn't be right, would it? I mean I know what

you said, about not trusting him. And everything I've heard about you, and everything I've seen, you don't do the 'staking a claim' thing. So, I'm wondering why it felt like it when I'm assuming you weren't."

She assumed wrong. But he hadn't yet weighed if it would be a detriment to his sanity if he clarified.

She searched his face, and it took everything in him to keep it passive while she did.

"Never mind." She shook her head, catching her bottom lip. "I'm just rambling. I do that sometimes. I suppose I just need something else to think about other..." her voice hitched. "Other than..." Blinking, she reached for the remote on the side table.

While she flipped through channels, he couldn't help feeling he'd missed his chance. That she'd offered herself and in trying to not fuck up, he *had* fucked up.

Seconds ticked by. Each one keeping time with his thumping heart.

Screw it!

If she needed something to distract her, who was he to deny her that. If it made him weak, so be it.

He rolled over. Supporting his weight on his knees and elbows, he straddled her, then took the remote and tossed it onto the floor, ignoring her little protest. "What...?"

He silenced her with his lips, just pressing them to hers. It could stay innocent if that's what she wanted. She could turn away––he wouldn't push it. But she didn't. And though it was only a couple seconds, it felt like a heart-pounding, dick-thickening decade before she opened her mouth and finally, *finally* touched her tongue to his.

He suppressed a moan, because too eager, too desperate just wouldn't be cool. No getting twisted over this woman.

Bullshit.

He was twisted.

He was desperate.

She angled her mouth, giving him deeper access. Then she sucked on his upper lip, and the goddamn earth shifted, rocked his foundation, rattled his fucking brain. He shifted closer, and she melted into him, giving him more tongue, more smooth, delectable skin against his. Her nails dug into his arms, igniting his need. And want. And just plain old-fashioned, carnal lust.

He pushed an arm under her, hooking her around the waist, pulling her even closer. Then, finding that spot between her thighs with his own, putting pressure on and rubbing her just right until she gasped in pleasure against his mouth.

Christ, now he needed in—more than he could remember.

He kissed her neck, down along her collarbone to her breastbone. Then starting low on that belly, scraped her tee shirt up over those naked breasts.

Those perfect, beautiful breasts.

And yes, like he'd guessed, her nipples were dusky pink, standing like little soldiers begging to take orders. He took one in his mouth and sucked, scraping his teeth and tongue over the sensitive bud, while he rolled the other between his fingers. She squirmed, making sexy, desperate noises deep in her throat, rubbing herself against his leg.

It was a long time ago he'd come this close to losing it with a woman.

She did that to him.

"I want this off," he ordered, tugging her tank, needing to see more of her naked. He didn't care how this was going to complicate things, he needed her. And clearly in this moment, she needed him.

Arching her back, she crossed her arms and slipped it off over her head, while he hooked his fingers into her pants, dragging them down her firm legs and ankles.

Then he paused to admire.

She was sensational.

Completely vulnerable and available—that beautiful body his

to have. Holy Christ, he was living every dirty fantasy he'd had about her and it was better than he could imagine.

Starting at her belly button, he worked a path, kissing and tasting down her flat, smooth belly, down the tender flesh of her inner thigh, right to where the silky auburn patch hid what he wanted.

Her.

Every inch of her naked flesh fueled him--burned hot and bright, consuming him. He slid back off the bed onto his knees and pulled her down to the edge.

He was a man needing to worship.

Having experienced the shit he had, he'd never been one for religion, despite his Catholic upbringing. But in this moment, in this woman, he found it—a Goddess.

She hitched her legs, bringing them together in front of his face, hiding herself. It was cute she was a little shy, looking at him through her lashes with those Fuck Me eyes, her pupils dilated with desire.

This was his one shot—probably his *only* fucking shot ever to blow her mind. Because he already knew deep in his cells he'd want more. Didn't give a rat's ass what her reason was to forget the day, he had her now and he wanted this.

Needed this.

"You sure?" he asked, his voice cracking, praying she didn't change her mind.

She licked her lips, which did unspeakable things to his cock, hesitating for one heart-stopping moment before nodding.

Placing his hands on the insides of her knees, he spread his fingers, smoothed them up her inner thighs, parting them. Her neatly-waxed, pretty little triangular patch confirmed she was a genuine redhead, not that he ever doubted.

"Say it, Red," he growled. "Tell me you want it."

She squirmed again, a flush moving over her breasts and face.

He pulled away a fraction, steeling against the possibility she wouldn't go through with it.

"Yes!" she breathed, writing against his palms. "God...this is probably the worst, most stupidest idea ever, but yes, I want this."

His tortured dick almost exploded. So much blood pumped straight to it, leaving him lightheaded and slightly drunk.

"Shit's going to get seriously complicated."

"It doesn't have to, it's just sex, right...so we can forget today."

Forget today? Maybe temporarily, but forget having her?

He doubted it.

"But if you're not into this," she whispered, trying to close her legs, then raising herself up to rest on her elbows, she continued. "If you'd rather we didn't..." That voice was husky, a whole load of sexy, and just a teeny bit shaky. With need or nerves, he couldn't say. "Do *you* want this?"

Yeah, he wanted—more than he cared to admit.

For his answer, he kissed her inner thigh midway down, delighting when she shivered. Then slowly, using his stubble and his lips, kissed to where he wanted to be. When he couldn't stand it anymore, he dove in, and latched on. She tasted so good, he almost cried while she bucked and writhed and squirmed against his face. Her fists balled, she clutched the sheets and made adorable noises that resonated with his soul and every male chromosome.

He sensed she was close. Her legs stiffened and moments later the first one hit her. Arching off the bed, her head back in an auburn cloud, she let out a hoarse cry that almost did him in. Her coming apart on his face, he didn't know if he'd ever experienced anything more beautiful, more mesmerizing. Or turned him on more.

Drowning.

He was fucking drowning.

Whatever came after this was worth it. Easing her through it, making it last, he only waited a moment before sending her soaring again while his cock throbbed and twitched, needing in. He would never forget this moment, and he would make damn sure she wouldn't either.

As she came down the second time, he reached in his bag for a condom. Ripped the foil with his teeth and rolled it on himself, his jaw tightening as he did so. He hitched her higher up the bed, positioned himself over her and ran a hand under her head, gripping her hair.

Her eyes were still glazed — he was pretty sure his were hazy with lust too. "I fuck hard, Red. You need to let me know if I hurt you."

"I like it hard," she answered, swallowing. "I like it a little rough."

Christ!

Could she be any more perfect?

He took her mouth, devouring her as he entered a little bit at a time, easing himself in. He was so damn hard, and she was tight, and hot, and so fucking good he shuddered before he began to move, trying to keep it slow while she adjusted. Trying to make it last.

Best intentions and all that shit.

His body took over, nullifying his brain, nothing but sensation: fierce, intense, mind-blowing pleasure.

Nothing but her.

It wasn't long before that familiar tingling began at the base of his spine. Slowing down, he circled her little bud, needing to make her go first. His fingers matched the rhythm of his momentum.

"Oh, God," she cried, wrapping her legs around his back, while she clung to him. He let go, and in seconds followed her. Growling into her neck, his whole body went taut, his vision went white, stars exploded in his brain, and he was pretty sure for a moment he glimpsed the Almighty.

Yeah—he'd found his religion.

Then he collapsed, burying his face in her hair while his heart drummed against her breasts. It was a while before either of them could breathe normally.

"Damn," he said against her shoulder. "You're going to be the death of me."

She didn't answer.

"Red?"

It took immense effort to lift his head, and even more to shake strands of her hair that stuck to his skin so he could actually see the woman. She'd passed out—dead to the world in his arms.

"Mission accomplished, I guess," he half chuckled.

A long time later, when he felt his legs could hold him, he rolled off and stumbled to the bathroom to deal with the condom. After taking care of business, knotting the rubber and splashing water on his face, he toweled off and returned to the bed. Stood there for a moment just watching. Girl hadn't moved.

He sighed.

He climbed in, then splayed a hand over her stomach, touching his lips to her shoulder he whispered softly, "Complicated."

In the process of trying to blow her mind, he succeeded in blowing his own and he wanted to remember it. He reached for his phone then curled up against her. Holding his arm out in front, he centered their faces, with just a little bit of breast and took a photo —something he'd never done before. Then setting his phone back on the side table, he let out a deep, long breath, closed his eyes, and fell asleep.

And didn't dream.

* * *

He woke up to the sun streaming through the sheers, her scent filling his senses, her gorgeous curves, the memory of her taste and the hot shit they'd done together filling his head.

His cock jumped beneath the sheets, and it wasn't just normal morning wood. He needed more of her. He rolled onto his side and smiled. Opening his eyes, he saw an empty space.

What the hell?

He stared at that spot and found a long red hair.

As he fully woke, he heard the muted sound of the shower running, and lay back, way too relieved for something that should be classified as casual. He picked up his phone, pulled up the photo he'd taken and replayed last night in his head. Every little noise she made, how she bit her lip when she was about to come, the way she clung to him when she did.

Girl was ballsy and feisty, not afraid to get in a man's face, and after an initial moment of shyness, it showed in bed too. And damn if he didn't love that.

But he knew women. She might be feeling that morning-after awkwardness, and there was one assured way to mitigate that: a repeat, the sooner the better.

On the way to the bathroom, he stopped at his bag for a condom. If things went the way he wanted, he'd have to stock up on more.

He tried the door handle, silently fist pumping it wasn't locked. Then entering he placed the condom on the edge of the vanity within easy reach and slid open the shower.

She turned, a little startled as he stepped in.

"Morning, Tomato Head."

"Hey." She gave a little half smile, fluttering her wet, spiky lashes.

He gave her no time to think. Curling one hand around her waist, the other up over her chest, he slid his hand up slowly until his thumb rested under her chin. Tilting her head and tugging gently, he pulled that sexy body, those perfect tits up close, skin sliding against wet, slippery skin and went straight for her mouth.

He kissed her soft.

Then he kissed her hard, exploring her with his tongue, sucking on her lips until they were both panting, and had to break for air. He dipped and lifted her. Her legs clamped around his waist, and her arms slid around his neck, holding on.

"I want you again," he said, his voice rough and just a bit cracked. "You cool with that?"

"Yes." She blinked water from her lashes and licked her lips. "I'm most definitely cool with that."

Then up against the shower wall, her legs around him, in the most impolite, dirtiest way possible, he showed her exactly how cool they were together.

Nuclear detonation cool.

Chapter Eighteen

"Cody had a Bitcoin wallet?" Helen asked, staring at the file on Carmine's laptop. He sat across from her, eating eggs over medium with a large side of sausage and bacon while she nibbled on scrambled eggs and buttered toast. Apparently, the man did not do carbs, which would explain the zero fat on those rock-solid muscles. Though she did worry about his cholesterol.

They'd chosen the same diner as the day before as it was within walking distance from the hotel and the food was good.

And today—yay—the ubiquitous Missy wasn't on shift.

Torque had texted first thing that morning. Carmine's wheels were in transport from Redding and the car should be ready by noon. So, basically they were just killing time before they checked out of the hotel.

"That doesn't make any sense," she went on. "I mean, if he had cryptocurrency why would he need to steal from me? Can't you just sell it like stocks or whatever and cash out?"

"That's the theory, but I'm not sure the Bitcoin was his," he said holding his coffee cup between both hands and sipping, staring at her intently. Like he was scrutinizing her face, or the bruises that were now much more obvious in the warm light of day.

But his eyes were different--softer. It made her a feel little off balance, but it also set her heart fluttering, and she shifted slightly in her seat. His ability to give excellent orgasms frightened her. She loved sex, and almost always got off with a man, but she had no idea how intense her orgasms could be. Until he'd shown her. She definitely wanted more. But she couldn't read him. Other than those stunning eyes, that were now soft and focused on her, his face gave nothing else away. It was disconcerting.

"Your position is still that this is your friend Snake's Bitcoin?"

"My *client* Snake, and maybe. The thing with cryptocurrency is, it's anonymous. It ultimately belongs to the person with the keys."

"Keys?"

"They're like an account number. You need those and a password to access the wallet. There are no names attached, so in theory whomever has both owns the account."

"Hmm." She wriggled her nose, then swallowed a bite of toast. "And we're absolutely sure that what Snake wanted was this Bitcoin thingy?"

"Nope, not sure at all. I'll admit he hasn't shared with me what was on the drive. Just that he needed it back."

"So..." She pursed her lips, trying to ignore the way he was studying her and how uncomfortable it made her, in a good way. "Indulge me here for a minute. We're not even sure that *this* thumb drive is the one that he says was stolen from him. But for argument's sake let's just say it is. What if he's really freaked out about that video and *not* the wallet? What if Cody suspected Snake of human trafficking? Because really, think about it, who has a name like Snake unless perhaps he is one?"

He pulled his lips in over his teeth, like he was trying not to smile, but then made a circular *go on* motion with his fork.

"Okay so here's my theory. Say Cody stole the thumb drive

intending to blackmail Snake with the video and set up the Bitcoin thingy for a place to deposit the funds."

Carmine seemed to consider that while he chewed on a mouthful of sausage, swallowed, then shook his head in the negative. "Doesn't make sense."

"Why not?"

"Because the timeline doesn't fit. The video was added to the drive after it was stolen. Which means Cody added it, not Snake."

"How do you know that?"

He placed his fork on his plate, then wiped his hands on a napkin before turning his laptop so they could both see the screen. His finger moved over the trackpad, then he clicked a few buttons and pointed it out. "See the date?"

Holy poop.

It *had* been added later. But the big question of the day remained; how did Cody get it?

Her shoulders slumped and she turned to look across the room. They were the only people in the diner, having apparently missed the morning rush due to their activities in the shower which then led to further phenomenal activities on the bed. But his statement forced her to consider something she really didn't want to believe. Things were not looking good for Cody. That perhaps he was both villain and victim in this drama.

"No," she stated, shaking her head. "I refuse to believe Cody's the bad guy in this."

Carmines eyes narrowed as he regarded her across the table.

"I know all the evidence points that way, and Cody definitely had his dick moments, but not those kind of dick moments. There's something we're missing. We don't even know whose voice that is on the video or if Cody was with him when it was filmed."

"I'll give you that, but I've got to know, why are you still defending him?" There was a definite frostiness in his tone that made her take notice. "You're wasting your emotions on a man who is a thief and an addict, and I'm *not* being a dick when I remind you, he stole from you."

She nibbled on her lip.

"And he stole from your parents."

"In all honesty?" Helen blew out a breath, then grabbed a strand of hair and twirled it around her index finger. "That's an assumption I'm making because of how I felt about him in that moment and the circumstances, the timing, and the fact my mom can't find Nana's ring. I'm not completely one hundred percent sure he did steal it. But, even if he did, those were soft, easy things for him to steal. God, I hate to think that I'm a soft, easy target or my parents are for that matter, but compared to human trafficking...really?"

"You're rationalizing. Remember, the Cody you thought you knew wasn't the Cody you actually knew. Your first instinct is usually correct. Go with that." His eyes, though green and stunning, had become pointed and hard.

She met them, refusing to shrink from what she already knew, having pondered that exact thing endlessly. How had she missed *all* the signs? If Cody had needed rehab, she would've stood by him—she'd loved him and isn't that what you do when you love?

"Anyway," she said, trying to steer the conversation as Carmine's mood had stepped into the shadows. "I think we need to talk to Vasily. This is his department, being head of the Russians and all that."

"*I* need to talk to Melnikov."

"'I'? What do you mean 'I'?"

"You're not getting involved in that, Red."

"Um...excuse me?" She sat back in the booth, because she didn't take kindly to being excluded. "I'm already involved, remember? I've seen those girls, their faces. I've also seen the prick who trafficked those girls and I know he was a friend or associate or whatever of that horrible Boris person who was also in the other video. Thank you for getting rid of him by the way. However, I'll remind *you*, it was me that almost had my head blown off by someone who may or may not be connected to Boris and that other creature."

"I don't need the reminding, Red, and FYI, I didn't get rid of Boris. That was all Vasily, which is exactly why you are not getting involved." He punctuated by stabbing his finger on the white Formica table. "I'll deal with him when we get back to the city."

She eyed him wondering where that softness had gone. Or if her presence had reached its sell-by date and was beginning to smell. Or like a hangover he'd been forced to suffer because he'd run out of aspirin.

"What's crawled up your butt all of a sudden?"

He held her gaze, then took a deep breath. "What are you talking about?"

"The big mood swing. You've gone all stony-faced and unapproachable again."

The space between his dark eyebrows creased as he looked at her.

"Are you in a secret relationship I should know about?" *Like with the mysterious Jazz-slash-Jasmine?* "And having morning-after regrets?"

"That's kind of offensive, asking me that, and a little late. One if I was in a relationship, it wouldn't be a secret and two, I don't cheat. That's the reason I'm not in a relationship. I happen to like variety."

"Okay." She tried to put that aside. The reminder she was the latest, but not the last was a very real slap of reality. "Just so you know, your mood swings are making me dizzy and I feel like I'm an inconvenience you can't wait to get rid of. So, who's Jaz?"

He blinked as she caught him off guard.

"A woman," he answered softly, after several, thumping heartbeats. "But we're not talking about her."

Now *she* blinked. "Why not?"

He held her gaze across the table, long enough for her to

suddenly not want to know. But it was too late, she couldn't escape it. It was in his eyes—pain. And whatever reason they weren't together didn't matter anymore.

"Okay," she said again, trying to ignore how hard her heart was beating. "You're right. It's none of my business. But that doesn't diminish that I'm sensing you want to be rid of me."

His eyes never faltered. "If 'getting rid of you' as you call it means keeping you out of trouble, so be it. It amounts to the same thing. I'm just trying to protect you."

"What if I don't want you to protect me?"

"Doesn't matter what you want. You're my responsibility and it's what I do."

"You're not responsible for me."

"I am."

"I may be small in body, Carmine. But I'm a big girl and I can make decisions for myself. I can also take care of myself, so you can stop being so...alpha."

He snorted. "Alpha is what's kept me alive. And might I add," he said pointedly. "You didn't mind alpha last night, or this morning for that matter."

Heat charged up her face as she nibbled on her lip. "Okay, um yeah. About that... we need to keep that just between us."

"What?" Those handsome nostrils flared, and his tone had a definite edge to it.

"I just think..."

"You ashamed you fucked me, Red?" His gaze constricted and fixed her to her seat.

"Why would you even say that!" How could she be? What he'd done, how he'd made her feel and her body react was...astounding. "You know that's not it."

"Then what is it?"

She had protective friends. Terra had warned her and if she knew Helen was half-way falling for him and he went about doing his usual, Terra would resent him. She didn't want that.

"You one of those chicks who uses a man for his cock, then she gets what she needs, wants nothing more to do with him?"

"Stop it. That's not it either. And you don't need to be so crude."

"This is what's crude, Red." He moved forward and rested his elbows on the table. "Crude is you thinking I'd run my mouth to anyone about fucking you. It's nobody's business."

"That's good, then. I just thought it needed verbalizing, you know so there weren't any misunderstandings, since I don't know you that well."

"Since you don't know me that well,' I'll tell you something about me. I'm friends with ninety-five percent of the women I've fucked. The only exceptions are the ones who got weird, who had some hang-ups about hooking up. And since I don't know *you* that well, I'm asking, do you fall into that five percent, Red? You got a hang up about hooking up with a man you virtually begged to fuck?"

Begged?

Holy hell.

"I don't." She wiped her mouth with her napkin and pushed her plate away, her appetite having died. "But the way *you're* acting tells me *you're* pigeonholing me into that five percent. Am *I* right?" She slid along the bench but paused at the edge. "Let me ask you this, Carmine. In which percentile does the lovely Jaz fall? The five...or the ninety-five?"

He growled. "Don't go there."

"Why? Did she get weird? Or maybe you did?"

His eyes snapped to hers. "I was wondering where that bitch part of you had gone. You're stepping into shit you know nothing about."

"Then enlighten me, so I can understand why you call out her name in your dreams."

His sucked in those slightly hollowed cheeks, and his gaze got hard and glittery. All the while questions ran through her head.

What did this mystery woman look like? Was she gorgeous and exciting? With a name like Jaz, probably.

"I don't talk about her."

"Why not?"

"Because it hurts too fucking much."

Whoa.

"She's the only woman I've ever loved."

Holy hell.

She pulled in a hard, short breath. They'd crossed a line and there was no going back. His subtext was clear, he didn't have to say it, even if he'd just stabbed her in the heart. She didn't want him to verbalize that his feelings would never be anything close to what he felt for Jaz.

Unwilling to hear anymore, she made to stand, but his fist clamped around her upper arm. "Stay," he ordered. "You asked, now you're going to get."

"It's...it's okay...you don't need to explain."

His grip on her arm tightened to the point that it hurt. Then after a long moment the pressure on her bones relaxed and he shook his head abruptly, but he didn't let go.

"For some reason I can't fathom, I feel like I do. I feel like I owe you this because you helped me last night too. Therefore, I'll clarify."

The heat from his hand was searing into her skin, but she needed the physical contact to keep her grounded.

"We were in the Army together, and as I said, in love. Forbidden as fuck because I outranked her, but we didn't care. Once our deployments were over and our time was up, we were going to get married. Use our skills to start a business."

She could hardly get the words out, her chest felt impaled. "What happened?"

"She died."

Oh...shit.

"We got ambushed and everyone but me got blown to hell."

"Carmine..."

"Left me scarred and not only my body. It hardened me much more than just being in country did. I still see it. I still dream it, as you are now aware. I went in a different man than when I came out. Afghanistan changed me. Her death changed me, and I'll never be that man again. And there you have it." He loosened his fingers, then released her hand. The spot where his grip had been throbbed, but she avoided rubbing it. It didn't seem right in the face of what he'd been through.

"I'm sorry," she murmured, fighting the burn behind her eyes. "I didn't know."

"No, but now you are one of the few who do."

One of the few? She didn't know what to do with that, but on some level it felt good he'd trusted her with something so profound and so personal.

"And now you know me a little better than you did five minutes ago."

She nodded and their eyes met and held while she searched his. She saw scars on his soul, the pain and the guilt he carried.

"What?" he eventually asked.

"You wonder why."

His brows came together. "I'm sorry?"

"What unconscious choice did you make in that moment that kept you alive, and not them."

A flicker of some unknown emotion moved across his face, evident in the way he clenched his jaw and swallowed.

"But maybe it wasn't anything *you* did."

"What?"

"You see, and I know this sounds whacky, but indulge me for a moment. I don't believe in organized religion, but this is how I make sense of it. I do believe there is a divine source and that we all have a divine purpose. We're all connected. Not only to the divine but to each other by invisible cords, like a giant, incredibly complex spiderweb. And when your cord gets pulled, that's when we're put into action and we complete our purpose and return to the 'mother ship'" — she made quotation marks in the air — "for lack of a better word. Your cord wasn't pulled that day. Therefore, your purpose hasn't completed yet. There are still big, very important things in store for you."

He stared at her, then chuffed shaking his head. "You're right about one thing."

"What's that."

"It does sound whacky."

"It's what I believe."

"You done eating?" He put his laptop to sleep and closed it. "My car is ready."

She nodded, hooking her purse strap over her shoulder.

"For the record," she said, getting to her feet, "I may have made a whacky statement just now, but as far as last night goes, I did not beg."

Out of the corner of her eye, she saw him pause. Then he took a step closer, caging her between the table and his body.

"Calling bullshit," he murmured, leaning in. That irresistible body heat enveloped her as he came closer, stopping just a breath from her lips. "You begged."

"I did not." Her chin tipped upwards, as she was pulled closer to his energy, bringer her mouth even closer.

"Nothing wrong with wanting sex in a shitty situation, Tomato Head. It's a great way to cope, and in fact I encourage it as I find it hella hot." Then he got even closer, and dropped his voice even lower, his breath a sensual, hot whisper against her lips. "I find *you* hella hot."

Then he gave a smirk that set her pulse to rapid-fire. But if she thought he was going to kiss her, she was disappointed. He stepped away, leaving her hanging and clutching the table for support.

Hella hot?

Those words made her giddy and her feet stick to the vinyl

floor. Several seconds passed before she snapped out of the spell they cast and followed him in a daze.

As soon as he'd paid, Carmine pulled out his phone. With his other hand on the back of her neck, gently massaging, he walked her out--keeping it there while he checked in with his men.

Status reports, he'd explained, were a protocol not to be ignored when one was in the field. Himself included.

She pretended to window shop at a charming little antique store while she digested his words. They were nice to hear, and great for her ego, but he was what he was. He'd spelled it out for her. He was not boyfriend material.

Not that she was looking, right? But where did that leave them when this little road trip was over?

Engrossed in her thoughts, she hadn't noticed he'd hung up and jumped a little when he asked, "See anything you like, Red?"

Other than him? She caught his reflected gaze in the window.

"No." She shook her head and smiled a little. He was definitely something she liked, but she wasn't going to say that out loud.

"Want to go in?" He continued to watch her, like he was trying to sort through her thoughts and dig inside her brain.

"I'm good, just lost in thought."

"Thought I smelled burning."

"Ha-ha!" She pointed a finger at him and adopted an accent. "You funny man."

His eyes crinkled in their corners, but he said nothing and they didn't talk again until they returned to the hotel. Once inside their room and after he'd used the bathroom, he said, "I'm going to get my car and stop by the sheriff to pick up the paperwork for Falk. Stay inside while I'm gone, and keep the door locked."

"I thought I was going with?"

"Nope."

"Why not?"

"It's safer here."

"That doesn't make sense. We just walked from the diner to

here. Aren't you being overprotective?"

"With your ability to find trouble?" Hooking his fingers into the waistband of her shorts, he pulled her close. The warmth of his skin against her belly felt delicious, setting her stomach aflutter.

"Oh, I know," she teased, "you don't want me to see Torque. Jealous?"

Possession flashed in his eyes, and she knew she wasn't wrong. One of his palms smoothed a path up her neck, tipping her chin so she was forced to look at him.

"It wasn't him making you come last night, and this morning. I'd say of the two of us, he should be the jealous one."

Heat filled her face, not just from the reminder, but from the way he was looking at her. Like he was remembering their carnal activities too.

"Forty minutes peace of mind." His voice had gone low and husky, which triggered something X-rated in her and made her panties get wet. "That's all I'm asking, like I did last night when I wrote you a note. Stay in the room. Will you do that for me?"

His eyes had darkened and were blazing with what she'd come to know as his *sexy* look. They were focused on her mouth-- making it go dry. She licked her lips.

He sucked air through his teeth. "Don't do that, I'll never get out of here."

Assuming she wanted him to. Her hormones responded to that hiss, making her legs quivery and her insides melt like butter on a hot day. How could he do that with just a glance, just the back of his fingers on her skin. Her arms slid around his neck, as if compelled, she pressed against him.

"Fuck, Red." He groaned deep in the back of his throat, then slid a hand to her buttock and squeezed. Leaning in, he took her top lip, sucking it between his. "You're wicked and addictive. You started this, but I'm the one who can't seem to stay away. And I *should* stay away."

"Why?"

"You make me want to do filthy, dirty things to your gorgeous body."

"Like what kind of filthy things?"

He unbuttoned her shorts, and slowly lowered the zip. "Like slipping my fingers into your panties kind of things." His flat palm grazed down her stomach, just breaching the top of her underwear. Then he stopped. She squirmed against him, pressing into his hand.

"You want more?"

"Yes." Her body didn't care her heart was on the line, it craved more. It craved him.

"How much more?" He was breathing harder now too.

"All the way."

"Tell me what you want, Helen."

Her breath hitched at the use of her name, how it seemed to roll off his tongue like tequila.

"I want your mouth."

"Where do you want my mouth?"

"Down there."

"Say it," he growled.

The intensity and the need in his voice sparked wildfires and made her core clench.

"Between my legs."

With a soft, satisfied laugh, he guided her shorts and panties down her thighs, caressing her tender skin as he helped her step out of them. Then, he lifted her and tossed her onto the bed. Heat gleamed in his eyes when he dropped to his knees in front of her, he took each leg one at a time, resting them over his shoulders.

He closed his eyes and bowed his head for moment. She almost got the impression he was praying—or worshipping which was totally hella hot.

"You're spoiling me woman," he said when he opened them again, catching her gaze. His voice was like gravel.

Actually, she was the one being spoiled—for all men forever

after. This was further confirmed when he connected with her core, the heat from his mouth and tongue sent explosions of pleasure through her body.

"Mmm," she mewled, biting her top lip and squirming her bottom across the fabric closer to his mouth. Then he clamped down in earnest.

"Oh...my...God!" she cried out at the sensations rocketing through her. Her heels dug into his back, every nerve ending, every part screamed for release as he teased and tasted until she spiraled, free-falling into bliss.

She was panting, still flying when she reached to unbuckle his belt. There was a fat, hard ridge in his jeans but he grasped her hand and stopped her. "Damn," he muttered and dropped his head like he was in pain.

"What's wrong?" she asked, needing him inside her five minutes ago.

"We're out of condoms, babe. I wasn't expecting that to turn me on so much or need to fuck you again so soon. This was supposed to be just for you."

His consideration, his selflessness made her heart jump, and her want him even more.

She sat up and took his face between her hands. "I have no funky little critters crawling in my coochie, Carmine. And like most modern woman my age, I'm on birth control."

"Funky little...?" He chuckled. "Thank God for that." But then he got serious again, and pulled in a breath through his nose, letting it out quickly. "I never fuck without a condom. You want me without one?"

She nodded. "I do."

Reaching behind him, he grabbed his collar, and yanked his tee shirt over his head. Then he dropped his jeans and found her mouth. She could taste herself on his tongue and that too was hella hot. He was so big, and so hard, yet his skin was soft, like hot silk as he slid into her. Thrusting, slowly at first until they found a rhythm, then harder and harder still as she felt him get closer. The headboard thumped against the wall with the force of his thrusts. It built again, different than before, but no less intense. Like a wave gaining momentum the closer it got to shore. As she crested, then crashed, her walls clamped around him. She bucked and arched her back. A moment later, he let out a low, feral groan as he pulled out. With his pulsing, twitching cock in his fist he shot hot spurts over her stomach below her belly button—marking her. It was filthy, and decadent, and beautiful and *hella hot*. Her new favorite phrase.

She dropped back onto the bed, and he shook a little as he lay over her, resting on his forearms and kissed her—long, and deep and wet, their skin sticky with sweat and other things.

"Still wondering what I want to do to you?" he asked when he finally spoke again.

"I think I have a decent idea."

"Because if it's not clear" — He pulled away to look in her eyes — "I'm happy to show you again. You just gotta let me recover first."

She giggled.

"Not joking, woman. You keep that up, you're going to kill me."

"I don't want to kill you...yet. I think I'm beginning to like you."

He snorted. "I already like you, Red." Then, as he moved away to pull up his jeans, he continued very softly, like she wasn't meant to hear. "Too much."

Leaving them unzipped, he rounded the corner into the bathroom. She heard water running then several moments later he came back with a warm, wet face cloth. Bending over, her, he gently wiped her stomach, cleaning away the evidence of his marking. As the water cooled and evaporated, her nipples puckered again. He stared at them, working his jaw. "We're going to need more condoms."

God, she sure hoped so.

He'd called her addictive, but she was pretty sure it was his hooks that were deeply imbedded in her flesh. And to break free was going to hurt her.

"I like this look on you," he murmured, his face serious as he smoothed the cloth down between her legs. "Freshly fucked, and soft. Even more beautiful than you usually are."

Her breath caught. "You think I'm beautiful?" she asked, not being coy. She sincerely needed to know, as she liked that look on him too.

He blew out a quick breath, then the left side of his mouth lifted. "Ridiculously beautiful, Red."

She wanted to believe him, but she needed to be careful. Not read anything into this, other than just sex. He'd told her. *He'd never be that man again.* The one who fell in love with Jaz.

She had to remember that.

"I think you're the beautiful one."

"What am I going to do with you?" he whispered, before he dropped his forehead to hers. Then after a long moment, he sighed. "I gotta get my car. We're meeting Snake at the clubhouse in a couple hours."

"What happens after that?"

"We go home."

Go home.

For some reason that filled her with a feeling of dread. Going home felt like the end. They'd go back to normal, back to their lives, and their little affair would be over. Here she had him to herself. In San Francisco she couldn't expect exclusivity, but exclusivity was all she could handle. Like he'd said before, he liked variety.

"Stop thinking."

"What?"

"You're thinking too hard," he said, taking her face in his hands. "I can see it on your face."

"Nope." she gave him a small smile. "Not a thought inside my empty head."

His eyes got serious. "One, your head's not empty. And two, thinking too hard over what's happening here is going to ruin this."

Her nose wrinkled up.

"Don't ruin this," he reiterated. "You hear me?"

Okay. Got it. Fair warning.

"I hear you."

He studied her for one moment more. Then, seemingly satisfied with what he saw in her expression, he planted a long, solid kiss on her forehead just above her left eyebrow.

A kiss that felt too chaste after what they'd just done. Almost like goodbye.

Still holding her eyes, he stepped away and buttoned his jeans. With a tap to his ass, he checked he had his wallet and room key. At the threshold, he stopped. Something played in his eyes, like he wanted to say something important. But then shook his head ever so slightly.

Don't say it.

She understood what this was, and that it was almost over. But she couldn't bare if he said it.

"See you in a few," he said all business again. The softness she'd seen in his gaze, in his features only a few moments before was gone. "Stay safe." With that, he moved out of her line of sight and shut the door.

"God," she groaned flopping onto her back. What had she done? What Terra had warned her not to do—and now she was going to pay for it. *Dearly.* If only she was one of those women who could separate their heart from their vagina's. But alas, she wasn't.

Rolling sideways off the bed, she schlepped to the bathroom. Brushed her hair, then her teeth, and added another layer of mascara and a touch of lip gloss. After which she changed into her jeans and trainers. Despite the heat, wearing shorts to a testosterone-drenched biker compound in the middle of the backwoods probably wasn't the smartest idea.

She turned on the TV mostly for background noise but watched a little daytime; a show about the rescue of an adorable raccoon and its babies. Then, when that was over, she stepped outside onto the balcony to send a text to Terra.

How did the filming go?

After no response, she tossed her phone aside and plopped onto one of the chairs situated outside their balcony door. She'd just planted her feet on the iron railing when the door opened.

"Thomas," Carmine growled into his phone, like he was barely hanging onto his patience. "Send the damn stills from the surveillance footage to my email, and do it now, please. I need to check them out before I meet with Snake. My gut's telling me something's not right and I don't want to walk in blind."

She couldn't hear the other side of the conversation, but his turn in mood again had her head spinning. That last moment aside, hadn't he left her happy? What had happened since?

He joined her on the patio and sat in the chair next to her and opened his laptop. His screensaver populated and her heart plummeted. It wasn't a standard one supplied by the manufacturer. It was a photo of a woman's face. Obviously uploaded by him. An unexpected slice of pain knifed through her when she realized what she was looking at, sharper than she was prepared for and she bit back a gasp.

For a moment she thought it was the doctor from the hospital, but the face was different. But like the doctor, the woman was blonde with blue eyes and straight shoulder-length hair. Tucked behind her hair was single blossom; jasmine. She was looking over her shoulder at the camera, exuding the lazy, satisfied, post-coital glow of a woman in love.

And who was loved back.

Surprise tears threatened, but she turned her head away, looking down the street. Weird, but now she almost wished he hadn't told her about Jaz. Knowing how much he loved her made it that much harder, but no way would she let him see her cry. Not over this. And if she had any doubt before, there was none now. He'd said it. He'd never be that man again.

"Okay, it just came in," Carmine said, still speaking to Thomas. When she'd collected herself and turned back, he was studying several attached photos. One in particular appeared to interest him most. He zoomed in, then his body locked tight. "Shit," he cursed, still studying the photo intently. "While you're at it, there's a file on my desk labelled Madden, Thomas Jr."

Helen's ears went on high alert. That was the dirty congressman who had recently been arrested for murder. Why did Carmine have a file on him?

"There's a name inside. Viktor something. There isn't much but I want you to dig deeper. Look specifically for connections to Snake, or any member of the club."

Carmine paused, and she assumed he was listening, but his attention came to her, his eyes narrowing slightly. She found it fascinating watching him work. The way his mind worked, the intelligence in his gaze and command he wielded so easily. His army training, no doubt.

"Before you do that though, find out who owns that truck transporting the girls."

After he hung up, he closed his eyes and massaged the back of his neck. It was a while before he opened them again.

"This is important, Red," he said, his tone grave. "I need to reiterate that what we know stays between us, understood? Not a word to Torque or Snake, or anyone in the club about the video, until we know who filmed it."

"You want to tell me what's happened since you left?"

"Torque wasn't at the garage when I got there. His mechanic said he tore out of there about ten minutes before. Something about bad shit happening at the clubhouse, and I can't get a hold of Snake to see what's up."

He indicated his laptop and adjusted the angle of the screen. "What do you see?"

It was a still from the video taken at the shootout. Of the biker. The photo wasn't clear, but then again neither had the video been. After staring at it for several seconds she saw it. It was in the way he held his head, slightly forward like he was leading with his chin.

"It's him again! The dude in both videos." She looked at him, her eyes getting wide, then back at the screen. "His name is Viktor?"

He nodded.

He wore one of those old school helmets with a lip the Germans used in World War One and large goggles, but the nose was the same. Long, with a bit of a bulb on the end. Nothing about his face raised alarms, but that in itself was alarming. The man was so ordinary, he didn't attract attention. You wouldn't give him a second glance if you passed him in the street or stood next to him in a bar. Yet she'd seen the evil that lived inside him.

"Does this mean Viktor is a member of Snake's club?" she asked, staring at Carmine.

"I don't think so, Red," he said, sending the video to his Dropbox. Then he removed a second thumb drive from his pocket and stuck it in the USB port. This one was silver, and she watched him drag the video from his desktop onto the drive. When the transfer was complete, he deleted the one on his computer, emptied his trash and shut it down.

"So then why is he wearing a cut with their emblem on it?" she asked.

"That's a good question. A biker's cut is his badge of honor. They don't lend them out and you can't just buy one. They're earned."

"So then where did he get it?"

"I'll give you one guess."

"Holy hell. Cody's brother-in-law."

"Indeed. The enigmatic and missing Hunter."

Chapter Nineteen

Biker compounds were generally noisy entities. Every one he'd visited had been alive and loud with activity, music, heavy drinking and often public sex. But as he pulled the Jeep through the wide farm gates and up a narrow dirt road guarded by tall, fat sugar pines, Carmine's instincts prickled again.

Shit was definitely not right.

He hadn't wanted to bring Helen, but he'd had no choice. Leaving her alone and unprotected at the Hotel wasn't a game plan. Not when he knew Viktor was still out there. And she was part of this, whether he dug it or not.

They entered a clearing that was overshadowed by a huge, slightly rundown barn that under normal circumstances would have been painted red and trimmed with white—a regular symbol of rural Americana. Only this one was a deep forest green, like the pines surrounding it.

Next to it was a series of greenhouses, running about half the length of a soccer field where they grew and processed the marijuana. The air was so full of it, he could taste it.

They parked next to a red Ford Explorer and a silver Lincoln Navigator, the only other cars in the lot, avoiding the line of wicked-looking Harleys with their front wheels facing forward, ready for a quick exit. He breathed in deep, though it didn't do much to relieve the heavy sense of gloom hanging around the place. For security purposes, he set a pin on their location and sent it to Thomas.

As it turned out their arrival wasn't undetected. Two men in their early twenties with scraggly goatees smoked cigarettes near the main door. Their leather cuts which had yet to lose their shine donned "Prospect" rockers sewn onto the back. Both were armed with assault rifles, currently pointed at them, and one was on the phone. Carmine suspected someone would be out to greet them soon.

He glanced at Helen and said in a low, careful voice, "This is not good. Sit tight, keep your hands where they can see them and don't make any fast movements."

She glanced at him. "Is this normal...this kind of reception?"

"Wasn't greeted by guns last time I was here."

"What do you think is happening?"

"Whatever it is, it's not good, Red. Guess we'll find out soon enough."

Prospect number one, the older and chunkier of the two came closer and made a motion for Carmine to open his window. He lowered it halfway.

"We're here to see Snake. Tell him Niccoterra is here."

Prospect number one nodded at prospect number two who repeated what he said into the phone. Then he called across to Carmine, "Stay in the car."

"Maybe we should just go," Helen said. "I'm not getting the warm and fuzzies."

Neither was he.

"Unless they turn us away, they're not going to let us leave until they know what we're about. But whatever happens, you listen to what I say, do what I ask, no questions. For real this time, got it?"

"My mother was right."

Carmine's brow furrowed and he turned to look at her. "About what?"

"It's polite to call ahead."

He snort-laughed and gave a half head shake. The woman amazed him. With a lethal looking AR pointed in their faces most would be scared stupid, chomping on their gelled fingernails. This one was cracking jokes.

"I'll keep that in mind next time."

"If there is one."

They sat in silence until a side door burst open and Torque exited. Which would explain why the biker hadn't been at his garage earlier when he picked up his car. As he got closer the tightness of the man's jaw, the way he worked it and his grim expression became notable.

"Not a good time, Niccoterra." The timbre in his voice raised Carmine's already stiff hairs at the back of his neck. "We got a situation."

"Only here to give Snake what he hired me to find. Then we'll get out of your hair."

"Give whatever it is to me." Torque held out his hand.

Carmine shook his head. "Can't do. I need to give it to him personally. *His* orders."

Torque's head tipped to the side, his eyes narrowing. Pulling his phone from a pocket in his cut, he thumbed through it then put it to his ear. Carmine could hear the tinny sound ringing and going to voicemail, but Torque tried again. The second time, Snake answered.

After several moments of taking Snake's verbal abuse via cell tower, and keeping his eyes locked on Carmine, Torque said, "Niccoterra says he's got something he can only hand personally to you."

Again, he listened, then without looking at the prospects, he ordered, "Stand down." To Carmine he indicated with his head. "Follow me."

Carmine put his hand on Helen's thigh and squeezed while he closed his window. "Give me a second with him, Red." When she acknowledged, he opened his door and then shut it behind him so she couldn't hear what he needed to say.

"Wait," he called after Torque, who had already started to walk away.

"What?"

"Just need to clarify so there's no problems down the line. She's mine. Nobody touches her. I need your word."

"Don't got time for a pissing contest."

"Ain't no pissing contest, Torque. It's them inside I'm worried about."

Bikers were notorious bastards when it came to unclaimed women in their territory, especially their clubhouse. They were considered fair game and he needed to impress upon Torque, Helen was not.

Torque held his gaze, his face solemn, and Carmine read in his expression that he understood. The man cast his eyes to Helen. "Already knew that, asshole. You made it clear yesterday and even if she weren't, she'd still be under my protection. None of my brothers would touch her. She's not club snatch material. Too classy for that."

Jesus.

Club snatch.

Carmine cringed inwardly, but it didn't surprise him. These were hard, crass men and Torque was no different, but he had earned a measure of Carmine's respect in his declaration of protection.

"Worth repeating," he said all the same.

"Understood." Torque dipped his chin in agreement.

With that out of the way, Carmine looked back at Helen, and

curled his finger. She climbed out her side and came around. When she stood next to him, she gave Torque a little wave.

"Trouble," he greeted her with no smile.

Shit *must* be serious if the dude had lost his flirt. The air was thick with whatever it was, and he wasn't talking about the marijuana stench. However, to further emphasize his point, he took Helen's hand in his. It was cool and small, but her fingers gripped his back firmly.

"What's happening?" he asked Torque's back.

"You'll find out," he answered as he led them past the prospects along a cracked concrete path marked with dandelions muscling their yellow crowns towards the sunlight.

They stepped through a side door reinforced with rebar into a large room. There was a pool table and several mismatched, overused couches arranged in a circle. On one end, under industrial-size windows stood a crescent-shaped bar with a small crowd of grizzly, tattooed men draped around it. Scary-looking assholes, he had to admit if he were one to intimidate easily—which he was not.

He only recognized one—Kai—the other biker who'd shown up at the cabin. He stood out because he was minus his skull cap and cleanly shaved—both on his dome and his face. There was a wicked looking demon inked into his scalp. Kinda gave him the creeps.

The dude eyed them particularly cold and hard, his heavy-lidded black orbs following them as they made progress through the room. Next to him was an attractive brunette with long straight dark hair. Next to her, was a bottle-blonde with two-inch black roots wearing a denim vest with "PROPERTY OF SNAKE" sewn into the fabric. Beverly, he reckoned.

Their faces all wore a similar expression to Torque's as they looked back—tight with emotions barely kept in check. Whatever the situation that Torque mentioned, it was dire.

These men were powder kegs waiting to be lit, and he

suspected it wouldn't take much to set them off. Helen inched closer, gripping his fingers a little harder.

"You good?" he asked her.

That adorable nose wrinkled. "It's silly, but I just got a weird vibe. The hair at the back of my neck is standing up, you know?"

Yeah—he knew and wished again he hadn't brought her.

Instinctive hand-gripping reactions were all too often not silly and he checked out the men again, but they reached the opposite corner of big room without incident. The conversation at the bar resumed as they stepped into a dingy hallway laid with a carpet that hadn't been cleaned since installation day. The only light came from high, dirt-speckled windows as they approached two doors in the back.

Torque stopped, his head bowed, his face stony. "Fair warning," he said in a low, solemn voice. "You should know this going in. One of our brother's has been slaughtered."

Holy shit.

Hunter.

"We found his head this morning dumped outside the compound."

Helen gasped, her hand covering her mouth. "Did you say...? Ohmigod, that's horrible."

Torque cleared his throat. "Horrible don't begin to describe it, Trouble."

Carmine swallowed; that explained the Grim Reaper reception. "Any clue how he got like that?"

Torque's faded denim blue gaze, simmering with a deep-seated anger met his. "Not yet," he clipped. "But the fucker left a calling card."

"What's that?"

"A dead rat."

The band around Carmine's chest notched tighter as he flashed on something he remembered from when they found

Cody. "There was one at the cabin as well," he said, his heart beating faster.

Torque's eyes narrowed. "What?"

"You didn't see it? It was left by the front door, half eaten and covered in flies. I kicked it to the side of the porch."

The air around them bristled with charged electricity.

"What are you saying?" Torque's tone was ice cold. "My brother was a rat?"

"Not saying anything, Torque. Just relaying facts. I got something that may interest you—may be related to what's going on here. You'll want to see it, but first I gotta talk to Snake."

At that moment, Snake's voice broke through. "Find her! I don't care what you gotta do to get it done, just fucking find her!" A long series of rough coughing followed.

Torque closed his eyes, releasing a long breath before he knocked.

"Come," Snake called, half-coughing.

Torque pushed the door open and they entered a small office thick with cigarette smoke. Carmine clenched his jaw at the assault on his lungs and nostrils. Man needed to quit that shit, though he had a feeling it was already too late.

Snake bent over a desk, cell pressed to his ear, resting his weight on a fist. His shoulders were rounded, as though hell had taken a dump on them.

"Look everywhere. Every fucken where! You get me? Not one inch goes unchecked. Do it." Then he hung up and tossed his phone onto his desk.

When he looked up, his eyes were red-rimmed, and despite his gin-blossomed nose, the rest of him was an unnatural gray.

"Candy's still missing," he said to the room in general, but the remark was clearly aimed at Torque. "Her car is at the house but she ain't there. Phone goes straight to voicemail. Work ain't heard from her. If those motherfuckers" — He jabbed the air — "have her, I swear, by all that's unholy, hell will feel like a fucken vacation."

"Who are these motherfuckers you speak of?" Carmine asked.

Snake's head jerked towards him, like he'd only just realized he had company other than Torque, who had moved over and sat on the arm of a paisley couch that had seen better days—and asses.

"You got it?"

Carmine nodded.

"Give it to me."

He pulled the black thumb drive from his pocket, stepped forward and laid it on the desk on top of a few invoices.

"Where did that little shithole hide it, 'cause it sure as fuck wasn't in that piece of shit cabin."

"Does it matter?" He did not want to divulge Helen's part in it. The atmosphere in the room was too tight for that. "You got it back."

"Yeah it matters." Snakes face went hard, his eyes glittery. "In case you haven't noticed, Niccoterra, shit's gone down and I don't got time to fuck with you. You see that cooler there?" He pointed at a cheap, white styrofoam cooler, the ones you can buy at a liquor store for a buck ninety-nine. "I'm dealing with *that!* That contains Hunter's head. *His fucking head*! And now his old lady is missing. So just tell me where the fuck he hid it."

"Snake..."

Snake yanked open a draw and as he reached inside Carmine caught a glimpse of the butt end of a Ruger.

Jesus! He stepped in front of Helen. "Fucking hell, Snake," he barked. "There's no need for that."

"Tell me, Niccoterra." He pointed the Ruger at his forehead, his hand shaking. "I'm itching to kill someone. Give me a reason."

"He gave it to me." Helen jumped in, surprising the crap out of him.

"Red, what the fuck?" He gritted out. "What did I tell you?"

"He did what?" The rest of Snake's face turned as red as his nose. Out his peripheral, Carmine saw Torque spring to his feet, ready to take his president's back—or try to defuse the situation, he couldn't tell.

He half-turned, putting himself between them. "Back off."

"Ain't backing off until I know what's happening."

"You had it the whole fucken time?" Snake roared.

Adrenaline surged through Carmine's system, as he checked Snake's desk for anything that would serve as a weapon should shit go even further south. The only thing of note was a Harley Davidson letter opener and a laptop out of his reach. No match for a 9MM between the eyes.

Helen nodded, looking Snake straight in the eye. Not one pretty lash flickered.

If they survived this, he was going to kill her! After he punish-fucked her into the end of next week. What the hell was up with this chick—*Jee...sus*!

"Everybody needs to calm down," Helen said like she was addressing a group of kindergartners instead of two dangerous assholes about to embark on a killing spree. "There's an explanation if you'd just let me."

Snake's stared, then blinked several times. He scraped a hand through his hair, then waved the gun, in a "go on" gesture.

Carmine's heart seized. The woman had balls the size of cantaloupes, taking on two men who combined were four times her weight. If circumstances were different, he'd be ridiculously proud of her.

"I did have it. But" — She held up a finger — "and it's very important you pay attention to the *but*. Carmine didn't know anything about it until *after* I got attacked in Sawmill. I didn't even know I had it until after I got attacked."

"You got attacked for *this*?" Snake picked up the thumb drive and held it up in the air. His gaze bouncing between her and him.

"I believe so."

There was a long, tense semi-silence while Snake sucked in air through his flared nostrils.

"All right, lady. You got the floor. Explain the fuck away."

"Okay, so there was this shoot out in San Fran, I'm sure you've heard about that? You know, the one where someone dressed as one of *your guys* shot at us?" Her pretty little brows rose in question.

Snake's eye twitched, but he grunted, "Yeah. Niccoterra told me about that."

"Okay, good, then I don't have to explain that part. But what I do need to explain, and I've been thinking hard about this and I can only come to one conclusion. You see, I never change my purse, and Cody knows that."

"What the fuck has your purse got to do with it?" Snake barked.

"He must have dropped that thing in my purse during...um...a moment of confusion before we were shot at."

"Confusion before it happened?" This was asked by Torque who'd moved closer, taking a position behind her.

"We" — She wiggled her finger between herself and Carmine — "had a...slight misunderstanding and things got a little physical."

Misunderstanding?

"This I gotta hear," Torque said.

Carmine snorted. "Bit my ear. It still hurts."

"Is that right?" There was a definite look of admiration on Torque's face that for some reason he didn't find annoying.

"Motherfuckers, focus!" Snake banged his fist on the desk. The letter opener jumped.

"Oh, okay sorry," Helen continued. "Anyway, Cody called me a couple nights ago. Said he was injured and he sure as hell sounded injured. Like a *lot* injured. I thought he just wanted me to bring him drugs, because he had that coke problem, but then he said he'd pay me the money he owed me if I did. And because he was my ex, and even though he kind of fucked me over, I was worried about him and I decided I would."

"But what he really wanted was what was in your purse?" Torque asked.

"That's what I'm thinking," Helen answered.

"And you knew nothing about it?" Snake's eyes slanted over to Carmine, narrowing to dangerous slits.

He shook his head. "I didn't."

"He didn't," Helen reiterated.

"And somebody tried to mug you in Sawmill for this thing you didn't know you had?"

"That's what happened. The only reason I came was because I wanted my money and to know what Cody did with my Nana's ring."

"What's so important about your Nana's ring?" Snake asked.

"Nana escaped the Nazi's when she was teenager and all she had was that ring. So, it means a lot to my family and I believe Cody took it."

"Fuck." Torque mumble behind him. "The Nazis?"

"Yes, if any of you find it, please, I'd be so grateful if you returned it."

"If we find it, you'll get it, Trouble."

"Thank you."

"What's on the thumb drive, Prez and why did the little runt take it?" Torque asked, surprising everyone.

"None of your fucking business." Snake dragged his eyes away from Helen and looked at his Sergeant at Arms.

"Respect, man, but it is my business. If whatever is on that thing is tied to what happened at the cabin and to Hunter, it's all our business."

The two men held a stare-off. Surprisingly, Snake was the first to break, dropping his head in defeat. Man must be sicker than he looks.

"Our Bitcoin account," he finally said. "The little prick stole it."

Torque's denim blue eyes grew wide as he dragged his hands through his long, blonde hair. "Jesus! Is everything still in there?"

"He didn't have the password."

"Are you sure? Why else would he steal it?"

"Fuck." Snake's ruddy face turned back to an ugly shade of grey. Then with shaky fingers picked up the drive and shoved it into the black laptop covered in pornographic hot-chicks-on-bikes stickers. "He doesn't know the password. He can't fucken' know the password. Jesus, how could he know that? Did he tell you he took any money?" He growled this looking at Helen.

"No, God no. Cody never told me anything. I still don't have *my* money."

"Argh," he growled which resulted in another fit of coughing.

"Fucking hell, Snake," Torque complained. "You need to listen to the damn doc and quit that shit."

"Shut the fuck up," he uttered while pecking at the keyboard. "We're all dying anyway!" He pecked again, slower.

"*No!*" he wheezed, and he collapsed into his chair, reaching for the pack of cigarettes on his desk. "That little mother fucking prick changed the password. This is a goddamn nightmare." He flicked a Bic lighter and lit up. After taking a long drag, he put a palm to his head. It was shaking again.

"You gave him the password?"

"It might've been on a piece of paper on my desk."

"And not in the safe? You've gotta be kidding me."

"Quit it, Torque. I can't fucken deal with your shit right now." Two trails of smoke streamed from his nostrils. "We got eighty percent of our brothers out looking for Hunter's old lady, but Jesus, we need that password. All our money's in that wallet."

To his side, Torque pulled in several deep breaths, held them, before letting them out. "Niccoterra!" he said, making a clear attempt to keep his shit together. "You said you had something to show us."

He nodded. He had his own personal issues with Torque, but he couldn't deny the dude's restraint in a shit storm—his ability to focus on what needed to be done and wondered how he wasn't president of this comical bunch of morons instead of Snake. Probably would be soon by the looks of things.

Removing his phone from his back pocket, he pulled up the email Thomas had sent earlier with the photos of Viktor, he tapped on the best one.

"Look at this," he said and passed it to Torque as Snake still had his head in his shaking hands and wasn't looking so good. He watched Torque's eyes carefully as he looked at the photo, as the realization set in.

"That's Hunter's cut and his bike!" he said like all the air had been punched from his lungs. "But that ain't him riding it." Carmine held his eyes for a long moment, read the grief, the anger, and the pain swirling in them. "Who is that motherfucker?"

"Viktor Sokolov."

Snake lifted his head from his hands and stared at him. Torque passed him the phone. "The Russians? Are you saying the fucken Russians killed Hunter?"

"I think either a new independent faction of the Russians or Sokolov is freelancing. You know that name?"

They both shook in the negative.

"How can you be so damned sure?" Snake stared at him.

"Because Vasily Melnikov's in charge of the rest of them on the west coast and this prick doesn't belong to him."

"What else do you know?" Torque asked.

"Not much, but it ties in with another case I worked, and my men are digging deep."

"What case?"

"The shady politician who went down for murder and rape."

"That Madden dude?" Snake's brows came together.

Carmine nodded.

"But why? Marijuana isn't the Russian's gig. They generally do guns and girls."

Exactly.

"Could be they were after money to finance themselves. My other case went badly for Viktor and his partner, Boris. Could be they're getting desperate, and in my opinion the dead rat is a warning. But it could also be a distraction."

"I agree." Torque nodded, tugging on his short beard. "This isn't about the grow. This is about something else, much dirtier." He turned to look at his president, his eyes narrowed. "What was Hunter into outside of the club?"

"How the fuck am I supposed to know?"

"You're president, Snake. You brought him in. You're supposed to know what sidelines he had."

"In case you've forgotten asshole, we took a vote. We *all* patched him in. Besides I don't know every damn detail of every damn brother's private life now, do I?"

"If it fucks with the club you oughta know. You gotta have some clue. What are you keeping from us?"

"You questioning my leadership, Torque?" Snake stood up so fast his chair shot backwards. "Today? When we got our *patched in* brother's head in a cheap-ass cooler and his woman is missing?"

The two men stood across the desk from each other, neither backing off. Snake puffing and wheezing through his flared nostrils. Torque, cold and hard, jaw set like a rock, fists clenched at his side. The tension was so tight, so combustible, a cockroach's fart would blow them all to Kingdom Come.

Carmine's instinct was to keep himself between them and Helen who for some reason had her nose in her phone. But he didn't dare move for fear of tripping some kind of invisible tension wire, sending them launching at each other.

"Uh, gentlemen?" Helen spoke up, making his heart almost explode.

Snake growled at the interruption, but neither men broke their stare-off.

"Gentlemen!"

Fuck!

This woman.

"What!" they snapped.

"I think I might be able to help with the Bitcoin Wallet thingy."

It took several long seconds, before first Torque blinked, then dragged his eyes from Snake to focus on her. Snake followed suit half a second later, brow creased. The tension suffocating the room eased considerably as they took their attention off each other and put it onto her.

"What're you talking about, Trouble?"

"Try entering this." She held out her phone showing them her screen on which there was a series of letters and characters.

PW*&%#@2241.

"I thought Cody butt-texted me the morning he died. But what if it wasn't a butt text? What if it was deliberate and he changed the password to protect the account from whomever killed him? What if this is the new password?"

Chapter Twenty

It wasn't until they were back in the Jeep when she showed him the second text.

Duncan gift vid tovas Menlo.

"I think what he was saying is don't come, give the video to Vas Melnikov. You know how auto-correct can be so annoying?"

Carmine squinted at it for while then he beamed. "You're a genius, Red." Those stunning sea glass eyes aimed straight at her, crinkling delightfully in the corners.

Despite the recent dire news, and morning activities aside, a warm flush of pride and pleasure rushed up her neck as she absorbed the compliment.

"You think so?"

"Fucking genius," he repeated as he started the engine. "I would never have figured that out."

She giggled. Mostly for stress release, partly in relief, but also because she was pretty sure she was glowing like the tomato he so often called her.

"I guess once you know the context, it makes it easier. I just had to think like an autocorrect bot. Cody was trying to warn me, probably right before...." She paused, then blew out air. "He gets giant kudos for that."

It was green and peaceful, the trees so tall and the air, other than being laced with the skunky-sweet smell of marijuana, was crisp and clean.

"Yeah. Probably why he destroyed his phone. Didn't want those texts traced back to you."

A red-tailed hawk circled above, its distinctive tail feathers a contrast against the indigo sky. For a moment her spirit soared along with it.

"But why does he want us to give the video to Vasily? I didn't even know he knew him."

"Don't know what that connection is yet."

They'd come to the gate and he stopped, checking the road before merging. "But at least we know now it was Hunter who filmed it."

"Yep, both Snake and Torque verified that. Maybe Hunter sent Cody the video by mistake."

"Why by mistake, Tomato Head?"

"Well, I mean think about it. Cody...Candy? Candy is his wife or old woman, or *whatever* biker's ladies are called. So maybe he meant to send it to Candy, but he was in a hurry or in danger and sent it to Cody instead?"

Carmine took his eyes off the road for a moment to stare at her. "That makes perfect sense."

"Especially since she's missing now too."

They were interrupted by his phone ringing. The onboard screen displayed the name *Thomas*.

"Yo," Carmine answered. "You're on speaker."

"Hi, Helen," Thomas said with a lot of smile in his voice. "Boss man treating you well?"

She giggled but before she could answer, Carmine interrupted, "What you got, Thomas?"

"Ooh, okay, so that's how it is."

"Thomas," he growled.

"I got the license plate of that delivery truck. Belongs to an Albert King out of Redding. But the problem is, that plate should be on a 1997 Subaru Outback and not a delivery truck. And Albert King is deceased, may he rest in peace."

"Figures plates are stolen. If I were trafficking women, I wouldn't use a legit one either. Albert King got any relatives?"

"Funny you should ask. He has two grandsons from his only daughter who is also deceased. One being a John King. He's the oldest with an address in Redding and he happens to own one vehicle and one motorcycle. Want to guess what type of motorcycle?"

"Shit, a Harley?"

"Ding ding ding. Winner winner, chicken dinner."

Carmine rolled his eyes, but Helen couldn't help chuckling.

"And the other?"

"Grandson number two, King's half-brother, is Helen's mystery date from yesterday. James Falk."

Holy...hell.

"The guy who attacked me?"

"One and the same."

They'd rounded a corner. Up ahead about half a mile away on the side of the road was a dot of red. Carmine's brow wrinkled and he slowed a bit.

"You know what Falk looks like, but I'm gonna email you King's driver's license photo so you can pick him out of a crowd. Ugly bastard."

"Do either belong to any known club?"

The red dot turned into the butt end of a Ford Explorer, like the one they'd parked next to earlier. It wasn't in its spot when they'd left.

"King's been associated with one in San Francisco, but not a patched member. However, that intel isn't recent. Don't have any more on him, we're still digging."

"Means he could be nomad. What about here in Redding?"

"No known as of yet."

"And the video? You have a chance to clean it up yet? Get any geographical markers?"

"Managed to isolate the voice, and running it through some recognition programs—"

"Forget that. We know who filmed it, I need a location."

"Oh, okay...uh, I haven't brightened the video enough yet to get any markers. The quality is poor and it's tricky."

The red Explorer was nose deep in a shallow ditch and covered by tree branches. As they got closer Helen realized there was a dark cloud of hair slumped over the wheel.

"Is that one of the women from the clubhouse?" she asked.

"Looks like it. Stand by for a second, Thomas."

"Roger that."

He put Thomas on mute, then pulled up next to the Jeep.

"Red, get ready to call 911."

Carmine jumped out of the Jeep, slid down the embankment and checked the door of the Explorer. Locked. He knocked on the window but a blur of movement in the bushes to his left became a dark hooded figure bearing down on him. The air snapped with a strange, electrical buzz. Carmine jerked, then collapsed, disappearing from her sightline.

"Oh, fuckohfuck*ohfuck*!" Helen yelled, trying to scramble across the seat but she was trapped by her seatbelt. "*Carmine!*"

Dammit.

Her fingers fumbled, not finding the release button. Then it popped and she was on her knees, halfway across the console when the man with a grey ski mask appeared behind the door, blocking her exit.

"There you are, bitch."

What—he was after her?

Reversing course, she scrambled backwards, but not fast

enough. He tried for one of her ankles, but she evaded and kicked him hard under the chin.

He grunted, then yelled, "Cunt!" as he yanked her hard.

"No, *no!*" She braced her free foot against the panel next to the dash, but he was too strong, and too big, his hands like massive vice grips cutting into her flesh.

She hadn't pressed 911! And her phone was now on the Jeep's floor.

Thomas.

He was still on mute.

She grabbed the steering wheel and clung for dear life with one hand as she stabbed at the onboard screen with her other, hoping against hope she'd hit the right button. The brute dislodged her foot and she went flying out the car, landing on her tailbone.

Ow, fuck!

Sharp pine cones dug into her back, but she ignored the pain and twisted to try to loosen his grip. He never let go.

She had one shot left. Pray God, she'd hit the button.

"Thomas," Her breath hitched. What if she missed. What if he was going to kill her—or worse—rape her. "Thomas...God, Thomas, HELP!"

"What the fuck you talking, bitch? Give me the thumb drive."

This was still about the thumb drive? Of course it was. She started to laugh. A hysterical, out of control laugh. Her attacker grunted, surprise widening his eyes.

"I don't have it, you stupid moron. It's gone."

"Aargh!" he yelled in her face, assaulting her with his foul breath and pressing down hard on her chest.

Holy hell, he was going to crush her, snap her bones like dried-up twigs. But then a dirty cloth smothered her face. It smelled sharp, sweet, almost like nail polish.

Then it all went black.

Chapter Twenty-One

Cold.

So, so cold. And dark. Where was she? Nausea exacerbated by each pulse of her heart climbed up her throat. Helen swallowed but it didn't help. Just the opposite. A smell—sharp and sickly sweet was stuck in her nose and gullet, but it was layered with something else. Like dirt. Wet dirt.

She gagged.

"Oh God, don't throw up. Please don't throw up, it's bad enough down here."

Down here?

Where—hell?

It was too cold for hell, and what was wrong with her—hearing thoughts she didn't even think? She didn't even sound like herself.

Attempting to move, it became clear she was in an awkward position with one arm trapped beneath her body. But she also seemed to be lying on something, or maybe in something? God—dirt. It was filling her nostrils. If she could just make herself roll...?

Okay.

Roll.

Whatever synapses in her brain were still working, they were not communicating with her body parts. Shit, she had to move or she was going to suffocate on *dirt*. Okay—try again.

Brain, command body to move.

Deep breath, move shoulder back, roll. Goddammit, stupid body...roll.

Oh, yes. Hallelujah!

Now on her back, painful pins and needles prickled as the blood flooded into her limb. It made her twitch, and she shook her arm to alleviate the sensations overtaking her entire left side. There was a sliver of light far above her and a corresponding beam hitting the dirt off to her left. Not the moon—too weirdly shaped.

Then, what?

Why was it so cold? Where was she?

"Carmine?" she croaked as she maneuvered into a sitting position. "Oh God, my head." Another wave of nausea hit her, and she dropped her skull between her knees to fight it off.

"Problem of the day."

What?

She definitely didn't think that.

"I'm hearing voices now?" she said to the dark. Wasn't that a sign of a concussion, or serious brain damage?

"Just mine."

Helen studied the area around her, not seeing anything.

"Over here."

Then she saw it, a slight disturbance in the darkness off to her right. As her eyes adjusted, she made out a darker human form against the wall.

"You're not Carmine."

"Nope."

"Who are you?"

"I'm Candy, and the headache will eventually get better," the form said slowly. "But it never seems to go fully away. Just when you think you're okay, the hunger starts. Then the thirst. But I guess I'm lucky it rained a little, otherwise I'd be in really bad shape."

Helen squinted in the dark. "Where are we?"

"Look around, hon. You tell me."

She looked up, and stared at the small patch of light, peaking through. That definitely wasn't a ceiling—and considering the dirt and the smell?

"Some kind of pit?"

"Uh huh." Her voice had an unnatural, slow calm to it, like she'd resigned herself to being here. Or maybe she just didn't have the strength left to do anything about it. "One with a bunch of dead animals in it judging by the smell."

"Is that what it is? Death?"

She'd never met Candy, so she couldn't picture her, and she couldn't see much except she was of medium build with darkish hair.

"And whatever they used to knock you out. It stays with you. I'm thinking chloroform, but I'm no chemist."

"There was a man with me. Do you know anything about him?"

"Sorry. It's just us."

"How long have you been here?"

"Two days, give or take."

"You wouldn't happen to have any water, would you?"

Candy just stared, until she closed her eyes. "Only what drips from up there. Let's hope it rains again soon. What's your name?"

"I'm Helen."

"Helen?"

"Yes, Cody's Helen."

"Oh fuck, hon...how did you get thrown down here? What are you even doing here? I'd thought you'd broken up."

"We had."

"Yet, you're here?"

"Yes." Her voice caught a little. "I came because Cody needed help and...they're looking for you, by the way. The club. They know you're missing...and..."

"My husband, Hunter?" she whispered. There was so much hope in her voice, it broke Helen's heart. "Do you know anything about him?"

Helen's face screwed up, both at the thumping in her head and in sympathy. But saying the words wasn't going to be nearly as hard as hearing them.

"I'm really sorry to be the one to tell you, but it's my understanding that they're um...that they're both dead." Her own voice faded out as her throat tightened. "I'm so sorry."

There was a sharp expulsion of air, which was followed with, "Your understanding...both of them?"

"Cody, I know for sure because we found him at your cabin." Oh, God, this was hard. Helen swallowed and took another breath before she answered. "But Hunter, that's what I was told."

"Oh, God *nooo*." Candy released a keen that struck a knife through her already aching heart. "Oh no, *no*. What happened to them?"

She didn't answer. The poor woman didn't need to know her husband's body had been separated from his head which was then delivered in a cheap Styrofoam cooler. Or in Cody's case that he only had half his head left. Instead she afforded her the space to grieve, doing some of her own for the man she once loved, but mostly worrying and aching for the one who was missing.

After a while, the soft keening gave way to sniffles and by that time her eyes had adjusted enough she could see Candy wipe her nose with her sleeve.

"At best I thought Hunter would be stuck in a pit or...or something like me, you know?" she said. "But I guess deep down I knew something worse had happened. He always found a way to get in touch and I hadn't heard from him."

"Why were they in San Francisco?" Helen asked mostly to keep her mind occupied, to counter the cold seeping into her bones. How Candy had stood it for two days was beyond her.

"Hunter had business and Cody wanted to see you. He said he needed to make amends."

"Amends?" she scoffed. Funny how that turned out, but now wasn't the time to bring it up considering Cody was lying in a morgue.

"I know he stole from you."

What?

"My brother was spiraling, and after you kicked him out, well, things got bad. And I don't blame you for kicking him out, I would've done the same. You should know that," she said wiping her eyes again. "But you should also know you're the reason he got help."

"Help?"

"My old man had a contact, someone who had connections and he helped get Cody into a rehab facility. That damn waiting list is so long it's a wonder anyone gets help before it's too late."

She understood that. Terra's mom had the same problem. "I didn't know, but I'm glad he did," she said, her throat tight. It was impossible for her not to respond to another person's tears. She was just built like that and Cody had been a shit, but he didn't deserve to be a dead shit.

Adjusting her sweater so it covered her shoulders, she rubbed her arms and stood, needing to move, to get her blood flowing and counteract the cold creeping into her bones. But also, so she could think.

"After he completed rehab," Candy continued, "Hunter got him a job working for the club, doing their books. Kept an eye on him. Kept him straight. It's not fair." She started crying again. "They're both gone. My whole family's gone. Who did this?"

"We were trying to figure that out." The floor was layered with gross smelling dirt and musty leaves and as she stood and walked around, other crunchy things. The tiny skeletons of animals unfortunate enough to find themselves in the same predicament—left to starve and die.

"Right before we were ambushed, a name was mentioned, John King. Do you know him?"

"King?" Candy sniffed and shook her head. "But all the brothers have road names. You don't always get to know their real ones."

"Figures."

The walls were concrete and too smooth to scale, except for a series of metal protrusions with sharp edges. Helen ran her fingers over them. Probably the remains of a ladder that had been removed —to prevent captives from escaping no doubt. She considered the distance from the ground to the sliver of light.

"How high do you think these walls are?"

"Too high."

"No seriously—how high?" She moved to stand up against the concrete. "I'm five-two. Take my height and use it as a template."

Candy's eyes moved from the top of her head to the trap door, calculating. "Fourteen, maybe fifteen feet."

We're getting out of here, Candy."

"I've already tried climbing those metal things you're checking out. It's not happening."

"I was cheerleading captain in high school."

"Congratulations?" Candy responded sarcastically, but Helen could tell her interest perked. "But how does that help?"

"There's two of us now. What are you—five-six? If I can get on your shoulders, all I need is a couple of those nubs to be long enough to support my foot. Maybe I could monkey up to that door and pop it, pull myself out."

"Yeah right."

"Won't know until we try."

Candy looked up, to where Helen was looking, then back at her. "You think you can do that?" Her voice reflected the teeniest amount of hope as she pushed to her feet, albeit wobbly.

"I'm pretty sure, unless that door is locked. Then we're fucked."

"You know" — she scratched her chin — "It could work."

"You've been down here a while, do you think you can handle me?"

Candy gave her a side glance. "You don't weigh much more than a starving alley cat. Besides, I'm a fucking biker chick. Hell yes, I can do this." She dropped her head back and sighed.

"I like your attitude."

"I like your mind. Oh, I need water. Water's up there. Eyes on the prize, Candy. Eyes on the prize. Okay, how are we going to do this? You're going to have to bear with me, I'm not very strong right now."

"I don't need strength as much as I need steady."

"Say again?"

"Lean your back against the wall. Come down a little so your thighs are bent and your feet a little apart."

Candy did as Helen asked. "Like this?"

"Yes, exactly, but dig your feet in."

"Got it."

"Now cup your hands, one hand under the other and I'm going to use them as a step to get onto your shoulder. When I push off, use my momentum to help force me up. We clear?"

It took several attempts.

The first couple times Helen lost her balance and she tumbled into the dirt. Fortunately, it was thick enough to cushion her fall. On the third, she found her balance on Candy's shoulders, and gripped a nub to steady herself.

"I need your head."

"What?"

"I need to stand on your head."

"Do it already."

She didn't wait and for once was grateful she was small. But that extra foot gave her what she needed to get another decent foothold on a protuberance she'd eyed. And as she pushed off of that, she shoved her fingers between the gap in the door and the concrete.

Searing white hot pain shot through her fingernail.

"Ow...*fuck*!" She cried, but managed to find a grip.

"What happened?" Candy called.

She couldn't speak. She could barely breathe, but neither could she let go. They were so close.

"Helen?"

She sobbed, her breath catching. Good God—that hurt.

Fuck.

Breathe.

"Helen, you okay?"

"Ya," she gritted through her teeth. "I'm okay." She had to be. Her foot had begun to slip off the tiny edge of iron and her leg started to shake. It was now or never.

She clung to the concrete, ignoring the pain and using the adrenaline it produced. Adjusting her foot, she got better footing and put her available hand flat against the trapdoor and pushed.

Holy hell, it moved!

A fatter sliver of light sliced her vision, with no sign of a lock or chain. She tried again, with everything she had. Surprisingly, the door wasn't as heavy as expected, nor was it blocked by vegetation. It swung open another couple of feet.

With both hands, and breathing through the pain in her finger, she clung to the edge. And toeing those protruding metal nubs with the tips of her trainers, she climbed the rest of the way, wriggling through the opening.

When she was out, she rolled onto her back, cushioned by a thick blanket of dead pine needles and soft green vegetation.

And sobbed.

"You okay?" Candy called after a moment.

"Just need...a minute."

"You did it! Oh my God, you're out. You're my fucking hero. You hear that Helen? You're my fucking hero."

She gripped her finger. The tip of her nail had ripped off halfway down the bed, leaving it bloody and exposed. It didn't matter how much it hurt, nothing could eclipse the joy of seeing the sky again. She was free.

They were free.

Like the birds and the bears and the rest of the critters in this forest. Over the buzzing in her head, she became aware of how noisy it was.

"Helen, you good?"

"I'm good." Except she now understood why pulling fingernails was such a popular form of torture.

"Don't leave me down here, please I beg you."

"Are you kidding?" Helen responded to the desperation in her voice, wiping her tears with her shoulder. "I'm not leaving you." She peeked down into the pit. "Besides, we have a better chance together than we do alone. How many hours of daylight do you think we have?"

Candy squinted at the light. "It's kind of hard to tell, but maybe two, three at the most."

"Then I better get moving." She pushed into a sitting position. "I'm going to find something to get you out."

"Okay, just don't get lost. Leave a trail of breadcrumbs, mark the trees before you leave and as you go."

Good point, but as it turns out, she didn't have to go far. Only a couple feet actually. She let out a sob-laugh. Leaning against a tree for all the world to see was the detached ladder.

She stared at it, thinking it was going to disappear on her like some weird apparition caused from lack of water or the hellish pain in her finger.

Was it really so easy—or was it some kind of cruel joke her mind was playing on her?

But no, it was solid and real and after an inspection of the rungs for damage or rust, it seemed in decent shape. It was heavy, but she maneuvered it into the hole and dropped it in. Moments later she helped Candy crawl out.

Then they hugged and cried.

"Oh, my God, thank you so much," Candy sobbed into her shoulder. "I mean it when I say you're my hero. I thought I was going to die in there."

She pulled away and Helen studied Candy's heart-shaped face and lovely long lashed brown eyes that were red from tears. Her boyfriend jeans and black strap cut long-sleeved tee shirt were filthy and she stank like death as she was sure she did too, but they were alive.

"Come on," she said. "We gotta get away from that hole." Then she stopped and looked around. There was nothing but trees and low growing foliage. "Oh hell, which way do we go? I have to find Carmine."

"We go west," Candy said, leaning her butt up against a tree, bent at the waist still breathing a little hard. "But first water."

"I agree with water, but why west?"

"Redding's west. Until I get some kind of geographical clue, I don't know which direction Sawmill is."

Helen searched the treetops. West would be smart. However. "I can't leave him, Candy. I have to try to find him. He's got to be close."

"Why do you think he's close?"

"That," Helen pointed to the pit, "by the looks of it, is an old fire bunker. There's probably a ranger's station or a cabin nearby. Maybe that's where they're keeping him."

"You're crazy." Candy eyed her, eyes wide, shaking her head. "You know that, right? We should try to find a road, flag someone down. Call the club for help." She pulled off a chunk of moss, and holding it above her head, she squeezed. Moisture flowed down her thumb into her mouth.

"That's safe?" Helen asked, watching her.

"Safer than any water you'll find in a stream. There's something in the moss that keeps it sterile. Just watch out for any tiny critters."

Helen copied her. She almost cried as it slaked down her dry throat. It was cold and clean and in that moment the best she'd ever drunk.

"Don't take this the wrong way, but what if it's someone in the club who did this?"

Candy paused, then turned her head to regard her. "Why do you say that?"

"We were ambushed right after we left the clubhouse. There was a car...a red Explorer that had an accident and we stopped to help..."

"A red Explorer? That's Marisol's car—Kai's woman."

"Kai?"

The woman in the car was Kai's woman? Well then, where the hell was he? Did he know she'd driven off the road?

"Not my favorite brother, but he stuck to Hunter like glue. He's a scary asshole, got those black eyes that look right through you.

Yeah, she'd noticed that too.

"And that demon tattoo on his skull." Candy gave a dramatic shudder. "I've seen some weird ink on some of those dudes, but that tattoo?"

She was listening, but it was hard to pay attention as she'd just caught her nail on some moss—again.

"Candy," she swallowed. "I need you for a second."

"What, hon?"

She held out her hand. "Rip this off."

"Ugh." Candy's eyes bugged wide at the sight of the separated nail. Then she blew out a long breath. "Just the thought of that makes me want to puke."

"Please, I need you to. I can't do it myself."

She sighed and her skin beneath all that dirt got paler. "Close your eyes."

Helen did as such, then held out her finger and braced herself. She felt Candy grip it, then a small touch of heat. She realized it was her hot breath, but before she could think, there was a jerk and white-hot agony shot up her arm.

"Oh, *fuuuuuck*!" she squealed, and dropped to her knees. It was so much worse that when she first injured it. Then she'd had adrenaline on her side. "Holy hell," she gasped. "Did you use your teeth?" A wave of nausea rose up from her stomach and whatever fluid she'd consumed exited her mouth and splashed on the forest floor.

Candy didn't look so hot either. Her butt was against the trunk of a red fir as she spat out the nail, then rinsed her mouth. "I'm sorry, I didn't know how else to do it."

"It's all good," she said, her voice coming out shaky. It's all... oh, wow it hurts." She scooted down the tree to her bottom and cried, holding her finger above her heart, putting pressure just beneath the nail. Then after a minute, still nauseated, her heart still thumping, but with the shock somewhat lessened, she rose.

Dismissing the lightheadedness, she grabbed more moss and squeezed cool water over her finger. The cold against the heat of the pain made her gasp.

"You should wrap that," Candy said, ripping the string from her hoodie. "I'll find you a leaf." To which she plucked a broad one from a nearby bush Helen couldn't identify and formed a roll, then slipped it over her finger.

While Candy adjusted the leaf, Helen asked, "What did your husband think of him?"

"Who, Kai? Didn't talk much about him but he kept him close."

"Did he say why?"

She shook her head. "Those dudes will gossip like teenage girls, but when it came to club stuff, their mouths shut tighter than a virgin's knees." Then as something dawned, her expression changed. "You said you got ambushed when you stopped at Marisol's car?"

"Yeah, like a mile down from the compound's entrance."

"You didn't see who though?"

"He had a ski mask on, but he was big, and had a stun gun."

"Hmm. They used one on me too, then that chemical...whatever it was."

Candy finished tying off the leaf and studied her work. "That should do for now."

Helen nodded. "So, what do you say? We go find a road and hopefully some food?"

"Food, oh God yes. I'm so hungry I could eat a pinecone."

"Theoretically you can eat the nuts in a pinecone. I have them on my salad all the time."

They did in fact find some golden current berries and dandelion leaves. They consumed all they could find but not much else.

They'd been foraging for a few minutes when, Candy asked, "What happened to Marisol?"

"Don't know. She was slumped over the wheel and Carmine got out to check. Everything happened so fast and next, I was in that pit with you. God, I hope she's okay."

"No sign of her...?" Candy stopped suddenly. About fifty yards ahead peeking through the trees was a slice of road. They stared at each other for a moment before approaching cautiously. It was a dirt road and marked with fresh tire tracks.

"We're going to need weapons," Helen muttered. "Just in case those aren't friendly tires."

Candy gave a weak laugh. "What is it exactly you're planning to do?"

"We'll figure it out if we come across them."

"That's what I'm worried about. Sticks? We can poke them to death. Or rocks?"

"Poking's good. I can do poking."

Helen found a good one. Sharper on one end and knobby and heavy enough on the other to do damage if necessary. She was testing it when a movement out of the corner of her eye made her jump. Two large forms carrying assault rifles stepped from behind a tree.

"Holy fuck!" Her heart almost exploded in her chest as she back pedaled, trying to put distance between them, but bumping into Candy instead.

"Yo," the one closest to her said in a gruff voice. "Where do you think you're going?"

Chapter Twenty-Two

"Eh, *mooschena*."

Something nudged his leg, hard enough to jog his senses. He began to surface from a dark tunnel that smelled like moldy hay.

As he woke, he found himself eyeball to a concrete floor, lashes flickering, vision limited. The rough, dirty surface dug into his cheek, making it throb, hurting more when he moved.

The faint drum of a voice echoed in his head. A strange *female* voice—making sounds...or were those words? He couldn't tell, they all jumbled together.

Where was he—Afghanistan?

His heart slammed into his throat, thundered in his ears. He'd been captured! Blinking hard, trying to clear his vision which was tinged with red, he breathed through the nausea and listened.

"Mooschena, you alive?"

Not Pashto or Farsi. Heavily accented English. He almost sobbed—he wasn't in country. Not anymore. Hadn't been in three years.

So then where?

It came back slowly, his last memory. The tall trees, the red Ford, chick over the steering wheel...Helen.

Yelling.

His eye popped wide.

Helen!

Where was Helen?

Another nudge.

"*Mooscheena!*"

He knew that word. Russian.

He attempted to roll off his face onto his side, to get a better look. His arms were stuck, tied behind his back at his wrists.

"You okay?"

A pale face, slightly familiar and framed with stringy brown hair and dull, pale eyes stared at him through wooden slats. They were wide enough apart for an arm to poke through. Her back was to the wall, but she reached through from her side nudging his boot. He looked at her hand, then saw his ankles were zipped-tied.

"Where's Helen?" he croaked, his mouth tasting like a horse had given birth, then died in it. He blinked again, clearing some of the red — blood he guessed — and got a better sense of his surroundings.

Two cells. Walls of cinder blocks with razor wire on top. More like stalls. His, the smaller cell, approximately eight by eight feet, and a second much larger one that contained several women and a blue porta-potty. Neither had windows, merely some kind of grate high up that allowed for fresh air.

"Helen?" he asked, looking back at the woman. He recognized her now—the one who spat at the prick in the video on the thumb drive. "The woman I was with? Red hair, small?"

"Not here." She shook her head.

Then where? His fear level spiked at the same time a hollow-ness filled his chest. Christ, was she alive? She had to be—they'd use her for leverage. He had to believe that.

"What's your name?"

"Irina. You?"

"Carmine. How long have I been here?"

"Few hours. Not long."

"And you, how long have you been here?"

"Maybe week, little more."

"There were more of you."

Irina waved a hand at the rest of the women who had gathered closer to the bars. "*Da*, we fewer now."

At least half were missing. In another cage perhaps? He counted five women in total and their expressions solemn and hopeless beneath the dirt.

"Sell us like dogs. Keep us like this, so behave better." She let out a mirthless chuff that bordered on despair. "Better to shoot us."

A door somewhere banged. His head jerked towards the sound. From a different building, but not far away. Then he heard men's voices speaking English. Two at least.

"They come. Know you're wake."

His gaze moved back to her.

"Camera," Irina stated, her eyes darting to a corner where he now saw a red light. "Watch all the time."

Chatter rose amongst the girls. They'd stayed mostly silent until now. Two scuttled back into the corner, hiding under a sparse blanket. Irina's face screwed up, a tear rolled down through the dirt and dripped off her chin, but she remained where she was. "They come. One, sometimes two get taken."

"Maybe this time they're here for me."

"Maybe. Either way not good."

No. Probably not. And he didn't have much time, he needed to use it wisely.

"How many women to begin with?"

"Twenty. Some sold right away. Ugly ones, fat ones come here. Get sold to ugly, fat men who can't find woman."

"Where're you from Irina?"

"Chudovo, small town in Russia." She nodded towards the women. "Some from Ukraine, others Poland. Take to Russia, put on ship, then here."

"How do they find you?"

"Nanny job on internet."

"What?"

"*Da*. American family look for nanny." Her voice cracked, and she paused for a moment. "Pay for ticket, but it's lie. Go for interview, give you tea, drug you."

Shit.

"The interview, they're Americans?"

"Man and woman. Say want give opportunity to poor farm girl."

The door behind him on the far end of the stable opened.

"*Stupid* farm girl."

"I'm getting you out of here."

She stared at him, then shook her head, a tear rolling down her cheek, defeat heavy in her features. "Don't make promise, Karamine. No one get out of here. Unless dead or slave."

Booted footsteps headed towards them. He twisted his neck to get a better angle. One tall and lean, the other not as tall but bulky, both faces covered with ski masks. He'd bet his left nut, the taller one, based on the way he carried his head was Viktor. The other —King?

A key produced from the pocket of the bulkier man was shoved into a lock, then his cage door squeaked open. They approached from behind, a cloth bag was placed over his head, then tightened around his neck. It was suffocating, panic-inducing. Each breath sucked the bag in, then puffed it out as he exhaled.

Stay calm. Stay the fuck calm. He pulled on his training. Breathe steady, think of Helen.

They grasped him underneath his armpits and yanked him up. The plastic zip ties around his wrists cut deeper into his flesh. He groaned against the pain as they dragged him, the tip of his boots scraping the concrete.

Helen.

Her face, her smile.

Her laugh.

Her smell.

The door banged shut again, and he was dropped like a sack of hot shit onto something hard, deep and bowl-shaped. A wheelbarrow? He lay on his hands, his legs hung over a sharp edge that dug into the tender flesh behind his knees. Even if he could push himself up, it wouldn't be enough leverage to roll out.

Keep thinking of Helen.

Her pretty legs in shorts.

Her flat, smooth stomach.

Honeysuckle.

The container was lifted, then the sensation of movement. Cooler, fresh air tickled his skin. A bumpy, uneven ride, his head banging on the metal edge.

One, two, three...twenty-two, twenty-three, twenty-four... Warmer air, no breeze, door shutting. More floating.

Then he was tipped, his skull hitting something hard. Teeth sliced into his lip and blood filled his mouth. He growled low in his throat and rolled onto his stomach, gagging. The thumping in his head, compounded now with that crack, felt like a bass drum at a rock concert. He was lifted, then placed on something, like a chair. Someone grabbed his arms, added more zip ties until he couldn't move.

Finally, someone removed the bag. He sucked in air like a man drowning and spat out blood.

"Ain't so pretty now, are you?" A deep, definitely American voice from behind him said. He didn't bother turning his head, instead studied the room. Big, dark, warmer than the stables. Smelled like oil. Garage maybe.

"Where is she?"

"Somewhere safe."

Safe for whom? Judging how they treated women, he seriously didn't think it was for her.

"Want to see her."

The dick laughed. It was ugly, and evil and echoed off the walls, hurting his head.

"Look at the asshole, making demands."

There was another, gruffer laugh from behind him.

"Tell us what we wanna know, and we'll think about it."

Hope gave him the strength to lift his head. It took effort, like it weighed more than the barbells he bench-pressed at his gym. The movement made lightning bolts pierce his brain, and the need to puke was strong. Probably had a concussion. The other prick–– Viktor he presumed––was still behind him and flipped on a row of stark fluorescent lights, which didn't help. None came through narrow windows on the far side, above double garage doors. By his estimate he'd been here, wherever here was, at least seven or eight hours. Seven hours since his phone call with Thomas. Time enough?

"What you wanna know, prick?"

"Who knows about the video?"

"What video?"

A stinging blow landed across his shoulder blades. He hissed.

"Oh, that video," he grunted. "Where's the girl?"

"We can play it this way all evening. I got time. But I ain't got patience, so go ahead, piss me off. I get off hurting people." And to prove his point, he hit him again. Same spot.

Shit!

The prick circled in front of him, a looming dark figure, grey ski mask, faded black jeans, shiny motor-cycle boots.

With a thick, heavy tread and a highly polished silver toe-strip.

He'd seen those boots. That motherfucker Kai! He almost laughed. Would've if his head hadn't hurt so much. Asshole went to all that trouble to hide his identity and his shoes gave him away.

He held something long and tapered. Out of his functioning eye, Carmine recognized it as a police baton.

"Who else knows about the video?"

"It's in cyberspace, fuckface. A bunch of people know about it."

Whack—just above his knee. Aah...*Jesus.*

Breathe—breathe. He wheezed through the pain. Bile rose in the back his throat. "Where's Helen?"

"Somewhere you'll never find her."

Whack. "Who has it?"

It rushed up his throat—blood and bile, burning an acid path, filling his mouth.

The man jumped back. "Watch the boots, asshole!" More blows landed, two in rapid succession high on his left thigh, inches from his balls.

Despite his punishing army training, he couldn't help it—he cried out. Holy Christ...he was only human.

Where the hell were his people? If he lived, he was gonna castrate this fucker, bleed him out and leave him to die.

"Killed Hunter," he grunted between hard breaths.

"So what."

"And Cody. Why?"

King-slash-Kai paused in his slow circle around him. Behind the ski mask, those dead eyes locked with his. They were so black you couldn't differentiate his pupils.

"Was your...club brother."

King spat at his feet. "Fucker was no brother. He's a fucking snitch."

Snitch?

Well, what do you know? That put a whole new spin on things. "For who?"

"Doesn't matter who," King snapped back, his pitch a touch higher, and raised his arm. 'Who has. The. Video."

Carmine forced out a laugh even though it almost made him stroke out. Probably going to die anyway. "The FBI."

Whack. Across his chest. He felt a rib crack and his lungs seized. Jesus, no oxygen.

"Think I'm stupid enough to believe that?" King ranted.

Dying—couldn't breathe. An old trick his uncle taught him when he'd fallen off a swing as a kid and had the wind knocked out of him—breathe out. He expelled whatever air was left in him, and his lungs responded, sucking in hard, wheezy, *painful* breaths.

"I...do," he added when he had enough gas in his tank. "Don't...have... money either."

Whack.

"Aagh, *fuck!*" he sobbed. Then another—lower, near his kidney.

"You want to know where the girl is?" The tone in King's voice suggested he was becoming unhinged, which almost certainly wasn't a good thing for his survival. "In a hole, with the worms, you piece of shit."

A hole.

No.

"Tell me what I want to know you might get to see her. Though you don't deserve nothing for getting my little brother locked up again."

"No point if she's dead."

"She ain't dead...yet."

Ah. He let that seep through him. Not dead yet. He could hold on. "It's all falling apart for you, isn't it," he grunted. "No money, a video of your crimes. Outsmarted by a fast-thinking pasty little coke-head and a snitch."

Whack.

"*Ungh!*"

His head dropped forward and bloody spit dribbled from the corner of his mouth while he braced for the next one. Strangely it didn't come. Then he heard why.

Thunder—the kind that originated from Harley pipes. Lots of them.

"What the fuck, Viktor? Is that the club?"

Carmine rolled his head to the side as he had no strength left to lift it. A curse in Russian spewed from the other man as he jumped onto a crate to look through the window. A door somewhere to his left burst open and a stream of men stormed in.

"On the ground!" Badger's deep voice boomed above the chaos. "Nuts to the dirt!"

"Fuck you!" The prick yelled and rushed at them with his baton. A short burst of automatic fire followed, then a high-pitched scream. A bullet took half of Kai-slash-King's silver-toed foot off in a spray of red mist. Carmine watched the separated half fly across the room, roll to a stop in a patch of dirty oil.

"Jesus, old man." Torque called when they had them face down on the concrete. "Cool it, we want 'em alive."

"Eh! Who you calling old man?" a wheezy voice answered as more people entered the garage. One being his uncle Billy, who literally barreled into the room, leaving no room for speculation why his mafia moniker was The Barrel. But no one called him old without getting their head clocked.

That wheezy protest belonged to Alfie Cadora—their weapons dealer and distant cousin to Gianni Cadora. His pounding head and split lip couldn't stop the grin from spreading when the shrunken form stepped into view.

Alfie took a position next to Badger and Torque, armed to his dentures with an assault rifle that was almost as tall as him.

Billy broke away from the mayhem and hustled to his side. "Jesus, son," he said, taking his face gently in his big, sausage fingers. "What did he do?"

"Cut me free," he hissed, each breath ripping through him like fire from his ribs.

Billy released his grip on him and pulled a Swiss army knife from his pocket and sawed, making short work of the zip-ties tearing into his flesh.

"You got my girl?" he croaked, his throat parched and raw. Christ, he needed water. "You got Helen?"

"In a moment, son." Billy turned his head nodded to someone he couldn't see outside. "We need to get this mess contained first."

Just then Badger pulled the ski mask off King, confirming indeed it was Kai and ignoring the man's whiny howl. "Fuck...it hurts. I'm bleeding to death."

"Shut up, you bag full of dog shit," Torque barked. "You think you get any sympathy from us?" He nudged his leg with his own combat boot, eliciting a wail from the big baby.

"Jeez, you're even uglier than your mug shot," Thomas added. "Like we thought, Boss. Johnny-the-piece-of-dog-shit-King."

"You're gonna love prison, man," Badger smirked. "Better stock up on the K-Y."

"He's ours," Torque snapped, his face chiseled. "We deal with him."

"Boss?

"He killed one of ours, took his woman, he gets club justice."

"Can't argue." Carmine agreed on a grunt. "But somebody needs...to answer me...the fuck now. Where's Helen?"

Everything seemed to stop and there was a period of silence as his men turned to the door. Badger whistled. It wasn't long, but as each second ticked by, his heart pounded harder, doing a number on his ribs. His men gave nothing away and he was fucking petrified, on the verge of a heart attack when he saw two female figures step through the door.

The taller woman spotted King on the ground and rushed to him. "You fucking cocksucker! You killed my old man." She started kicking King in the head until Torque pulled her away.

"We got it, Candy. We got it."

"He needs to die!"

"I know, darlin'."

263

He ripped his eyes from the drama as he was more interested in the other woman. There was no mistaking that beautiful hair. The sight of her propagated a rush of emotion that surged through his veins, overwhelming him. The back of his eyeballs stung. And fuck him, he almost broke down and cried.

"Hey," he murmured when she was close enough to hear. "Whassup?"

She cupped his face in her hands and stared at him. She was filthy, smelled like dirt and pine needles, but she was the best damn thing he'd ever laid eyes on.

"Whassup witchou," she said, her voice hitching.

His vision blurred in his working eye. Her voice in his ear was sweeter than any angel choir.

"You're safe." She wrapped her arms around him, crying. Pressing his head gently to her breast, she rained kisses on the top of his head. "God, Carmine...I didn't know if you were alive."

His Red was crying.

His tough, beautiful, feisty Red was shedding tears—for him. He ached and bled and stank like vomit, but she clutched him in her arms like she didn't mind, like she never wanted to let go.

He didn't want her to let go.

"Take's...more than a prick...like him to kill me."

She half laughed, half cried and, still shaking, clutched him harder to her soft chest. It hurt, but not more than he already did.

"There's five women...locked up," he said to Billy. "I'd show, but my legs.... stable...barn near here."

Those thick Italian brows rose an inch while Billy regarded him. "We saw a stable when we arrived." You're telling me there are female prisoners in there?"

"One...Irina. Tell her...you're with me. Tell her I keep my promises."

Billy shook his head in astonishment, then put a hand on his shoulder. "I'll find them. Thomas," he bellowed at the small crowd guarding King and Viktor.

"Yo!" Thomas snapped to attention.

"Come with me. Bring your weapon."

Thomas looked at Carmine and nodded. He could trust his uncle to be mindful of the women, and not frighten them further. But also, he wasn't feeling so good. Shit was getting woozy, besides his head wanting to explode.

"I need a kiss, Tomato Head." If he died, he wanted her lips on him.

"I'm filthy," she returned.

"And I smell like honeysuckle?"

"No, you most definitely don't." Gently, she brought her lips to the corner of his mouth—the only spot on his face that didn't hurt––and laid soft, beautiful kisses on his skin.

"I was so scared they killed you," she murmured.

"Same." For some reason, his mouth wouldn't work anymore and there was a thick fog blanketing him.

The last thing he heard was, "Carmine...ohmigod, Carmine—what's wrong?"

Chapter Twenty-Three

She'd wanted to go straight to the hospital. Torque insisted they go to the clubhouse.

"You'll want to be clean so they'll let you see him," he explained. And he was right. No doctor would allow the crud she carried on her body to be transferred to their patient.

She, Candy and a couple of the woman piled into one of the Jeeps with Thomas driving. The other three, including Irina went with Alfie and Badger. They followed Torque and another brother named Mug in an old police cruiser with Viktor and Kai chained in the back. *They* were escorted by more of the brothers on Harleys while Billy followed the ambulance in Carmine's Jeep they'd recovered from behind the barn.

When they arrived at the compound, a rugged, quiet man with a dark beard and hair pulled back into a man-bun named Doc was waiting for them.

"He was an army doctor," Candy explained. "He kinda checked out after Afghanistan. Lives alone on club land in his RV. I guess it's an arrangement that works for all of us."

Beverly who was the blonde with the black roots and a few other women, except for Marisol were also waiting with sandwiches and a pile of clothes. She'd rallied the old ladies and pulled together enough items to provide for her and the girls. When Candy crawled out of the Jeep, Beverly rushed to her.

"God, Candy. I'm so sorry. So, so sorry."

Candy clung to her and sobbed. She'd cried in the pit, but now in these surroundings on home ground in the safety of Beverly's arms, she really let loose.

Helen realized how much of a tough lady she was, having kept it together for both their sakes while they were out there trying to survive.

After they'd showered and while the other women were being fed, she and Candy were called to Snake's office. As they entered, two brothers were leaving and stopped to hug Candy. "Sorry, honey," one of them said. "We can't bring them back, but we'll do our best by you."

"Thanks, Mug." Candy gave a weak smile then Helen followed her in. Torque, Snake, Alfie, Thomas and Badger all sat waiting for them. After giving their side of events and answering questions, there was a long moment of silence.

"Right under our noses," Snake finally said, leaning forward on his desk, resting on his elbows, seemingly spent. "The fucker was running girls in our backyard right under *our fucken noses*. Less than four miles from here. How did we not see this?"

"Seems like Hunter did," Torque answered. "That's why they killed him."

"And Cody," Candy added softly. "They killed my brother too."

"Yeah, darlin'. Cody too. And I'm an asshole for thinking he stole our money," Snake said. "Kai confessed to taking the thumb drive and setting your brother up, but Cody did us a solid by stealing it back and changing the password. That won't be forgotten."

"So that's why they went to San Francisco?" This came from Candy. "To get the thumb drive back?"

"Not sure about that but it seems so. Knew he'd be the one I'd blame. I had my reservations about hiring him and Hunter knew that too so I'm deducing they tried to take care of shit themselves. That's on me and I'm sorry." Snake stood and came around the desk. "We'll take care of you, darlin'. You don't need to worry about a thing from here on out."

Candy nodded, tears spilling from her eyes. She stood and went into Snake's outstretched arms. Helen felt her own eyes stinging and as she swiped a tear from her cheek, she caught Torque watching her.

"You alright?" he asked.

"Mm hm," she confirmed. "I just need to get to the hospital."

"Let Doc take a look at your finger first."

She sighed, but agreed, then let Torque lead her to a small sterile room behind the great room which seemed to be some kind of surgery.

Now that she could see Doc clearly, she was surprised how good-looking he was behind all that facial hair, but she sensed a brokenness that defied his tall, muscular frame.

He greeted her with, "When was your last tetanus shot?"

"Oh...hey, um, hello to you too. I'm Helen."

He grunted in response but when she didn't answer his question, raised an arched brow.

"I honestly don't remember."

"Probably high school then. You need one."

"Really?"

Another grunt.

"Can I have my own doctor do it? It's not that I don't trust you, it's just that I don't know you and, um, well, I don't even know if your license is up to date but I guess circumstances being what they are, that's neither here nor there. But I really don't like needles and I've heard tetanus shots are painful and I've had enough pain for one day already."

"Nope," he uttered, then pumped soap from a dispenser and

washed his hands at a stainless steel sink. This she took as a good sign. "You've already been exposed long enough. You should get it now. Lockjaw is no joke."

"Okay." She sighed, and took some comfort in the fact he pulled a pair of gloves from a box and donned them.

She endured the shot digging her fingers into the gurney he had her sit on, then another as he gave her a local anesthetic on her finger. He was silent while he cleaned and dressed her finger, but she managed to catch his eye when she thanked him. They were filled with a deep sadness and she couldn't help wondering what his story was.

Fucking war. That's what.

After that, she hugged Candy goodbye and Badger drove her to the hospital.

"Two cracked ribs," Billy said, when they approached him in the hospital waiting room. "Five stitches, a mild concussion and multiple contusions. Which is just fancy doctor speak for bruises."

"He's going to be okay?"

Billy nodded. "He got lucky." Stress lines radiated from his eyes and across his brow. Though he was calm, anger seemed to pulse off his rotund form. "No serious damage, but they're keeping him here to make sure everything's working right."

"Oh, thank God," she said, taking a seat on the waiting room bench. He joined her, resting his elbows on his knees, looking as exhausted as she felt.

"He's banged up but he's gonna be fine."

"Will I be able to see him?"

"Probably, when they're done poking him."

She reached over and took his hand in her uninjured one. It was big and warm and calloused.

"Thank you," she said when he turned his head to look at her. "For...you know."

He squeezed her fingers, patting them with his other before releasing her. "No need for that."

"There's plenty of need. Those...those people..."

"They're not people. They're scum." Billy's lip curled in disgust.

She couldn't disagree. Not after what she'd seen and experienced firsthand.

"What happens to those girls?" she enquired, meeting his cinnamon eyes. "I asked Torque but he's staying pretty tight-lipped."

"They'll be taken care of. Nobody's gonna touch them. You have my word." He continued to hold her gaze. Shelley considered Billy like a dad, loved him as such. If she trusted him like Carmine did, it was good enough for her.

"If it hadn't been you...if it had been them we came across, I...I..."

"I know kiddo."

"What they did to him..." Her voice caught.

"I hate to say this, but that boy has been through worse." He patted her knee.

Helen lifted her eyes to his face.

"You've seen his scars?"

She had indeed, and a hot rush of shame filled her, because she hadn't the courage to ask further about them. Not after she'd seen the pain in his eyes when he spoke of the ambush that killed Jaz.

"He hasn't told me much," she whispered.

"Shrapnel." Billy's chest expanded as if fortifying himself against the memory. "Shredded him." Billy closed his eyes, working his jaw, like the pain was his. "He's lucky his spine wasn't severed, lucky he's alive, though for a while he sure as hell worked hard not to be." At this point Billy turned back to her. "But he came through."

Helen's nose scrunched as the significance of his words sunk in. She wondered if Billy knew what they meant to a woman like her. The actual damage they did. Though when she glanced at him, he was staring at a spot on the floor lost in his thoughts and seemed not to notice.

Was it wrong to be envious of a dead woman? One who'd captured Carmine's heart so completely he'd wanted to die after he'd lost her. Even years after her death, she still had a hold on him.

"I'm glad he did," she choked out.

"Me too, kiddo. Me too." Billy ran his hands through his thinning hair. It was still dark, with only a hint of gray at the temples. They were quiet for a while watching the hospital staff doing their thing, checking on patients.

"How did you find us?" Helen asked eventually, more as a way of taking her mind off her damaged heart.

"GPS tracker."

"In the Jeep?"

"Nope." He side-eyed her. "Under his skin. They all have 'em."

"GPS's in their bodies? Are you kidding?"

"The kind of work he does is dangerous." He angled his head, chin pointed in her direction. "Wish he didn't, but I ain't in any position to tell him what to do."

At that moment, an African-American nurse in sensible black shoes and a bun situated low on her nape stepped up. "You can see him now," she addressed them with a solemn expression. "Just don't stay too long. He needs to rest."

"Is he conscious?" Helen asked, getting to her feet.

"If he is, it won't be for long. We've given him meds to make him more comfortable. They should knock him out."

"Thank you for helping him."

The nurse smiled, transforming her face into something quite lovely. "Just doing my job, sister, but it's good to know you appreciate it. Room two-oh-two."

"You coming?" she asked Billy who had remained seated after the nurse left.

"Go, kiddo. He needs to see your pretty face more than he does mine."

"You certain?"

He gave a tired nod. "I'll sort out rooms for us nearby."

With that, she patted him on the shoulder then walked the short distance to Carmine's ward down the hall. Once there, she knocked on his door.

"Hello?"

Carmines eyes were shut. There was an IV needle shoved into the tender flesh near his elbow, as the area around his wrists were bandaged. No doubt torn from the zip-ties they'd restrained him with. He looked so vulnerable it made her heart squeeze. Those sharp cheekbones and those slightly indented cheeks with the creases near his mouth that she found so attractive and endearing, were puffy and bruised. A cut above his eye was sewn together in neat, tiny stitches, yet even damaged he was beautiful.

"You still awake?" she asked softly, curling her fingers under his. There was no response, but feeling his warmth, his roughened skin against hers, soothed her.

"I'm sorry they did that to you but I'm so glad you're going to be okay."

She studied him carefully for any sign of recognition, but he showed none.

"You probably can't hear me, Carmine, and God knows I wouldn't have the courage to say this if you were awake, but I realized when I was in that hole that ...I'm falling for you...*have* fallen for you. That finding you was the only thing that mattered. Life is too short to not be honest about..."

There was a squeeze on her fingers. She sucked in a sharp breath.

Was he conscious?

He stirred, kind of sleepily, moving his shoulders a little like he was settling in, getting comfortable.

His grip on her finger tightened, and his lashes flickered as if struggling to open them, without quite managing it.

But he could manage a word.

"Jaz..."

The one she didn't expect to hear, but the one she was most afraid of. She stopped breathing.

He was thinking of Jaz?

Not her.

"Oh..." she gasped. It was like he'd taken a meat cleaver and slowly, excruciatingly carved her heart in two. It was a while before she could breathe again, if one could call it breathing. It was more a series of shaky little hitches her chest involuntarily made in response.

"Holy hell... oh." Tears she could no longer control cut a salty path down her face. "Okay," she whispered at last, swallowing. "I get you, and I'm sorry. You have no idea how sorry."

She began to unhook her finger, pull it loose, but his tightened around hers.

"No," he groaned. "Jaz..." Her gaze darted to his face, the two cleaved pieces of her heart thumping in her throat. His eyes were closed, his lips parted, his brow furrowed as though even with the meds, the pain persisted. But perhaps not physical pain.

Emotional.

Did it matter? He didn't want her. Sexually, yes. But not the way he still wanted the only woman he'd loved.

Her palm trembled as she wiped the river from her cheeks, then pulled her hand free from his. He groaned again. In a fog, she drifted to the sink in the private bathroom and turned the cold water on. It ran for several seconds before she could make herself move to splash some on her face.

The fluorescent lighting was unflattering at best. Her skin was pale and the bruising on her cheekbone didn't help.

Who gave a shit anyway?

Leaving the bathroom, she returned to his bed for a last look.

"So long, handsome," she choked out, smoothing the hair from his brow. "I wish you love. So much love."

Then, wiping the last tears from her cheeks, she pushed

through the door headed towards Billy. He'd been joined by Badger.

"All good?" the senior asked, tilting his head and giving her a look that seemed to see past her carefully pasted on facade.

"All good," she lied. Avoiding their eyes, she kept walking. "He's asleep." As she passed by, she sensed, rather than saw them stare at her. To direct their attention away, she asked Billy, "We sorted for rooms?"

"We are," he affirmed. "You okay? You're paler than you were before you went in there. You wanna get checked out while we're here?"

She shook her head. "Just need a bed to collapse in."

"I hear that." He matched her steps, then laid a big paw on the small of her back. That left Badger to take up the rear and his curious greys burning holes into the back of her skull as Billy led her out of the hospital.

Carmine's Jeep was parked close by. Billy climbed into the driver's seat. The hotel was only a mile away; Badger followed in the same Jeep he'd driven her in from the compound.

They checked in and with overnight bag in hand, which miraculously was still in the car, but not her purse. She walked the couple doors down from Billy's room.

"See you in the morning, kiddo," Billy said as he stepped through his door.

She was about to use her room key, wanting a bath, a bed and a good, soul-cleansing cry, when Badger called from down the hall.

"Yo, Helen, wait up."

He had a long, loping stance and was built solid with an aura that suggested he could take a beating. And probably had. He carried a white plastic drugstore bag, which he presented to her. Inside was her purse and phone.

"Found those inside that house. Thought you'd want them, but you should check with your credit card company in case they used them."

She nodded. "I thought they were lost. Thank you, Badger."

"You're welcome, Helen." He nodded, his face chiseled and solemn. He started to leave, but stopped and turned back, waiting until she lifted her eyes to his.

"I just gotta say, what you went through, the way you two ladies kept it together, that takes balls. You got my respect."

Respect? She blinked.

"We had no choice, Badger. I wasn't going to die down there where my family would never find me."

"As I said, respect. You need anything, you say something. Okay?"

"Okay... and again, thank you."

Then with a last nod, he turned on his heel, leaving her staring after his back.

Respect was nice. In fact, it was very nice, but it barely registered on her Feel Better scale. A different emotion—from a different man was preferable, but that wasn't happening. The ache in her heart confirmed it.

Inside, ensuring the deadbolt was turned and the sliding bolt in place, she ran a bath, pouring the entire mini bottle of shower gel into the steaming water. Though she'd showered and didn't physically smell, eau de pit was stuck inside her nose.

While the tub filled, she raided the mini-bar. No tequila, but there were two tiny bottles of Jack Daniels and two of Maker's Mark. After grabbing them and marrying her phone to its charger, she stripped, kicking Beverly's clothes aside and stepped into the tub. Cracking the seal on the first bottle, she took a sip. As it burned down her throat, she finally allowed herself to really cry.

For Cody.

For what she'd been through. For those women. For what Candy had lost, and what she'd lost. And for what she'd never have.

She sipped again.

And cried some more.

Cracked the second bottle, repeated, and rinsed.

After an interminable amount of time, the bottles empty, the water in the tub cold, and fresh out of tears, she climbed out and wrapped herself in a fluffy white robe. She retrieved her phone off the side table and read the texts she'd received. Most were worried.

Terra: *WTF why aren't you answering? Where are you? Are you still with C?*

Mom: *Honey, I'm worried. Call me.*

Ben: *Hey, you wanna meet at Chucks tonight?*

Terra: *Everyone's going nuts. Including Z, C's not answering either!*

Shelley: *Oh good God I just heard from Billy. Call me when you can talk.*

She sent a group text to her parents, Terra and Shelley. *I'm safe. Going to sleep talk tomorrow.*

To Ben: *Not back yet.*

Then put it on silent and slipped naked beneath the sheets, with her hair still damp.

It felt empty. She'd spent one night with him. So how could she miss his arm curled around her waist, her back against his chest? His nose in her hair. How could she need his warmth, his smell, his hard, scarred body? And how could she fall for someone who was in love with a ghost?

Fuck her life.

* * *

The following morning, a sliver broke through the black-out drapes, piercing the floor like Carmine's somnolent words had pierced her heart.

Unable to sleep, she finally gave up and threw open the curtains. The specter of a snowcapped Mount Shasta commanded the landscape. Though majestic, it wasn't the Golden Gate Bridge, or any of the other landmarks she longed for. She picked up her phone and booked a flight home.

It wasn't hard to convince Billy why she needed to leave.

"I have to get back to work," she said, nibbling on a slice of bacon, hiding her swollen, cried-out eyes behind cheap Jackie O sunglasses she'd bought at the small hotel gift shop. "Unfortunately bills don't pay themselves and I don't make money unless I sell."

"I hear you, kiddo, but if you want, Badger can drive you. Save you the airfare."

"It's okay, it's not that much. I'm grateful but I know you all need to deal with your stuff here and I'm just in the way." And she had a need to be with people who loved her.

"Understood. You've been through it too. Need a ride to the airport?"

She took a sip of her coffee, her second of the morning. "I'll Uber it."

"Had enough of us, eh?" His thick, black brow arched.

"Of course not...it's just..." She bit her lip to stop it from trembling. It's just that she needed space to cauterize her wounds.

Billy stopped chewing on his waffle and regarded her intently. It was a moment before he spoke and when he did, his gruff voice carried concern. "What happened last night, when you were alone with him?"

Oof!

She breathed in deep, yet stealthily behind her cup. One would think having anguished over it all night, the reminder wouldn't hurt as much. One would be wrong. But she couldn't lie either. Even hidden behind her sunglasses Billy would see right through, and it didn't feel good anyway. She blinked until the threatening tears stopped, swallowed her masticated bacon, following it with another sip of coffee. Then pushed back from the table, dabbed at her mouth with a napkin, folded it, and neatly placed it back on her plate.

He never took those questioning cinnamon eyes off her, which were now weary and sad. Leaning in, she kissed his thinning crown.

"The truth happened, Billy." she said softly. "Thank you for everything. I'll guess I'll see you around."

Ten minutes later, she checked out of the hotel.

Chapter Twenty-Four

Two days later he woke up with it.

The same feeling he'd had the day Jaz and the rest of his squad got blown into nonexistence. A sense of anticipation—or as he now recognized it in twenty-twenty hindsight —disconnection.

He couldn't pin it then, thought it had been the disagreement he and Jaz had on how to proceed with their mission. He hadn't trusted the intel they'd gotten from a local. Jaz had.

He'd felt it again when his mom had her stroke. She'd stumbled on the stairs outside his apartment. Insisted she was fine—but that feeling. Thank fuck he'd listened to his intuition then and took her to the ER, in time for them to give her the right meds to reverse any damage done.

But today?

Staring at the faded gray ceiling, he had no sense of today.

Only that he needed out of this hospital.

"Aagh," he groaned as he inched into a sitting position, trying to ignore the marching band that had taken up residence in the lump in his skull. Perhaps that was the source of his feeling, or the dissipating effects of his dream.

Shit—his dream.

A shudder rumbled down his spine. Helen got eaten by a worm that popped out of the earth like that movie *Tremors*. It had terrified him as a kid. He'd tried to hold on to her, but she'd slipped away, calling his name. He was pretty sure he'd screamed hers.

He sat up, too damaged to do anything. It hurt to breathe, it hurt to move—damn, it hurt to think. He'd had no control over what they'd given him when he was admitted, but insisted they pull his IV earlier or he'd do it himself.

Couldn't deny he regretted it, but he wasn't going to become dependent.

Where the hell was Billy? Where the hell was she? He needed out. He needed her.

"What are you doing?" The grumpy nurse snapped as she entered his ward. They'd had an altercation earlier over the needle in his arm and the tube in his dick.

"Going home, away from that lovely attitude."

"Oh no, mister." She shook her head. The bun situated in her nape jiggled. "You have not been discharged. You are not getting your beat-up ass out of that bed."

"I have to take a piss."

"Well then, that's different. But there's a button next to your bed you're supposed to use to call for help. Your ribs are cracked, not your fingers. Next time, use them."

"Whatever," he grouched, waving her offer off to help him shuffle. Because shuffle was all he could manage, the muscles in his thighs screaming.

Oh, Jesus. Every step.

But no more fucking plastic tubes in his cock, thank you very much. It took a while, but he relieved his bladder, happy to note there was no blood in his urine. At least two of his organs still worked as they should.

When he was done, he exited the bathroom and hobbled towards his clothes.

"Wrong way, buddy." Nurse *Imawhoopyoass* blocked his passage. "Bed's that way."

"Not happening, going home. Pass my shoes, please?" He was afraid if he leaned forward to put them on his feet, he'd keep going until his skull connected with the ugly-ass gray vinyl floor. Another concussion wasn't on his agenda.

"Not happening," she mimicked him, planting her hands on her plump hips. "Bed, now! Do it."

He held a palm to his forehead. "Don't yell. My head hurts."

"I wasn't yelling, but that's exactly why you need to be back in bed. That thick, handsome skull needs to rest. You do know you got a knob the size of Idaho on it?"

Yeah, that too.

"Flattery ain't gonna work, babe. What I need is to go home."

And Helen.

Dammit, he needed Helen.

"Don't 'babe' me, I'm old enough to be your mother, for heaven's sake. Crawl back between the sheets, or I'll call for backup and we'll make you do it."

Carmine closed his eyes, and took a somewhat deep breath, because bruises and cracked ribs. Truth was, he could barely breathe, let alone walk. But it went against his nature to give her the pleasure of being right.

"You've got ten seconds."

"Fine!" he growled, wincing. "I'll do it, if you'll go away and leave me in peace."

Where was his team? They could jail-break him out, appropriate a goddam gurney and roll him to his car.

"I'm not going anywhere, *babe,*" she smirked, helping him lift his legs into the bed. "It's my job to not leave you in peace. Get used to it."

"Ungh," he groaned, collapsing back on his pillows, spent.

She adjusted them, then ensuring he was at optimum comfort, handed over the TV remote. "So you can catch up on General Hospital."

He rolled his eyes, but spared her a half smile.

"Sure you don't want anything stronger?" she asked, her tone a touch softer. "It's no fun suffering like that."

"Don't wanna be an opioid stat."

"I've got news for you, handsome. You're too ornery to be a stat. One more day isn't going to get you addicted. Why don't we give you a little something else to help you sleep, rest that brain and your body and we go from there, hmm?"

Sleep?

Yeah, he could do that.

"Oral only, no fucking penetration."

She chuckled pleasantly, showing white teeth against lovely chocolate skin. She was quite attractive when she smiled. "Okay, Prince Charming, you got it." Then she slunk out of his ward to get his meds. Leaving him with his lingering thoughts on oral and a gorgeous little tomato-head.

Where the hell was she?

* * *

He awoke hours later to a play-by-play of a Sharks game—SAP Center going nuts and knew at least his uncle was there. Billy was a rabid hockey fan. Prying open his working eye, a slo-mo replay of Hertl sneaking a puck past an unfortunate and stunned-looking goalie came into focus.

But he wasn't interested in that.

After rolling his head from one side to the other, it became clear what he was interested in, was nowhere to be seen. At least not in his room. Disappointment left him feeling deflated.

Billy shifted his head from the screen to look at him.

"Hey, son." he said, his fingers tapping at his phone. Scooting his rump out of the well-used hospital armchair, he closed the small distance separating them. "How ya doin'?"

"Where is she?" His voice sounded rusty. How long had he been asleep?

Billy opened his mouth to speak, but hesitated, closing it again, pushing out his lips like he did when he chose his words carefully. "She went home, son."

Home?

What. The fuck?

Carmine kept his breathing steady, yet there was a sharpness in his chest that he suspected had nothing to do with his cracked ribs. He closed his eyes. She left without saying goodbye?

Billy poured a cup of water from the plastic pitcher next to his bed, then pressed a button. The mechanics whirred softly as the bed raised to an upright position.

"How's she doing...she okay?" he finally asked after taking a sip and when he knew his voice wouldn't crack.

"Don't know, son. But she wanted to be with family."

Of course—couldn't blame her for that. He was fortunate to have his uncle with him. But that didn't mean he liked it. In fact, it pissed him the hell off. He needed her.

"When shit gets rough," he said, unable to keep the bitterness out of his tone.

His uncle's eyes narrowed, and he focused hard on him. "You're banged up, drugged up, and for that reason I'm gonna give you a pass on that comment. But don't be an unreasonable asshole, doin' her a disservice. She don't deserve that."

"Then why'd she run?"

"Run?" Billy's thick black brows rose an inch, wrinkling that impressive forehead. "You must not remember her dragging her filthy, dirt covered ass in behind myself and Alfie when we rescued you."

Fuck. How hard had he cracked his head? Now that Billy reminded him, a mushy picture formed. She'd kissed him, held him to her breast and he'd noted at the time how she'd looked. How could he forget that?

Fucking drugs. He hated them with a passion.

"This was right after she pulled a magic trick." Billy apparently wasn't done. "Got herself and another woman out of a cement fire-bunker buried deep, ripping her fingernail from its bed. We found them in the woods, son. Know what she said when we found her?"

"Uh..."

"'You gotta help me find him.'"

Damn.

"She didn't ask for a hot bath. She didn't ask for help with her finger, or to be taken to the nearest damn hospital. She said, *you gotta help me find him.*"

"Shit." He swallowed hard, duly chastised. "I'm a dick."

"Won't argue with that," Billy's tone softened. "But I will add 'injured' and 'medicated' to 'dick.'"

"I didn't know."

"No," Billy confirmed, then briefed him on the details.

"How's she doing?" Carmine repeated, unable to bring himself to ask the unfathomable.

"Physically, okay. She wasn't raped if that's what you're really asking, but emotionally—that's another question."

"What do you mean?"

"She spent time with you, and went in okay, but came out not okay."

A sinking feeling filled his chest as the stitches in his brow pulled. "She say why?"

"No, son."

"Where's my phone?"

"Destroyed."

"What?"

"Your computer too."

His stomach dropped. Damn.

"Badger's working on getting new ones."

"I need a sit-rep. Text everyone, tell them to be here in an hour."

"Did that when you woke up." Billy glanced at his watch. "They'll be here in twenty."

* * *

His men arrived first, and Thomas handed him his new phone. First thing he did was check all his incoming. Nothing from her, not even a text, he thumbed one of his own. *Missed your goodbye, Red.*

As it whooshed, Alfie trailed in, sporting a grin that raised his ears an inch higher on his skull. Carmine scrutinized the older Cadora, noting the glassy eyes, then swung his gaze to his team. Badger pulled in his lips then looked to the ceiling.

"Are you high, Alfie?"

"Heh heh," the old fart wheezed a cackle. To which everyone burst out laughing.

"As a fucking kite." Thomas emitted a noise that Carmine had come to know as his laugh. Like an engine turning over but not quite catching. "He pigged out on Bev's brownies."

"Heh heh. Gave me a boner," Alfie added, still grinning, and doing a couple lewd hip thrusts that sent his men over the edge.

He had to admit, it was funny, and cracked a grin.

At that point Torque swaggered in, chin tipping each of his men. Spotting Alfie, he fist-bumped the old man.

"Still got it, eh?"

"Heh heh."

That spawned another roar of hilarity. When they finally settled down and with the pleasantries over, Alfie took a seat in the armchair next to Billy while everyone else stood. Then things got serious.

"Reiterating Kai is ours," Torque demanded, seating his ass

against the windowsill, muscular arms crossed in front. "No negotiating about that."

"He's yours." Carmine agreed.

"And the women want no feds involved. They're worried they'll be deported. Irina said they wanted to come here for a reason. That reason still stands and none of them have family to go back to. They can't stay with us. The State finds out we're harboring illegals, we lose our permit to grow."

"We'll take Sokolov and the women back with us to the city. Vasily Melnikov will know what to do with them."

"As long as he treats them right."

"He will." Melnikov had a reputation. As head of the Russian mafia, he would. But he respected the man and he didn't mistreat the women in his stable.

"What about Kai's woman?" Carmine added.

"Marisol? She disappeared and so has her car. None of the women have heard from her, which I'm not digging."

"Think she was involved in the trafficking somehow?" Badger stepped forward. "She wasn't at the house when we raided."

"Not sure," Carmine returned. "Irina said there was a couple involved in scamming them. Could be her."

"She could also be dead," Thomas stated.

"Uh huh." Carmine grimaced as he shifted position, trying to relieve the pressure on his ribs. "But until I know she is, I'm presuming she's involved somehow. Could be the brunette in the video." He looked at Torque. "You got a last name for her?"

"Price. Lives in Redding but I don't have an address."

He nodded, then caught Badger's eyes. "On it, Boss," his man acknowledged. He was grateful his men could read his mind. All this thinking was making his head pound.

"Is there anything else?"

Torques jaw rippled a moment before he answered. "We haven't found the rest of Hunter yet."

Carmine's stomach turned. "No disrespect, but plenty of bear in the woods looking for MREs. Ugly, but an easy way to dispose of a body."

"Ahead of you, Niccoterra. Got brothers doing just that. Just don't mention it to Candy. She don't need to know her man could be bear scat."

"Goes without saying." Carmine rubbed his temple, then dropped his eyes to his new phone. No new notifications. Her silence shouldn't piss him off, but it did.

No.

If he really analyzed it, he was hurt. Felt blown off like a high school prank date.

"What you want us to do next boss?" Thomas asked, recapturing his attention.

"Get Sokolov to Melnikov along with video of the ranger's station, the cells they kept the women in, the hole, all of it. I want him to get a full picture. Alfie?"

"Eh?"

"You bring your caddie?"

Alfie cackled again. "How you think we got da weapons here?" The man was too shrunken to drive as he couldn't see over the dash, but Alfie's 1973 Caddie was legendary. Black and as big as a boat, it came with a chauffeur and a false bottom in its trunk. That false bottom usually carried a shoulder-mounted grenade launcher among other weapons.

"Billy and I will take two of the women. Alfie can take the rest." He caught Torques eyes. "You good with that?"

"Fucking perfect."

"Good." He looked at his men. "Now get your asses out of my room. Tomorrow you break me out of this place."

After he made arrangements with Billy to collect him in the morning, Torque was the last to move.

Carmine caught his eye. "A moment?"

The biker nodded. Then stopped at the side of his bed. When the door closed behind Alfie, the dude looked at him.

"Just wanted to say the club's help is appreciated."

Torque paused before he spoke like he was weighing his words. "It goes both ways." His lips pulled back in a grimace. "Do your end, we'll do ours."

"Excellent." Carmine swallowed. What he needed to say was a long time coming. "What happened in the past..."

"As much as this fucking pains me to say," Torque cut him off, "I'm not gonna lie, it hurt. But once I cleared my head, I came to the uncomfortable realization it wasn't your fault. It wasn't Lilly's either. *I* fucked up. I acknowledge that and I've lived with it. Letting her go was close to the worst thing I've ever done. But it *was* on me."

The weight of Torque's acknowledgment hung heavy in the air and several beats passed as the two men looked at each other. He let it settle, then in an attempt to lighten the atmosphere, Carmine joked, "You suggesting I was the rebound fuck?'

Torque cracked a grin. "Ain't suggesting, motherfucker. But I'd say it was more like a revenge fuck."

Carmine scoffed. Truth be told, he *was* the revenge fuck and had no illusions about it at the time. He'd been grieving Jaz, going through his own shit, and nailed every female willing just to feel alive. Lilly's agenda was her own thing. At the time he didn't question it, or her.

"Let's move past that, yeah?" Torque said. "Water under the bridge."

He nodded. "Done."

"When was the...last time you saw her?" The slight hesitation carried a lot of regret, and he realized the dude maybe wasn't quite over her. He compared it to losing Jaz and didn't know which was worse: losing someone living, or someone dead.

"Not in a long while."

"Her old man is dying."

This wasn't news. He'd already guessed it, but let Torque continue. "Snake hasn't told her."

"That's messed up, but it's between them."

"It is. There are things I'm not willing to get into about what went down, but their pride is roadblocking both from reaching out, and he don't have much time. Lilly should know."

Carmine contemplated that for a moment. "Perfect time for you to reach out."

"Don't know where she is."

"I can help with that."

The biker blinked, looked down, then nodded. Gratitude flickered in his eyes.

"You know," he finally said, tucking his thumbs into his pockets. "For an ugly fucker, you're not a terrible human. Still don't mean I like you."

Carmine smirked. "Same, asshole."

"I'll be in touch." Torque tipped his chin, then left.

When the door clicked shut behind him, Carmine laid his head back on his pillow and sighed. He hoped things worked out for them. He checked his phone again. Nothing.

Hell, he hoped things worked out for himself.

Chapter Twenty-Five

Vasily's office was situated on the thirtieth floor in downtown San Francisco. It was a clear day, and Carmine could see all the way to an approaching fog bank out in the Pacific. He stepped back from the wall-to-ceiling glass window framing the bay and turned to watch the small gathering.

Vasily, along with the five women, sat at a large U-shaped couch and were deep in conversation. They seemed relaxed, at ease with him, but most of all relieved. A couple were even smiling. This was good.

Before long, the man stood and sauntered towards him and his uncle, stone-faced. He leaned his ass against a large glass desk, arms folded across a crisp, white button-down, Ferragamos crossed at the ankles.

"I have an apartment I can house them in, and they'll be okay for now until I can make better arrangements. You did right by bringing them to me. They're not comfortable dealing with the government and I can help."

Sweet relief flowed through Carmine at handing over responsibility of the women. At handing over Viktor? Well that was another story, but he had enough on his plate, and this was more the crime boss's area of expertise. Viktor and the deceased Boris had encroached on his territory, violated his beliefs and he knew Vasily wasn't one to let it stand. He'd counted on that.

"Thank you," he said.

"You ain't gonna exploit 'em?" Billy asked, scrutinizing Vasily through narrowed eyes from his position on the dark leather couch opposite. "Because I made a promise and I intend to make sure that promise is kept."

"I don't exploit women," Vasily said, meeting Billy's hot cinnamon gaze with his own chilly pewter one. "I give them choices. What they do is up to them. If they choose to work for me directly, for a small percentage I house them, feed them, protect them and they get medical."

"By directly you mean hooking?"

"If you want to put it that way, yes. But it's their choice. They mentioned they came here to be nannies. Some of my women are in need of childcare, I can make it so it's good for everyone. If they choose to go home, I can help with that too."

"Also for a small fee?"

"I'm a cold asshole most of the time, Mr. Niccoterra. But these women have been through it. I'm not inclined to make a profit off helping them. I'm not my brother."

"Hmm," Billy grunted, eyeing him skeptically.

"And since we're talking about my brother, let me take this opportunity to apologize for Dean's actions." Vasily pushed away from the desk and stuck both hands in his Brooks Brothers pockets. "What he and Boris did to you and Shelley was beyond the pale. I don't run the operation the same way."

"My nephew doesn't think you do and just this once, because I trust him, I'm gonna give you the chance to prove yourself. If I hear otherwise, you know I ain't gonna be happy."

"I respect that. We can work well together if we put the past behind us. I think you and I have more in common than most people would understand. I don't like scum, and from what I understand, neither do you."

Billy grunted again but said nothing further.

At that point Vasily caught Carmine's eye. "Regarding our other matter, Viktor. I'm gonna give him a day to stew before I interrogate."

"Appreciate it," Carmine returned, then reached out and held out his hand. "I'll be in touch."

Vasily took it, then shook his uncle's as well and escorted them across the highly-polished oak floors laid with soft white rugs. They said goodbye to the girls and Irina gave him a clumsy kiss on the cheek. "You kept promise, *Karamine*. I...we," she indicated all the women, "never forget you."

"I'll never forget you ladies either. Take care of yourselves."

As the door shut behind them, they stepped to the elevator. Billy, pushing the 'down' button, said, "Well, that went better than I thought. Perhaps too well. Sure you can trust him to do right by those women?"

Carmine cocked an eyebrow, wincing when the forgotten stitches above his eye stung.

"My experience with the Russians ain't as dandy as yours," Billy qualified.

"Nope."

"I don't know enough about that fucker."

Indeed, Vasily was an enigma. He'd taken over from his brother, Dean who was currently rotting in a federal prison for kidnapping Shelley and putting a hit on Billy. But ten years ago Vasily had disappeared and his whereabouts for those ten years before he resurfaced were suspect. Carmine had done a deep search on the man. Every detail was generic. Wouldn't look like it to the average citizen, but he'd seen enough whitewashed personas for it to raise flags. Like it had been authored and not actually lived. To his knowledge, Vasily was not a whitewashed individual. Far from it. But he'd kept this knowledge to himself, thinking there'd be a time when he could use it to his advantage.

"He's their best option. He speaks their language and has connections I wish I had."

Billy made a noise.

"Do you really trust me, Uncle, or was that just blabbermouthing for his benefit?"

"You know I do, son. It's just that you might not be thinking straight right now."

He definitely wasn't, he'd give Billy that. Besides every part of his body hurting, complete and total radio silence from one *particular* woman had him fucked up like a soup sandwich. The time they'd spent together wasn't much, but he'd gotten a good sense of her. Girl wasn't the quiet type, *so what the fuck?*

They rode the elevator down to the underground garage, then continued in silence as they walked to the Jeep. Billy drove through the mid-afternoon city traffic, cursing at an Uber driver who cut in front of him. They parked in their own underground garage, and as Carmine reached for what was left of his bag, Billy stopped him. "Let me get that for you son."

"Hmm," he grunted in appreciation.

They took the elevator instead of the usual stairs, for which he was grateful as well. Sitting for hours on the drive down had caused his muscles to stiffen and he could barely walk the short distance to his apartment.

"You gonna be okay alone?" Billy asked, pausing outside his apartment door. "You want me to camp in your spare?"

"Fuck, no. Your snoring is the stuff they make horror movies from."

"Up yours, you little shit," Billy tossed him the middle as he continued up the one floor of stairs to his home. "I'll check on you tomorrow."

"Make it late tomorrow."

Because he needed to sleep for like a week. He unlocked the front door and stepped inside. They'd bought this building together after he'd been discharged from the army and spent time together fixing it up. His uncle had the penthouse as he'd fronted the most money, but Carmine liked his unit. Two bedrooms, two bathrooms, with a large balcony and views of both bridges. Rent from their other tenants covered the mortgage and the bakery did well. A good investment, and with his own business, he had plenty of cash.

He shouldn't want for anything.

But he did, and he hadn't realized it until lately. A warm, particular, sexy little woman in his bed.

Shuffling across hardwood floors to his bedroom, he dropped his bag and sat on the edge of his king-sized bed.

Disconnected.

He reached into his back pocket and pulled out his new phone, stared at it before dropping his head in frustration. Why didn't she answer?

Red? I miss you.

He scrolled further down. Found Verity's number. *She home?*

Her response didn't come immediately. While waiting, he undressed. In his medicine cabinet, he had a sleeping aid. After he hit the light switch in the bathroom, he turned and stopped short. His reflection shocked him.

Jesus, no wonder he hurt so bad!

Purplish-black bruises covered fifty percent of his torso and upper thighs. The swelling on his eye had receded, thanks to the ice he'd packed all day, but that too had turned black and was over-scored with stitches and the butterfly bandage on his cheekbone.

He sucked down two pills, drank water straight from the faucet, took a quick shower, then crawled between his empty sheets.

Verity's reply had come in. *According to GPS on car she is. You want me to remove it?* For the first time all day he felt somewhat okay. *Nope*, he responded. *I'll get to it.*

That bodacious little badass could try to avoid him, but he intended to catch up with her. Find out what her problem was. As he eased back onto his bed, staring at the crown molding around his ceiling.

When he'd had her, something had happened. A switch had flipped, a faucet had turned on, a fucking dam broke. Whatever metaphor worked. Though truthfully, it had started before. When they'd first met. The moment he'd kissed her, it had solidified. But having had her only meant he wanted more, left him in a situation that was unsatisfactory.

And that needed fixing ASAP.

Chapter Twenty-Six

Anna put her on bereavement leave. Which was fine as all she did the first day back was sleep and cry and ignore her phone anyway. After that she spent the next two days ignoring her phone and scouring all the known pawn shops in the city and some on the peninsula.

Nada.

Day four, she flew back to Redding for Cody and Hunter's funerals and cried some more. Torque invited her back to the clubhouse for the wake, but she declined. Instead, while waiting for her return flight, she finally found her courage to read his texts.

Missed your goodbye, Red.

Red?

I miss you.

What the fuck, woman?

Do I need to beg?

Okay, You're a five percenter. I get it.

The last text hurt. Because she missed him too. Desperately. But could she shift to the ninety-five side? Not as a lover, but as a friend? There was only one way to find out. And that's how she found herself on the first half of day six making Nana's chicken soup.

At 2 that afternoon, she stood at his doorstep, elbow ready to press his buzzer. She hesitated, fast losing her courage. Maybe she'd just leave the soup and her cousin's fabulous rosemary ciabatta bread outside his door and text him it was there. It was a start, right? But she'd barely finished the thought when Carmine's front door sprung open.

"Yes?" A tall, lean, cool-as-a-cucumber Barbie-like blonde with frosty blue eyes, but minus the disproportionately large boobs blocked his doorway. Though she wasn't currently dressed in a white lab coat or scrubs, it only took a second for her to place her face. The beautiful, yet chilly doctor from the hospital when Brady got shot.

How the hell had she known Helen was there? Did he have cameras?

"Oh...okay." Helen barely breathed, her heart stuttering to a stop as she took in the woman's minuscule clothing. "Uh...hi." This wasn't what she expected, or planned for, though in hindsight, it's exactly what she should've expected.

"Can I help you?" the blonde asked.

Her white denim shorts were so short, you could almost read her nether-lips, and her pink crocheted cropped top stopped just below her ribcage showing off a naked belly. Clearly official doctor-patient business wasn't on the agenda—unless it was *sexy* doctor-patient business. Helen was grateful that except for taste-testing Nana's soup, she hadn't eaten yet.

"I'm sorry." She swallowed. "I didn't mean to intrude, I just brought this for...for him. I thought he might not want...or be able to cook, you know, for himself. I didn't realize he'd be...busy."

The blonde made no effort to take the items she held out. Instead, looked down at Helen, which wasn't hard to do, she was that much taller.

"Quite the little feeder, aren't you?"

"Excuse me...the what?"

"Feed...er," the blonde re-iterated. "Wasn't it you that brought him food at the hospital when his employee got shot?"

Ugh.

"Yeah, that was me, and yes, I guess I am." Helen wrinkled her nose and looked down to where her little Fiat was parked, wishing she could teleport herself into the driver's seat. Feeding people was her thing, and she wasn't going to apologize for it, especially not to this one.

"Well, um." She brought her attention back to the items she held. "Okay, I guess I'll just leave this here."

Knees bent, she rested on her haunches, butt to heels. Sliding the pot inside the threshold, she placed the brown paper bag with the bread on top.

"Who are you talking to, Jules?" Carmine asked from somewhere deep inside his apartment.

Helen looked between the blonde's long, malnourished legs and cast her eyes over dark wood floors, past the corner of an open-plan kitchen down a hall. Two naked feet, which led to two naked knees appeared in her sightline. First her mouth went dry, then her throat closed tight.

Carmine's dark curls glistened with moisture as he finger-combed them back out of his face. The movement made a black towel wrapped low around his waist slip. He grabbed it before it dropped, but it was clear he was naked underneath. She'd caught a glimpse of large, serious looking bruises staining his skin and his happy trail. The one she'd had her fingers in just a few days ago.

Had this one's fingers been entangled in that happy trail too? Actually, never mind—she didn't want to know.

Jules side stepped and opened his front door further, facilitating his view of Helen's still crouched form. Their eyes clashed. His widened a fraction, then little furrows formed between his brows.

"Helen." There was a definite note of surprise in his voice, along with a slight crack.

"I...uh..." Her throat constricted painfully, and his Adam's apple bobbed in a way that suggested he was having difficulty digesting the knowledge she was there.

Clearly, she'd made a mistake. That had become glaringly obvious as she pushed off her haunches and rose. She couldn't do it. She couldn't want him as much as she did and share him. It just wasn't going to happen.

"I made soup for you," she said softly, tucking her hair behind her ear while not looking at either of them. Disappointment and heartache burrowed a hole through her stomach into her chest, which surely showed on her face but was not for their personal entertainment.

"Enjoy," she said and spun on her heel. This man wasn't hers, never would be, and what happened in Sawmill would stay there. The end.

"Helen, wait!"

She didn't want to stop, but her imbecilic feet halted before she reached the stairs no matter how much her brain told them to keep moving.

He followed her outside, hands on his hips, looking badass as all get out and just as beautiful. In spite of his bruises which looked even starker in the cold light of day. It was horrifying to see what they'd done to him. Just how much punishment he'd taken.

"Just wait for a fucking second."

"I've got to go."

"One minute."

To hear what? Nothing good apparently judging by his tone.

But he was so commanding, like a Roman general in half a toga, and with those striking green eyes trained on her, she had no choice.

Without looking directly at him, she asked, "What do you want?"

"Come inside," he said.

She shook her head and mouthed *No*.

Not while she *was still in there.*

"You left without saying goodbye." Those perfectly sculpted lips flattened in displeasure. "With no explanation. I want one."

"I did give an explanation."

"To my uncle. Not to me. You blew me off, Helen. I want to know why."

A sad scoff escaped as she picked at the strap on her purse. "I was trying to fix that. I brought you my Nana's chicken soup. And if you knew anything about my Nana and her cooking, you'd surmise after eating it that I'm not blowing you off. But you don't, so I can't blame you for thinking that."

He processed that for a minute, his face solemn. "Why, Red?"

"Why was I trying to fix it?"

He opened his mouth to speak, but the blonde poked her head out from behind him, carrying a large brown bag, laid a hand on his shoulder and kissed his cheek. She at least had the decency to put on a light sweater that covered her belly. "Gonna head out, honey. I'll check in with you later."

He seemed to tense a little at her touch, and the good news was he didn't lean into her kiss, or even turn his head when he answered. Instead he kept his eyes solid on Helen. "Thanks Jules."

"No problem, sweetie."

Jules cast her eyes to Helen, something playing in them as she passed by that wasn't quite friendly, but not overtly rude either. More curious, or protective maybe.

She couldn't tell what he was thinking though while he watched her from the top of the stairs, but his mood stayed dark.

"Would you please come inside? I'm not dressed to have this conversation out in the open." Indeed, he had chill bumps all over his torso from the cool San Francisco breeze, and to further prove his point, his nipples were puckered. As she didn't want him to catch pneumonia, she relented.

"All right, but I can't stay long."

He stepped aside as she ascended the stairs again then followed her in and closed the door behind them. The slow click as the lock engaged seemed super loud over the muted television noises coming from his bedroom. What were they doing in there and why was he only wearing a towel?

Her soup was still where she left it. She retrieved it, mostly so she could avoid his eyes. His apartment was clean and masculine, like him. Also larger than she expected. Soft dove gray walls, with sleek furnishings and another large TV mounted opposite his couch. What stood out was a collage of individually framed black and white photos. She focused on one, then another, and then another.

Jaz was in them.

All of them.

Her heart broke a little more. It didn't matter where he was, who he was with, the woman he'd loved would always be there.

Helen believed in signs. If the blonde's presence hadn't slapped her in the forehead, this did. She'd bet her only pair of Jimmy Choos the beautiful Jaz was also next to his bed, though she certainly didn't want to think about that.

There was only so much in-your-face hurtful reality her heart could take, and her eyes burned at the reminder. But she was done shedding tears.

Carefully, she placed the soup on his polished concrete counter and turned. He'd come up behind her and was only inches away. Close enough she felt his warmth, and anger for that matter, radiating across the small distance separating them. It also gave her a close up view of the dark patches defiling his chest. They were starting to change color, from purplish black to blueish green.

She hadn't intended to touch him, yet her fingers found themselves brushing his skin, wanting to ease his pain.

"I'm sorry they hurt you," she said, catching his eyes.

He hissed as they slid across his warm skin and silky chest hair.

"Oh." She jerked her hand away. "Sorry."

But he caught it mid-snatch, then uncurled her fingers and placed it flat on his chest right over his thumping heart. His palm over hers, he kept it locked in place, his skin so warm beneath her hand. And just for a beat, the expression in his eyes softened before he closed them.

"You're confusing me, Carmine."

His nostrils flared before he opened them again. She searched, looking deep for a clue to what really computed in that brain, getting no read whatsoever, only that he was struggling with his anger.

"I'm confusing you?" he scoffed. "You should be in *my* head. You leave without saying goodbye, you ignore me, then show up on my doorstep with food that I didn't ask for. What I asked for Helen, is an explanation. What am I supposed to think?"

"Oh, wow, okay." She balked at his tone and tried to yank her hand from his chest. He pressed harder against it, curling his fingers around hers. "There's no need to be a jerk. And by the way, I don't appreciate you lumping me in with your weird ones."

"Really?" His brows raised in question while he continued to glare at her. "How would you describe your behavior?"

"There are a number of ways I would describe it, but you've already made up your mind, haven't you? This was a mistake. I'm sorry I came." Then she looked down at the towel. Suddenly it all became clear. Jules and her skinny, long-as-a-racehorse legs aside, his under-the-influence, yet honest utterance in the hospital, the photos on his wall and his laptop only confirmed what she already knew. She couldn't do it.

"Actually, um...no. No. I'm not sorry."

He blinked, then brought his brows together. "What the hell does that mean?"

"It doesn't matter."

"For the love of Christ, Helen, it does fucking matter," he

yelled, then looked away and shook his head. "This about Jules? You're questioning why she was here?"

Yes, she was, though it wasn't her place. And she really didn't want to know.

"You have every right to have anyone you want in your apartment, how you want. In a towel...or...or naked or whatever. That's really none of my business, is it? And I know that, and I get it, so there's no need for you to get so angry."

"Angry?" He exhaled hard. "I'll tell you what I'm angry about." He removed her hand from his chest, released it like he was throwing it away and took a step back. "You and me." He pointed at her, his temper flaring. "*We* went through something together. Something bad. And you left when I was out of it in a fucking hospital bed. I wake up, you're not there, had no clue where you were. Had to hear it from my uncle. You left me hanging, Red, and you've got the balls to question why Jules was here?"

She cleared her throat, then thrust her chin up. "I had my reasons for leaving."

"*What* reasons?" He closed the distance between them, forcing her against the counter, but still leaving a space between. The heat of his anger was a furnace, burning her, but there was another layer in his voice. Something that sounded like...desperation? But what she knew about him, he wasn't a man to get desperate.

"What reasons, Helen?" he repeated, lower this time. "Give me that at least."

Her eyes went to the side, landing on the photo of Jaz. A timely reminder of why she'd run. Why couldn't she just say it? Nothing could be harder than being down that pit and not knowing where he was? But—

"I can't...I...I just wanted to bring you soup, to let you know I was thinking about you. And I've done that, so I'm going to go." Before she allowed her emotions to get ahead of her, and she burst into tears, because wouldn't that be wonderful.

"You were thinking about me," he said sarcastically.

"I was."

"Great, because it sure as fuck didn't feel like it."

"You can be as sarcastic as you want, or believe whatever you want, Carmine." She scooted out from between him and the counter and put distance between them because it physically hurt being so close. She wanted to touch him, soothe him, but at what cost? "You think I don't care? You're wrong." A rogue tear rolled down her cheek. She ignored it, pretended it wasn't there. "So very wrong. But look around you, Carmine. Look inside your heart, inside your dreams, look at your walls, your computer, look *everywhere*. I'm not sure what it is you're hoping to hear from me, but until you're ready to let her go...I can't...I can't."

"Can't what?"

Compete with a ghost.

"Allow myself to fall any harder for you."

"What?" He seemed to stagger at her words and caught himself by gripping the counter. "What did you say?"

"I wish you nothing but the best. Enjoy your soup. There's no need to return the pot."

This time she kept going, because she was too afraid to hear what she couldn't hear. "Red, don't fucking leave!"

She pushed through his door and jogged down the stairs to the street. The tears were falling freely, but he would not see her wipe them away.

The further she got, the more her vision blurred, and she slipped on the last step, one foot sliding forward. But she saved herself by grabbing onto the handrail, though not before her butt hit the brick.

"Helen, dammit!"

She pulled herself up and continued on until she reached her car half a block down. Beeping the locks open, she stumbled in, slammed the door and relocked it. By some miracle, she stuck the key into the ignition on the first try and started the engine. Not even waiting for a gap, she darted into traffic and didn't look behind her, not wanting to see if he'd followed her down.

Or to be more precise, if he hadn't.

Because that would be intolerable.

Chapter Twenty-Seven

B ecause he'd promised his mother, he booked a flight to Hawaii.

But not before he sat on his couch eating her soup and replaying every word she'd said. Over and over. And Over.

Allow myself to fall any harder for you.

He was fucking this up and he couldn't afford to. His future depended on it.

By divine intervention or just dumb luck he'd found an out-of-the-way beachfront Airbnb—a last minute cancellation on the other side of Diamond Head, far from the human hustle of Waikiki. Blocked out seven days to heal. Seven days of sun and ocean—to decompress, get strong. Clear his head.

Should've been idyllic, except for that aching, empty chasm in his chest the size of the crater behind him that wouldn't go away. No matter how much he rubbed the spot over his heart, the gnawing ever-present sensation stuck to his ribs.

He missed her.

It was as basic as that.

Helen.

He missed *her*.

After Jaz died, he'd gone a little crazy. Trying to find ways to deal with her loss he'd done everything to keep her alive, to hold onto everything her. To avoid that sense of disloyalty that pervaded his every cell to the very core if he found another woman even slightly attractive. His shrink called it survivor's guilt. Sex was different. He didn't feel anything for them, like most males, he could separate his dick from his heart. But not with Helen.

The cold hard truth was, Jazz was gone. And she'd never been a selfish person—one of the things he'd loved about her. She wouldn't want him to lose out on someone worthy. And if he didn't get his shit sorted, he would.

He'd lose his Red before he even got started. His obnoxiously beautiful tomato head had wisely called him on it. Though it'd taken him a minute to figure out what she'd said before she ran out on him.

Hence the reason he was here. Seven hundred and sixty-one feet above sea level. Forearms planted on his knees, hands hanging loose between them—admiring the sapphire splendor of the Pacific spread out before him.

He and Jazz had come here after they'd first begun. Two horn-dog army grunts fucking like monkeys, swimming, surfing—generally in that order, but the last day they'd raced each other up the crater. He'd won, but only by a few steps. Jaz proclaiming she'd *let* him in order to save his ego. He chuckled at how she'd ribbed him. "You're getting slow, soldier. Must be all the jungle sex making your legs wobbly."

Because of Helen, the memory wasn't accompanied with any of the usual chest tightening cramps they so often came with. It was accompanied with fondness. Like what had happened at the cabin when they'd found Cody and Helen had asked about his dead. Somehow, being with her made it tolerable.

Perhaps her whacky theory had merit, that he still had a purpose. The divine hadn't pulled his string that day because it had been to meet Helen and save those girls. And in the process, he'd fallen for her.

How could he give that up?

Dammit—he squeezed his eyes shut.

He couldn't.

A lump in his throat that had seemed ever present since she'd run out of his apartment thickened, and he swallowed hard.

On the other hand, his life was dangerous. Full of seedy fuckers who committed seedier acts. Cleaning up after, or hunting stupid, irresponsible assholes and the shit stain that left on his soul wasn't conducive to maintaining a healthy relationship. If his shrink was right, which he'd refused to believe until this moment, he'd surmised his career choice was deliberate and meant to keep women on the dark side emotionally. To lessen the risk of falling for another. It had worked—until now. Until Red had crawled beneath his skin and burrowed deep, consuming him.

If he wasn't a selfish man, he'd admit Helen was better off without the stench of that shit stain defiling her pretty presence— yet she made him clean again. He dragged a finger over his eyes and pinched the bridge of his nose, unsurprised to find some moisture pooling in the corners.

But he *was* a selfish man, and he wasn't better off without her.

"Need you in my life, Red," he murmured. "You're not getting away."

He stood and took a drink of icy water from his thermal flask. Today was his last full day before returning to San Francisco. He was going to try to enjoy what was left of it.

He took the first step of the return journey when the breeze hit a lull and the air went eerily still.

It's time to move on, soldier. Don't fuck it up.

Goosebumps exploded over his skin while the hair at the back of his neck stood ramrod straight. Those words were not in his head. They rang loud and clear—a tuning fork displacing the airwaves around him. He spun around, eyes scanning the rim of the crater, the bushes, then the stairs, searching.

There was nobody.

Not even a bird.

Not even a damn cricket.

* * *

Later, outside on the flower-drenched patio, he sipped from his beer bottle and watched the waves break, his nostrils filled with the salty air. A spectacular palette of oranges and pinks colored the lower half of the sky when a tiny splash of white off to the side caught his eye.

He wouldn't ordinarily have paid attention, as his field of vision was dominated by an overgrown pink hibiscus and wild plumerias, but for some reason it drew his eye—a single, tiny star-shaped blossom on a bush ten feet away. He got up to examine it.

Jasmine flowering season was long past.

"No fucking way," he murmured, shaking his head. Not daring to blink, he was afraid it would disappear if he looked away. It didn't. He was compelled to pick it and sniff its gentle scent.

"Hit me over the head, why don't you, babe."

That's what it took, soldier.

Grabbing his beer, he walked down a short, shell and gravel path, across the warm sand to the water's edge. He sat, knees up, arms draped over them twirling the blossom between his fingers until the tide peaked and turned, and the moon played peek-a-boo on the horizon. At last he was ready.

"Lima Charlie, babe," he whispered into the wind, shoving his long-empty bottle into the sand and getting to his feet. *Message received.*

The water was refreshing around his ankles after the warm, humid air. He kissed the blossom and drew in its fading scent one last time.

"I'll see you in paradise, Sargent Jasmine Hyde. Rest in peace."

Then he dropped it, holding it in his gaze until it disappeared in the frothy foam of the gentle waves. He stood at attention, saluted, then retrieved the empty beer bottle and walked back slowly to the house, breathing easier, and with a small measure of peace for the first time in three years.

Since that day his life irreversibly changed.

Onward, soldier. It's all good.

"Roger that," he whispered.

His phone rang in his pocket and he answered without checking the caller ID.

"Yo."

"I hear you're looking for something I might have," Vasily said.

Chapter Twenty-Eight

Helen finished her shift at Provocative acknowledging it had been the longest, horriblest of weeks. One which she chose not to participate in Karaoke night, despite both Terra and Shelley egging her to go. Somehow the thrill had gone, to quote the fabulous B.B. King. But hey, such was heartbreak. One had to deal or die, right?

She parked, grabbed her grocery bags and schlepped to her door. She gave it the necessary shove, then having locked the deadbolt behind her, her fingers lingered on the sliding bolt. Out of defiance, she refused to lock it. Perhaps she'd ask Petey to remove it. The threat was no longer, and the constant reminder hurt too much.

After stashing her groceries, changing into sweats and putting away her shoes, she was about to drown herself in wine and dive into Netflix when her door knocker sounded. She sighed, contemplating not opening to whomever was on the other side.

Nevertheless, she stepped up to her peephole. Her head jerked back when she recognized the faded jeans fitted to a very shapely butt and the back-to-back skulls of a Double RMC cut.

"Hey," she said, opening the door a crack and trying to sound normal, like outlaw bikers showed up at her door every other day.

"Hey yourself." He turned and smiled, setting those blue eyes twinkling. "What's up, Trouble?"

"Um...what are you doing here?"

"Don't look so worried," he chuckled. "I'm not here to tread on toes. I got something for you. Wanted to give it to you after the funeral, but you left 'fore I could." He dug into his cut and pulled out a white envelope from an inside pocket. "Just rode into town and wasn't sure you'd be home, but thought I'd give it a try."

"Well, you got lucky. I am home." She smiled. Though she had to wonder how he knew where she lived. Probably Candy, she guessed. Regardless, she stepped out of the way and invited him in. "What is it?"

"Niccoterra here?" he said by way of an answer, looking around her living room.

Unfortunately, not. "Uh, no. I haven't heard from him."

"Hmm," he grunted, then handed her the envelope. "Open it."

It was fat and reasonably heavy. She dug a nail under the flap and tore it open, then gasped. There was a wad of hundred-dollar bills stuffed inside.

"What's this?"

"Some of it's the money Cody stole from you. Candy wanted you to have it back. And there's a little extra in there from the club for helping us out with the password."

More than a little extra by the looks of things. "Are you serious right now?" Her mouth dropped open. "You rode all the way from Sawmill to give me this?"

"Well, I was coming for something else, figured I'd kill two birds."

"I don't know what to say."

"Don't need to say anything." He grinned. "Except maybe offer me a drink."

"Ohmigod, of course. I'm so rude. You want coffee, wine?"

"You got beer?"

She nodded, then showed him into her little kitchen and opened her fridge. Pulled out a bottle of IPA from a local micro-brewery and handed it to him.

"So what was this other thing you were here for?"

"A girl." He removed a pocket-knife from inside of his cut and used a notch in it to pop the top.

"How did that go?"

"It hasn't." He sighed and scraped his hand over his short beard before taking a long pull on his beer and tossing the top into her garbage can. It was then she noticed how road-weary he looked. Tension lines fanned from his eyes and there was a fatigued shadow in them. Five hours in traffic on a big, badass Harley would do that to any man. "I haven't seen her yet," he continued. "Planning on it tomorrow."

"Well, I can tell you're exhausted. Where are you spending the night, Torque?"

"The nearest motel. Got any ideas?"

"Yes." Considering what he'd just done for her, she felt it only appropriate. "My couch, if you want." Anyway, it wasn't like she had a man in her life to worry about getting jealous or anything, right?

"Like I said, don't wanna step on anyone's toes, Trouble. Niccoterra and I just made our peace and I'm not gonna be the one to fuck that up."

"There are no toes to step on, Torque. We're not together."

His eyebrows raised. "Since when?"

Since forever, really. "Since Sawmill."

"Hmm." He grunted again, regarding her with narrowed eyes. "If that's true, dude's an idiot."

Dude's just still in love with a dead woman. But she kept her thoughts to herself. They had their own story and she didn't want to add to any bad feelings that may have lingered.

"Appreciate the offer. I am beat, and my first option didn't pan out and the thought of looking for a room right now doesn't appeal."

They got caught up on gossip while she sipped her wine and he finished his beer. After which he'd retrieved a few things from his saddlebags, then she let him use her shower. While he did, she pulled sheets and blankets from her hall closet and made up a bed on her couch. She fixed the coffeemaker for the next day and then when Torque was situated with the TV remote in hand, she took her own shower. By the time she got out and came to say good-night, he was asleep. One long leg draped on the couch, the other planted on the floor with the remote still clutched across his naked chest. She turned the TV off and tip-toed to her bedroom.

The envelope he'd given her lay on her bed, fat with cash. She counted, then re-counted just to be sure her eyes weren't playing ticks. Seven thousand dollars! Two from Candy and five from the club.

With images of hundred-dollar bills still stuck to the insides of her eyelids, she fell asleep. It felt like only five minutes later that someone was shooting off cannons.

Adrenaline surged through her system as she stumbled out of bed and into her living room. She was faced with Torque's naked, strong back yanking her door open. Of course, it didn't give the slightest resistance.

"What the fuck, motherfucker?" Torque growled, one arm stretched out in front of him while he held the knob with his other. The violence in his tone was scary as hell. But she couldn't see who he was talking to.

"You just had to, didn't you?"

Holy poop!

Carmine?

"You couldn't resist getting payback."

"You're a fool, Niccoterra."

"Lower the gun, Torque."

Gun?

Did he say gun?

"Not 'til you tell me what it is you want, asshole."

"You spin me a line with that shit about Lilly?"

"Wasn't shit."

Gun? What the holy hell?

"Then what was it?"

"You here about that?"

"You know why I'm here. Step out of my way."

"You gonna do her harm?"

"What?"

"Are. You. Going. To do her harm?"

"Of course not," Carmine snapped. "Though I may kill you."

There was silence. Torque's big form blocked the doorway and she could only assume they were glaring at each other. With testosterone setting the air on fire, what seemed like an eternity passed until something relented in Torque's posture.

"Jesus, you're an obstinate butthead." He moved and jerked the gun in a circular motion, waving Carmine in. "Get your stupid ass inside 'fore I shoot it full of holes. You need to wake the fucken neighbors?" Torque shoved his weapon into his jean's waistband. "She don't need that. Neither do I."

"What are you doing here?"

"Taking care of business."

"Helen's not business, Torque. Don't talk about her like that."

"You know, I really ought to kill you," the dude said, shutting her front door. "Put you out of your misery. Would be the kind thing to do. Good thing for you I'm not a kind man."

"What's happening?" Helen peered from behind her door, her heart in her throat. Both at the prospect of seeing Carmine's beautiful face, which she'd thought she'd never see at her door again, but also because he looked like he wanted to kill Torque for being at her door. "Why are you here?"

He seemed stunned as he took her in. His eyes dropped to her big, ugly tee shirt and then lower to her naked legs and she felt them rake and burn every inch of her skin. She swallowed.

A silence stretched between them until she couldn't stand it, looking between the two men. "Um, somebody tell me what the hell is going on and why you two are wanting to kill each other."

"I guess I'm asking the same question."

"Not that I answer to you." She folded her arms and stuck out her hip in her best *I don't give a crap attitude,* but inside was silently rejoicing he actually sounded a little jealous. "Torque needed a place to crash. I offered. Now it's your turn."

"You ran out on me."

"Oh?" She planted her hands on her hips. "That was a week ago and it does not give you the right to bang on my door and barge in here acting like...like this."

"I get that, but we need to talk."

He glanced at Torque, and the message was clear. Carmine wanted him to leave, but she wasn't going to ask him to. That was up to him.

"We can talk tomorrow. At a reasonable hour, like reasonable people."

"Fuck, Helen." He let out a long breath, almost like he was deflating. "I just got off a plane. Came straight here from the airport 'cause I had to see you. You want me on my knees?"

Torque sighed, then shook his head, but said nothing and walked into her room. A moment later the bathroom door shut.

She stared at Carmine, trying to gauge him as she took a seat on the arm of her couch, her hands steepled between her thighs, her hair covering her face. There was so much she wanted him to say, yet she was so afraid she wouldn't hear what she needed. One thing she'd learned was never to get her hopes up.

But before he could get started, or perhaps he was waiting for a cue from her, Torque returned.

"I'm out," he said, and stalked to the couch to retrieve his henley lying on the side table next to where she sat.

Helen looked up at him. "Torque, you don't need to leave."

"Trouble, no offense," he answered, pulling his shirt on along with his cut. "As much as I'd find it amusing as hell to watch this butthead get it handed to him, I got a feeling you wouldn't appreciate an audience. Words need to be said between you two, shit needs to be handled, and I got enough of my own problems to sort out." He snagged his helmet from the coffee table. "Wanna tell me where that nearest motel is?"

"You're not guaranteed to find anything at this hour," Carmine said.

"Got any *other* suggestions, motherfucker?"

Carmine dug into his pocket and tossed something that Toque snatched out the air. It was a key.

Was that his apartment key?

"Use my spare room," he confirmed while thumbing through his contacts, then typing something. "Just sent you my address and the alarm code."

Torque eyed him. "Not booby-trapped, is it?"

Carmine gave a charming, lopsided grimace which looked a lot like an apology and set those butterflies in her stomach a-fluttering. "Not today." Helen marveled at how dudes had their own secret code and so often were able to get over their issues with just a few curse words and insults.

Torque responded with his own smirk, accompanied by another head shake and started for the door.

"Torque?" Helen called, halting him in place. "Thank you, you know for…"

"No problem, Trouble. Catch you later." Then he leaned towards her and mussed up her hair like he would a little sister and murmured softly, "Don't let this asshole fuck it up, but throw him a bone, would ya?" Then he headed for her entrance nodding at Carmine as he passed.

The moment they were alone, the air changed. It became more dynamic––charged. Not like when he and Torque were about to

317

face off. That was full of male aggression and hormones. No, this was different. Heavier, emotional.

"You really have no right, you know," she said, getting to her feet. "I don't know what you think you're doing, but whatever it is, you have no right."

"I know that, Red." He took a step closer, something soft and pleading in his eyes. Something that made her heart crawl into her throat. Yet it was something that also made her very afraid.

"To use your words, I'm here to try and fix that."

"Assuming there's something to fix."

"Isn't there? You see, I'm really hoping there is."

"What is it you want?" she asked wearily. And by God, don't let it be that he was hoping they could be friends, for the sake of *their* friends. So things wouldn't be awkward and uncomfortable when he showed up with another woman at whatever social function, like Shelley's engagement party. She steeled herself at the possibility.

"You said something to me, before you ran. What did you mean by it?"

"What...what did I say?"

"You said" — He cleared his throat, then swiped his hand over his face, like he was nervous — "You said you couldn't allow yourself to fall any harder."

Her gaze caught on his for a long moment before she turned away and focused on a spot on the front door. "What do you care?"

"I care, Helen." He was close enough he could pull her into his arms if he wanted. But he seemed to be holding back. "I care so fucking much. More than I..."

"Don't play with me," she whispered, emotion thick in her voice. "I don't need that...I can't take that."

"Play with you? I'd never do that. I couldn't do that. Not to you. But for the love of Christ, just tell me what you meant."

This was it. The death-by-fire moment. One she wouldn't

normally have a problem with as she'd so often jumped into a raging metaphorical fire, feet first without even thinking how her heart could get burned. Yet telling *this* man how she felt and what she wanted? The risk was exponentially higher if he didn't want her in return. But he was here, asking her, facing her, looking like he really needed her answer.

"I meant, I can't fall for a man who will never love me," she blurted, her eyes stinging, and imagining now was the time he'd turn and run screaming for the hills. Because who the hell needed a needy bitch like her emoting to a dude who clearly wasn't available. "For a man who's still in love with someone else."

"Helen, I..." He came closer, until he was in her space.

"No." She put a hand to his warm, hard chest, curling her fingers against his flesh. Because now she'd started, she was not going to hold the words back. "I need a man who puts me ahead of a memory. Ahead of a woman who isn't alive anymore, because *I am*." Tears spilled down her cheeks, and her voice was so tight, her throat hurt. "I'm alive Carmine. And I'm so, so sorry you lost her, but I can't be a substitute or second to a woman who isn't here anymore."

"Red..."

"Yes okay, I'm kooky and obviously suck at relationships, but no matter what, I'm still worthy of being someone's number one. Someone who wants to give me kids and a cat and maybe a dog..."

He captured her face between his hands, spread his fingers across her cheeks and covered her mouth with his. His tongue slipped between her lips, hot and wet, and slippery. Tasting familiar, of man and whiskey. He groaned deep in his throat. The simple sound ignited her blood and her body, and despite her best intentions, she melted. She always did when he touched her. There was no denying their chemistry and there was no stopping what her body wanted. One hand dropped to her lower back, then slid further, lifting up her tee shirt and dipping under, he clasped her ass cheek over her panties. Then he ground his already solid cock against her, hissing as he did so. But she pushed against his chest, breaking away.

"No," she whispered, panting hard. "Stop, I can't just be—"

"You're not," he cut her off, growling a little in what seemed like his need to make her understand. You're not *just* anything. Don't you get it? I'm trying to show you that I want those things too."

"You do...why?"

He squished his eyebrows together. "Why? You serious right now?"

"I mean..." she began, then stopped again and bit her lip.

"Helen," he said, his voice low, cracking with pent up emotion. "I feel so much for you. And every day I spend with you, I feel more. This thing inside me, that's you, it's growing, it's taking over my head. You *are* kooky and you *do* make me crazy, and you have since that day we met. Remember that?"

She laugh-sobbed, then nodded.

"You dissed me." With his index finger that shook slightly, he gently moved a strand off her face and tucked it behind her ear. "Normally I'd blow that off, but I think it's what made me pay attention. I couldn't stop thinking about you. I still see you flipping this gorgeous hair and your eyes flashing, carrying Terra's guitar. You're so beautiful, you stopped my world. You make me *want* to love again."

She gave herself a moment to let that sink in, her lashes fluttering as it did.

"I want to be that man who gives you kids and cats and dogs and see wherever this thing takes us. Whether it's up or down or sideways I want it to be with you."

She looked at him, holding her breath.

"I can't share, Carmine."

"Hell, no. God knows I couldn't share you." His body gave an involuntary shudder. "When I thought you and Torque...when I saw his bike outside...no it would kill me. And anyway, I never want my heating vents sardined."

She giggled into a sob.

He lay his forehead on hers. "What do *you* want, Red?" he asked, his voice rough.

A blast of air left her lungs, then she wrinkled her nose, before sucking in another more tortured one. "You shattered me."

"What?"

"You asked me why I ran. In the hospital, you were asleep. I was telling you how I felt and you called for *her.* You'd passed out in my arms and yet you called *her* name. I didn't think there was any room for me in there." She put her palm on his chest, where his heart was. Heat from his skin seeped through her fingers. His palm landed on top of hers and he held it there over the steady beat. "And when I brought you soup, there was Jules."

"Red..."

"And you were naked...well almost naked because the towel doesn't count, not really. And you were so comfortable being naked I thought you'd just...you know...and I...you didn't say you hadn't." She swallowed at the hurt it had caused her. "I didn't know what to think. You were so angry, and I couldn't stick around thinking you had."

"Jules was there as a doctor checking on me. I swear. I'm not saying we haven't, but I have no interest in seeing her again in that capacity."

"What about the towel?" she asked, still skeptical.

He exhaled hard. "I was hoping to avoid that part, but since were here. I hadn't showered in days. I was nasty. Hurting and depressed and majorly pissed at you for blowing me off. Jules wanted to check my lungs for pneumonia but wouldn't until I showered. That's where you came in. I'd literally just stepped out and heard voices. I thought it was those goddam political assholes who leave flyers on my door and pollute my property."

"Oh." She felt a warm, pink flush move over her face and put her hand to her forehead, shielding her embarrassment. "Oh Lordy, now I feel so stupid."

He took her hand and started sucking on the tip of her ring finger, pulling it into his mouth, circling it with his tongue. "You're adorable when you're embarrassed," he whispered.

The hot slippery contact sent waves of desire straight between her thighs. She squirmed, clenching them together, needing some sort of friction. The kind only he could provide.

"But what do I have to do to get you to answer my question?"

"Yes," she whispered back, tilting her chin. "*Yes!*"

"Yes?"

"You're everything I want, and it scares me to death I feel this much for you in such a short time. I'm trusting you with my heart, Carmine, and I couldn't take it if you were just messing with me."

"Red, I'm trusting you with mine too," he said against her lips. "You're the only one I want to take a chance with. I never thought I could fall for someone again. In all honesty, I didn't want to, and did my best not to, but the truth is, I was cooked the moment I saw you."

Her breath hitched, then she lifted her chin higher. Their lips met, and he kissed her softly and tenderly until her toes curled. Then he deepened it, teasing her with more tongue, nipping at her lips until they were both breathing hard.

"I need you," she said, frantically unbuttoning his shirt, tugging it loose and smoothing the fabric from his shoulders. Hooking her fingers into his belt, she tugged him into her room, blood rushing in anticipation. At the edge of her bed, he pulled her tee shirt over her head. Beneath she wore only a pair of boyfriend-cut black panties with crisscross spaghetti straps hugging her hips.

He pulled in air, smoothing a calloused palm over her flat belly and ribcage, cupping a breast. He took its rosy peak into his mouth, sucking hard. Heat suffused her veins, making her gasp and drop her head back.

"God, you're so beautiful Helen, it hurts to look at you."

She responded by putting her hand against his cheek and grazing her fingers through his hair. "Told you before, you're the beautiful one."

"No." He shook his head, his eyes blazing as he gently pushed her back until she lay in front of him. "No. Not me. You."

Their gazes locked as he slid his hands up her thighs until his fingers found her panties. They hooked into those little straps, dragging them down, which he followed with soft licks and kisses on her thighs. Shoving her underwear under her pillow, he touched the delicate insides of her knees, caressing her skin, moving higher until she flushed and squirmed with a want she'd never felt so strongly before.

She needed him naked. She needed his skin on hers and, unzipping his pants, she pushed her hand in and palmed his impressive erection.

"Helen," he groaned, his throat bobbing as she stroked him over his Jockey's. She removed those too. He kicked them off and lay next to her, taking her mouth again with his, but teasing and stroking her with his fingers until he brought her to climax. Then again, with his tongue and teeth.

He took his time, like he wanted to savor her, watch her come undone, watch how she arched her back and neck, gasping his name.

At last, when he rolled on the condom, he was shaking as he fought to maintain his control, then moved between her thighs. He entered her with short, restrained strokes as she adjusted and took all of him. Again, they kissed, their tongues matching the rhythm of their bodies, until it grew in pace and intensity they had to break for air.

"Woman," he growled when she sensed he was close. Shifting his position so one elbow supported his weight, he placed his other hand under her head with his thumb on her cheekbone. "Look at me," he commanded. When her eyes met and held his, she knew they were glazed with heat, and need as his were. Then his thrusts deepened and increased, grew wilder and less controlled. "Keep looking at me. I want you to see how much I want you. What you do to me."

"God...Carmine," she panted, her body tightening as her orgasm began to surge. His words sent her over, into a free fall of pleasure so extraordinary her mind went blank and she thought her heart would explode. He went with her, and she watched his body go taut as he gave in to his own release, and it was beautiful and intense, and the best thing she'd ever witnessed.

Long moments later, when it was over, and their breathing had slowed, he remained wrapped around her, his head in her hair, his breath fanning her neck, filling her with everything that was him.

Everything she needed.

Everything she had ever wanted.

* * *

The sunlight woke him first. Helen was on her stomach, her face buried in her pillow and angled towards him, lips slightly parted. Hair draped over her cheekbone and fluttered each time she breathed. Gently, he moved it aside with his index finger, wanting to see all of her. Her pretty, curved lashes slightly darker, but of the same hue as her hair, the pale blue undertones of her skin and those fat lips that spawned his fantasies.

With Jaz it had taken time. Shared experiences along with an understanding of Army life had brought them close, then made them inseparable.

But with Helen, one look and he'd fallen hard and fast.

How had that happened?

Did it matter?

Frankly, no, but he was happy it had.

Happy.

A word he hadn't used in conjunction with himself in a long time, but it felt good—felt right.

He rolled over as smoothly as he could, not wanting to disturb her. Did his business in the bathroom, then on his way back to the bed snagged his pants from the floor. The way things turned out, he was kinda glad he hadn't given it to her last night. It was the one detour he'd made on his way to her apartment from the airport. Retrieving it, he took her right ring finger, the one closest to him and pushed it on.

Of course it fit perfectly.

She stirred a little at the disturbance, then her lids fluttered open, giving him a full blast of those extraordinary eyes.

"Hmm," she mumbled sleepily, then smiled. "You're still here."

"Where would I go, Red?"

"Thought maybe I dreamed last night. Well, the last part anyway."

"No dream." He grinned back, that muscle in his chest bursting with emotions he couldn't describe and wondering how long it would take for her to realize what was on her finger. It was kind of fun waiting. "That was as real and, might I add, as awesome as it gets."

She giggled, then whispered shyly, "Have to tinkle." She attempted to pull the sheet around her, but he caught her hand and stopped her.

"No, Tomato Head. Every inch of you is beautiful. Don't hide your body, not from me."

Her nose wrinkled as she pushed her hair from her face. "'Kay." A soft shade of pink moved up her neck and joined the sleepy flush still on her cheeks. "Be right back."

At some point she'd put her panties back on, but since they displayed her ass perfectly with just the right amount of jiggle, he didn't mind. Wasn't going to be wearing them long anyway.

At the bathroom door she stopped and checked him out over her shoulder and caught him ogling. Then, sexy as hell with her hair all mussed from sleep, her gaze dropped to his crotch and she licked her thoroughly kissed and slightly swollen lips.

"Watch it, Red," he growled, feeling shit start to stir in his groin. "You keep doing that, you may not make it in there."

She laughed and stepped over the threshold, quickly shutting the door behind her.

While he waited, seeking another condom from his pocket and trying not to think about his dick, he arranged a pillow and settled back against the iron gate headboard and checked his phone.

Torque had texted him. He'd left his apartment keys under the big potted plant at his door and was en route to meet Lilly. Brady checked out of the hospital with the intention of spending a week with his mother. And Irina sent him a photo of the impromptu daycare she and the other girls had set up in Vasily's second apartment.

All was well in the world.

He glanced at the door when he heard the toilet flush then the faucet running. When it finally opened, he pretended to be engrossed in his phone. Nevertheless, out the corner of his eye, he saw Helen looking at her hand.

"*Am* I still dreaming?" she asked, tucking a strand of hair behind her ears. Her voice was husky and cracked a little.

He turned to look at her, unable to keep the smile playing on his lips.

"Not as far as I can tell. Look pretty lucid to me."

"You found Nana's ring?"

He said nothing, instead waited for her to join him. She seemed frozen, her feet cemented to the floor, her eyes wide and unsure. As if she was convinced she *was* still dreaming.

"How did you do this?"

"Come here," he said, holding out his hand. As she put hers in his, he tugged her onto the bed, then pushed the kick-ass hand-made quilt out of the way and guided her into straddling his lap.

"Where was it?"

"You were right." He gripped her hips and adjusted her position. "Cody did take it."

"But how did you find it?"

"I put the word out. Figured you'd already contacted the pawn shops so I went a different route, called my network of shady contacts. Was surprised as hell when I got a call back. Cody used it as collateral for rehab."

"What?"

"You heard of the Sunshine Institute?"

"That fancy rehab center that Terra's mom went to?"

"Vasily owns the land it's on and finances the center."

"Vasily?" Her mouth dropped open. "As in Melnikov?"

"The same."

She wrinkled her nose. "Wait, I don't understand."

Her hair was draped over her magnificent breasts, and he hooked his thumbs behind the silky strands and moved it behind her shoulders.

"Sometimes patients don't have cash, but they might have access to collateral like cars, or property or anything of value. He holds a lien on it until they pay it off. If they don't, he sells it and the money goes back into the Institute." He leaned in and kissed the bump on her collar bone, running his tongue into the dip in her throat.

"Mmm," she said angling her neck to give him more access. "That's quite unconventional."

"I've come to learn he's an unconventional man."

"I'll say." She went still, and a moment later put her soft palms on either side of his face, studying him. "How much did Cody owe?"

Damn. This was the part he hadn't looked forward to. He'd done it because he'd wanted to and didn't need her feeling she owed him.

"Doesn't matter, Red."

"It does to me."

"I made a small donation."

"Small?"

"Mm hm."

"Exactly how small?"

"It's tax deductible."

She exhaled a breath, then nibbled on her lip. "You're not going to tell me, are you?"

"Nope."

"I see," she said, sitting back, looking suddenly serious. "Well... in that case I'm just going to have to torture it out of you."

He chuckled. "And how do you propose to do that?"

"I have my ways, mister." A mischievous smile danced on her mouth. Then, scooting her hips slightly backwards, her silky thigh skin rubbed against his legs. He was already hard and standing tall from those stunning breasts in his face, so close and within reach, when she put her hands on his thighs and looked at him from beneath her lashes.

"What on earth am I going to do with this?" she purred, licking her lips. "It's so handsome when it stands to attention, I could just stare at it for days. Or maybe..." she paused, biting her lip.

"Maybe what?" His mouth went suddenly dry.

"I'll just tease it a little with the tip of my tongue, see what I can make it do." To which she put her pink, delicious tip to his, just barely touching and circled it around.

"Woman," was all he could manage as his cock jumped, his heart beginning to pound, forcing more blood into his loins. Making him want her more if that was possible, which somehow it was. He rested his head against the headboard, reaching up to grab the edge, while hissing through his teeth. "Mmm...fuuuuck, Helen! Torture me all you want, but I'm never telling."

She gave him a slow, sexy smile that spurned visions in his head. Visions of what she had yet to do to him. He'd gone down plenty on her, but this was the first time she'd reciprocated. Then she proceeded to make that fantasy a reality–– torturing him with pleasure. With her tongue, her lips, her hands and when he couldn't take it anymore, his body on fire, he gripped her waist and hoisted her hot little ass off him and onto her back. Then he proceeded to torture her in return.

After which, still drenched in the exquisite gratification they gave and took in equal measure, bodies sated, they made coffee and breakfast and spent the rest of the day in bed.

He never told her how much.

Suffice it to say, it was a fuck of a lot. But she was worth it.

Thank you for reading.

If you enjoyed this book, please consider leaving a review. Even if it's just one line. It really helps other readers find my work. 🖤